MIDNIGHT ETERNAL

(SKY BROOKS WORLD: ETHAN BOOK 7)

MCKENZIE HUNTER

A J CONNOR

McKenzie Hunter

Midnight Eternal

McKenzieHunter@McKenzieHunter.com

ISBN: 978-1-946457-17-2

CHAPTER 1

I paced back and forth across the living room, my battered muscles knotted with tension. I was under doctor's orders to rest, but I couldn't sit still. There was too much at stake, too much still unknown for me to sit around doing nothing, and yet until I knew more, I couldn't get out and face the pack's problems.

It had been four hours since I'd learned that some of the most powerful people in North America were missing. The Alphas and Betas of the Southern and Eastern packs had disappeared, along with the Master of the Northern Seethe. If it had just been Demetrius, then I would have been fine with it—the vampire was a force of evil by anyone's standards. As for Cole, the East Coast Alpha, I might reluctantly have accepted the need to find him, but I wouldn't have been doing it with any enthusiasm. He had been plotting to kill me and take my place as Beta of the Midwest pack for years. Hell, he'd recently challenged for my place knowing full well that I was in no state to fight, leading Sky to accept the fight on my behalf.

He had a full-on anti-Ethan approach to life, was willing to sacrifice me and my mate for his own power, and if he turned up dead in a ditch then I wouldn't mourn him. But Joan, the Alpha of the Southern Pack, was one of the best weres I knew, brave and compassionate, and there were others caught up in this who didn't deserve to share a fate with Cole. Whatever was going on, I needed to know more about it. I needed to fight back.

I ran my fingers through my hair and stalked back and forth while Sky watched me with anxious eyes.

"Why Demetrius?" I said, thinking out loud. Everyone else who had gone missing was a were, so why pick off the vampire? And why not come for me and Sebastian, the Beta and Alpha of the most powerful pack in North America?

"You said this is worse than the Red Blood," Sky said.

I nodded, looked at her, and took a long breath, trying and failing to calm both of us. I could hear her heart racing and feel her tension through the mating bond we shared. Both told me that the attempt to soothe her hadn't worked.

I sat next to her on the sofa and mustered my thoughts. There was a lot that could be said about the people I suspected were behind this; the challenge was narrowing it down to the parts she needed to know. That was hard to do while I was knotted up with frustration. I sank back into the soft cushions of the sofa, which offered no comfort worth having, and started to explain.

"It happened seven years ago. We were accused of abducting and killing off smaller packs in the area in an effort to assert our dominance and let our presence be known." I ran my hand across my jaw, considering how this fit in with what Sky had seen since she joined the pack. "The accusation wasn't taken lightly. We didn't have a problem with smaller packs in the past."

That had changed when one of the smaller packs attacked Sky. Now we didn't allow them in our territory—packs there faced the choice to join us or leave. If they didn't like that choice, then the brutal consequences were on them. "We had to look into it, but the trail went cold. Someone was picking off the Alphas of the smaller packs, along with their Betas and a few of the thirds. We couldn't find the culprit."

Sky's heart beat harder at the mention of thirds, panic rising through her. She must be thinking about Winter, the Midwest's third, and now I felt like an idiot for not thinking of her myself. I grabbed my phone off the coffee table and called her number. The phone only rang for a second before connecting.

"I'm fine," Winter said, her calm tone at odds with the speed at which she had answered. "Sebastian called already. Don't worry about me. If someone comes through my door, they will be exiting without body parts that I assure you they will likely miss. That is, if they manage to leave."

There was a click of metal as Winter tapped one of the many swords and knives that decorated her apartment, all of which were as razor-sharp and carefully weighted as they were polished and well presented. There was no need to say anything more—she had this under control. Reassured, I hung up and tossed the phone on the table.

"Winter's fine," I said, then got back to my story. "They were missing, and the trail was cold. We had no idea who was taking them, until they made a fatal mistake. They took a witch."

"A witch? Were they just collecting supernaturals?"

I shook my head. "No, they were hunting were-animals. For sport, and people paid a lot of money for the privilege. The witches were just for entertainment.

"Asking a level one witch to perform magic equivalent to the tricks that a children's magician or cruise ship entertainer does is insulting to them. It's about as insulting as someone wanting to keep one of us as a pet. Or hunt us like natural animals."

I gritted my teeth at the thought of the pain and indignity. The way these people wanted to treat us was sickening. We weren't novelties for the pleasure of others, and anyone who tried to do that to me would feel the consequences in the sharpness of my claws and teeth. I closed my eyes as I tried to calm the anger running through me.

"David and Trent ask Josh to perform magic all the time," Sky said, sounding a little embarrassed.

I opened my eyes and gave her a half-smile. "Josh isn't that easily offended. Besides, he likes Trent and David."

Somebody had to, aside from Sky. I certainly didn't have time for her nosy, gossiping neighbors and their shallow, self-indulgent lives.

"Who took the witches and the were-animals?" Sky asked.

"Ronan Everest. We still don't know how he found out about us and why he went the route he did. I guess he'd planned to find success in the underground entertainment industry. He gave hunters the opportunity to hunt animals that were smarter than the ones you find in nature. We had no idea what he was going to use the witches for, other than entertainment. He knew enough about were-animals and our dynamics to know to go after the smaller packs. They didn't have the same resources as the larger ones. I'm not sure that he wouldn't have become more confident and tried the larger packs. The smaller packs could have been practice."

"You were able to find his location by tracking the witch's blood?"

I nodded. I could still remember the smell of it in my nose as the hunt picked up speed, hurtling toward a violent confrontation.

"The witches were more than happy to help us do it."

Sky hesitated for a moment before her next question.

"Is he still alive?"

I shook my head. "Nor are any of the people who thought it was okay to hunt us."

They had deserved everything they got, and I'd relished my part in delivering it.

"You think it's a copycat? A friend, maybe even someone who worked with him in the past?"

"It seemed as if he was working alone. He'd had a few Hunters help capture were-animals, but they were just work-for-hire, not part of his plan."

"What happened to them?"

"Chris is what happened to them. She's dedicated to her job and even more so to the reputation of Hunters. Others working for humans and ultimately hurting people in the otherworld wasn't good for business. She can be ruthless when crossed."

Satisfying as it was to remember how that had ended, thinking back on it filled me with a sense of dread. We had been vulnerable, we had lost good people, and we had almost lost many more. The whole pack had been at risk, and now it looked like it was happening again. Except that now the stakes were higher. It wasn't just my pack at risk, it was Sky, the love of my life. If these bastards thought I'd fought hard before, they hadn't seen anything yet.

I kept expecting to hear from Sebastian. As Alpha of our pack, he would be planning how to respond to this latest crisis, gathering information and coordinating our resources to deal with whoever had revived the rogue hunt. But another hour passed without the phone ringing, while I paced the room, fists clenched, teeth gritted, my raging emotions stirring my body into a storm of untapped energy.

"Sebastian should have called by now," I said. "Something's wrong. I have to go see."

I snatched my phone off the table and headed for the door. Sky grabbed her things and started to follow, a movement which stopped me in my tracks. This was meant to be about keeping her safe, not leading her into danger.

"Sky, you can't go."

"Ethan, we don't have time to debate this. It's not a bad idea to have someone to back you up. If Sebastian is in danger, I can help."

"I can't do anything while worrying about you."

"We can spend time arguing about this, or we can go. I can take care of myself."

I clenched my jaw, biting back my instinctive responses, all of which would have led to a futile fight in which neither of us would be willing to give ground. Reluctantly, I nodded my agreement and we headed out to the car.

As I raced through the shadowy streets, the world around us gray and gloomy, I fought to stay calm despite the tension gripping me. To keep myself focused, I talked to Sky about what we would do when we reached Sebastian's house, how we would ensure that she stayed safe while we checked to see if the enemy had come for him. Sky listened in silence, but even with my eyes fixed on the road I could tell that she was humoring me, letting the words flow while I worked through my anxiety about her safety. It was immensely frustrating, knowing that nothing I said would change her behavior, but I loved her for that willfulness, and even more for the fact that she was trying to help me manage my mood.

"Sky, I need you to be careful," I said at last.

She nodded. It was as good as I was going to get.

We drove down the long driveway to Sebastian's house, past the densely planted trees that protected his home from view and gave him somewhere to run without the pack. The house itself was a large building made from sand-colored bricks, with pillars out front adding to its neoclassical air. Huge windows looked out across meticulously manicured shrubbery and woodland beyond, a construction of restrained but imposing civilization with an intimate view of the wild, just like its owner.

As I stepped out of the car, I saw the front door hanging wide, light spilling out over the porch. The door had been smashed open, scattering splinters of wood across the foyer floor. I stepped carefully inside, Sky close behind me, and broken glass from the windows crunched beneath my shoes. A sharp, toxic scent made me gag, and I covered my nose to stifle it.

"Gas?" I asked.

If Sky had an answer, then she didn't give it. Like me, she was staring at the ruin that had been made here, the tiled floor littered with chunks of plaster and sprays of blood, the walls marred by body-shaped holes.

I crouched to get a better scent of the blood, which was almost obliterated by the acrid gas. I knew Sebastian's scent, knew the distinct notes of his blood, and this wasn't it. Relieved, I rose and walked across the room, heading for the kitchen.

A movement made me stop in the doorway. A pale figure turned and flung up a hand. A bolt of magic shot at me, only to burst in a bright flash as Sky raised a protective field.

Ariel gasped as she saw who she had fired her magic at, and a hand went to her mouth as she made a muffled apology. The leader of the witches' Creed was dressed in a white, airy shift dress that exposed parts of her toned shoulders as well as a hefty hint of her pink lace push-up bra. Its mid-thigh length revealed toned legs leading down to a pair of pastel-print stilettos. This wasn't the outfit of someone planning an assault and kidnapping.

"What are you doing here?" I asked.

"I had a meeting with Sebastian," she replied. "He told me to just let myself in when I arrived."

I looked around the room and took a deep breath, registering the scents of roasted meat and spices, the bottle of red wine and two glasses resting on the counter. I'd known that something was going on between Sebastian and Ariel but hadn't realized it had gotten to the "let yourself in" stage. Had he given her a key already? That would be one way to solidify our alliance with the Creed.

"Meeting?" Sky asked, raising an eyebrow.

"I haven't been here long," Ariel said, ignoring the implied question. "Once I realized he wasn't here, I erected a ward to protect me while I investigated." She shook her head, heavy with emotion. "I should have known something would happen to him when London informed me of the other missing were-animals."

There was another smell in the room, apart from food and blood. An unnatural, chemical smell that made me think of the infirmary. Some sort of medicine had been in use here, and given the context, I was betting on a tranquilizer. It took a huge dose to knock out a were, but combine it with silver and you could keep one of us down for a long count. The more I saw, the more certain I became that Sebastian was the latest victim of whoever was making weres disappear, and that they were using human technology, not supernatural powers to do it.

We followed the trail of destruction out of the kitchen and into the next room. Avant-garde art and nature scenes decorated neutral-colored walls, which were spattered with blood, as was the sturdy dark-wood furniture. A large coffee table had been flipped over and one of its legs snapped off. The wall-mounted television had a web of pale cracks spread across its screen. In a corner of the room, the missing table leg lay battered and bloody, apparently having been used to beat someone.

My worry for Sebastian was tinged with pride at seeing how hard he'd fought.

My phone rang and Quinn's name flashed up on the screen. I answered immediately.

"What's wrong?" I asked.

"Sebastian's gone," Quinn said, his voice strangled by panic.

"I know—"

"No… you don't understand. When everyone started going missing, he said he had a tracker with him. I had him for a while and then it just shut off."

As the leader of the Worgen, a small pack we had absorbed a few months before, Quinn was our lead tech guy, the arch-nerd of a band of expert hackers. No technology he put in place would have simply failed.

"You think they found it?"

"Maybe, but it's in his mouth. It's a cap that goes over the tooth. Sebastian said it was uncomfortable, but he'd wear it just in case."

"It was moving from the house, right?"

"Yes. But then it stopped. If he'd lost it, then its position would be stagnant. It just went blank on my screen."

My brow furrowed as I tried to put together the story of what had happened here, from the broken door through the carnage in several rooms to the tracker tooth switching off somewhere outside the house. But before I could construct a neat narrative, there was a sound from the back of the house, a muffled thud followed by a creak.

"I'll call you back," I said, then hung up.

Careful not to tread on the broken glass, I walked silently toward the back door. Sky and Ariel followed me. I stopped in the hallway and turned to look at Sky, about to tell her to stay behind, but the look she shot me said just how futile that would be. This was no time to argue among ourselves. Reluctantly, I accepted that she was coming along no matter what I did.

I backtracked and headed out the side door of the house. Sounds were coming from both the front and the back, quietly revealing the arrival of several unannounced visitors.

I doubted that Sebastian had told these people to let themselves in.

Ariel slipped off her heels and headed for the front, magic shining between her fingers like fiercely blazing sparks.

Sky and I crept through the growing darkness. The smells of iron, gunfire, and cheap cologne cut through the soft and familiar evergreen woods. Wind whistled through the branches, shaking leaves and making the long grass hiss, while small animals scampered unseen through the twilight. Through it all came the unmistakable rhythm of booted feet.

I headed east while Sky went west, spreading out to see what we could find. As I stalked toward the edge of the wood, the footsteps came closer, quiet enough to avoid detection by human ears, but nowhere near quiet enough to evade a were.

The bushes to my left rustled as a man in combat fatigues emerged, a pistol in his hand. I sprang at him, knocking the pistol from his hand and sending him staggering back. He found his balance quickly and lashed out at me with a high kick that spoke to years of martial arts training. I jerked back, caught his leg as it went past, and twisted hard, venting my stored-up anger into that movement. Tendons tore as I bent his leg back on itself, and he cried out with pain, the sound slicing through the air like a ragged blade.

Rushing footsteps made me turn, letting go of my first attacker and turning to deal with a second. He came at me with an assault rifle raised, swinging the butt like a club. As I stepped aside, one of his hands went to his belt, pulling out a long, ugly knife. Before he could bring it around, I grabbed his head and twisted. There was a snap and he fell to the ground.

A blow from behind knocked me to the ground. I rolled to all fours and looked up to see another guy dressed for combat, bringing a gun to bear. It had been adapted with a bulky ammo clip and something like a silencer on the muzzle, and his finger was on the trigger before I had a chance to think.

I leapt right. There were two soft thuds from the gun, and a pair of hefty darts buried themselves in the turf where I had been. The guy turned, but this time I was ahead of him, grabbing the gun by the barrel and wrenching it from his hands with all my fury. I flung it away, but that kept my hands busy long enough for him to deliver a pair of strong punches to my gut. The pain my body was already dealing with returned twice over, and I started to buckle, but I wasn't going to let him beat me; my anger was stronger than that. My own fist lashed out, punching him in the throat. He gasped and grasped at his neck, face going red as he struggled for breath.

I brought my foot up, then slammed the heel down hard on his ankle. There was a satisfying crunch and he fell to the ground, still clutching his throat with one hand. The other hand drew a pistol from his belt, a far more conventional gun than the one he had used before. I kicked his arm and his shot went wild, the crack of gunfire punching through the night. Then I kicked the gun away and sank to crouch over him, raising my fist ready for a killing blow.

Footsteps rushed toward me. I looked up to see Sky, but also four more of these mystery mercenaries, all pointing assault rifles at me. The shadows fell the wrong way for me to tell if they were regular guns or more tranquilizers. Either way, I didn't like the idea of getting shot.

"Put your hands up," one of them shouted. "Now, dammit!"

I watched them, considering my options. They weren't close enough for me to reach them without getting shot at all. Perhaps if I took out two, then Sky could deal with the others, assuming no more arrived in the meantime, but it was a plan that could easily go wrong, if plan wasn't too strong a word.

"I said now!" The soldier cocked his gun.

I stood and looked at Sky, still trying to work out how far to obey them, whether to raise my hands to buy time or go for something bolder. The rush of adrenaline was still flowing through me, along with the satisfaction at venting my anger after a long and frustrating evening. I really wanted to punch more of them and had to keep reminding myself that it might not be the smartest move.

The thud of a dart gun was accompanied by a sharp pain in my arm. I looked down to see a bulky dart protruding from my bicep. I blinked at it in confusion as drugs flooded my veins, making my head spin and my thoughts tumble across each other in disjointed fragments. My legs felt numb, muscles quivering like Jell-O, and I stumbled as I tried to keep them under me. It was no use. My legs gave way and I fell face first on the ground.

I sensed rather than saw magic rippling through the air. Sky was using her powers to fight our attackers, but I couldn't make sense of the sounds. There was shouting, thuds, the crack of bullets, footsteps and crashes. Was she winning? Had she been hurt? Was Ariel back to help?

A huge sense of weariness overtook me, as if I had been awake for a week and was now lying down for the first time, struggling to keep my eyes open while my body told me to rest. The sights and sounds around me had a distant, dream-like quality, as if everything was happening far away or to someone else. Was that the stab of another dart hitting me, or just the prickling of my skin? I couldn't tell any more.

The magic and the violence had stopped. People were talking. Something about names and women. There was a woman I had to look after. Sky, that was it. She was in danger, I needed to help, but I couldn't even lift my hand.

Then a needle slid into my upper arm and I stopped even caring. My eyelids finally surrendered to their own terrible gravity and I sank into unconsciousness.

$\mathcal{I}$ woke face down in the back of a van, my arms bound tightly behind me, legs still weak from the drugs the mercenaries had knocked me out with. My face was pressed against the cold corrugated metal of the floor and my cheek was wet with my own drool. The van rattled and bumped over poorly kept roads, jolting my injuries from the fight in which I had been captured and the ones from the fight before that. Apparently this was my life now, an endless series of battles against different opponents. I wouldn't have minded that too much if only I had won the last one.

My brain was still fuzzy, fragments of memory failing to find each other in a fog of drugs and exhaustion. I kept my eyes closed and tried to ignore the pain, to focus on remembering where I was and what was happening to me.

"I thought he was meant to be tough," someone said as he prodded me with a booted toe. I ignored the far from gentle nudge. If my captors thought that I was unconscious, then they were more likely to leave me alone, which gave me more of a chance to learn about them, plan an escape, or just work out where the hell I was and what was happening.

As we jolted over a pothole, I was briefly flung from the

floor of the van, then smacked back down onto it, my jaw colliding with the metal. My teeth dug into my lip and the salty taste of blood filled my senses, enlivening me. It seemed that the jolt had shaken something loose in my mind, because the memories came tumbling back—the missing weres; racing to Sebastian's house; the carnage we found there; the fight at the edge of the woods; and then…

Another jolt. This time my knees took the brunt of the impact, and in doing so told me that they had been bruised when I fell after being drugged. The pain was made more bearable by the fading haze of those drugs, but I still felt like the vehicle was giving me a terrible beating.

I opened my eyes and tried to look around, but it was difficult with my face pressed against the floor, and that made the situation more frustrating. The only light was what little of the headlights' glow came in through the windshield of the van, but that was enough for me to make out the shapes of three men up front and at least another three in the back with me, their assault rifles across their laps. I was outnumbered, unarmed, and bound. Escape didn't look likely, for now at least. My anger at what had happened would have to stay bottled up inside, growing in strength until I could unleash it later.

I wondered what had happened to Sky, worrying at what harm they might have done to her. She had still been fighting back when I went down, hadn't she? Or had she? The image of Sky, bound and battered and face down in the back of another van, filled me with pain and anger. If they hurt her then I was going to make every last one of them pay in blood. No one hurt my mate and got away with it.

"I think he's awake," one of the men said, leaning over to look at me. "His eyes are open."

No point in hiding it anymore. I flexed my hands and wrists, which were bound with a pair of cold, heavy cuffs. The restraints were fitted tightly, giving me almost no wiggle room. If I could change into my wolf form then I would have the advantage here, with these guys unable to use their guns effectively in the confines of the van. But the bindings were too tight for that, and the weight of the handcuffs told me that they were iridium, which would prevent me from using my magic. Whoever had planned this, they knew what they were doing.

The rumble of the vehicle's tires changed as we turned off the road and onto some other hard surface. Then we came to a halt, the engine switched off, and a gate clanged shut behind us.

"All out," the driver said. "Including the prey."

I was so used to being the predator in any given situation, it took me a moment to realize that he was talking about me. Then the back doors of the van were flung open and I was hauled out.

I found myself standing on the weed-strewn concrete loading yard of a processing plant. The place was enclosed by a rusty wire mesh fence topped with recently added barbed wire. The enclosure was large, holding a series of looming buildings, all of them with broken, grimy windows that marked years of neglect. A sign hanging lopsidedly off one of the buildings read "KITSBORO CORP," presumably the current or former owners of this place. Stark white light spilled from the nearest building, and that was where my captors led me.

This building had been some kind of chemical production facility. Pieces of broken-down machinery lay piled up in one corner of the cavernous space, while in another, reclaimed parts were set up to brew something with the same acrid smell I had noticed at Sebastian's house. From the way my body responded to just a hint of it, I guessed that was the hefty tranquilizer I had been stunned with. Along another wall were racks of guns and gym equipment, while opposite were portable storage units that looked to have been turned into temporary accommodation, with bunk beds visible through the open doors.

There were a few men and women in combat fatigues scattered around the place, eating, working out, even playing cards. But the ones who caught my attention stood in the middle of the room, a pair of women, one's hair red, the other's dark. The redhead had a hunting rifle slung over one shoulder and a cold smile on her face. Her companion stood with her arms folded, watching in curiosity as I was brought in.

"This is him?" the dark-haired woman asked as I was dragged in front of them.

"Yes, ma'am," one of the mercenaries said.

"I'd expected something more… I don't know, wild looking. After everything we've been told, I imagined some hairy, savage beast, flailing out of control."

Her tone was clear cut, the sort of voice that came from an upbringing of money and privilege.

"Release my hands and I'll give you all the savage you want," I growled. The way they looked at me, like I was some toy waiting to be played with, made me want to smack the smiles off both of their faces.

"Oh, he'll do," the redhead said. "Look at the fire in his eyes, he's practically spitting blood. And those muscles…"

She ran a hand across my chest, then down my bicep. I heard her heart beat faster, but if that was a sign of attraction then it wasn't a healthy kind.

"Be careful, Sonja," the dark-haired woman said. "He could get you while you're up close."

"Don't be such a pussy, Bethany." The redhead rolled her eyes. "This fine hunk of man meat is nicely wrapped up, just like we ordered. Our customers are going to get their money's worth."

"Our customers, not you."

"Hey, you remember the deal." Sonja grinned and laid a

hand on Bethany's shoulder. "I get to be part of the hunt too. That's why I helped arrange all of this." She flashed me a look of cold contempt. "That and revenge."

After what I had heard so far, it actually felt good to know that there was something personal here, that I wasn't just going to be hunted for profit. Not that it made a difference to how badly I was going to tear these two up when I got the chance, but I despised them a little less now.

"Revenge for what?" I asked. "Did I ruin your coming out party when you were sixteen and now you want to settle the score, or did daddy just tell you that monsters ate your great-great-uncle a hundred years ago?"

"Revenge for Ronan." Bethany's voice wavered as her expression screwed up into one of pure malice. "You remember Ronan, right? Ronan who you monsters killed."

So there it was, just like I'd predicted. Ronan Everest, coming back to bite me from beyond the grave. At least when vampires did that, they had the decency to put in the hard work themselves and put their necks where I could rip them open. It seemed that Everest was just bones and dirt, but he was still here to make my life difficult.

"I remember Ronan Everest," I said in a steely tone. "He tried to hunt me and my friends for sport."

"You and your friends are monsters!" Bethany's voice rose and her hands clenched at her sides, but she didn't come any closer to me. She might be plotting my death, but she wasn't a woman with the courage to do her own violence.

"Ronan was the one hunting innocent people for pleasure. By my standards, that makes him the monster."

"You're a liar and a beast and you're going to die for what you did." She was practically panting with anger, spittle flying from her lips.

"There, there." Sonja took Bethany's hand and held it between both of hers. "It's going to be okay. I promise."

As Bethany closed her eyes and took deep breaths, Sonja

turned her attention to me. Her expression was filled with slow-burning menace, but something else too, hidden beneath her performance of anger. Sonja was just crazy enough to enjoy this.

"Ronan, he was friends with Bethany's brother," she explained. "The two of them, they even had a thing going on, back in the day. So this matters to her. You matter to her.

"And it's personal for me too. I met Bethany through another friend of Ronan's, a guy named Dexter who I used to do jobs for. And you knew Dexter too, right?"

I sighed in exasperation. It was like being haunted by the ghosts of assholes past, but unlike Scrooge, I didn't think I'd get to wake in the morning and find out that it was all a dream.

"That makes sense, at least," I said. "Dexter was a vicious little prick who thought that he could experiment on people for fun and profit. Of course all of this would be inspired by him."

"The inspiration was Ronan's, but the knowledge we needed to track you all down again and effectively contain you... Well, let's just say that Dexter left me a little something in his will."

I shrugged casually, putting on a show of confidence. I didn't have the power to do much in this situation, and few things frustrated me more than that, but at least I could try to keep them off balance, to look like I had a plan to get out of this. Anything that kept them guessing was a drain on their mental energy, and that would work in my favor.

"Whatever. Shall we get this over with? I've got appointments tomorrow."

Sonja laughed. "Oh no, we're not ready yet. We've got some very special clients coming in for the occasion, and I don't want to damage the goods before they even arrive. For now, think of yourself as our guest. These fine folks will see you to where you're staying, and I hope you have a lovely night."

"Is there room service? Because I skipped dinner."

"Room service would imply that you have a room. For a creature like you, I figure cage service is more appropriate." She nodded to the guards. "Take him away."

CHAPTER 3

I was led at gunpoint into another of the large buildings that made up the abandoned processing plant. This one looked like it had served as a warehouse, with its bare walls, scuffed concrete floor, and a high ceiling from which our footsteps echoed around the cavernous space. Neon strip lights had been hung from some of the ceiling beams, their harsh glare casting weblike shadows from the lines of cages that filled the center of the space. In that emptiness, I felt less like I was walking into a room and more like I was walking out onto a stage, to stand exposed and vulnerable before an audience just out of view.

There probably was an audience for this place, as security cameras stared at us with unblinking scrutiny from positions in the corners of the room. Whoever had put them there didn't just want to watch the place, they wanted everyone inside it to know that they were being watched. They wanted us all to be on our best behavior, to believe that any plan or scheme we had would be futile because they would see it. But I wasn't so easily intimidated.

I had been part of enough court cases involving security

camera footage to know that it didn't reveal everything. There were always blind spots that could conceal covert movement. For security guards watching in real time, there were choices about which screen to pay attention to at any given moment. And of course, the weak link in so many security systems: Sometimes people simply didn't watch those screens at all. Sure, I needed to be wary of those blank electronic eyes, but that didn't mean I was under their control.

As my guards marched me toward the cages, I was hit by a dozen familiar scents. Most were the fur and sweat of weres I knew, which would have brought me comfort in better circumstances, but there was also the grave dust rot and rancid blood that was the harbinger of vampires.

Sebastian sat with his back against the bars of the first cage we passed. His face was bruised, his shirt torn and bloodstained, and his swollen lips stayed shut as I passed him, but cold determination shone in his eyes. Other weres filled the cages around him, our missing Alphas and Betas. Some snarled at the guards, others reached out toward them. Joan caught my eye and offered a reassuring smile, despite the desperate circumstances we were trapped in.

"Keep your fingers to yourselves," one of the guards said, lashing out with a truncheon at an outstretched hand. "Unless you want me to break them."

"Let us out of here!" Cole bellowed from a cage near the center. He shook the bars hard, but nothing looked even close to breaking loose.

"You want a beating?" one of the guards snapped back. "Because that's what you'll get if you keep up this shit."

For a group who had to keep their living goods intact, these guards were remarkably free and easy with the promises of violence. I wondered if they were nothing more than hollow threats, or if a certain amount of bruising and bloodying was just a normal expectation once you got into kidnapping and human trafficking. It wasn't like they needed us to look pretty.

I was led to a cage on the far side from Sebastian, probably a deliberate effort to keep us apart. These people knew a lot about us, and putting together the people most likely to effectively cooperate was a bad idea for them. The cuffs were removed from my wrists, and I had half a second to consider whether escape was possible before that opportunity vanished and I was shoved into the empty cage. The door clanged shut, a key turned in the lock, and I was trapped.

I'd been through some painful and unsettling situations, had lost control of myself to magic and nearly died more than once, but nothing I had been through unsettled my inner wolf more than that cage. Some deep, abiding animal instinct understood that a place like this had only one purpose: to contain and control me, to prevent me from running free. I could smell other weres around me, a pack in the making, people I should be running and hunting with, but I was cut off, constricted, an animal prisoner in an animal trap.

I fought to contain that panicky instinct, to keep control of my senses. I had to keep my head here. Panic was contagious, and as long as we were trapped in these cages, all it could lead to was frenzied beasts battering themselves futilely against the bars.

"So here you are at last," a cold voice said from the next cage. "I was starting to think that you hadn't received an invitation to this little party."

Demetrius's onyx eyes stared at me with all the disdain I had grown used to. In the cage next to him sat Alexander, the Master of the South. The heads of two vampire Seethes weren't the sort of targets I would have mixed in with a pack of weres, but maybe some of Bethany and Sonja's customers had stranger tastes.

"Looks like they invited all the cool kids," I said. "And the cold-blooded ones too."

"I'm glad you find this amusing." Demetrius's sneer turned into a snarl of fury. "Because it's quite clearly your fault."

"What, you think I arranged my own kidnapping?" My body ached in a dozen places, my inner animal was howling for release, and a bunch of maniacs were planning on hunting me and my friends for sport. I really didn't have the time or patience for Demetrius's bullshit. "Maybe decided to lock up a few friends and acquaintances with me?"

"You might as well have, with the amount of chaos your pack has caused in recent years. The battles, the public court cases, the vast and powerful magical rituals, these things draw attention. The supernatural world stayed hidden for decades, but you've drawn the attention of outsiders onto all of us."

"These people were after us already. They're following on from the same rogue hunters who came after us before."

"And their hunt has been made a hundred times easier by your reckless endeavors. You might as well have stuck a sign up on the road into Chicago saying 'here be monsters.'"

"And you've been so damn careful?" I glared at him. "Half the problems we've had to fight were brought on by you and your people. Or have you forgotten the times you tried to kill us?"

"Tried to cut away the rotten flesh that threatens to infect us all. If I had destroyed the Midwest Pack five years ago, my people would have been ten times safer than they are now."

"Safer to murder innocent people out of hunger for blood."

"Safer to live as we are made."

It didn't matter what I said, Demetrius was immune to any line of reason that didn't end with the conclusion that he was right. I knew that my pack had made mistakes, just like anybody did, and we had spent a lot of time over the past year cleaning up those messes. We took responsibility in that way. If anything bad happened because of Demetrius and his people, apparently that was somebody else's fault.

The chaos around the pack had come from doing the right things, fixing the threats and problems that we faced, keeping ourselves safe, often keeping innocent people safe as well. These hunters hadn't been drawn by those problems, though they had probably used them to gather more intelligence on us. They had been drawn by their own desire to murder with impunity, using our monstrous side to justify killing people. The sort of people who behaved like that would do their worst no matter what I did.

At least Sky wasn't here. Some part of my mind had half-expected the clang of a cage door at any moment, as the same group who had captured me brought her in. The more time that passed, the clearer it became that it wasn't going to happen. Either she had fought them off, or she hadn't been on their list.

Given their ability to overcome me, the second option seemed more likely. They knew who the Alphas and Betas of the packs were, knew that rounding them up would give them the cream of the crop of weres. Perhaps they had also been counting on depriving the packs of leadership, leaving them uncoordinated, unable to respond until it was too late. If that was the plan, they had missed something important: that the mate of an Alpha or a Beta also shared their rank. In Sky's case, that meant there was still someone with status, confidence, and the skills to lead the pack, alongside the other senior weres. Sky was about to get another chance to step up and prove herself, and I was confident that she would live up to it.

More than that, I was relieved to know that she was safe. I had every intention of breaking out and making my captors pay, but there was no guarantee that would work out. At least I could be sure that, whatever happened to me, Sky wouldn't be hunted down by the real monsters of this scenario—the hunters.

Her safety gave me some comfort to cling onto as I curled up in the bottom of my cage, weary from fighting and worn down by the beating I had taken, and drifted off to sleep.

<hr>

I woke to the sound of raised voices. Cole was arguing with someone, and whoever it was, I instinctively wanted to take their side. Anything the manipulative Alpha of the East Coast Pack was saying had to be wrong in some way.

I stretched my arms and legs and was pleased to find that my aches were a lot less intense than on the previous day, despite a night spent sleeping on cold concrete. I thanked the universe at large for my were healing ability.

A guard stood in the middle of the collection of cages, a tray in one hand and a taser in the other. He was facing Cole's cage, and Cole was glaring back out at him, teeth bared, eyes flashing with anger.

"You call that food?" Cole snarled. "It's just more slop so you can keep us weak for hunting."

"You don't want it?" the guard answered. "Don't have it."

The tray landed face down with a clang, spattering the dusty concrete floor with Cole's breakfast. Looking around, I saw that several of my fellow captives already had trays in their cells and were eating like they hadn't fed in months, wolfing down slices of cheap bread, scrambled eggs, and plastic beakers of water. A stewardess's cart sat within reach of my cell, loaded up with more of the trays. At least our captors weren't letting us starve to death, though that wasn't much reassurance given what they intended instead.

"I'm going to tear you apart," Cole said, reaching for the

guard. "I'm going to get out of this cage and rip you to pieces."

It was more dramatic than I usually expected from Cole. Where was the manipulator who twisted the rules to get his way and who had tried to turn my own pack against me? Apparently his captors had left his subtlety behind when they snatched him from his home.

I found myself smiling despite the circumstances. It was satisfying to see Cole put out like this, to see his usual composure collapse as his inner wolf was overrun by the panic that came from being caged. He might not be the sort of heartless killer Demetrius was, but Cole was selfish and manipulative. There was no one in the world who I despised more, so his frustration gave me something to enjoy.

"You're going to kill me?" the guard said with a cruel laugh. "From behind those bars?"

"Not just you," Cole replied. "I'm coming for your friends and your family, I'm going to—"

His words were cut short in a crackle of electricity as the guard shoved a taser into Cole's arm. Cole let out a grunt, then a gurgle, then slumped over, twitching on the floor of his cage.

"Threaten my family, you hairy bastard?" The guard slid a key into the lock of the cage. Four of his colleagues approached from the outskirts of the room, descending like vultures as the door of the cage swung open on smoothly oiled hinges.

I half expected this to turn into a trap, for Cole to leap to his feet and attack the guards. I had seen weres shake off taser strikes before and keep on fighting, and Cole was one of the toughest of us. But either he had been weakened during his capture or these guards carried special heavy-duty stun weapons, because Cole just lay on the floor of his cage, groaning and twitching as the guards walked in.

The one who had tasered him leaned over to speak.

"You need to learn your place," he said. "You're not here to be fed. You're not here for your dignity. You're not here to make conversation or threats or pathetic schemes for how you're going to get your revenge. You're here to die like the beast you are, and everything before that will be what a beast deserves too."

He spat in Cole's face, then swung a kick at him. Cole grunted in pain, then arched his back as another guard kicked him from behind. With five of them clustered around Cole in the confines of the cage, I couldn't clearly see what was going on, but I heard the thuds of their boots as well as Cole's gasps and moans, and I saw the rise and fall of batons as they bludgeoned his head and shoulders.

I couldn't take pleasure in seeing Cole suffer like this. However hateful he might be, he was one of us. Here and now, he was on the receiving end of all the hatred these hired soldiers held for me and my kind. This beating could easily have landed on me, if I had been awake and in the mood to mouth off when they came around. The sounds of pain made me wince.

I looked away.

My gaze was immediately caught by the cart sitting outside my cage. While it was mostly filled with trays of food, it was used for other purposes too, as the bottom shelf held tools, tape, and pieces of scrap, including a couple of lengths of stiff wire—the sort of wire that could be used to pick a lock.

I glanced over my shoulder. For once, Cole was making himself useful, as the guards were still occupied with beating him. That gave me a few moments.

The gaps between the bars of my cell were just big enough to get my arm through almost the whole way to my shoulder. Crouching low in the cage, I pressed up against those bars and stretched, reaching for the bottom of the cart.

It was at the limits of my reach, and I had to strain, all the while listening for any gap in the brutality behind me.

My fingers brushed the scraps of wire, but I couldn't quite catch them between finger and thumb. I tried to catch them between my index and middle fingers, but it was hard to maintain a grip, and the wires fell to the floor.

The sound of the wires hitting the ground seemed unreasonably loud from where I crouched, and I looked around, sure that the guards would have heard it, but they were still occupied in making Cole's life miserable.

The wires had fallen at the edge of my reach. I managed to brush them with the very tips of my fingers, rolling them across the concrete toward me. At last, they came properly within reach. I caught them between finger and thumb and drew them into my cage, just as the guards emerged from dealing with Cole.

"Remember," the lead guard said, pointing at Cole as he looked at the rest of us, "this is what you get if you fuck around."

Cole's cage door clanged shut, the lock clicked into place, and the guards set to handing out the rest of the meals, leaving Cole with only the trampled remnants that had been spilled on the floor outside where he lay.

When the guards were all gone, Cole got back to his feet. The beating had been long and brutal sounding, and I had expected him to come up bruised and bleeding, spitting teeth. Instead, he looked little worse than he had before the taser struck him. He clutched his stomach and groaned melodramatically, but there was no sign that anything was broken. Surely these guards were tougher than this?

I didn't have time to consider how Cole had gotten off so lightly. Though I'd only taken scraps of wire from the cart, there was still a risk that the guards would notice that something was missing, or that someone would go back over the security footage and see what I'd been doing. If I was going to escape, I had to take a chance now and hope that no one was watching.

Summoning up the skills I'd been taught by a hired master thief, I bent the wires into suitable shapes and slid them into the lock, probing for the points of resistance. There was a click from inside the chamber, and then another. I kept working, using the sense of tension and resistance to guide my hands while I watched the doors for any sign of trouble.

"What are you doing?" Demetrius hissed.

"Trying to concentrate," I said, keeping my back to him.

One final click, a tug on the wire, and the bolt slid back. Grinning in triumph, I pocketed the wires and took one last look around me.

It was time to get out of this place.

CHAPTER 4

I sat with one hand on the cage door, holding it in place while I considered my next move. It was one thing to get out of my prison, another to know what I would do with that freedom.

There were three exits from the warehouse, and I had only seen the guards use one of them. That could mean that the other two were less used, and so better for making an escape, but it could also mean that they were locked or sealed shut, making them useless for my purposes. Not knowing how quickly someone would notice my escape, or how quickly they could respond, I had to make a choice between a possible dead end and one where I would almost certainly face opposition.

Then there was the question of who to take with me, if anyone. Everyone in this place had skills that could be valuable in making an escape, even if, in some cases, I was never going to acknowledge that out loud. There was an argument that letting out more people would also give me an advantage, as more bodies meant a better chance of overcoming the guards, if they got in our way.

The downside was that numbers were harder to hide. If I

went on my own, then they might not notice my absence for a while, and I might be able to sneak out of the facility unseen. Taking more people made it more likely that the alarm would be raised and that we would be seen. What I gained in strength, I would lose in stealth.

I looked across the cages once more. Many of the people here were friends of mine, and as Beta of a major pack, I owed a debt of loyalty to everyone except the vampires. Even Cole, much as I loathed him, was one of us, and today that meant he was on my side. I didn't like the idea of leaving them behind, but the alternative was worse. The last time hunters had come after us like this, we had lost good people. If one of us didn't get out and bring help, then there was almost no chance of us all getting out of this alive.

I eased the cage door open and slid out, then quietly closed it behind me.

"Well, well, well," Demetrius whispered. "It seems that the Beta has some tricks up his sleeve. Come, get us out of here and we'll make these barbarians regret the day they first picked up a gun."

I shook my head. "Not happening."

"Oh, so you're letting your were-beast friends out first, even though our cages are closer?" Alexander glared at me from between the bars. "I should have known that a were would put tribalism above all of our wellbeing."

"I'm not letting anyone else out," I whispered, hoping that they would lower their voices. I didn't want them to draw attention.

"What?" Demetrius's tone rose in outrage.

"I've got a better chance of escaping alone," I said. "I'll get help and bring it back."

"While they beat us and hunt us? I think not!" Demetrius, his face full of fury, gripped the bars as he glared at me. "Let us out or I will shout this place down."

I froze, halfway to the rear door, and turned to stare at

him. Was he so childish and selfish that he would risk my getaway, and with it everyone's lives, just to make sure things were done his way?

Of course he was.

I didn't have time for this nonsense, but I couldn't ignore it.

"If you start shouting, you ensure that this fails," I hissed angrily. "At least if I get out then you stand a chance."

"I stand a chance if you let me out to fight." Demetrius rattled the bars of his cage, but at least he had lowered his voice again. "Let me out, now."

"Ethan's right," Cole said, to my surprise. "We need someone to get out for help, and I wouldn't trust either of you to do it. The moment you're clear, you'll kill Ethan and leave the rest of us to rot."

It was good to see that Cole had my back for once. I didn't usually trust his motives, but on this occasion I figured that they had to be self-interest. He wanted to get out of here in one piece as much as I did, and he was smart enough to see that I was a better bet for that than the vampires' demands for a mass escape. Whether he could persuade them was another matter.

"We can't be trusted?" Demetrius turned his baleful gaze on Cole. "That's rich. I can practically smell the treachery coming off of you, hound."

"No one can ever trust a vampire, even your own kind. All you care about is your self-interest, your own self-indulgence."

"This coming from one of the creatures who brought this down on us?"

"At least we're up front about our intentions."

Coming from Cole, that was so much bullshit and bluster that it made me start to doubt his honesty. But what could his motive be if not to get out of here? He was as trapped as the rest of us, and the guards clearly didn't have much taste for him.

Alexander's voice rose shrilly as he joined Demetrius in arguing back at Cole.

"This is just the sort of garbage you get from weres. Growling like beasts, full of self-pity and self-righteousness, dogs whimpering for someone to tell them what to do. They need to be beaten into place, or they bring trouble like today down on all of us."

If Cole had meant to quiet the vampires, then he had completely failed. They were making enough noise that they risked drawing attention, whether that was still their plan or not. I couldn't risk sticking around to settle the issue, I just had to act.

"It's not a debate," I snapped. "I'm going. Try not to screw it up for everyone."

I ran to one of the doors at the back of the warehouse, while the vampires hissed angry words to each other, trying to decide how to deal with my disobedience—did they accept my plan as their best chance now that I was going, or scream the place down and hope I took them with me next time? Thankfully, they settled for silence.

The door handle turned and I pushed, but something was blocking it from the outside, and it barely moved more than an inch. Cursing, I ran to the other rear door and tried that. For a moment, it wouldn't give, and I thought I would have to risk going out the front way. Then there was a crunch as rust gave way and the door burst open, spilling me into daylight.

I found myself standing on a patch of open ground covered with broken concrete. Weeds grew between the cracks, and in places bushes had sprung up, tough, wiry things covered in thorns. A heap of old oil barrels were rusting in the open halfway to the wire fence, which was topped with a thick tangle of newly installed barbed wire.

If I had any kind of cutting tool, I would have headed straight for the fence and cut my way through, but a couple of scraps of wire would not help with that, and without something to cover the barbed wire, I couldn't get over without getting badly cut and probably too tangled to keep moving. That meant that I was going to have to work my way around the compound and find the main gate.

It felt good to be out of the cage, and I relished the freedom of being able to move more than five feet at a time, but I was gripped by the tension of my circumstances. If I was caught now, then our captors would tighten the security around our cages. My freedom, and that of my fellow captives, depended on me making a quick escape unobserved, from a prison I knew almost nothing about. And with cameras watching the cages, it was only a matter of time before someone looked at a screen, noticed I was missing, and sent people to catch me.

I ran along the back of the warehouse, to a gap between it and another large building. Peering around the corner, I saw a central loading and unloading area, in which at least a dozen of the mercenaries were milling around near a selection of trucks and cars. None of them seemed to be in a rush or on high alert, which was a good sign, but they were all armed.

If I could get around the next building unseen, then I would be most of the way to the gate. The only other options were doubling back the way I had come or rushing straight into the mercenaries guarding us, and neither seemed like a good idea. So I needed to get across the gap between the buildings unseen, around the corner, and hope that there weren't too many guards between me and the gate. There were a lot of unspoken ifs in that plan, and I had to hope that none of them got between me and freedom.

I tensed, watching the movement of the mercenaries, waiting for a moment when no one was looking my way. At last, everyone had their backs turned, attention drawn by the arrival of a large white van. I dashed across the gap between the buildings, running low to reduce the risk of being noticed if anyone turned around. I reached the other building at a sprint and stopped with my back against the wall, hidden from my opponents once more, while I caught my breath and listened for signs of a reaction.

No shout of alarm had been raised, no booted footfalls thundered toward me. I was still clear.

I walked along the back of the building, stepping around clumps of weeds and abandoned, rotting crates. This place had been lying neglected for years, only to be brought back into use as an improvised prison. It probably belonged to one of the people behind the hunt, a suitably out of the way location to run this operation from. Maybe when this was done, we could buy up the property, turn it into another out-of-town base for the pack. That would be a satisfying way to mark Bethany and Sonja's defeat. Assuming we did beat them.

I was almost at the far corner of the building when two mercenaries rounded the corner. They were laughing and talking, clearly not expecting any trouble, and they froze as they saw me.

The moment it took them to take in my existence was the moment I needed. My clothes ripped as I let my wolf form emerge, muscles straining, bones twisting, fur and claws thrusting from my skin. Even as that power rippled through me, I leapt at the mercenaries. I couldn't give them time to work out what was happening.

The closest one was the faster to react. He grabbed the assault rifle that hung from his shoulder, swinging it around.

I was faster, getting inside his guard before he could aim the gun at me. I grabbed the wrist of his gun hand between my teeth and twisted. The rifle fell onto the ground as he grunted in pain.

The other mercenary swung his rifle around, the butt heading for my head. I ducked, jerked back, and pulled his companion into the way, so that the weapon slammed into his chest.

One man was momentarily stunned and the other pulling back his weapon for another strike. I slashed at him with claws, and the world became a jumble of movement and pain, of lunging and dodging, shoving and striking. He opened his mouth wide to shout for help, but before he could get a word out, I flung my whole body at him, flattening him against the back of the building and knocking the breath from his lungs.

The other guy was back in the fight now, grabbing at me from behind. I kicked out, slashing at him with my back claws. I heard the tearing of cloth and felt the hot spatter of blood.

The one pressed against the building drew a silver combat knife, the smell of the metal drawing panic from my inner beast as he stabbed at me. I flung myself back, landing on his companion, who let out a low grunt of pain.

The guy with the knife was about to call out again. I couldn't let that happen. I flung myself straight at him, dodging right as the knife point flicked out to intercept me. The blade ran along my shoulder, drawing a clear, searing flash of pain but not cutting deep. Even without that sharp edge, silver would have burned, and the wound was agonizing, but I pushed on past, desperate to stop him before he could get a better angle with the blade. My teeth closed around his throat, he let out a brief gasp, and then my jaws clamped shut.

I had never liked the taste of human blood. Weres that did were the ones that went mad, giving in to that long-buried monster of our ancient ancestors. They went on killing sprees and had to be hunted down by their own packs, a tragedy no one liked to consider, much less talk about. Now I had that taste in my mouth, salty and bitter, pouring from the man I had killed. A moment of dizziness came over me as I stepped back, letting his body fall to the ground, and held my mouth open, letting most of the blood run out.

I turned to face the other man, who was drawing himself to his feet. Horror filled his face at the sight of me, blood dripping from canine jaws, teeth gleaming through that crimson coat, eyes blazing with aggression. I was confirmation of everything he had ever been told about weres, about how we were merciless monsters, savage beasts only worthy of being hunted down. I was the nightmare fuel of horror films and cheap paperback novels. I was every ancestral memory of desperate fights for survival, buried deep in the lizard part of his brain.

That panic worked in my favor. Already injured and now faced with an avatar of brutal death, he gave in to his deepest instincts. For some people, that would have been to run or to shout for help, but those sorts of people seldom ended up working as soldiers for hire. This guy's instinct was to fight.

He drew a knife with his uninjured hand, and again I saw the flash of silver in the sunlight. These people knew what they were up against, in theory at least, and they had come equipped for it.

Despite his injuries, he came at me, the knife blade steady, giving away nothing of his intentions. I stood my ground, equally steady, muscles bunched and claws bared. A dribble of blood ran between my teeth and spattered in the dirt.

He was good, but not good enough. At the last moment, his eyes flicked left, showing me which way he was going. As the knife flashed out, I was already in motion, dodging around the attack. My claws whipped up, one catching his arm below the wrist, the other raking his chest. The knife clattered on the concrete as he stood for a moment, staring down in disbelief at his wounds. Then he collapsed.

Now that the fight was over, I was intensely aware of the

pain in my shoulder, where the silver knife had cut me. The knife had left some trace of that silver coating, a particularly cruel and effective way to hurt a were. It burned like molten metal in the wound, from which blood ran freely. My best hope was for the blood to flush out the silver, and so give me a chance to start healing, but I couldn't wait for that to happen.

There were still no sounds of alarm. No one had heard our struggle. I might yet make it out of the complex, but there was no time for subtlety. Just get to the gates and get out.

I peered around the corner of the building. Sure enough, there was the front gate, past another of these large processing buildings, the length of a football field away from where I stood. I could only half see the gateway, but that was enough to see that the gates were open, giving me a chance if I could get past the guards. Two of them were in sight, leaning against a jeep and smoking, looking out of the compound, not in toward where I stood.

This was as good as it was going to get.

I loped out on four paws from behind the building, picking up speed as I went. The blood ran faster and my wounded shoulder ached, but I was committed now. I passed the end of the first building, picking up to a sprint, paws pounding the concrete, heart beating fast. I was racing past the second building, the gateway so close I could smell the guards' cigarettes, freedom less than fifty yards from me.

Then Sonja stepped out into my path, three more mercenaries behind her, all with pistols aimed at me.

CHAPTER 5

Sonja treated me to a cold, contemptuous smile. Her red hair blazed in the sunshine, a bright contrast to the drab camouflage colors in which she and her soldiers were dressed.

"Stop," she snapped, her Glock aimed firmly at my head.

I skidded to a halt only a dozen feet from her. Blood dripped from my lips as I let out a low, menacing growl.

"You think that scares me?" Sonja laughed. "I've killed worse than you all by myself, and as you can see, I'm not alone today."

My chest tightened and I pawed at the ground, my growl turning from a threat into a way to vent my frustration. I had come so close, only to be stopped with freedom in sight. Should I keep going, try to get past them, or was that just going to get me killed?

"Turn back into your human disguise," Sonja said. "We'll take you back to your cell. You can boast to your little friends about how close you came, get everyone psyched up for what's to come. Or…"

She cocked the hammer on her pistol, that click carrying its own unspoken threat.

I eyed her and the men and women backing her up. Four shooters, four guns. Even if I moved fast enough to surprise them, somehow got past without being hit, they would keep shooting all the way to the gate and beyond. Assuming that she hadn't hired amateurs, I would end up riddled with bullets, and I didn't like my chances of escaping that way.

Was that any worse than surrender, though? If I went back to the cage, I would just be waiting to be taken out and hunted. Sure, I might have another day or two first, but now that I had picked the lock once, I doubted I would get another chance at escape like that again. There was a ruthless efficiency to Sonja's movements that showed someone capable of learning quickly from her mistakes.

As I watched her, her gaze steady behind the gun, I saw another possibility. She stood ahead of her mercenaries, commanding the situation, and that meant she could get in their way. If I charged straight at her, it would be hard for the others to get a shot in. She would get a shot at me on the way, but unless she got both accurate and lucky, that wouldn't take me out in my wolf form. Once I was on her, no one would be able to shoot for fear of hitting the wrong person. And if I could get my claws around the throat of the woman in charge, maybe I could use that threat to get out.

It wasn't a great plan, and it was definitely going to hurt, but I was feeling desperate, and a painful plan was better than giving in.

"Well?" Sonja asked, twitching the tip of her gun to reinforce the threat. "What's it going to be?"

I didn't even tense my muscles in preparation, just leapt straight at her, using all the strength I could from a standing start. Claws bared, jaws wide, I sailed through the air, a missile of muscle and furry.

A single gunshot cracked and a blaze of agony torn into my shoulder. Not just a bullet. A silver bullet.

I crashed into Sonja, tried to grab her with my uninjured

fore claw, but failed. The pain in my other shoulder was too much, the silver a shard of white-hot agony searing my nerves. I couldn't think, couldn't focus, just thrashed wildly with my legs. I felt as though the pain lay in my very soul, burning out from the center along every single nerve, reducing me to ruin.

I thudded to the ground, the impact shifting the bullet inside my shoulder, sending more pain through me. I howled, a piercing, ragged noise that echoed around the rundown processing plant.

Sonja, who had landed beside me, pulled herself to her feet. I was faintly aware of other shapes around us, her mercenaries closing in, guns pointed at me.

"Stupid mutt," Sonja said, pushing back hair that had fallen across her face. "Did you really think that I hadn't planned for you?"

I writhed on the ground, my body curling in around that unbearable agony. I had been so stupid, so arrogant, not thinking that what she had done with knives she might do with bullets too. This whole place was designed to contain people like me, to rob us of every advantage we had, to hold us ready for the hunt. Whatever concept of sportsmanship they might claim to follow later, it wouldn't apply here. This was a perfectly constructed prison camp.

"Take him to Frayn," Sonja said, holstering her pistol. "Get her to dig out the bullet and clean that other wound, then get him back in the cage to heal. I want him in good condition for the hunt.

"And someone check where he came from. Judging by the blood, someone's life insurance policy is about to pay out."

I was carried across the plant to a pair of cargo containers that had been joined end to end. The interior had been painted pristine white, with one container holding an operating theater, the other a ward of empty beds. With the devices attached to the walls and the cupboard full of medicines and instruments, it reminded me of the pack's infirmary, a place well equipped to deliver off-the-books medicine.

Frayn, the mercenaries' medic, was as professional in her role as they were in the part of killers. She assessed me calmly as I was laid out on the table, two mercenaries still pointing their guns at me, as if I was in any condition to try and escape again.

"Tie down those legs," Frayn said, pointing with a scalpel. "I'll need the fourth one free to operate."

Thick straps were wrapped around my hind legs and one at the front. With my free paw, I clawed at the table, unable to hold still through the terrible pain.

"I haven't treated many weres," Frayn said as she set up an IV drip on a stand by my head. "I assume that it will go better for you if I treat you in this state, rather than as a human?"

I nodded my head, as best I could while pressed down against the cold metal of the table.

"Excellent. That will make this more interesting."

With a swift snip of scissors, Frayn cut away the fur where my neck met my right shoulder. She slapped on shaving foam, then ran a cutthroat razor across, scraping away the foam and stubble. With my bare skin exposed, she found a vein, thrust a needle in on the first go, and attached it to the drip. Every movement was fast and assured. If treating a monster intimidated her, it didn't show.

"I'm giving you an anesthetic," she said. "Enough to numb the pain and let you lie still, but hopefully not enough to knock you out yet. This is still going to hurt, but having you awake increases my chance of success, so if you feel yourself drifting let out a growl. Understand?"

I nodded. Already, the pain was starting to ease off

around the knife wound, though the bullet was still a hideous blaze inside me.

"Good." Frayn picked up some sort of probe and what looked like a pair of long-nosed pliers. "Let's get started, shall we?"

I couldn't tell how long Frayn was working on me. With the pain, though muffled, still coursing through my body, it felt like hours, but in reality might only have been fifteen minutes. First, she extracted the bullet, a process that made me dizzy with pain as tools were forced down the hole the bullet had made. Despite her skill, it took two attempts to get a grip on that lump of silver amid torn muscles that writhed at its touch, and I could feel that poison every inch of the way as she dragged it out.

The bullet fell with a ting into a metal bowl. Frayn held it out in front of me, a silver lozenge covered in my own blood, smelling both familiar and awful.

"Fascinating, isn't it?" Frayn said. "How much carnage such a small thing can do. I spent some time in Basra, back when that war was young, and let me tell you, even an ordinary bullet can do extraordinary things."

With that bundle of agony gone, I sagged in relief on the operating table. I could almost have felt grateful to Frayn, if not for the fact that she was working for these assholes, not saving my life so much as preserving it a few days more.

I hadn't noticed that I was panting for breath, but my tongue hung out of my mouth, the salty taste reminding me that not all the blood here was mine.

Frayn talked while she worked, sometimes about what she was doing, sometimes about wounds she had seen in the past, medical horrors she had dealt with in war zones and crime-infested cities around the world. Her fascination with the details of her work was unsettling, talking about death and destruction with a tone not of shock or carefully fostered calm but of academic fascination, like a collector talking about their specimens. I didn't know if she needed a counselor or just a friend, but she sure needed someone to talk to who wasn't dealing with their own wounds.

By the time she had finished cleaning and stitching my injuries, I was starting to lose track of her words. Between the drugs and the blood loss, my grip on the world around me was fading, and I could feel sleep coming on. Remembering her instructions, I forced a quiet growl out between my teeth.

"Nap time, is it?" Frayn stood back, assessing me. "Fair enough, I'm done. But before you fade away, what blood type are you?"

I rolled my eyes, then looked down pointedly at my lupine snout.

"Ah, yes, of course. And we don't want you changing because you heal well this way, is that right?"

I nodded as best I could with a head that felt like lead.

"Well then." There was a squeaking noise, then Frayn held up a small whiteboard with blood types written on it. "Which one?"

I pointed at the appropriate letter.

"If only all my patients were so cooperative." Frayn drew a sachet of blood from a cold store and waved an IV needle at me. "All right, Mr. Charleston, now you can sleep."

I woke up in my cage, still in wolf form. Someone had left me clothes—jogging pants, a t-shirt, and canvas sneakers—and a tray of food. No point in putting me under the surgeon's knife if they were then going to let me freeze or starve to death.

I flexed my legs, testing how my body felt. A lot of dull aches, and a deeper pain where the bullet had been, but nothing as intense as I had feared, and certainly nothing that would seriously get in my way. The remnants of the drugs, along with my body's exhaustion at dealing with my wounds, had left me groggy, but not so bad that I couldn't pull myself together and deal with the hunger clawing at my guts.

Carefully, not wanting to risk tearing my stitches, I shifted to my human form. Everything seemed to be in place. For all her supposed lack of experience, Frayn knew how to handle were-animal wounds, and I wondered how many she considered "not many" to have treated. I also wondered how many of those had been captives taken for hunting, how often she had been complicit in murder. She had taken good care of me, but no one here was innocent.

As I pulled on my clothes, Demetrius watched me with a sneer from his cage.

"Enjoying the reverse strip show?" I asked.

"Much as I love to see you in pain, this is hardly a moment for pleasure," he replied. "You had a chance to get us out and you wasted it. If we die now, that is on you."

Normally, I would have risen to Demetrius's goading. The baseline disgust with which I viewed him made it hard to ignore his superior sneering and verbal barbs. But the same haze that softened my view of the rest of the world also took an edge off my anger. I cared more about eating than about putting the vampire in his place.

"I did my best," I said, peering at the food on my tray. Steak, eggs, beans, bread on the side. Plenty of protein to help me rebuild, and carbs to energize me. There was even a glass of orange juice and a lukewarm cup of coffee.

"Your best? You sound like a child begging for a participation trophy."

I didn't bother taking the plastic knife and fork to the steak, just picked it up and bit off a chunk. The meat was rare. Did our captors know my taste in food, or had they made an educated guess based on my nature? At this point, either could be true, and neither mattered. What was important was the surge of vitality that washed through me as I tasted meat.

"You should have taken us with you," Demetrius said, pressing against the bars of his cage.

His voice, normally so controlled, was shot through with frustration. Being caged didn't suit him any more than it suited me, and I had at least been out for a bit. My lack of response was clearly adding to his frustration, and that was reason enough to stay calm, eat my meal, and leave him unsatisfied.

"If you had let us out, we could have escaped by force," he said in a menacing hiss. "You think those people out there could stand against all of us combined? The strongest weres and vampires in North America against a cluster of humans with their pathetic bodies and their feeble weapons."

I scooped up a forkful of eggs while I considered what he was saying. Had I gotten it wrong? Could we have gotten out together?

Sonja had gotten to the gates before me, which meant that she knew something was wrong. My escape from the cage hadn't gone undetected for long, probably not long enough to let everyone out, given the time it took to pick my lock. So it wouldn't have been all these strong creatures together, just a handful of us.

Even if we had all gotten out, we wouldn't have known about the silver bullets. A weapon like that could have taken us all down before we even reached the gate. There would have been no catching guards by surprise if we had charged out together, just a mad rush for the exit, bullets flying at us. Ordinary bullets would have been enough to make that difficult, silver would have made it nearly impossible for anyone to get out.

Of course, the soldiers might not all have silver, but that was a big thing to gamble our lives on.

"Maybe," I said with a shrug. "But you're probably wrong."

"That's it?" Demetrius shrieked. "That's your whole answer, your whole justification? Maybe? Probably? You wretched creature!"

I turned my back on him and focused on eating. Demetrius kept ranting behind me, and the sound made me smile. If I was going to die, I could at least enjoy this moment first, hearing the vampire Master drive himself into an impotent frenzy.

Of course, if I lived then the memory would be all the sweeter, and I intended to live.

Dawn woke me the next morning, its light shining through the grubby skylights in the ceiling of our warehouse prison. Not long after, guards appeared, delivering trays of food. They were more careful this time, keeping the cart well out of reach. After days trapped in cages, we were all subdued, watching them with wariness rather than the hostility that had gotten Cole his beating.

The guards watched while we ate, then gathered up the trays. They seemed more tense than the previous day, and I didn't think that was just about my breakout, though they all looked my way from time to time. More was happening today. They were waiting for something.

At last, the main door opened again. Sonja and Bethany walked in, followed by Frayn pushing a cart of her own, this one laden not with food but with syringes.

"Today's the day," Sonja said with a clap of her hands. "Your chance to get out of your cages and run. Not run far, I expect, but how far depends on you. After all, there's no sport if there's no challenge."

At her shoulder, Bethany stood treating us to a deathly glare. For her, there was no fun to be had here, not even the psychotic sort that Sonja relished. This was about money and revenge, and I didn't know which took precedence. I feared Sonja more as a fighting opponent, but if we somehow got away today, Bethany was the one who would hunt us to the ends of the earth.

The thought of the hunt made my pulse race. Part of that was anticipation, as the prospect of getting out of these cages came with the chance, however slim, to turn this around. But more powerful than that was anger, the sheer fury that came from knowing that I was about to be hunted for sport. My throat went dry and my fingers twitched as I thought about wrapping them around Sonja's throat.

I flexed my arms and legs. Everything was stiff and aching from my recent fights. The places where Frayn had stitched me shut, though starting to heal, still threatened to burst open if I strained too hard. This wasn't the state I wanted to be in going into a fight, but it was the one I would have to deal with.

"Dr. Frayn has a little something for you," Sonja said as the doctor picked up a syringe. "Either you stick your arm out and let her inject you, or we shoot you down, then send her in to inject you." She patted the Glock on her hip. "Ethan knows how painful that can be, so take your cue from him."

The others turned to look at me. I hesitated. Those syringes could contain anything. On the other hand, how was I going to avoid the injection? Getting shot wouldn't make it any better.

Resentfully, I thrust my left arm between the bars of my cage.

"Good boy," Sonja said as the others followed my lead.

I ignored her mocking tone and let Frayn stick the needle in my arm. As the drug flowed through my system, I felt a sense of warmth, then a twitching in my muscles. My body was trying, against my will, to change into its were form.

"How…" I gasped as a spasm ran through my legs.

"Research," Frayn replied as she stuck a needle into another were. "And some outside help."

I might have accepted the injection, but I hadn't agreed to have my body changed in this way. I felt violated by this overriding of my own desires, this artificial enforcement of a natural process.

I fought against the transformation, as I had seen Sky fight against it under the influence of a full moon. Around me, other weres were changing, human bodies giving way to animal form, but I resisted, trying to keep my body as my own, taking inspiration from the woman I loved. I breathed deeply, slowed my pulse, fought back against the transformation.

But as hard as I fought, it was still coming. My legs spasmed and I fell to the floor, hands twitching against the concrete. My back twisted as bones grew and muscles turned, rippling into different but familiar shapes. My teeth elongated, sharp points pressing against my tongue, and fur bristled on my arms.

"No," I growled, still fighting the change. If Sky could do this, then I could too. I was my own master, the controller of my body, and no one was taking that from me.

Except that they were. Whatever was in the drug, it was too powerful for me to resist. I sank to all fours, shoes falling from paws, clawed hands losing their fingers. My snout extended, my ears pricked up, and my tale unfurled, twitching. At last I collapsed, my body exhausted by the forced transformation, and unconsciousness took hold.

I couldn't have been out for long, because everyone was where they had been when I passed out: Bethany, Sonja, and Frayn watching us with curiosity, the guards standing warily around, the rest of the captives lying or pacing in their cells.

I was a beast still, snarling in frustration, forced and trapped. I tried to turn back to my human form, but the change would not come. Whatever they had done to me, I was stuck this way, my body no longer my own to command. It was a bitter feeling, a sense of utter violation, and I felt as frustrated as I had ever been.

All the weres had changed. I could smell their animal nature, could feel the sense of connection that it brought. A feeling that normally brought comfort, but today brought only anger and humiliation. We looked at each other uncertainly, not knowing how to act. Weres changed to fight or to run free, to work together as a pack. With cold bars between us, none of that was possible.

"See, that wasn't so bad." Sonja stood at the bars of my cage, a dart gun in her hand, looking down at me with that same cold, superior smile I was growing all too used to. "Now it's time for a nap, and then the games can begin."

She pointed the gun at me. There was a thump and then another, a prick of darts piercing my flank. My legs, only just grown steady, wobbled again and then gave way as I fell unconscious.

CHAPTER 6

I was getting used to uncomfortable awakenings. This time, I could feel the prickle of pine needles through my fur and smell fresh loam and tree sap, a great improvement on the concrete and chemical dust of the processing plant. I was out in the woods, though which woods I didn't know. How far had my captors taken me? Had I been unconscious for days, hours, mere minutes?

I didn't seem to have been bound, which was a good start. If I was free to act, then I had a better chance of getting out of this alive. I readied myself mentally, determined to race off the moment things started looking dangerous.

I opened my eyes and looked around. The other weres were lying around me, all in animal form. The remnants of torn clothes we had been left in by our forced transformations had all been removed. Demetrius and Alexander sat under a tree, both rubbing their heads groggily. They looked like I felt—half asleep but waking up fast, energized by anger.

Across the clearing we lay in, Sonja and Bethany stood amid their guards, watching us with their familiar expressions of cold calculation and bitter hatred. Unfamiliar men and women stood with them, all dressed in some variation of woodland camouflage. They carried a range of weapons, including bows, crossbows, hunting rifles, and shotguns. Most wore expressions of excitement that bordered on hunger, though a couple looked less certain. The air smelled of silver.

"Is this it?" one of the men asked. "I'd expected something grander, not a bunch of sleepy critters and a couple of goths."

"Don't underestimate them," Bethany said. "You will never meet a stronger, more merciless, or more ingenious prey than these creatures."

"And you'll never get another chance like this," Sonja added excitedly. "How many people you know have ever hunted a werewolf or a vampire? When you go home, you will look at your peers and know that none of them have felt the same thrill as you, have overcome the same prey as you. You will be unique, unequaled, masters of the hunt."

"Secret masters," the man muttered. "What's the point if we can't talk about it?"

"Can't talk about it yet," Bethany said. "But sooner or later, their secret will come out. When the world eventually recognizes these monsters for what they are, you will be able to tell your friends that you helped keep the beasts in check. You won't just be the greatest hunters you know—you will be heroes."

"Heroes." The man ran a hand down his bow. "I like the sound of that."

"Good, because you signed a contract, and your nondisclosure agreement is as binding as our no refunds policy. Now, if you would like to take your places…"

Under the eyes of the guards, the hunters lined up, weapons at the ready, Sonja among them. They faced us in a line, fingers on triggers, arrows notched to bowstrings.

I tensed, waiting for the expectant silence to break. Should I just charge straight at them? That would surely be futile, with so many weapons pointing our way. Run off into the forest then and try to deal with them there. Perhaps we, the prey, could regroup once we were out of sight. We just needed a moment to talk, to plan, to prepare for the fight ahead…

"We want to make this a sporting challenge," Sonja said. "On that basis, prey, you have one minute to get away. On my mark…" She glanced down at a stopwatch. "Go!"

I didn't need more signal than that. There was no time to consult the others, so for now it was every man for himself.

Leaves flew from my paws as I dashed into the woods, leaving the clearing full of killers behind. For the first hundred yards, I could hear movement to either side, other weres racing between the trees. But soon we were scattered, spread too far apart for me to know who was near. The forest stretched out ahead of me, an unknown expanse of woodland in which I didn't know my way out, never mind my way home. I was alone.

But I was also angry, and that anger could be the fuel I needed. I would find a way to turn this around, to inflict on my enemies what they had wanted to do to me. I would make them the prey.

Then I felt a twinge in my shoulder and the hot oozing of blood through my fur. My stitches had split.

I stopped to look at the wound. It was smaller than it had been, only a slow flow of blood emerging. That would have given my presence away to a were-animal or a vampire, but these humans wouldn't catch the scent. With any luck, they wouldn't see the drops that had fallen in the leaf mulch either.

"There's one of 'em," a voice called from behind me.

I turned to see two men, both with bows, stalking after me through the undergrowth. They had come more quickly and quietly than I had expected. I wondered if Sonja's sixty seconds head start had been a lie, or if the sedative was still slowing me down. Most likely it was both, as my body felt like a weight dragging me into the dirt.

An arrow whistled past me, too close for comfort. I took off again, sprinting through the trees with the hunters on my trail.

I couldn't bet on running to get me out of this. For the hunt to work, Sonja and Bethany had to have set some sort of perimeter, to prevent us from just using our animal speed to get away. My best bet was to turn the table on my pursuers, to go from prey to predator. Right now, I was at a disadvantage, as they were armed, but that was something I could change.

Dashing through the trees, I kept my eyes open for the right sort of irregularity in the ground, the perfect sort of misshapen tree. After a few minutes, something caught my eye.

I stopped and ducked into a hollow between the roots of two closely grown trees. Grabbing branches between my teeth, I got nearby bushes spread in front of me, hiding me from the trail I had been following. I stopped and waited, ears pricked up, listening for sounds of pursuit.

No one was close yet. That gave me time for the next part of my plan. Settling down in the hollow, I closed my eyes and reached down inside, seeking my human form.

It was a strange and unsettling experience, forcing things this way. Usually, it was the wolf that I called upon in emergencies, drawing him out when my human form was not enough. But if I wanted to take the hunters' weapons, then I would need human hands, and that meant shifting form.

Years of practice had made it easy for me to become human, shedding the wolf body to return to normal life. But though I strained to make my body obey me, nothing seemed to happen. I tried again, focusing on the bright inner spark that was my human mind, reminding myself of how it felt to have arms and hands, to stand on two legs. I breathed deeply and let my inner truth flow.

Nothing. Whatever drug Frayn had used, it had trapped me in animal form.

Frustrated, I shifted in the dirt of my hideout and peered through the concealing leaves. Two people were coming, their footsteps heavy on the forest floor, probably the two I had previously seen. I couldn't do what I had been planning, but I could still use this opportunity to ambush them, and hopefully to lessen the odds against me.

For the first time since Sebastian's house, luck was on my side. The two hunters walked right in front of me, only a yard from my hiding place. They had their bows at the ready, arrows nocked, fingers ready to draw. I held my breath as I waited, afraid that one of them would turn and see me here, cornered in my own hiding place, but they were intent on the forest ahead.

"You think he kept runnin'?" one of them asked in a low whisper.

"Aye, I reckon so," the other answered in a Scottish accent. "But you saw that blood back there—yon beasty's hurting, and sooner or later he's gonna have to stop. That's when we'll get him."

Careful not to rustle the leaves, I crept out of my hiding place. The hunters' backs were to me, their bulky clothes and matching weapons giving me no way to choose between them. It would just be dumb luck for them who went down first.

I leapt, landing on the back of the Scotsman. He screamed and fell as my claws sank into the back of his neck. My other claws raked his back, but instead of tearing through flesh they scraped over something tough and flexible—body armor. The odds were even more stacked against me than I'd thought.

The Scot rolled over as he hit the ground. His initial

alarm had given way to a sort of grim determination, and he yanked a knife from his belt. Not a silver one this time—apparently those were reserved for the guards—but something long and wide and ugly, a blade designed to take a chunk out of whatever it hit.

He slashed at me, but I dodged the blow easily, adrenaline cutting through the fog that had lain across my mind. I snapped at him, catching his forearm between my teeth, and bit down hard. There was a crunch of breaking bone, that foul taste of human blood again, and another cry of pain from him, deeper this time. As he clutched at the arm, I clawed his face, leaving him screaming through a ragged, bloody mess.

It was no more than he deserved.

A strike to my flank drove me off the fallen Scotsman. I turned to see the other hunter, who had a long baton in his hand. It looked like the sort of weapon the police might use, except that wires ran from its base to a battery pack on his belt.

"Been wantin' a chance to try this," he said with a grin. "Guess you're gonna be that chance, boy."

He pressed a stud on the handle and electricity crackled around the tip of the baton, bright sparks flying in the still air. He swung at me and I backed off, away from the chemical smell of the baton and the glint of malice in his eyes. If that thing packed a punch like the guards' tasers, I really didn't want to be on the receiving end of it.

I turned and ran. Behind me, there was the thud of something being dropped, then the twang of a bowstring. Pain tore through my thigh, making me stumble on a weakened leg, and I looked down to see an arrow protruding through my fur.

Slowed by the arrow wound, I stumbled on through the woods, barely able to put weight on that leg. I needed a place to hide again, some way to deal with the wound.

Suddenly, the ground gave way beneath my forepaw. I stopped abruptly and look down.

In front of me, branches had fallen across a hole in the ground, and leaves had fallen across them, covering the gap. I had almost run into a natural pit trap.

I doubled back, then flung myself down beneath a thick stand of bushes. There, I lay in the dirt, blood running from my wounded leg. I gritted my teeth against the pain, but that left me with no way to grip the arrow and pull it out. I needed human hands.

I took a deep breath and closed my eyes, ready to try and force the change again. This time I focused on the wolf, not bullying or cajoling it but pleading with it to retreat, to let my human form return. Filled with panic and pain, the wolf resisted. It was my natural form in a time of crisis, and some part of my mind thought that it was what I needed.

I had to suppress that instinct, to bring conscious choice to the forefront. I slowed my pulse and looked my inner wolf in the eye, offering all the reassurance I could. Things would be well, I told it, despite the evidence of my own body. Things would be well if it just let me take control.

However Frayn's drug had been riling the inner wolf, forcing my body to take that shape, it was starting to weaken. I felt a twinge in my foreleg, then my shoulder, the beginnings of a change. I took more deep breaths, urging the transformation to flow through me, pulling my body back into human form. The change seemed excruciatingly slow, with blood running from my leg and a hunter on my trail, but at last muscles twisted, bones reformed, fur withdrew, and I lay in human form, battered and bleeding but in control.

"Come out, come out," the hunter called between the trees. "I see the blood trail, boy. I'm gonna get you soon. You'll be better off runnin', we both know that."

I hated it, but he was right. I couldn't just wait and fight him, not with an arrow sticking out of my thigh, and he was too close now to take the time and deal with that. But perhaps if I ran the right way, then I could lead him into the pit I had seen.

From a sprinter's crouch, I dashed out of the bushes and back onto the forest trail. Pretending to duck and weave in case of a shot, I dodged around the pit.

Just as I reached the far side, there was the thrum of a bowstring and the whistle of an arrow. This time it hit me in the shoulder, a fresh burst of pain in an already tender place. My human body couldn't take a battering and keep going like I could when I was a wolf. The pain and shock stunned me and I fell beside the hole.

At least I had gotten around my trap. Now the hunter stalked closer, slinging his bow and drawing a long, slender knife, like an old-fashioned bayonet.

"Well, well, well," he said, looking over at me. "Reckon you were prettier as a beast."

He came closer to the pit edge—three steps away, two, one. His foot hovered over the edge of disaster.

He pulled it back and sidestepped around the pit.

"What, you thought I wouldn't notice that?" He laughed. "Been huntin' my whole life, boy. I ain't that easy to kill."

He stood over me with a look of malicious glee, the knife glinting in a beam of sunlight between the trees. I was bleeding from both my wounds, the arrows throbbing strands of pain that ran through my flesh. The ground was growing sticky under me and I could feel my strength seeping out with my blood.

The hunter leaned over. "Let's get this done with, go see if I can catch me more prey."

I kicked with my good foot, slamming it up into his stomach. His body armor absorbed most of the blow and made my toes throb at the impact, but it was still enough to make him double over. I swung my fist into the side of his head, knocking him down in the dirt next to me.

He rolled over, the knife in his hand, trying to get back to his feet. Fighting back the wave of pain that came with every movement, I flung myself on top of him. The knife slashed at my face, so close I felt the wind of its passing against my cheek. Then I had hold of his wrist, twisted and jerked. The knife flew free and vanished into the pit.

His other fist smashed into my chest, and I winced, but two could play at that game. I punched him in the face, smashing his nose in, then punched him again, and again, battering away until he stopped moving. Both my fists were sore and bloody, but for the first time since entering the woods, I was free of pursuit.

I staggered to my feet. Noises came to me from elsewhere in the forest, sounds of fighting from multiple directions. It gave me hope that I wasn't the only one to have turned the tables on our pursuers. The problem was, I didn't know which was the best way to go. Following the sounds of any fight could as easily lead me to enemies as to friends.

I stumbled through the trees, trying to rally my thoughts. Which way to go? What to do? How best to get out of this mess? If I could find Sebastian, maybe we could work together, but I couldn't catch his scent, couldn't even begin to work out in which direction I might find him. It was hard to concentrate, pain and weariness dragging me down. I could barely begin to pull a plan together.

Struggling to keep myself upright, I leaned against a tree. I would just take a moment to catch my breath, to muster my thoughts, to regain my strength…

"Is the person who did this to you still out there?"

It was Sky's voice. For a long moment, I couldn't believe it, but then I caught her scent through the blood and fallen leaves, felt that magnetic draw between us. Looking up, I saw her approaching me. I never tired of seeing Sky, but I had never been more pleased to see her than I was right then. A minute before, I had been desperate, my strength fading. I hadn't known if I would make it through this alive, never mind whether she was safe. And here she was, the love of my life turning up like hope out of the blue, coming for me in my moment of most terrible need. She was more than just a woman. She was a miracle.

I smiled faintly, overcome by both relief and physical weakness. "Yes, but they are in desperate need of medical attention."

"Did they shoot you while you were like this?" She looked horrified. I could hardly blame her.

"I changed after I was hit in the leg. It's easier to pull out." Not that I had managed to take it out. I shifted slightly and muscles moved around the arrow in my thigh, making me draw a sharp breath at the pain. "The second one I got after I'd changed. Both men are down. One severely injured and the other dead. Or that was my assumption."

Sky leaned in and kissed me lightly on the lips. In spite of everything, the taste of her was intoxicating, a moment of pleasure after days of struggle and frustration. She had come to save me.

"Close your eyes," she whispered.

I shook my head and forced a grin. "Not a chance. I want to see your face when you do it."

"I just saw a couple of people mauled by animals. I can handle a little blood from an arrow."

She snapped the head off the arrow protruding through my shoulder, then pulled the rest out the back. It hurt like hell, but not as much as the one in my thigh; she had to push through the muscle to get a hold of the head and break it off. After everything else I had been through, it would have been unbearable without her there.

It was fantastic to see Sky again, to feel the strength that always came when I was around her, to know that she had gotten through the confrontation at Sebastian's house unharmed. More than that, I was proud to see her charging to the rescue, emerging from the woods to save me and the other captive weres. Her dogged determination, which had sometimes caused me so much stress, had become the difference between me living or bleeding out in the woods. I would have rather been the rescuer than the one being saved, but if I was going to be rescued by anyone, then I was happy it was Sky.

I looked down at the blood covering me.

"I should try to change," I said. Now that I didn't need my hands, I would gain more from the healing that came in my wolf form.

"If you can do it."

I called back the wolf form that I had so recently dismissed, urging it to take hold of me. Muscles strained and flesh trembled as my injured body shifted from one shape to another, blood flowing as wounds stretched. Encumbered by blood loss, injury, and the aftereffects of multiple drugs, the experience of changing, usually so smooth, had become awkward and painful, but I forced myself through. Soon I was on all fours, standing at Sky's feet.

As she led me through the forest, I finally got some understanding of what had happened. The trees were full of the familiar scents of pack members, a whole force of them who had come to our rescue. They had overcome our captors and the hunters they served, arriving just in time to save anyone from being hunted to death. My relief at having lived through the ordeal was matched only by my pride at the way the pack had performed. Even without me and Sebastian there to lead them, they had seen the problem, found out where their enemies were, and acted decisively to deal with them. I didn't know if any of us would have survived without that, but I was sure that some of us would have died.

This was what it meant to be part of a pack—knowing that someone always had your back.

With my body still racked by pain, I had to stop several times before we reached the edge of the forest and the cars waiting there. It was frustrating, but hardly surprising. I gritted my teeth and pushed on through the pain.

At the tree line, Josh approached us, with Gavin and London behind him. He knelt in front of me, his face full of concern, and touched a hand to my head, then across my fur, feeling the openings of the arrow wounds on my shoulder and leg. We weren't normally so intimate with each other, but there was something comforting in his steady touch, a reassurance that I would be okay. For all our differences, Josh and I were closer than ever before, and he had sprung into action to save me alongside Sky. I owed them more than I could ever repay, and knew that it was a debt that would never be called in. Like a pack, this was what family did, and my family, like my pack, stood strong.

Josh frowned but kept that gentle touch in place, and there was some magic in his voice that helped ease my pain. I still needed rest and treatment, but I knew that I could get through this.

"We have everyone except Cole," he said, glancing at London with a smile. "London did most of the cleanup. Once you return, we'll go over it again."

I could see the struggle on Sky's face. She knew that, if we were rescuing the other weres, then we should rescue Cole too, but she disliked him almost as much as I did. The temptation to leave him behind was strong.

Fortunately for Cole, Sky was a better person than me. She started to walk back into the trees. Unwilling to let her enter danger alone, I walked after her.

Sky unsheathed a sword hanging from her belt and looked down at me.

"I'll be fine, Ethan." She smiled, but that wasn't going to

stop me from following her. "Ethan, if I run into any trouble it will be harder for me because I'll be worrying about you. I came to get you, I can handle this."

She was right, and I hated it. Normally I was the one trying to get Sky to stay behind, to keep her safe because she was more vulnerable than me, but now the tables were turned. In my injured state, I would be more liability than help, and if we ran into trouble, then I might end up dead. I loathed the feeling of being protected, being the vulnerable one relegated to spectator status, but hating a thing didn't stop it from being true. Sky could kick ass as well as anyone in the pack, and I had to let her do it. I watched with a terrible squirming in my guts as she ran full pelt into the trees.

"Come on," Gavin said, opening the door of an SUV. "We need to get you home."

I shook my head and stood staring stubbornly at him. I wasn't going until Sky came back.

"You're going to have to," Gavin said. "Sky's in charge of this one, and her orders were to get injured people back to Dr. Jeremy for treatment as fast as we can. Demetrius and Alexander have gone off to lick their wounds with the Seethe, but all the weres are being taken back to the retreat. Unless the Alpha or Beta tells me otherwise, that's what I'm doing with you, and I don't think you're in a state to resist."

I glared at him, but he just grinned as he approached, ready to pick me up.

I wasn't going to let them do this. With a huge force of will, I made my body change again, strained muscles twisting and writhing until I stood human again. Stood probably wasn't the right word—I had to lean against the SUV just to keep from falling down—but at least I could give orders.

"We're not leaving until Sky returns," I hissed through gritted teeth.

"What a shock." Gavin grinned some more. "You going to sit down, at least?"

"I'm fine."

"You stubborn, self-obsessed ass," London snapped.

I turned my head, surprised by this sudden outburst.

"Your brother is worried sick," London continued, gesturing at Josh. "Even this ridiculous slab of meat"—she pointed at Gavin—"is encouraging you to rest. But no, you won't even sit down before you fall down. You'd rather make your friends watch you suffer."

I stared at her, open-mouthed. I had no idea that London was so strong-willed. She herself seemed a little surprised, though her glare never wavered from my face.

"Fine," I said, sinking into the SUV's back seat. "Does anyone have a dressing for these wounds?"

Gavin wasn't much of a medic, but he managed to stop the worst of the bleeding. By the time Sky emerged from the woods, a battered Cole leaning on her, I was as comfortable as I had been since the first arrow hit me. I watched as she eased Cole into the car. He looked even worse than me, his skin pale and body trembling. For once, I couldn't enjoy his misery. This had come at the hands of the hunters, and I wouldn't share in any triumph they might feel.

"Bethany?" I asked. I hadn't seen either of our lead captors in the woods, but if we had one of them alive, then we could learn more about how they found us and the drug that forced transformations.

"Dead," Cole said.

"Sonja?"

"Dead too," Sky said.

One last hope remained.

"Frayn?"

"What do you think?" Cole asked between lips turning blue. "They all got what they deserved."

I didn't feel sorry for any of them, but there was still a

sense of regret. If there was a connection between these hunters and the other forces arrayed against the pack, then we weren't going to find it. Sonja and Bethany's connections had died with them, along with the identity of the outside help that had led to Frayn's drug.

I just had to hope that no one else had that power.

I staggered into the pack house, leaning on Gavin for support, while others carried Cole in. We were both deposited on beds in the infirmary while Jeremy set to work on us.

Cole looked like death, his skin pale but warm. Though barely conscious, he got hold of Sky's hand and clung to it. Even in this state, he was finding ways to aggravate me, but when I caught Sky's eye she just shrugged. What was she going to do, shake off a man seeking comfort, one who had been badly injured helping us?

Kelly and Jeremy worked their way around the assorted injured weres who had come back from the hunt. They cleared silver from wounds, bandaged them, and set up IVs to flush out any silver remaining in our systems. Between his other patients, Jeremy's eyes kept flicking back to Cole. Something more was wrong there. Though Cole's injuries didn't look any worse than the rest of us, his pale and feverish body said that something was seriously amiss. We were recovering, our supernatural healing already kicking in, while Cole seemed to hover on the verge of death.

At last, Sky detached herself from Cole and came over to curl up next to me on the bed. I wrapped my arms around her, wincing as my injuries pressed against her body. A little pain wouldn't make me let go of Sky.

"You're going to make it worse," she warned me.

I rested my chin on top of her head and sighed contentedly. It was a huge relief to be with her again, knowing not only that I was safe but that she was too. A day before, I had been in the hands of kidnappers, not sure if I would survive, never mind whether I would see Sky again. Out of that darkness, she had emerged to save me, showing all the strength and courage that made me love her. Now I could finally rest with her in my arms, and I planned on enjoying the moment.

"I won't hurt anything," I said.

"Mmmm, I see you still think that a JD is very similar to an MD degree. I'm sure Dr. Jeremy will be very excited to know that. Maybe he should look over the contract for the next business venture?"

"Sky," I said, shrugging off her concerns. That one word summed up so many of our conversations—Sky fussing over things that were fine.

"I know what that means," she shot back.

I laughed, but my good humor didn't last long. Comforting as it was to be back with Sky, a worry still hung over all of us. Had we really caught all the hunters and the people working with them? Was this problem dealt with or would it, like so many others, rear its ugly head again?

I started pondering the options to find out more, but my eyelids were heavy, my thoughts fading to black. Within moments, I was asleep.

CHAPTER 7

The infirmary was as crowded as I had ever seen it. We were playing host to the injured Alphas and Betas of other packs, as well as our own weres who had been hurt during the rescue mission, and there were only so many beds to go around. While were-animal healing meant that some people were recovering quickly, no one was fully healed yet, and some were far worse off than others.

Mateo, the West Coast Alpha, had been riddled with silver dumdum bullets by one of Sonja's guards, and it was taking a painfully long time to flush the metal from his system, even before the wounds could start healing. Frayn had turned out to be more than just a doctor, turning some sort of chemical weapon on Tabby, the were-snow-leopard hacker who had joined us from the Worgen, and she lay twitching and thrashing in her bed. Jeremy thought that he could save her life but feared that some of the scarring might be permanent.

Worst was Cole. He slid in and out of consciousness, his skin pale and feverish. Though he didn't show Tabby's alarming spasms, he seemed constantly on the verge of death. There were times when I would have liked to see Cole's life end, but this wasn't one of them. He had fought alongside us, and now he was in the care of our pack, making it our duty to save him. The politics and personal grudges between us could wait for later.

After a few frustrating hours of working around crowded rows of beds, Jeremy had taken over an adjacent room, turning it into an overspill infirmary. Sebastian and I had persuaded him to move the two of us in there, so that we could at least have private conversations about the running of the pack, even as we lay wrapped up tight beneath the sheets, monitors strapped to our arms and IV drips filling us with whatever the doctor had ordered.

Rest didn't come easily. The kidnappings had highlighted a fresh threat, and I wanted to be up and about, making sure we had thoroughly destroyed it. But Jeremy and Kelly were insistent—until my body was better, my place was in bed.

"Once we get out of here, we need to do a thorough inventory of our vulnerabilities," Sebastian said, looking at me from the adjacent bed. "Check the state of potential threats and whether they're connected to the kidnappings. Put measures in place against anything that looks like it might cause trouble."

I'd been thinking similar things, in the moments when my body let me stay awake. If the past year had taught me anything, it was how easily a forgotten threat could catch us by surprise.

"Let's put a list together," I said.

"Start with the obvious." Sebastian typed a note into his Blackberry. "The kidnappers. What do we know?"

"Revival of a previous group, looking for money, revenge, and the thrill of the hunt. They were wealthy and well equipped, with good mercenary contacts."

"Do you think there are more of them out there?"

I considered everything I had heard from our kidnappers. Nothing had hinted at a wider network or someone else pulling their strings, so it seemed likely that the threat was resolved. On the other hand, we had thought this was over when we dealt with Ronan Everest, and his specter had returned to bite us on the ass, in the form of Bethany and Sonja.

"They're probably done," I said, "but we should look into their contacts, just in case there are more of them out there."

"I agree. Let's get Quinn on it. The Worgen can hack into their finances and communications, see where that takes us."

"Frayn's drug worries me more than the people involved. She said that she had outside help with it, but not who it came from or whether she shared the results with them. If someone has a way of forcing us to change, that could make staying hidden impossible."

"Agreed. That sounds like another one for Quinn, with some help from Jeremy to understand the scientific side."

He shot off a couple of messages, then looked at me again. "Who's next on the list?"

"Let's stick with the humans for now and talk about Red Blood."

"They must have lost some followers when that video of Sky didn't show her change."

I nodded. Intent on revealing supernatural creatures to the world, Red Blood had kidnapped Sky and filmed her under the full moon. It had taken a huge effort of will on her part to resist changing, and the memory of it still made me shudder. They had also tried to reveal us through a court case against Steven, one I had beaten despite all their attempts to corrupt the system.

"The problem is, we don't know how many followers they had," I said. "Or how many are die-hards. We saw some of them turn on the leaders when their promises failed, but most believers in conspiracy theories aren't so easily persuaded. They'll find a way to explain away the setbacks, so they can cling to the world they're invested in. It doesn't matter if it's the flat earth or anti-vax, evidence isn't going to change their minds."

"So we're stuck with them?"

"Probably. But are they a threat?"

Sebastian drummed his fingers against the sheets, his gaze distant as he balanced the odds.

"No supernatural powers, no clear organization, and we've discredited them in public. I think they're the least of our worries."

I agreed. Better to focus our efforts on more serious threats.

"What about the vampires?" I asked.

Sebastian let out a long breath.

"There's the million-dollar question," he said. "We're in a weird place with them right now. Demetrius keeps showing us his angry face, but lately he's the most cooperative he's been in the whole history of our relations with the Seethe."

"You call this cooperative?" I asked. "Every time we try to get a political decision, he's against us."

"But he turns up for those conversations. Ten years ago, he would have torn the throat out of anyone who even asked him to meet with the weres."

I hadn't thought about it that way, but Sebastian was right. Demetrius, who I was so used to thinking of as an enemy, was turning into something else. Not a friend, certainly not an ally, but a complication rather than an outright menace. It should have been a reassuring thought, but our long history of hostility made me uncomfortable at the idea of ever trusting him.

"Are you saying that he's not a threat?" I asked.

"Oh no," Sebastian said with a soft laugh. "Demetrius

would still tear us down given the chance. The difference is, he's not spending so much time making those chances."

"Do you think that being kidnapped together against the hunters might help? It's a way of building a bond, and our people rescued him in the end."

Sebastian pulled a face. "Maybe, though we could equally become a reminder of how those hunters wounded his pride. Let me work out how to approach that. It could require some delicate conversations."

"Are you saying I can't be delicate?" I asked in mock outrage.

"Around Demetrius?" Sebastian pulled a face.

We both laughed at that. The movement of my chest made my wounded shoulder ache, but it wasn't as bad as it had been the previous day, and it would be even better tomorrow. I felt increasingly ready to get out and face the world.

"How about rogue witches?" I asked, giving Sebastian a pointed look. His relationship with Ariel meant that we should have better insight into that world, but it also meant that we were vulnerable to bias, either in what she told him or in what he wanted to see.

"The Creed has that under control," he said.

"Really? Or is that just what you're being told?"

"Fine, I'll do some more probing."

"I bet you will."

He laughed, more likely at the awfulness of the pun than because it was actually funny.

"The elves are more likely to be trouble," he said.

"Really? Gideon seems sensible, and he has them under control now."

Sebastian shook his head.

"Elven politics are fluid and complicated, a constantly shifting game of power and position. So much of it happens behind the closed doors of Elysian; anything could happen there and we wouldn't know."

"So we can't count on Gideon?"

"I think he'll side with us as long as he's in charge, but there are no guarantees on how long that will last."

"So how do we keep track of it?"

"By getting out there and talking to elves."

He tapped a finger impatiently against the back of his Blackberry. I was feeling restless too, trapped in here while all these threats gathered against us. We should be out there, gathering intelligence, making plans, preparing the pack for whatever came next. Hell, if Red Blood or Sonja's hunters were still out there, then we should be taking the fight to them. Instead, we were stuck in bed, waiting, watching the world go by.

I looked under the bed. Someone had taken away my clothes, probably an attempt by Kelly to keep me here. She wasn't always subtle in her approach to patient care, because weres often needed a direct approach.

"Anything else?" I asked, turning my attention back to Sebastian.

"Faeries," he said.

That word stopped me cold. The power of those ancient, malevolent creatures had come close to destroying us, as they tried to grab the power of the spirit shade trapped inside Sky. It had been a bitter battle, one that had torn chunks out of the pack retreat and left me in a vulnerable state. If they came back now, there was no way we could stand against them.

"Do you think they're coming again?" I asked, remembering with dread how those monsters from the ancient past had emerged, bringing cruelty and violence down on our home.

"No reason to think they are, but we didn't expect it last time either."

"How would we even prepare for a thing like that?"

Sebastian shook his head sadly, in recognition of how small we were compared to the Faeries' strength. "Research, I suppose. Learn about them in case they ever return."

"Then let's get to it."

I had been lying around long enough, it was time to get back to pack business. My thigh gave a spasm of pain as I stood up, and that leg almost gave way, but I steadied myself. Pain I could stand, but the frustration of lying here doing nothing, while all these threats mounted around us, that was too much.

"You're right." Sebastian swung his legs over the side of the bed. "I'm sure I had a robe around here somewhere…"

He fumbled around under the bed but came up empty-handed. With a shrug, he wrapped a sheet around his waist, turning it into an improvised kilt.

I opened the door and stepped out naked into the corridor. It felt good to be up and about again. A day was more than enough time lying idle.

"What are you two doing out of bed?" Kelly strode through the infirmary doors and straight toward us. Dark-brown ringlets bouncing around her face couldn't undermine the seriousness of her scowl.

"We need to be up and about," Sebastian said. "We have work to do."

"You need to be resting," she said. "Look at the state you're in!"

I was intensely aware of the bandages and bruises that littered my body, of the wounds healing beneath the dressings and the damaged tissue deeper inside. Every step I took was a reminder written in pain. But I was on my feet, and that alone proved that I was well enough to be moving.

"Seriously?" Kelly snapped as we stood facing her, not letting ourselves be pushed around by the force of her personality. With an impatient frown, she reached up to prod my shoulder, a small nudge that forced me back with stumbling steps until I was leaning against the wall.

"And as for you"—she turned to Sebastian—"I thought there was at least one grownup around here, but maybe I was wrong."

Sebastian looked down calmly at her.

"Ethan and I have work to do," he said. "I'm sorry we can't take more time to rest."

"If you're so sorry then get back in there."

"No."

"Doctor's orders."

"You're a nurse, not a doctor."

"Do you think Jeremy will say anything different when I call for him?"

"The answer is still no."

Kelly folded her arms across her chest and stood looking back and forth between the pair of us. I wanted to find some clothes and then somewhere to sit down and work, as I didn't have the energy yet to stand around all day, but I wasn't going to let Kelly see any sign of that, so I straightened my back and stared right at her.

"Do you understand just how selfish you two are being?" Kelly was turning red with anger. "The whole pack went out to keep you safe. Jeremy and I spent hours stitching you up when you came home wounded. We've put hard work into keeping you alive, making sure that you heal properly, work that could have been spent on someone else, someone who actually appreciates our efforts and expertise. You are wasting Jeremy's time, one of the most precious resources this pack has right now, undoing his good work by not letting yourselves heal. You should both be ashamed."

I took a step back, overwhelmed by the force of her fury. Like London at the edge of the woods, she was showing unexpected reserves of inner strength, standing up to the leaders of her pack.

Maybe she was right. Our medical resources weren't limitless, and she and Jeremy knew how to get the best results out of them. If an extra day of rest meant that I would heal quicker, did I need to fight back my own impatience and go lie down?

"No, Kelly." Sebastian had stiffened, a brooding scowl crossing his face. "You need to understand your place. We are your Alpha and Beta, and we do not take orders from you."

Kelly blanched. She was a relatively new were but had been working with the pack for years before she turned. She understood the importance of hierarchy in our lives, and she understood that she had crossed a line.

Still, she wasn't ready to give up.

"Please," she said. "For your own sakes…"

"This isn't about us," I said, laying a hand on her shoulder. "We have work to do, work that's important in keeping the pack safe. There's only so much we can do while lying in bed."

"I promise," Sebastian said, "I'll take what rest I can, and I'll order Ethan to do the same. But we're the leaders of this pack and it's time for us to get out of the infirmary."

Kelly still frowned, but she didn't argue back. She just gave us both a sad look, one that made me feel far guiltier than all her strong words had.

But I was up now, with Sebastian's reminder that we needed to take the lead, and I wasn't going back to bed.

Kelly sighed and turned away.

"At least put some pants on," she called over her shoulder as she headed into the infirmary.

"I thought the sheet suited me," Sebastian said with a wry smile.

"I know nudity suits me," I said, grinning. "But it would be good to have pockets."

As I walked away, I caught one last glimpse of Kelly through the infirmary door. She shot me a look, eyes narrowed, that said this wasn't over. Sebastian would be hearing more about the need for rest. I, on the other hand, was getting as far away as I could from her guilt trips and pouting. I had my own way of healing, and it didn't involve lying flat on my back.

There was work to be done.

CHAPTER 8

After days locked up in a cage or the infirmary, it was good to get home. Nobody here was going to lock me up or force me back into bed. I could rest and recover at my own pace, while getting some work done. First though, I needed some exercise. I was frustrated at the world, my body twitchy after a day lying around in bed, and the best solution to both those things was to work out.

In an ideal world, I would have done that at the retreat. The gym there gave me more space and better equipment to work with. If I'd done that, I was sure that Kelly would have appeared within minutes, telling me that I needed to rest, that I shouldn't be straining my body after injuries. But how was I going to get better if I let my body atrophy?

I headed into a back room, where I kept weights and an exercise bike. The bike only got used in the worst possible weather, as I much preferred to get out for a run, but the weights got regular use if I was working from home.

I started with some push-ups, warming up my arms for the weights. But straight away I felt a deep and disconcerting ache, as the strain of holding up my weight passed through the injured shoulder. I fought against it, determined to work through the pain, but it only intensified, building to a sensation that reminded me of the moment before my knife wound had burst open in the woods. Maybe this wasn't such a good idea.

I grabbed dumbbells and started working with those instead, venting my frustration into every lift of my arms. After a few lifts, I sat down in a chair to take the weight off my injured leg; after all, I wasn't exercising that, so there was no sense in straining it. But again, my shoulder started to ache, the pain growing in intensity until I flung the weights down.

At least sit-ups shouldn't strain any part of my arm. I sat on the floor and started, soon settling into the rhythm. I still felt some bruises where I pressed against the floor, but that was the sort of injury I dealt with every day, and if my other wounds protested occasionally, at least nothing was threatening to rip open.

As I moved, some measure of satisfaction returned. I could do this. I hadn't been made completely useless by my experience of the past few days. Give me a couple more days like this and I would be back on form, never mind what Kelly said about resting.

Except that, less than a quarter of the way through my normal round of sit-ups, I was already getting tired. My body felt like a lead weight, my muscles trembling as I tried to do what I did every day. Sweating and straining, I kept going for a few more, before collapsing on the floor.

I swung my fist into the wall near my head, venting my frustration. That led to more pain as the scabs on my knuckles cracked open.

Cursing, I forced myself to my feet and limped to the bathroom, in search of a dressing for my bleeding knuckles. This whole situation was ridiculous. I could do better than this.

Except that, right now, I couldn't, and that made me feel

like I wasn't myself. As long as I wasn't able to work out, some essential part of me lay frustratingly out of reach.

I flopped down on a couch in the living room. Part of my brain just wanted to shut off and do nothing for the rest of the day, but as Sebastian and I had pointed out to Kelly, I had things I needed to do. I dragged myself out of the cushions, made a strong cup of coffee, and headed for the study, laptop in hand.

My first priority had to be the drug that had forced me to change. If that had gotten out into the world, it could be deadly for all weres. I remembered the terrible feeling of it, a hundred times more unpleasant than any change I had experienced before, a thing forced on me from outside, not drawn from my own inner nature. My body twisting and buckling as I tried to hold it back, to retain control over who I was, to remain me. It was one thing to be transformed by the full moon, a natural part of who we were, but this was something else. Where the moon felt like a comforting whisper from a long-lost lover, calling the animal out to run free, this felt like the whip crack of a Victorian circus master, using pain to drive the beast into action, to turn us into playthings for a cackling crowd.

I flicked through the indexes of books on plants, looking for those that had known effects on weres. Nothing in my supernatural herbals covered anything like this, but I knew how limited my collection was. I had never taken much interest in such things before and had relied on Jeremy for insight on medicinal plants. Now definitely wasn't the time to call on him for help, so instead I hopped online and ran a search for some of the books I didn't have. A couple were up on an auction sight, so I set automatic bids, with upper limits well beyond any reasonable price. I wasn't feeling reasonable anymore, too desperate to avoid this happening again.

With that done, I ran a search on Frayn. I figured that, if I had a look at the doctor's online presence, I might find clues to how she had made the drug. A couple of research papers with her name on them seemed like the most promising start, so I turned to those and began reading.

Within moments, my eyelids were drooping. The dense academic language, together with the weariness of my body, was pushing me into the fog of sleep. I gulped down the rest of my coffee and rubbed my eyes, trying to drive away the exhaustion.

A knocking snapped me out of a reverie, to find myself staring blankly at the screen. How long had I been like that? I grabbed the coffee cup and headed for the front door.

Josh stood on the doorstep, a bulging paper bag in his hand.

"Thought I'd come and see how you're doing," he said with a too-innocent smile.

"How did you know that I was home?" I asked, narrowing my eyes. It had only been a few hours, and Josh hadn't been at the retreat when I left.

"Sky called me," he admitted. "I told her she didn't need to worry about you, of course, but saying I'd check in was the easiest way to calm her down." He held up the bag. "Plus there's that great deli on the way over, so it's a win for me too."

I sighed and took a step back, letting him into the house. I should have been pleased to see him, but I felt exposed, my weakness no longer hidden from the world by the walls of my home. I was on display again, and not in a state I wanted anyone to see.

"I was going to make coffee," I said. "You want one?"

In the kitchen, I filled the espresso pot and put it on the stove, then got out a couple of plates. Josh loaded them up with the contents of his bag: sliced meat, cheeses, pickles, bagels, enough for a whole meal and more. The sight of the food made me realize how long it had been since I had eaten, and even as the coffee was brewing, I attacked the food with enthusiasm.

"Missed lunch, huh?" Josh asked.

"I got distracted," I admitted. "What time is it, anyway?"

"Nearly four."

I blinked in surprise. That couldn't be right, not unless I had fallen asleep in front of the computer. But a glance at the clock told me that I had lost half the afternoon.

A whistling from the stove announced that the coffee was ready.

"I'll get it," Josh said before I was halfway out of my seat. I watched with narrowed eyes as he grabbed cups from the cupboard and poured the thick, dark brew, then hunted for sugar to go in his.

"I can do that," I said.

"So can I," Josh said. "And I'm not going to bust a stitch if I stretch too far."

"I knew it," I snapped. "You're not just here to appease Sky —you're here to force me to rest."

"To help, not force." Josh smiled. "And I feel like you've earned a rest, after everything you've been through."

I snatched the cup he was holding and jumped up from my seat, ignoring his condescending smile. Any goodwill I'd been feeling toward him evaporated. He was an invader in my private space, trying to force me into something I didn't want.

"I decide when I rest," I said, glaring at him. "And right now, I'm going to work."

I strode out of the kitchen, heading for the study, with Josh trailing along behind.

"Can't you just sit and chat for a bit?" Josh asked. "I haven't seen you since we got you back from the woods."

"So you thought you'd mark the occasion by coming around to nag me? Great work."

I flung myself down in the seat behind my desk, my leg protesting at the swift strides that had brought me there.

"I was worried about you," Josh said, glaring at me across the desk, his hands planted on his hips. "We all were. Is that not allowed?"

"Oh, so now it's that you were worried? What happened to just catching up?"

"I can want both things at once. Not everything in life is a binary choice."

"Well here's a binary choice for you—get out of my house or get ignored."

I woke my laptop and opened the app I used for messaging contacts on the dark web. I wanted shaky rumors about experimental medicine, not another lecture on taking care of myself.

"Do you have to be an asshole about this stuff?" Josh demanded.

"Do you have to still be in my house?"

"How many times are we going to have this same damn conversation? You're always protecting and helping other people, so what's wrong with letting them help you?"

I didn't answer. I knew I was right, but my brain was too weary to summon up a smart response. I would just get on with my work, and sooner or later he would go away.

Josh pulled up a chair and sat facing me.

"How would you feel if it was me or Sky refusing your help?" he asked, his voice softer now. "Frustrated? Hurt? Angry even, because all you want to do is help, and we're being too damn stubborn about it? Well, that's how it feels to be on the other side. It feels completely disempowering. When we're in need, you get to come help, but when it's the other way around..."

He let the words trail off, letting me fill in the blank. When I needed help, I wouldn't admit it, any more than I would admit that I needed rest. The satisfaction I'd seen in

Sky when she rescued me, the pride I'd felt in her achievement, that was something I was keeping from her and Josh and the others around me. And it wasn't like they hadn't told me this before, or at least some part of it. But no matter how often it happened, my same old stubborn instincts came through.

I looked at Josh, feeling guilty at how I'd treated him, but also resentful at having to face those feelings. I pushed that resentment aside. It was an ugly parasite living in my life, one I was better off without.

"Maybe I could take some time to rest," I admitted. "And that food was pretty good."

"There's plenty of it still sitting in the kitchen."

I shut the laptop and stood up.

"This doesn't mean that I'm going to take the whole afternoon off."

"Of course not. Just some time to eat. And if you need a nap afterward, that's just a way of charging up before the real work."

We settled back in the kitchen, eating the food he had brought and drinking coffee. Having won as much of the argument as he needed to, Josh had the good grace to move the conversation on, telling me about an indie movie he had seen with London the previous night. It sounded like exactly the wrong film for me—something foreign and thoughtful, without any explosions or chases—but that wasn't the part that interested me.

"Things are going well with you and London," I said, nudging around the edge of a question.

"Yeah, they are," Josh said. "It feels much more like a real relationship this time, you know? Like something substantial."

"Have you talked about that with her?"

He burst out laughing. "I'm sorry, are you asking if I've talked about my feelings? Because coming from you—"

"Yeah, I get it," I said, with an embarrassed smile. "What can I say, Sky's been good for me. I might even be growing as a person."

"Let's not jump to conclusions."

"I'm just saying that—"

My thought was cut off by the buzzing of my phone. We'd had so many crises recently, I didn't dare not answer a call, in case some disaster had struck. The caller ID said this was David and Trent, Sky's neighbors, which made me even more worried. Why would they call me if not because something had gone wrong for her?

"What's happened?" I asked.

"Nothing, apparently," David said. "Unless you've been making plans in secret."

"Plans for what?" I asked. These two were aware of my nature, and of the dark world in which I lived, but they weren't usually a part of that. Had they somehow gotten drawn into pack politics, and if so, what part?

"Ask him about his tux," Trent called out in the background.

"Quiet, you," David hissed. "You'll panic the poor man." He brought his voice back to normal. "Plans for your wedding. You know, you and Sky, together forever, cake and flowers, a big white dress and a lovely party with all your closest friends."

I stared blankly at the phone. Sure, Sky and I had gotten engaged. I had wanted to let the world know that I loved her and that we would be together forever. But there was a gap between that and the reality of a wedding, a gap I hadn't even started to cross.

"I've been distracted by other things," I said. It was true, if also deceptive. This could have been the quietest moment in our lives, and I still wouldn't have been thinking about a wedding ceremony. Was it something I should have been concerned about? Sky had been raised in the human world, where wedding ceremonies were a bigger deal. Would she assume that I was busy with this stuff?

"Other things?" David's outrage was palpable. "Other things? This is the biggest day of Sky's life."

"And his," Trent called out.

"Yes, fine, Ethan's life too. Which makes his casual disregard all the more shocking."

"Look, guys," I said, cutting across their building wave of drama. "I don't know why you're suddenly so worked up about this, but it's not a big priority for me and Sky."

"Oh, really? Did she say that? Because let me tell you, any woman who says that her wedding isn't a priority, she is either lying or horribly ill."

Across the table, Josh was laughing at my discomfort. Apparently watching someone else give me grief was just the relief he had needed, whereas all I wanted was to be left in peace.

"Fine, I'll think about it," I said. "Happy now?"

"You'll *think* about it?" David repeated, as if it was the most outrageous thing he'd ever heard. "No, you need to act. Do you know how fast the good venues get booked up in this town? How far ahead the caterers have to be briefed? I bet you haven't even thought about which flowers will be in season."

"I don't even know what season it will be."

"You don't even know..." David's voice grew distant, as if he was holding the phone away in disgust. "You deal with this. I can't take any more."

There was a moment of fumbling, then Trent's voice came through, crisp and clear.

"Have you not set a date?" he asked. "Or at least short-listed some?"

I took a deep breath. "How many ways can I say this? I haven't made any plans. None."

"Well, that's just foolish. When you make contact with

reality, remember that David is the finest event planner in Chicago, and we would do anything to make Sky's day special."

He hung up.

I stared at the phone.

"Do you think they could make my day special by staying away?" I asked.

"It's okay, no one's expecting you to become groomzilla," Josh said with a laugh. "Let Sky deal with those lunatics. As long as you get yourself a tux in time, you'll be fine."

"But should I be thinking about a date, at least?" I hadn't even considered this stuff up until now, hadn't even been sure we would go through with a wedding when we were already mated, but David had managed to trip over my biggest anxiety. Sky's expectations, shaped by a human upbringing, were different from mine, and while I couldn't bend to every one of her wishes, I wanted to make her happy. The way David had talked about it, I feared that I was failing on that front.

"David and Trent are drama queens in the truest sense of the term," Josh said. "Don't worry about their priorities, focus on yours and Sky's. Has she said anything about a wedding?"

I shook my head. "Not that I remember."

"Then you've got nothing to worry about. Unless, of course..." Josh leaned forward conspiratorially. "...the big bad Beta is actually excited about his own wedding."

"I don't know," I admitted. "I haven't even thought about it."

But now my head was full of the things that went into planning a wedding. Visions of cakes, flowers, and tuxedos drifted across my mind's eye. To my surprise, the thought energized me, my mental weariness fading as I contemplated the chance to celebrate my life with Sky, to bind us together in marriage. The thought of her smiling at me, my mate and my wife.

After days of dealing with threats and injuries, it felt great to have something I could look forward to, something to occupy my mind that wasn't a threat to our survival. I grinned and reached for a bagel. I'd never been glad about dealing with David and Trent before, but they'd really raised my spirits.

Not that I was ever going to tell them that. The last thing they needed was encouragement.

CHAPTER 9

A couple of days based at home, working and doing some gentle exercise, left my body in a vastly improved state. I felt better than I would have staying in the infirmary, because I had my own comforts around me and was able to work without interruption. But I had to admit, Kelly hadn't been entirely wrong—some rest had helped. I just needed to do it on my own terms, more specifically on my own sofa.

Once the aches in my muscles receded and the wounds closed enough that I could take off the dressings, it felt like time to go running again. An ordinary human would still have been stuck in the hospital, waiting weeks for those wounds to heal, but ordinary humans didn't get hunted for sport or have to fight other supernatural beings. If not for our healing, I wasn't sure that weres would have survived into the modern world. I knew I would have been in a far worse state.

I stepped out of my house and paused at the edge of the woodlands, closed my eyes and took a deep breath. The scent of the forest filled my lungs, clear and refreshing. It felt like a source of healing in itself, nature reaching out to make me whole. This was the place where I felt most comfortable, most at one with my inner wolf: out in the wild, where the two of us could run free.

I stripped off my clothes, letting them fall in a heap in the dirt. Overhead, birds were wheeling, lifted on a brisk breeze. The wind ruffled my hair, the world reaching out to caress my skin, to welcome me back after days indoors.

Now came the real test of my healing, as I reached for my inner wolf. Slowly at first, my muscles turned and bones shifted, sinews stretched and fur started to emerge. I sank to all fours as my back arched and then straightened into a new shape, my paws pressing against the ground, each stone and clump of grass presented through the tough yet sensitive pads of my feet. I sniffed the air again, the scents even clearer and deeper, and tasted hints of pine sap on my tongue.

It was time to run.

I pushed off into a gentle lope, following what felt right, letting my legs set their own pace. Familiar paths drew me away from the house, into the shelter of the woodland. Though there were some aches and pains, none were intense enough to hold me back. I picked up speed, feeling my heart beat faster at the thrill of my own body in action, enjoying the freedom that came with the run.

Now I really started to feel my wounds. The leg that had been shot was weaker than my other hind leg, and it flashed with pain as I stretched out to push myself into a sprint. A burning pain swelled through my shoulder before settling into a steady blaze. Part of me wanted to stop, to curl up and make the pain go away, but I needed to know what I could achieve, needed to find my limits. I slowed my pace and kept running as those pains receded to a dull throb.

Those wounds were a reminder of what I had been through and how close I had come to death. There had always been a tension in the relationship between were-animals and humans, specifically those humans who knew about us. Some were filled with wonder, but more with fear, and that fear could so easily turn into anger or hate. That was what drove many hunters, a profession that Chris, my own ex, had once belonged to, before a vampire's bite saved her from death. It was certainly what drove the likes of Sonja and Bethany, as well as the people leading Red Blood. They couldn't just live at peace with something that wasn't like them; they had to control it, reveal it, kill it. They had to master the beast.

My pulse quickened as I remembered running from those hunters in the woods. Though I hadn't stopped to think about it then, part of me had expected that the end was coming, that I would never see Sky again. More than death itself, that was what I feared: missing out on my chance to be with her.

The threat of violence had always hung over me, and I had risked maiming or death every time I went to fight for the pack, or to defend my position in it. I was willing to risk myself for the sake of the people I loved, the people who relied on me. But now I was risking more than that. I was risking the loss of my promised future with the woman I loved. I was risking her happiness. I was risking all the promise we held together.

I slowed to a jog, loping across tree roots and around fallen branches, as I considered what that meant. Should I be more careful? Did I need to take fewer risks?

No. That wasn't who I was. That wasn't how I lived. I fought for Sky, as I did for all the other people in my life, and I couldn't let any of them down by letting fear master me. Especially not when life was becoming so good.

I remembered other times running through the woods, with Sky at my side. The smell of her. The sound of her breathing. The sense of her close to me, a presence I could feel in the world even at a distance, urging me on. To run with her made me feel happy in a way I had never felt alone.

Wolf and man both responded to her presence, gaining strength and energy from her. I had never expected to find this happiness, but now that I had, I knew that my life without her had always been incomplete, and that for years I hadn't known that a part of me was missing. Now we would spend the rest of our lives running together.

The surge of joy at that thought urged me to pick up my pace again. My injuries still ached, but the pain seemed less than before, or perhaps it just mattered less. What was an arrow wound compared to running with Sky? What was one day of being hunted compared to a lifetime with her?

By that point, my route had brought me back around, heading for the house. On a normal day, I could have run for twice as long, but this wasn't a normal day. Each pace took more effort than when I was healthy, and my reserves of energy were depleted. I needed to rest.

It was tempting to stop out there, to curl up under a tree and sleep. But while my wolf form was helpful for healing, so was the warmth and comfort of a real bed in the shelter of a house. It was time to show some of the sense Kelly thought I lacked.

I stopped, panting, at the edge of the woods and turned back into human form. The change took a little longer than normal, another symptom of how drained I was, but at least my body was doing what I asked. I flashed back to the start of the hunt, not being able to shift shapes, the horrifying feeling of my body being forced into a form against my will. But that disturbing and unnatural memory wasn't enough to scour away the happier feelings.

I scooped up my clothes and headed into the house. A long hot shower cleaned off the sweat and dirt, as well as easing some of my aches. Then I cooked a late dinner of steak, salad, and potatoes, before settling back onto the couch.

Sky hadn't been living with me for long, but it already felt strange to be at home for so long alone. I missed having her there with her dumb TV shows and her demands for cake to follow the steak. While I rested, she had been helping out with the pack more, filling the gap my absence left, and I didn't want to disturb that. But after everything that had happened, I was uneasy not even knowing where she was. I respected her independence, but there was no harm in asking when she would be home.

I turned on my phone and shot off a quick message to her, then settled back into the couch, weary and aching but content. I was on my way back to healthy, and soon Sky would be on her way home. What more could I want?

I woke up on the couch, my head tipped back and my phone lying by my hand. I must have fallen asleep there, with the television chattering away at low volume in the background. I glanced at the time—one in the morning, which meant I had been asleep for hours. The exhaustion had finally become too much for my body to resist.

If I was going to sleep, then I might as well be in bed. I got up, switched off the television, and headed for the bedroom. Sky wasn't home yet, but I was well past the point where it made sense to try to stay up and wait for her.

I cast off my clothes, climbed into bed, and lay there in the dark. Normally, I had no trouble getting to sleep, and I expected to be lost to the world in moments, but my unplanned nap on the couch had left me too well rested. My brain wasn't exactly buzzing, but it certainly wasn't ready to settle down yet. The obvious solution, and one that had worked for me many times before, would have been to work out, and I considered it for all of two seconds before admitting to how badly my body ached. Running through the woods earlier had been immensely satisfying, but it had also pushed my limits. If I tried to work out now, I would be setting my healing back, not helping myself to rest.

Frustrated, I turned on the light and picked up the book I had lying on the nightstand. If I couldn't tire myself out enough to sleep, maybe I could bore my brain there instead.

The book was one I had ordered as part of my research into how the hunters had forced us to transform. Part of a limited print run of a modern translation of an obscure medieval text, it was meant for academics, and either the original had been dull as dirt or the translator had sapped all the life out of the language. Either way, I hadn't gotten far with previous attempts to read it, finding excuses to give up and look elsewhere.

Books like this were one of the problems with trying to understand our supernatural lives. Living in secret, hiding our true selves, meant that there wasn't a lot of scientific research into how were-animals functioned. Modern medical textbooks didn't have a section on how to cure problems with changing, and no credible journal carried content about us. Historic sources were often all that was available, written at times when ordinary people had been more willing to believe, or when weres had been less discreet about keeping themselves hidden. So here I was, reading some medieval monk's theories on rare and unnatural plants. It was dull and probably irrelevant, but it was still one of the best leads left to me, offering the possibility that Frayn's drug had its origin in something older.

If I was hoping that the dull writing would send me to sleep, I was soon disappointed. Partway through, the writing style changed, and a footnote by the translator said that the handwriting in the original changed with it. Another monk had taken over from the first, and this one seemed to know what he was talking about. Mixed in with the usual misunderstandings, there were accurate references to the effects of certain herbs on werewolves and vampires, as well as descriptions of plants I had only seen during my rare trips into Elysian. I had finally found a halfway useful source.

Disappointingly, there was only one reference to an herb that could affect a were's transformation, something the monk referred to as "changeling's bane." He described thick leaves and a pale bulb, but gave no further details, and there was no illustration. Was this thing real, or merely rumor? And if it had existed seven hundred years ago, did it still exist now? It seemed unlikely that such a plant had been around for centuries without someone finding and using it against us, but if it had even existed once, it showed that a transforming herb was a real possibility.

I kept reading, hoping to find something else similar, but without luck. When the front door opened and I heard Sky walk into the house, I was about ready to give up, and still no closer to sleep.

The smell of Sky drifted through the house, the human scent of her skin mingling with her wolf pheromones and a hint of alcohol. The smell of her stirred me, but I stayed in bed, book in hand, while she cast off her clothes and went to take a shower.

A few minutes later, she crawled into bed beside me. I set the book aside and reached out to draw her naked body close. Even after the shower, I could smell the wolf of her along with the woman, and both sides of me grew thrilled at her presence as she rested her face in the curve of my neck.

She pressed in closer and trailed her lips across my chest, first a string of soft kisses, then her tongue running across my skin. I groaned in pleasure at her touch, her scent, the sight of her supple body pressed against mine.

I rolled onto my back, pulling her on top of me. Her lips ran on down my body, from my chest to my abs, teeth nipping at my skin, each touch a teasing promise of more to come.

My blood raced with desire for her. I drew her face to

mine and kissed her with a desperate hunger, something as wild as the wolf that had run through the woods hours before. With one hand, I tangled my fingers through her hair, while the other ran down her body, stroking her breasts, her side, and on down, over every curve. She was like something out of a fantasy, this perfect, passionate woman with an appetite to match mine and curves people would have killed for.

Then she pressed down, drawing me into her, and I shuddered in excitement at the fulfillment of that earlier promise and the prospect of something more. She rocked against me, slowly at first, then moving faster as our breath came in unison and we found our rhythm. She swayed above me in the light of the bedside lamp, breasts bared, hair hanging loose, lips parted in pleasure.

Her hands slid underneath me, digging into my back until her nails broke my skin, that small, brief pain only sharpening my awareness of my pleasure. At the scent of blood, Sky took a deep breath, her face lighting up with excitement, and I saw in her eye the flicker of the terait, that orange ring that was a testament to her vampire side. I saw a hunger in her as she moved harder against me, her hips rising and falling with a desperate urgency, trying to sate a longing that was no longer just lust.

I turned my head, exposing my neck to her. She sank her teeth in with as much passion as she had kissed me, and her lips worked hot against the wound as she lapped up my blood. She shuddered, clasping me tight, and my body rose in response. What had once appalled me was becoming part of our union, an extra act that I didn't understand but no longer resisted. It was something she only did with me, something that I would never allow another vampire to do. The act brought us closer together, bodies joining in more ways than one.

Her tongue licked the wound, sealing it, and she rose, one

hunger sated, but the other yet to be fulfilled. I wrapped my arms around her, pulling her close, kissing her with a renewed passion of my own. Then I spun her over, rolling with her, so that she lay on her back as I plunged into her. I pressed my face against her neck and ran my tongue along the trail of her pulse, then nipped at the skin, an imitation of what she had done to me. She shuddered and gasped, drawing me in close as she reached the peak of her passion, and a moment later I was there too. With a final thrust, a wave of pleasure swept over me, and I was spent.

For a long moment, I lay on top of Sky, our bodies still joined, hot and sweaty and wild. Then I rolled off and pulled her close.

Lying there in the night, with my mate pressed against me and the sheets tangled beneath us, a doubt crept over me. We hadn't talked about this growing habit of combining her blood drinking with sex. It had grown in frequency since our mating, as though it were a natural extension of our greater closeness, but was that really what was happening? Was this about us, or was it just about Sky and her vampire side taking control?

More than anything else, that was what I feared for Sky— that she might become something monstrous, like Demetrius. Could these moments be encouraging a bloodlust rather than sating it, drawing out something terrible that would be better left untapped?

But as I looked at Sky lying beside me, I realized how impossible that was. This was Sky, a woman of tenderness and compassion, not a bloodthirsty beast. We had found a way to channel her vampire side without anyone else being hurt, and done it in a way that brought us closer than ever. It was something to be celebrated, not feared.

I smiled as my heavy eyelids drooped shut and I finally sank back into sleep.

CHAPTER 10

I sat at the breakfast bar, coffee in one hand and e-reader in the other, the remains of breakfast in front of me while I caught up on the news. I had already been up for two hours, while Sky had only just lumbered into the kitchen, wearing fluffy socks, yoga pants, and a purple fitted t-shirt with a unicorn on it. It wasn't exactly an elegantly coordinated ensemble, but it was very Sky.

"So sexy," I said with a mocking grin. Of course, there was an element of truth in those words—Sky could dress in a collection of cardboard boxes and I would still find her hot—but I wasn't going to admit that right now.

Sky pulled a face, then grabbed a sausage off one of the plates spread across the table.

"Be happy I have on clothes."

"Is there a no-clothes option?" I raised my eyebrows. "If so, I want that one."

I got up and walked around the table to kiss her. Everything worked a little better than it had the previous day, my muscles less stiff, the aches less intense. I wasn't quite ready to ascribe healing properties to sex with Sky, but it certainly hadn't done me any harm. Kissing her good morning seemed like a good way to set the seal on that improvement.

I reached into my pocket and pulled out Sky's engagement ring, then set it down next to her plate. I'd taken it back to the shop where I bought it for repairs, earning a small look of disappointment from Etsuko, the friend of Claudia who ran the place. At least I assumed they were friends—her relaxed familiarity with my godmother spoke to a comfortable history together. Regardless of the connection, Etsuko had quickly repaired the ring, making it as perfectly fitted for Sky's finger as on the day I had bought it.

"You're not going to put it on me?" Sky asked, holding out her hand.

"I put it on you when I proposed. That's tradition. How hard is it to put it on your finger now?"

Sky stood, her arm still outstretched, while I faced her, my own arms folded. I couldn't even pretend to understand what the issue was here. This wasn't a proposal, just returning something that had been damaged and that I had gotten fixed. I'd thought I was doing a nice thing, but now she was looking at me like I'd done something wrong. I wasn't going to give into that, to the expectation that I should understand what the problem was without explanation, so I just stood there, looking back at her.

At last, Sky put her arm down. She slid the ring to the middle of the table, then sat down to eat her breakfast, glaring at me the whole time. When she was done, she cleared the table, putting plates and cutlery into the dishwasher and leftovers into the fridge, pointedly leaving only the ring where it sat.

Two could play that game. I picked up the ring, swept away a few crumbs, and then put the ring back where she had left it.

"Are you going to work today?" I asked.

Sky had recently started working with Josh at the pack's bar, and she seemed to be enjoying it. It was certainly a job with a lot of appeal, as much about encouraging social contacts and lifting up the party atmosphere as it was about administration and people management. Plus it meant that she got to work with a friend.

"I thought I'd go by the house first—"

"To check on Cole?" I asked, more sharply than I meant to. I knew that Sky didn't like Cole any more than I did, but his attempts to build a bond between them still played on my mind.

"He might die. It seems cruel to ignore him and let him be alone."

"Dr. Jeremy has been there around the clock, and so has Kelly. Just because his preferred guest is you doesn't mean being there is the right thing to do."

I sighed. Cole still hadn't shown any signs of recovering, and that had put off the awkward issue of the challenge he had issued to me, but it also meant that we were stuck with his presence at the pack house, a constant reminder of his dark and manipulative schemes. I wanted him out of our lives, but I wasn't going to get my way anytime soon, as even Jeremy couldn't work out what was wrong. If it had been up to me, we would have moved Cole home the moment we were free of the hunters, but he was too fragile to be moved, his health too uncertain, and that left me twitching with frustration.

"Where are we with finding out what they used to change you all?" Sky asked, shifting from one uncomfortable subject to another.

"We were all sedated," I said, rubbing a hand over my face, as if I could wash away the trauma of the forced transformation. "We awoke in animal form, unable to change back. I was in the woods when I regained the ability. We didn't have clothes and there wasn't an adequate sample of any substance in our system."

"Where does that leave us?"

"Screwed. If someone has the ability to force us to change and we're unable to stop it, what if it's done while we are in public?"

We had only just avoided being revealed to the public once, now we faced the same threat again, without even knowing where it came from.

"Maybe the formula died with Sonja and Bethany," Sky said.

"Let's hope so, but I'm looking into it."

I needed to get going, as I had work to do with the pack. But first, I needed to do something about the ring, which was still staring at me accusingly from the table. I gulped down my coffee, put the cup in the sink, and then picked up the ring, grinning as I did so. I wasn't going to give way to Sky's stubborn streak, but I had another way to end the moment.

I took her hand in mine and kissed the back of it. Then I turned it over and did the same to her palm, gazing intently at her the whole time. I stretched out each of her fingers in turn and kissed their tips, tasting her skin on my tongue. At the ring finger I paused, then nipped the tip between my teeth, just like I had nipped at the skin of her neck the night before. As she stood smiling at me, I dropped the ring into the palm of her hand and closed those pale fingers around it.

Before Sky could respond, I made for the door. All I heard from her was a high, incoherent noise of irritation. I laughed as I headed out.

<hr>

Sebastian was in his office at the retreat, his laptop open and his desk littered with papers. As I walked in, he looked up and raised an eyebrow.

"You look pleased with yourself," he said. "Are things going particularly well with Sky?"

I almost laughed out loud at that, remembering the way that I had left her standing speechless in the kitchen.

"You could say that."

I closed the door and took a seat across from Sebastian. It was the first chance we'd had for a proper meeting since getting out of the infirmary, and there was bound to be a lot to cover. There always was when you were running a pack.

"I'm glad to hear it," Sebastian said. "She's turning into ever more of an asset for the pack."

My smile softened, mischief giving way to pride.

"What did she do now?"

"I've been talking with the others about what happened after we were kidnapped, and it seems that Sky stepped up to take the lead. She rallied the pack and led them in finding and rescuing us. Without her, they might have arrived too late."

I'd picked up some of this from the way that Sky acted in the forest, and from things that the others had said, but it was still gratifying to hear it confirmed.

"She's finally accepted her responsibilities as the Beta's mate," I said.

"Perhaps, though I suspect she would have acted in much the same way even if she didn't have that position. This is Sky, after all, and her actions are seldom about who's in authority."

"Except to buck against the man."

"True."

"Still…" I leaned back in my seat, thinking about what I had heard. "If Sky has stepped up once, we can expect her to do it again. She's clearly found the confidence she needed as a were. Deliberately or not, it's good to see her growing into her position."

"I agree. Do you think we can try to expand upon this, put her in charge of other tasks for the pack?"

"Not yet," I said reluctantly. "She's just getting used to her job with Josh. Let's wait until something comes up that grabs her interest, then take the opportunity it brings."

"Good thinking." Sebastian ticked the top item off on a list in front of him. His fountain pen tapped against the next item and he let out a long, weary breath. "Then there's Cole."

I groaned. Of course there was Cole. There was always Cole, no matter how hard I tried to shake him off. If not for Sky, I would have killed him the last time he challenged me for the position of Midwest Beta. That lapse in judgment on my part meant that we were still burdened with his scheming.

"Let me guess," I said. "He wants to postpone the challenge while he recovers from his injuries, even though he didn't do the same for me."

"Hardly." Sebastian put the pen down and picked up a note written in Jeremy's messy scrawl. "He's been conscious barely half the time since we brought him back here. He's weak, feverish, apparently on the brink of death, and no one knows why."

"That's weird." I thought back to how Cole's injuries had looked as we left the woods behind. On the surface, his wounds had seemed no more extreme than mine.

"I agree." Sebastian looked up at me. "Could anything that happened while we were captured explain it?"

I thought back over everything I'd seen, but only one thing involving Cole stood out.

"There was that beating he took from the guards," I said. "But frankly, he came out of it better than he should have, for all the time and noise they put into it. Nothing about that would explain this."

"Could he have had a bad reaction to the drugs?"

"Has anyone else?"

Sebastian shook his head. "Of course, some people have unexpected allergies but…"

"But that's grasping at straws."

"And we can't do that. We need a proper answer, in case this happens to someone else."

That was a worry I shared with him. We had already seen one new weapon turned against us, transforming us into our animal forms. What if Frayn had been developing others, or Sonja and Bethany had found other sources of exotic toxins?

But while I was concerned about what this meant for the pack, I was relieved to hear that Cole was still out of action. It would be easier to do my job if I didn't have to keep an eye on him, or for the trouble he stirred up.

"Moving on…" Sebastian ticked Cole's name off his list. "Mason put out a bounty on you and Sky. Sky and I have dealt with it while you were recovering, but I thought you should know."

"What the hell?" I sat bolt upright, glaring furiously at him. If someone had tried to take a hit out against me and my mate, I should have been the first person Sebastian told. "How could you keep that from me?"

"There wasn't much time to tell you."

"But you had time to endanger Sky by recruiting her to help fix it?"

"I didn't need to do any recruiting. I just let Sky deal with it and then followed along to clean up afterward."

"You let her throw herself into danger without backup? That's even worse!"

I was on my feet now, fists planted on his desk, glaring down at him. I didn't often get angry at Sebastian, and I expected him to take it more seriously than this when I did. He sat smiling up at me, one eyebrow raised, like I was a small child who had just done something amusing. Where was the defensiveness? Where was the anger returned, or some sort of apology?

"You said yourself that we should let her take opportunities that grab her interest," he said. "It's a good way of supporting her in taking responsibility within the pack. Well, this was something that grabbed her interest."

"You…" I wanted to curse him out, but I could see how futile my anger was. Sebastian had used my own words against me, and worst of all, he was right. "You set this up deliberately, didn't you, discussing her achievements first, then coming back to this once I was off guard?"

"I wouldn't be much of an Alpha if I couldn't manage my Beta."

I snorted and sank back into my seat, shoulders hunched and legs sprawled out in front of me. I was at risk of sliding into childish petulance, a waste of both our time as well as my dignity.

"She needs to do things like this," Sebastian said more gently. "To take charge of real problems. To find her place in the pack. That way she'll be there to take the lead if something happens to both of us again."

"It's bad enough that you're right," I said. "You don't have to rub it in."

A knock on the door drew our attention away from that issue. Jeremy walked in, taking care to close the door again behind him.

"We need to talk about mental health," he said, taking a seat off to one side.

"If this is about trauma counseling again—" Sebastian began.

"Not your mental health. The pack's."

That got our attention. I sat up, the previous dispute forgotten.

"What about the pack's mental health?" Sebastian asked.

"We've been inadvertently building up a problem," Jeremy said. "And with so much going on, it's taken me this long to recognize it."

"Go on."

"It's your policy of expansion, absorbing smaller packs rather than letting them stay independent. It means that we've taken in a lot of talented people. They're natural leaders, or skilled professionals, or just very good at using their were-animal abilities."

"That sounds like the opposite of a problem," I said. "Just look at how much help the Worgen have been."

That wasn't a point I would have conceded to the Worgen themselves, with their Klingon conversations and their computer desks littered with action figures. But in the privacy of Sebastian's office, I was willing to admit that their computer skills had proven a huge asset to the pack.

"I'm not arguing against the benefits, I'm just pointing out the problem. Normally, some of these people would be leaders of their own packs—Alphas, Betas, Thirds, Fourths, Fifths. But here, those places are already taken, and there are no slots to fill below Steven. People aren't working at the level of authority they should be."

"You're finding problems where they don't exist," Sebastian said. "No one has complained about this."

"Sebastian," Jeremy said, a hardness in his voice that I seldom heard. "I don't question your judgment as a leader; please do me the service of respecting my judgment as a doctor. Just because people can't name their frustrations doesn't mean that they're not there. These people are weres, guided as much by their animal instincts as their human mind. They may not understand that they have been frustrated in this way, but that only makes it worse.

"And then there's Sky."

Sebastian and I looked at each other, then burst out laughing.

"What did I say about respecting my judgment?" Jeremy snapped.

"It's just..." Sebastian tapped his pen against the list on his desk. "Sky's ambitions aren't exactly being frustrated. If you wanted to prove your point then—"

"Her ambitions aren't the problem, her wild emotions are. We've discussed this before, remember? Her emotions are so powerful that, when they're not restrained, they affect everyone around her. What I hadn't recognized was that they're bringing out these underlying tensions. In a way, that's a good thing, as her raw passion is forcing us to address the issue. But in another way, it's disastrous, because it means that this pack could rip itself apart."

I pondered what he was saying. It made sense in theory, but in practice, I just hadn't seen it. Had I been so distracted by my own life that I'd missed the fault lines running through our lives? It wasn't a comfortable possibility to recognize, but it was a real one.

"Look at Ethan," Jeremy said, snapping me out of my thoughts. "In any other pack he would be an Alpha."

"I don't want to be an Alpha," I said.

"At all?"

I hesitated. I had to admit, there was an appeal to it. The thought of having ultimate authority, of calling the shots in my own territory, attracted me on the deep level where my inner wolf lived. But there were limits to that ambition.

"I'm not saying it has no appeal, but I've made my choice. I would rather stay here and be Sebastian's Beta than go to another pack."

"That we can work with," Jeremy said with a sigh. "But I can see it in your face. Even you feel a tremor of frustration at what you're giving up. Now imagine that but ten, twenty times stronger, running through goodness knows how many people in this pack. It's a time bomb waiting to explode."

Sebastian's expression had grown serious as Jeremy talked. He added two lines to a list on a different notebook, then looked up at the doctor.

"Thank you for bringing this to my attention, Jeremy, and

I'm sorry for the lack of respect. I'll consider what can be done."

———

I arrived home not long before dusk. Sky's car was in the driveway, her clothes scattered nearby. I smiled at the sight of them. This was the first time I knew of that she had felt the need for her wolf form so deeply that she cast aside her clothing as soon as she got home. I hoped that she was enjoying her run, that it was helping her deal with whatever issues were on her mind. Jeremy might be better than me at diagnosing mental health, but I knew one treatment that was always bound to help—running in animal form.

I got out of my car and went to gather the abandoned clothes. As I picked them up, I caught two scents. One was Sky's, soft and alluring; the other was much less appealing, a stink of graveyard and cologne that hung like a fine miasma over the things that Sky had been wearing.

The smell of Demetrius.

I clenched my fist around a handful of Sky's shirt. What did this mean? Had Demetrius hurt her, and now she was running off her pain and fear? If he had so much as caused her distress, I would rip his throat out. Without us, he would have been dead at the hands of the hunters, and now this was how he repaid the debt, coming back to menace members of the pack.

I took a deep breath. There was no sense winding myself up over facts I didn't have yet. I would hear the truth from Sky, and then I would work out how to deal with the Master of the Northern Seethe.

Gathering up Sky's clothes, I made my way to the edge of the forest and sat down beside a large tree. I waited there, the clothing heaped in my lap, soaking up the unsettling mixture of scents. Even the fresh, clear smell of the forest couldn't chase the vampire's stink away.

For twenty long minutes, I waited there alone beneath the trees, stewing in those smells and my thoughts as dusk closed in. At last, I heard paws padding through the forest, and Sky emerged in wolf form from between the trees. She walked over to me and laid herself down, lying half in my lap. It was good to see her there, safe and seemingly uninjured, but I needed more reassurance than that.

"Change," I said quietly.

She whimpered a refusal.

"Sky, change." My tone became tougher. I couldn't keep sitting here uncertain about what had happened. "Now. You've been out here for hours. Your clothes smell like Demetrius, and right now I'm itching to go over to his house and kick his ass. I should know why I'm doing it. What happened between you and Demetrius?"

Sky crawled out of my lap and onto all fours, then shifted to human form. She reached out a hand to take her shirt, but I clung onto it. What started as obstinacy on my part turned into something else as I took a moment to admire the shape of her body, the curve of her hips and the mounds of her breasts. How had I ever lived without this beauty in my life? And why hadn't I realized how stunning she was from the moment she appeared?

Sky snatched the shirt, pulled it on, and sat down next to me. She closed her eyes and rested her head against my shoulder, surrounding me in her scent. Fresh from running as her wolf, that scent was particularly strong, and I could feel my body responding to it, even as I listened to her heartbeat slowing to match mine. I gazed transfixed at those long, shapely legs, but now wasn't the time to get distracted in that way.

I stroked her hands, kissed her hair, then forced my

attention to the issue I had been brooding on this whole time.

"What happened?" I asked.

"Nothing."

"Sky, there is no way we are not having this conversation, and 'nothing' isn't going to cut it. You come home and go straight to the woods for hours. Something happened. What?"

"He said that I had killed Quell long before he did."

"Hmmm," I said, wanting to acknowledge the words but not sure yet what to say. Demetrius had probably said that to hurt Sky; he seldom said anything that wasn't meant to cut its target in some way. But he was old and cunning, his life built around manipulating others, and sometimes he understood people in ways that they didn't.

I squeezed Sky's hand, trying to show some sympathy for the problems she had brought on herself.

"I was expecting a little more than a 'hmmm,'" she whispered wearily.

I drew her around and lifted her up, placing her in my lap, legs straddling mine, the two of us facing each other inches apart. I needed her to understand the seriousness of my words as we discussed Quell.

"He was in love with you, Skylar," I said, using her whole name to hammer the point home. "It might have been platonic for you, but it wasn't for him. If he'd lived, he'd have spent his life looking for someone to fill his Sky-sized void. His donor looked so much like you it was creepy. It was like looking at a picture of you. When he went on his feeding binge, did the women not resemble you?"

Sky was silent for a long moment, her face sinking into sadness.

"It's not my fault," she said.

"I never said it was, but *you* think it is. No matter what I say to you, any comfort I attempt to give you won't be enough. I'll just pose the question: What could you have done to save him from those feelings? To make things better for him? Be with him?"

Sky hung her head, breaking eye contact. She couldn't even stand to look at me, to face the truth of the situation. Or was it something more? Our relationship had been the final nail in the coffin of Quell's hopes—she couldn't possibly think that we could have stayed a secret from him.

"He would have found out about me," I whispered. "Are you happy with me?"

"Of course I am."

I looked at her, frowning. That was hardly an enthusiastic answer. Bring up the subject of Quell, and suddenly her doubts about our relationship seemed to reappear. Even from beyond the grave, he was causing us problems, drawing Sky down a path of doubt and recrimination.

"This is your least favorable quality," I said.

"Hey!" She hit me in the chest, the blow a little too hard to just be playful. "The whole 'kicking a person while they are down' thing applies."

"It's not my intention to do it, but you've always had a Pollyanna way of looking at things. Willing to sacrifice your own safety and happiness for others. While most people find it endearing, I am not one of them."

"Hey!"

"You're the one who wanted total honesty, and that's it," I said, grinning. Despite the circumstances, it felt good to realize that openness could work to my advantage. "No filters. I love you, but every day when I walk through the door, I wonder what stray cat, dog, person, vampire, elf, fae, witch, or whoever you've picked up for the day with the intention of 'saving' will be there. The loyalty you have for the people you love is admirable, your best trait. The other thing, not so much."

"I got it. Let's move on."

Her snappy tone, defensive as it was, told me that I'd gotten through. Things would be all right in the end.

I kissed her, very aware that she was half naked and my body was responding to that. But the conversation wasn't over yet.

"Why did you agree to meet with Demetrius?" I asked. "Everyone doesn't deserve your time or sympathy. I tell people to go to hell all the time."

"Like you don't enjoy doing it."

I laughed. "I do. But there's a freedom to it. You should be more like me."

"If I were like you, I doubt we'd have ended up together."

I pondered that one for a moment, and the answer I found made me grin. "I don't know, I like me—it can't be too hard to be with me."

She let out a long, dramatic sigh. "It's exhausting."

She climbed out of my lap, still in nothing but her shirt, and headed to the house. A moment later, I heard the shower start up.

Taking her remaining clothes with me, I walked indoors. I abandoned the clothes at the bathroom door, then discarded my own alongside them. Through the glass of the shower, I could see Sky's body, the water running off of her, making her hair cling to her shoulders and her skin shine.

"Here, let me help," I said, stepping into the hot water.

"So kind," she said with a mocking smile.

Steam rose around us as I filled my hands with shower gel and ran them over her, leaving long trails of bubbles across her breasts, her belly, and on down her thighs. I knelt in front of her and kissed the softness between her legs, drawing a gasp. She ran her fingers through my hair, pulling me in, while my hands ran up the wetness of her legs.

I stood to find that her hands were now soapy too. She ran them across my chest, around my back, and on down, while we kissed each other in the flowing stream of water.

"You missed my back," she whispered, turning around.

I ran a trail of soap bubbles down her spine, and she arched her back. Then she bent forward and I pressed in closer, sliding into her, losing myself in the merging of our flesh. Steam billowed around us, filling the shower, as we moved against each other, moving faster and faster, while I ran my hands across her wet skin and around, cupping her breasts even as I pulled her closer.

My excitement was building, and hers with it, expressed in panting breaths and the racing of her heart. She flung her head back and let out a long moan of exhilaration, even as the heat within me reached its peak and we found our pleasure together.

We separated and reached for the soap, then helped each other to wash off—for real this time—each of us laughing as the other ran bubble-draped fingertips across sensitive skin.

"We should do this more often," I said in a low, sensuous growl.

"If you had your way, we would do this every time," she said. It didn't sound like an objection.

When we emerged, my phone was ringing. I hastily dried off my hands and then answered the call.

"We found out what was wrong with Cole," Sebastian said.

"Not an allergic reaction then?" I asked.

"Not a beating from the guards either."

"I don't suppose it's fatal?"

"No, thanks to Jeremy."

"Then well done, Jeremy. I guess."

"Ethan…"

"I know, I know." I needed to be grateful that Cole hadn't died in our care, and that we had identified a threat that could be used against us. But that gratitude was tempered by everything else I knew about Cole.

"The problem was caused by a parasite inside him. Jeremy

has gotten it out and sent us both pictures. You should take a look, then get over to the retreat. We need to keep an eye on what happens next."

I hung up and turned to Sky, who had wrapped herself in a big, fluffy towel with a cat on the corner.

"They found out what was wrong with Cole," I said, doing my best to treat it like a good thing. "He's healing."

CHAPTER 11

Cole sat on the edge of his infirmary bed, facing Sebastian across a three-dimensional chess game. For a guy who had apparently been on the brink of death three days before, he looked remarkably perky, his hands steady, skin no longer pale, a slight grin twitching at the corner of his mouth. The bad old Cole was back already, the real, manipulative Cole who hid beneath his mask of helpfulness and charm.

I glanced at the game, trying to assess the strategies in play. Despite Sebastian's best efforts to encourage me, I had never mastered this version, but I had learned enough about both the pieces and Sebastian's mannerisms while playing to know when he was setting a trap for someone. He had that look on his face now, thoughtful and restrained, while Cole's barely stifled grin showed that he was falling for Sebastian's strategy, all the while thinking that he was the cunning one. This was the difference between them and the reason why Sebastian would always be the better Alpha: Cole was too busy being proud of his cunning schemes to execute them with the sophistication needed in the long term.

Cole moved the wrong pawn forward, then looked up to where Sky and I stood in the doorway.

"Sky," he whispered in a seductive drawl, as if they were the only two people in the room. He gave her a small wave, then mouthed the words "Thank you."

I gritted my teeth and glared at him with all the disdain he deserved. Barely back to the land of the living, and here he was making moves on my mate again, right in front of me. I understood that part of it was a power play, an attempt to goad me into making a mistake he could later use against me, but that didn't mean that I was just going to smile and let it go.

Jeremy was standing in the corner of the room, frowning as he looked back and forth between a microscope and the chart sitting next to it. His slender face was crumpled, his silver hair tousled from where he had been running his hands through it. Sky went to stand by him, a reassuring and stable presence in a world that seemed to be heading ever faster toward chaos.

"I have no idea what this thing is that I found in Cole," he said.

"May I see it?" Sky asked.

Jeremy stepped aside to make space for her. I didn't feel a need to examine it more closely; I had already seen the photos that Jeremy sent to me and Sebastian. They depicted a cylindrical creature just over an inch long, not unlike a slug, but a slug that lived inside a person's body, leaking silver into their system. It was the silver that had incapacitated Cole all this time, and would have done the same for any were, leaving them crippled by the steady stream of poison.

While Sky examined the creature under the microscope, I went to watch the chess game. Cole was following through on the big plan his earlier moves had promised, but a hint of doubt already showed in his expression as he hunched forward, examining an unexpected move from Sebastian.

Their opposing strategies, which had previously danced around each other, were colliding, and while the state of the board currently looked well balanced, there was a tension around the table. Each player in turn stared at the board for a long, silent moment before making their move, the pieces landing in their new spaces with a click. As carefully planned moves were revealed, I watched Cole's face, looking for tells, trying to learn the minutiae of his expressions. If I could read him better, perhaps I could predict and even counter whatever schemes came out of him next.

"Perhaps we should save the rest of the game for later," he said, pressing his hand against his stomach. "I'm not feeling well."

It was almost laughable, a child's excuse for giving up on a game he couldn't win. I was sure that, before they could play again, the board would get knocked over or "accidentally" put away, saving Cole from the sting of defeat. Even in a small thing like this, he would rather cheat than lose.

"Of course," Sebastian said, moving the table out of the way. "I'll leave the board so you can study it. We can always learn something from the moves we made that didn't have favorable results, right?"

"I agree," Cole replied, his tone showing that he really didn't.

Sky had come over to watch the game, but now she stepped away. As she turned to leave, Cole said her name, again in the low, throaty voice of a seducer. Having been beaten at chess, he was turning to another game, and I almost laughed out loud at his petty attempts to protect his pride. But now I was thinking through my strategy, and part of that was hiding my true face from Cole, not letting him see what was coming, just as Sebastian had hidden his strategy in the game. So I glared at Cole, a look that said he was getting to me again. Let him think that he was winning, right up to the moment when he wasn't.

"What?" Sky snapped, looking back at him.

"Is there a way I can get a laptop?"

Jeremy grabbed a small laptop off a shelf and dropped it in Cole's lap. The swift, impatient silence of his movements said that Cole was testing his patience as well. He lowered the head of the bed, leaving Cole flat on his back, too surprised to protest.

"I need to check your bandages," he said.

"I looked at the wounds earlier," Cole said. "They're almost healed. Whatever you put on them worked its magic."

"I still need to see them."

Jeremy started undoing the dressings.

"Bye, Sky," Cole said as she headed out the door. His need for attention was tipping from frustrating into pathetic. Maybe if I learned to see it that way, I could stand to put up with him a little longer.

"We should fill you in on what's been happening while you were out of action," Sebastian said, watching as Jeremy unraveled Cole's bandages.

"That would be good," Cole said.

Sebastian started talking through the big issues in and around the pack, including our attempts to understand the drug that had changed us. It was an edited selection of highlights, chosen by the two of us so that we could leave Cole feeling informed without giving away things he might use against us, like the tensions within the Midwest Pack. As an outsider, he didn't need to know about that.

I had expected Cole to be full of questions, enthusiastically asking about what was happening, trying to make himself the center of things, bemoaning the time he had lost. Instead, he seemed strangely complacent about it all, untroubled by having lost days to the silver-secreting slug. Was he hiding how much it bothered him, or was there something else going on here?

The shape of the creature used on him added to my suspicions. It reminded me of the Tod Schlaf, the paralyzing parasite only found in the elven realm of Elysian. I didn't see any way that the hunters who had captured us would be working with elves, given their commitment to hunting the supernatural. So how had this thing come to be used against Cole?

While I considered the options, I half listened to the topics Sebastian covered. He noticeably steered clear of issues of leadership, which might have led onto the challenge Cole had issued against me while I was injured. But the topic hung in the air between us, its presence clear in the brief glances Cole shot my way. Was he waiting for me to bring it up, or to insist that he now face me in a challenge, while I had the advantage?

"Excuse me," Sebastian said, breaking away from the conversation to answer the buzzing of his phone. He stepped out of the infirmary, leaving me with Cole and Jeremy, who had just finished replacing the bandages.

"So what's next?" Cole asked, his steel-gray eyes challenging me.

Before I could work out how to answer, Jeremy stepped in, a syringe in his hand.

"Now you lie back," he said. "I need to give you a sedative to keep your muscles still while I search for more parasites."

"I'm sure that's not necessary," Cole said, flashing Jeremy a smile. "You've done a great job catching the problem, and now I should be getting back into action."

Sebastian returned to the room, pocketing his phone, and looked at me.

"We've been called to a meeting of the Council. We have to go right now."

I blinked in surprise. Normally the Council of senior weres gave days, if not weeks of notice, not hours.

"What's going on?" I asked.

"They'll tell us there, apparently. They want our full leadership group, and you, Jeremy."

"What's that?" Jeremy stuck the needle in Cole's arm.

"Hey!" Cole said. "There's a meeting. I should..."

He flopped back on the bed, arms and legs limp.

"It won't last long," Jeremy said. "Just long enough for Kelly to check you over. Sadly, it sounds like I'll need to be elsewhere." He smiled at me and Sebastian. "Shall we go?"

Normally, the Council met at the home of one of the packs. Today was different. Mateo, the West Coast Alpha, had rented a conference room at a hotel near an airport, putting us on neutral ground while making it easy for everyone to get there. Even having booked the space specially to accommodate everyone, it was crowded by the time we all got in. The Alphas and Betas sat around a central table, backed up by their Thirds, Fourths, and Fifths, as well as a few weres I didn't recognize. Despite that, space had been made at the table for Jeremy, alongside me and Sebastian. Something strange was going on.

Cole was noticeable by his absence, though the rest of the leadership of the East Coast Pack were all there.

"Where's Cole?" Mateo asked suspiciously.

"He's still receiving medical treatment," Sebastian said. "Unfortunately, that has him stuck in the infirmary."

"This is your doctor?" Niimi, the Canadian Alpha, pointed across the table at Jeremy.

"That's right," Sebastian said, smiling at her.

The atmosphere in the room seemed off. I had been to Council meetings before, and they were sometimes contentious, but never confrontational in the way this one was. The way we were positioned in the room, the way the others stared at us, the tone in which they spoke, none of it felt right. The only truly friendly face was Joan, representing the Southern Pack, and even her eyes held doubt. It was as if we were on trial. My back stiffened as I tensed, preparing for some sort of attack.

"Jeremy," Joan said, "could you please tell us about Cole's injuries and the treatment you've given him."

Jeremy explained the state in which Cole had come to us after his rescue from the hunters. He detailed the major wounds and general bruising he had acquired in captivity and the hunt, as well as the feverish symptoms that had initially proven so hard to explain. I didn't follow all the details of the treatments he had tried, but the blond woman sitting next to Niimi clearly did, as she tapped away on a tablet the whole time he was talking, making detailed notes. When Jeremy, described the silver-releasing slug, she looked up in interest. This was a new topic for her, as it was for almost everyone in the room, and one that offered a serious threat to weres.

When Jeremy's flow of medical jargon came to an end, Niimi turned to look at the woman.

"Well?"

"It all makes sense," the woman said, her voice touched by the lilt of Quebecois French. "I wouldn't have thought of everything Dr. Baker tried, and I might have used a different sedative while removing the slug, but there's nothing I would consider suspicious."

"Suspicious?" I asked, leaning forward with my elbows planted on the table. "What is this all about?"

Mateo cleared his throat, then looked at Sebastian, clearly uncomfortable with what he needed to say.

"Cole has made some serious accusations," Mateo said. "He says that he does not feel safe while in the home of your pack. He fears that you or your Beta might have him killed while he is at your mercy."

"That's outrageous!" I snapped. "If Cole has a problem with us, then the son of a bitch should tell us to our faces, not sneak around like this."

The outrage burning inside me was so strong that I could barely keep myself still; I wanted to leap out of my seat, jump into the car, and race home to have this out with Cole. After everything we had done for him, all the space we had made for him in our pack, all the behavior we had put up with, this was how he responded?

"Your hostility is hardly a defense," Niimi said, unfolding her muscular arms as she stared steadily at me. "I see now why Cole doesn't feel safe."

"If he doesn't feel safe, then why doesn't he leave?" I snapped. "Why are we stuck with his arrogant attitude and using up our resources to look after him?"

"As your doctor explained, Cole is unwell. He has been unable to travel."

I could hardly argue with that, especially after Jeremy had sedated Cole to spite him a few hours before. But it was a view that missed the point of the situation. Cole had been constantly hanging around our pack for months, meddling in our business. He wasn't just in our infirmary because of the hunters, he was there out of habit.

Sebastian put a hand on my shoulder, restraining my next outburst. In spite of the provocative accusation leveled against us, he maintained a steady, professional smile.

"Has Cole offered any evidence that we intent to hurt him?" he asked.

"Only your history, and your attitudes toward him," Mateo said. "Second-hand evidence, perhaps, but that's all he would have if you had not yet made your move."

"That seems like very little on which to raise these accusations."

"Perhaps," Niimi said. "But it is easy to believe them, given the recent history of your pack."

"Our history?"

"So many wild events revolve around you. Death.

Destruction. The risk of exposing us all. You are reckless, and the rest of us must face the consequences."

"That hardly seems relevant to this."

"If your recklessness and aggression have caused so many other problems, why couldn't they be turned against a political opponent?"

It was ridiculous. They were connecting together every problem we had faced for years, many of them inflicted on us from the outside, and turning it into some conspiratorial web. What next, blame us for tanking the economy?

"I know you wouldn't hurt someone in your care," Joan said, taking a conciliatory tone, "but you have to admit, you don't look good right now."

I glared at her. She at least should have been on our side.

"This is nonsense," I snapped. "Cole causes trouble for our pack every time he visits, but we tolerate him because he's an Alpha, and because just occasionally he pulls his weight. Now it turns out that the asshole's been whispering behind our backs, trying to make us look bad to the rest of you."

"Your tone is only making his point," Niimi said.

"My tone is hardly—"

"Ethan," Sebastian cut me off. "Everyone understands your opinion."

I slumped back in my seat. The strain in his voice had cut through my temper, leaving me with the sting of guilt. My instinctive response to any attack was to fight back, but here and now, that was making things worse for us. I folded my arms across my chest and pressed my lips tight together, determined to sit back and let him work his charm.

"You mentioned our history with Cole," Sebastian said. "Is there something in particular there that bothers you?"

"He challenged Ethan's position," Niimi said. "Then, before he could fight the challenge, he ended up in your infirmary, strangely worse off than other people who had been caught by the hunters."

"As Jeremy explained, the slug—"

"Is something you could have obtained from Elysian, given your alliance with Gideon of the elves."

"That seems an extraordinary step to take just to put off a challenge."

"You have taken extraordinary steps before, to protect him." Niimi pointed at me.

"Excuse me?"

Mateo cleared his throat again.

"You twice rejected challenges by Cole against Ethan," he said.

"That was within our laws at the time."

"But it was unusual, and doing it twice..." Mateo's voice trailed off. "You can see, I am sure, why people might wonder what other extraordinary measures you would take to protect your protege."

"We might also wonder what that says about your judgment," Niimi added. "And your position as Elite Alpha."

If I had been on the receiving end of all this, I would have been shouting back at them now. Even as I sat next to Sebastian, I was struggling to keep my temper in check. But he kept his calm, let out a deep breath, and looked steadily at each of the other Alphas in turn.

"I understand your concerns," he said, his expression serious, his voice low. "I understand how you have come to them. But consider all the years that you have known me, and how I have acted during that time. I won't ask you, on that basis, to abandon all your worries, but if I promise you now that Cole will be safe in my care, is my word on this good enough?"

"Yes," Joan said firmly.

"I believe you will honor what you say," Mateo said.

Around them, other weres nodded their approval.

Niimi watched Sebastian for a long moment, as if weighing him up before a fight.

"You know that we are watching," she said. "If nothing else, that should hold you back from harming Cole. I can accept this."

It seemed as if the whole room let out a sigh of relief.

"If this is done, then we should get going," Sebastian said. "I have a lot to deal with back at my pack."

"Just remember, we will be watching your pack carefully," Niimi said. "Do not force us to meet like this again."

As the meeting broke up, I couldn't help dwelling on the events that had led up to this. For years, I had been telling Sebastian that Cole couldn't be trusted, but he had still let him spend time with our pack. Now Cole had come after us, his schemes emerging from hints and shadows into an open attack, undermining our credibility and breaking the bonds of trust between us and the leaders of other packs. Being proved right should have been satisfying, but it came at too high a cost. Instead, I felt frustrated, embittered, betrayed.

As we headed for our cars, I looked at Gavin, Winter, Steven, and Jeremy. They all walked stiffly, except for Gavin, who loped across the parking lot with an arrogant, aggressive prowl. What had they made of the meeting and the accusations made there? And how would that affect the already tense dynamics within our pack? I expected this group to take our side, but there were hundreds of weres in the Midwest Pack now, and if any them saw things Cole's way, then the tensions we already faced would grow even deeper.

It almost didn't matter what Cole had hoped to achieve by telling the Council that he feared for his life, or whether he had met his goals. He had planted more seeds of trouble, both within and around the Midwest Pack.

CHAPTER 12

For the drive back to the retreat, Sebastian made sure that he and Jeremy were in my car, while the others traveled with Steven. We headed out onto the highway, the hum of the engine and the feel of the steering wheel helping to calm my rage, while he sat next to me, staring out of the window, drumming his fingers against his knee. Ten minutes out from the hotel, he finally spoke.

"Tell me again about Cole's injuries," he said, loud and clear to be heard in the back seat.

Jeremy leaned forward to reply.

"What do you want to know?"

"Could he have inflicted them on himself?"

That was an ugly thought, and not one I had seriously considered. Apparently Sebastian hadn't either, until now.

"Theoretically." Jeremy sat back, running a hand through his hair. "Almost everyone who was injured in the hunt had at least one injury from behind, as you would expect when being pursued by armed attackers. Cole's injuries were all to the front, which could just have meant that he fought back— plenty of you had injuries like that. But in theory, yes, I suppose he could have caused them."

"You're saying he was working with Bethany and Sonja?" I asked.

"I'm considering it," Sebastian said.

"Then why get himself kidnapped at all?"

"To cover up his involvement in getting rid of opponents. Think about it. Several of the victims, including you and me, stood in his way in increasing his power among the weres. By having the hunters take us out, he would have cleared his path to what he wanted, while keeping his hands clean. And if he was also kidnapped, no one could blame him."

It would help explain a few things, like how Bethany and Sonja had known so much about us, and why the loud beating Cole had received in his cage had led to so little damage. Even the deaths of everyone in charge of the hunt made sense if Cole had been running around covering his tracks during the rescue. It was certainly a story I wanted to believe, given the light it painted Cole in, but there were holes in the narrative.

"What about the vampires?" I asked. "They weren't in his way. If anything, they were people he could have used against us in the future."

"Getting rid of Demetrius would make Sky happy, and we all know how Cole feels about her. Perhaps he was planning on telling her later that he had helped to get Demetrius caught, or perhaps he hoped to kill the vampire himself during the hunt, as a way of winning her around."

I wasn't worried that those tactics might somehow impress Sky; our bond was too strong for that. But it was unsettling to remember that it wasn't enough for Cole to try to steal my pack, he wanted to steal my relationship too. How had he become so focused on the things in my life? It was like having my own private stalker, if that stalker had claws and a taste for deceitful scheming.

"And Alexander?" I asked, wondering what the other vampire Master had to do with this.

"He was captured alongside Demetrius, during a private meeting between them. A lucky find, not someone on their list."

The pieces fit together. Even the use of the silver slug added to the picture. If Cole came back more hurt than the rest of us, then he could play the role of the martyr, as well as having an extra excuse to stay with our pack. That in turn let him set up today's meeting, to undermine our reputation and make it politically impossible to move against him.

"He could have gotten the slug from Liam," I said. "Take us out and Gideon loses some of his strength, opening up the leadership of the elves."

"So it's not just Cole's game we're playing here."

We drove on in silence, the road rolling by beneath us. I let my mind sink into the experience of driving, my own private meditation, a way to clear my thoughts. There was a lot to deal with. Part of me felt frustrated and angry at the leaders of the other packs for buying into Cole's lies. But I had to remember that he had played them carefully, probably sowing the seeds of distrust over many months. Cole's schemes looked crude and clumsy from where I sat, but they were more convincing from another perspective, and that was how he had gotten his way. It was maddening, and made worse by the fact that I had no idea how to repair the damage.

"The problem is how to deal with Cole," Sebastian said at last. "After the Council meeting, he's virtually untouchable. If we kill him, then it looks like his conspiracy theory was right. If we kick him out, then we're covering our tracks."

"So what do we do?" I asked. I had no answers of my own, and I needed to hear one from him, to know that my Alpha had a way out of this mess.

"Damned if I know." Sebastian looked back at Jeremy. "Not a word of this to anyone, understand? It needs to be dealt with discreetly."

"Of course," Jeremy said. "I've juggled enough internal organs to learn how important it is to handle things with care."

By the time we got back to the pack retreat, we didn't have a long-term plan to get rid of Cole, but we at least had our strategy straight for dealing with him in the short term. He would be expecting an angry response to what he had done, and we had to give him that or rouse his suspicions. Given my very real fury at his behavior, I was more than happy with the plan.

"Where's Cole?" Sebastian snapped as the two of us strode into the infirmary.

"Sparring in the basement, I think," Kelly said.

"I thought he was sedated."

"For half an hour while I checked for more slugs. You've been gone all day."

If Cole was well enough to be up and fighting, then he was well enough to face the consequences of his actions. Together, Sebastian and I strode through the house and down to the sparring room.

As we headed down the stairs, the scents from the room hit me. Cole and Sky, sweat and blood, the woman I loved and the man I hated mingled together in the air. My anger came through stronger. Cole was pushing boundaries again, drawing Sky into his sphere, looking to forge a bond with her. My mate wasn't his to steal, but he was still trying.

The two of them stood facing each other, close together in the center of the room, swords in hand. Sky had a cut on her leg, while Cole had one on his arm and two diagonal cuts running from chest to pelvis. All were shallow wounds, the sort that weres accepted as a hazard of training and that would easily heal on any of us. Still, the sight of Sky's blood added to my mounting temper.

Cole smiled smugly at us. "I'm guessing, by the gloomy looks on your faces, you two received really bad news. Do you mind sharing?"

"You should fear for your life!" I snapped, standing close enough that I could have grabbed the sword from his hand and run him through.

"You felt concerned enough for your safety while in my house to notify the Council?" Sebastian barked. "Really?"

Cole smiled over my shoulder at the Alpha.

"I've always thought the Council was unnecessary," he said, "and that we were capable of policing ourselves, but over the years as the Midwest's power increased, the secrets that shrouded you all increased, and you seemed to be looked upon as some great influence. A sovereignty that so many follow blindly. Overlooking, or rather tolerating your flaws because you are the Elite. Given what seems like unchecked power and the adulations of a deity. You are a man. A man who is capable of being flawed and having weaknesses." His gaze shifted to me. "Ethan is your fatal weakness. Always has been. The cost of keeping his secrets is your reputation and confidence in your ability to lead without bias."

None of us said a word. I wanted to punch him in the face, to shoot out my claws and tear his smug face to shreds. But part of our strategy was to let him talk, to give him all the space he needed to give himself away. Cole was so pleased with his own cleverness, sooner or later he would cross a line and show what he really was.

"The Council is more powerful than you, possessing the ability to strip you of your status of Alpha and Elite if you prove to be a threat to the pack, to other Alphas." He gave a choking laugh. "You protect Ethan, the Council protects us. You benefit from the protections you extend to Ethan. After all, your pack's strength lies in the fact he is powerful and possesses magic. So does his mate and his brother, who is a blood ally. You would do anything to maintain that status quo, and so would Ethan. Is it so unthinkable that you would poison me, while I was in your home, in your hospital? I've made no secret of my desire for his position and eventually yours."

He turned his eyes upon Sky, his gaze running up and down her, as openly lascivious as he had ever been, but with a strand of cruelty beneath the lust.

"And my desire for Sky. I'm sure none of that sits well with any of you. Would it be beyond what we know of you and what you are capable of to allow me to die of a little accident? An affliction that even Dr. Jeremy couldn't fix? So yes, I feared for my life."

Cole's hypocrisy was staggering. He was the one who had been scheming against us this whole time, plotting to take over our pack even as he pretended to be a friend and ally. Now he was accusing us of exactly the sort of underhanded behavior we'd seen from him, and doing it all with the smug pretense of complete sincerity. The worst part of it all was that I could have stopped this, if only I'd killed him when he challenged me for the Beta position. Sympathy had made me weak, and now Cole was abusing the opportunity he had been given. Instead of becoming better than the person he had been, he was revealing himself as even worse.

"You know goddamn well we would never do anything like that," Sebastian snarled.

Cole shrugged and smiled at the other Alpha, looking utterly pleased with himself.

"Do I? No one knows what to expect from a pack that wields as much power as you do. We can't afford to underestimate the lengths you will go to, to protect your pack secrets and maintain your stranglehold on power. We all know power can corrupt the most honorable person and push them to do the unthinkable when they feel at risk of losing it.

Sebastian, you have been corrupted. No one would put anything past you, which is why I felt compelled to notify the Council and they so readily addressed it. Do you think those accusations would have been so easily accepted if they were about any other pack?

"If it weren't for them, I would've been falsely accused by Sky and you would have punished me accordingly. How unfair would that be for me?"

For all that he was trying to play a part, Cole couldn't keep from smirking. He was so proud of himself, so sure that he had the upper hand, and in the aftermath of the Council meeting he did. I knew I shouldn't touch him, but I badly wanted to hurt him, just like he was hurting my pack by dragging its name through the mud.

Cole put the sword he had been using into its place on the wall, straightened his clothes, and then lifted his shirt to draw attention to the cuts he had received while sparring, as if they were one more sign of our hostility toward him.

"You don't feel safe here?" Sebastian said. "Then leave."

He stood facing Cole, the amber of his wolf's eyes flashing, fists clenched at his sides. Sebastian's anger was as real as my own, but I was sure that the decision to let it show was carefully calculated, part of giving Cole what he wanted, for now.

"Easy," Cole said, with a mischievous half-smile, growing ever calmer in the face of our wrath.

Sebastian stared at him, eyes narrowed, a growl rumbling from his chest. He looked as ready to strike Cole as I was.

Cole drew in a deep breath.

"You want my head on a platter right now, don't you?" he said. "Yet you can't do anything to me, can you? I think the Council is ready to accept that you've ruled with unchecked power for too long. The secrets you kept from everyone except Ethan. The murder of the leader of the Creed, only to replace her with your puppet."

"You don't know Ariel very well. She'll never be anyone's puppet."

"Yet, she's come to your rescue, formed an alliance with your pack. She's in a position of power because Josh got rid of Marcia."

Cole knew the truth as well as any of us. Josh hadn't gone after the leaders of the Creed for Ariel's sake—we hadn't even known her when he'd flown into his rage—he had gone after them because of the horrifying experiments they had conducted on ordinary people, experiments designed to increase their power in the supernatural world. But it would be easy enough for Cole to tell a different version of the story, far easier than it was for us to prove him wrong.

"I didn't orchestrate that," Sebastian said. "It just happened."

"You still benefited from it." Now Cole was starting to look angry, his words emerging through clenched teeth. Was he frustrated that Sebastian had an answer to his slander, or did Sebastian's very presence anger him, a reminder that he wasn't at the top of the heap? "The Midwest Pack reigns, and people treat you like a god and you enjoy the spoils of it. Unchecked power and freedom that should have been reined in long ago."

"Is that what you think you are doing, reining me in?" Sebastian moved closer, so that he stood only inches from Cole. Words could have turned to violence in a moment.

"I seem to remember only one Alpha ever being removed from his position," Cole said with a cruel smile. "Am I remembering correctly?"

When the only response was silence, he kept talking.

"Yes, there was one. About twenty years ago. He was found unfit to lead. They rarely remove anyone from their position, but I wonder how they would feel if I expressed my concern for my life while recovering from injuries in your home? And here I am, barely healed, and you attack me. It probably wouldn't work in your favor that my recovery was hindered by a creature from the dark forest. Hmmm… who can get in and out of the forest without any problem?"

He looked at me and then at Sky, and in that moment I was certain that we were right. Cole had obtained that silver-secreting slug creature and turned it on himself, all so that he could reach this moment.

"The secrets you all keep may protect your pack, but they always cast doubts. Others admire your position but are distrustful of your process. I guess that's the trade-off."

"What do you want, Cole," Sebastian asked, "my position or Ethan's?"

"You don't see it, do you? Sebastian, you are a true Alpha. You deserve the credit for what you've built. It was hard-earned. At one time I'd have willingly admitted that you were the foundation of the Midwest. A beacon of strength and a testament to its greatness. That was the past. Now you have become an infestation—a termite whittling away at the very core of this pack. All of it could have been avoided. You chose the wrong path. You aren't good for the Midwest Pack, not for any of us. I am the future of this pack, and you are the past. But your talents won't be wasted; I think you will be a good Beta."

"I'd leave the pack before I'd be a Beta for you," Sebastian said, his voice icy cold. "*But* that's something I will never have to consider. If you are under any illusions that you can fill my shoes, let me set those straight right now. You are quite impressed with yourself and have feelings of grandeur because you were at the top of the game in the minor leagues. Good for you. I'm the majors and so far out of your league, you can only dream of doing what I've successfully done. This pack isn't what it is by accident, as you pointed out. It rose under my leadership but I guarantee it would fall under yours. Even if I were on my death bed, and you were having the best day of your life, I still wouldn't be worried about you being a better leader than I am." He stepped forward again, leaving only inches between him and Cole. "I'm confident enough to say the same about Ethan as well."

Cole's composure cracked beneath the onslaught of Sebastian's will, the sheer power of his strength as Elite Alpha.

"You can't hurt me," Cole blurted out. "Believe me, you will lose your position if you touch me."

Sebastian stared at him like he wanted him dead. Despite our discussion in the car, I thought for a moment that he might attack.

"You may want to take my head off," Cole said in a low rasp, "but if you do, you will surely lose your position."

Sebastian took a serious of ragged breaths, then stepped back. "When I'm done with you, I think you would have preferred that I'd taken your head off and saved you the misery."

Beside me, Sky's heart was beating as fast as mine. She wanted Cole punished every bit as much as I did, as much as Sebastian did, and like us, she was struggling to contain her anger. Cole's campaign of harassment and his attacks on the pack had hurt her, and she was struggling with that pain.

"Ethan," Cole purred, his confidence returning as he moved toward me. "I enjoyed the day I had with Sky. If we had more time, I do believe I would have gotten what I wanted from her before she—"

I grabbed him by the throat and slammed him against the wall, my hand tightening around his windpipe, squeezing out the air. He could plot and scheme if he wanted, make plans to kill me and usurp Sebastian, and I would do my best to hold my temper. But for him to talk about Sky like that, to keep pushing her to be with him, to try to steal my fiancée, my mate, the love of my life, that was too much. All I could see was his face as he gasped for air. All I could hear was the thunder of blood in my veins and the rasping of my breath.

The world was a red room filled with blood and fury, and rage would have its way.

Somewhere in the distance, Sebastian was calling my name, but I ignored him. It didn't matter. Nothing mattered except for slicing the cancer that was Cole out of the body of our pack.

"Ethan! Let him go! Now!" Sebastian's voice grew more piercing, but it barely registered in my mind. Only Cole mattered, and the time had finally come to deal with him.

"Ethan, please," a softer voice said. Sky's voice.

My hand trembled around Cole's throat. I wanted to kill him, for Sky's sake more than any other. But she was the one begging me to stop. I didn't know if I had the will to let go, but I definitely didn't have the will to hurt her.

I dropped Cole. Sky stepped closer and I drew her to me, but those scents were still there, hers and Cole's intertwined.

"You smell like him," I said quietly, struggling to master myself. Cole hadn't just sparred so that he could spend time with her. He had fought her to show the world that there was something between them, to leave her with his scent. To mark his territory.

But Sky would never be with Cole. Even if it weren't for the deep bond between us, she loathed him and his deceitful ways. It seemed like he would never give up on her though, no matter how clearly she made her feelings known, and that meant that these power plays of his would continue, as he pursued a prey he would never catch. I couldn't change his behavior, but I could change mine. I could stop playing his twisted game of jealousy. I could let it go.

I kissed Sky on the forehead, then the cheek, and finally the lips. The taste of her skin soothed me, the warmth of her body pressing against mine.

Cole had gone too far. We might not be able to hurt him, but we didn't have to accept him here anymore. He had shown his true face too clearly for that to continue, no matter the political consequences.

"Get out of our city," I said, turning my back on him to head up the stairs.

There was a moment of silence, and then the terrible, soft, wet sound of a blade punching through flesh.

I turned back to see Sky facing Cole with a look of pure fury, the katana she had been practicing with driven into his stomach. Whatever he had done to tip her over the brink, he hadn't expected it to go this far. His face was a picture of pure shock as his hands grasped the bloodstained blade.

Shock ran through me too. What had Sky done?

She pulled the sword free then drove it into Cole again. He sank to his knees, blood streaming to the floor, mouth hanging open.

Sky drew the blade out once more, took a step back, and raised the katana, ready to chop off his head. In that moment, with the smell of blood in my nostrils, I grew thrilled at the thought of finally being rid of him. Though part of my mind worried about the consequences, about the other packs watching us and how they would respond to his death, that inner voice was far quieter than the one that wanted to see Cole dead. Like Sky, I was giving way to my anger, casting aside all rational thought, and for a moment I didn't care.

"Sky!" Sebastian grabbed her arm a moment before she could make the killing blow. I felt her fury as if it were my own as she grappled with our Alpha, trying to break loose and finish what she had begun. But though she strained against him, Sebastian was stronger, and he was determined to save us from disaster. Cole deserved to die, but doing it like this, here and now, would be terrible for Sky and for the pack.

At last she relented and let Sebastian take the blade from her. Cole flopped back, sprawling across the mat of the sparring room, blood pooling on the canvas. His strength was fading, eyes growing blank.

Sebastian knelt next to him and cursed under his breath. For a moment, the future hung in the balance, as he considered the same possibilities rushing through my mind. Was there a way that we could get away with letting Cole die like this? Was there any outcome that didn't spell disaster for the Midwest Pack?

He sighed, drew a knife from a sheath on his leg, ran it across his hand, and pressed his own wound onto Cole's. Then his body twisted, his suit ripping as he turned from man into wolf and collapsed next to Cole. The joining of blood and their wolf spirits would keep the other Alpha going a little longer. If we moved fast, then Cole might live, and Sky wouldn't have to face the worst consequences of what she had done.

"Go get Dr. Jeremy, Sky," I said.

I hated the words even as I spoke them. I wished that I could let Cole die. Sky had struck a blow for the pack, attacking one of our greatest threats, and I was proud of her for protecting the people she loved. But it was a rash, impulsive act that could draw down the anger of the other packs, that could see Sky cast out or worse, and I couldn't bear to see that happen.

I looked at Cole as he lay on the floor, skin pale, life seeping out of him. For days, he had used that elven parasite to make it seem like his life was in danger. Now the threat was real, and I had no pity for him, only anger. He had brought this on himself. In a just world, we would have let him die.

But sometimes there were no good choices, only bad and worse ones.

CHAPTER 13

As I approached the infirmary, I smiled to myself. It should have been an odd way to respond, given what the place meant to me; the space where I had ended up after all my worst injuries, where I saw my friends in sickness and pain. But today, I was going to see something that made me happy. I was going to see Cole looking miserable, and I was going to make things even worse for him.

In the hour or so since Jeremy and Kelly had gotten Cole up to the infirmary, I had been considering the ramifications of Sky's actions. Stabbing Cole had been a bad idea, one that could cause us a host of problems depending on how the other packs reacted. But it also presented an opportunity for me, one that I could easily have missed while I was preoccupied with politics and with finding someone to clean up the blood in the sparring room. The sooner I took that opportunity, the better.

Gavin and Winter were standing in the doorway of the infirmary, sentinels watching the patient's actions as much as they were protecting him. Both looked bored, but their eyes lit up when they saw me approaching.

"Sebastian told us not to let in anyone who might hurt Cole," Winter said. "Does that include you?"

"Not right now." I smiled widely at her, comfortable that my words would have the ring of truth. After all, I didn't need to hurt Cole right now. That could wait for later.

"In you go then," Gavin said, a mischievous glint in his eyes.

I felt their gaze following me as I stepped into the room. In some ways, this would be even better for the presence of an audience.

Cole was sitting on the edge of a bed, bandages wrapped around his abdomen, pressing a thick dressing against the wounds. I was sure that more would be going on underneath, including Jeremy's careful stitching. An IV was running blood into Cole's arm, but he still looked pale as a ghost.

Kelly looked up from tending to those bandages. Seeing me, she frowned.

"I don't want any trouble in here," she said with surprising menace for such a petite woman.

"I promise, no trouble," I said. "I'm just here to talk."

"Get him out of here," Cole growled. "His bitch mate was the one who did this to me."

Kelly narrowed her eyes at Cole, then took a step back and offered him the sort of false smile a waitress gives to a constantly complaining customer.

"I'm sorry," she said, "but it's not up to me who comes into the infirmary. I just treat the injuries."

Cole's glare shifted from her to me. It seemed that pain and blood loss had robbed him of some of his defiance. This wasn't the arrogant schemer I was used to dealing with, but a man struggling with the world.

"What do you want?" he snarled at me.

"I've come to challenge you," I said. "For the position of Alpha of the East Coast Pack."

Cole snorted, then burst out laughing. The laughter cut

abruptly short as he felt some pain in his gut and clutched a hand to his bandages.

"You don't want to be East Coast Alpha," he said. "You tell anyone who will listen how much you like working with Sebastian. You're such a pathetic little kiss ass, it's embarrassing to hear."

"I've had a change of heart," I said. "Decided to expand my horizons, step up to my full potential. Jeremy tells me that it's not good for my mental health to stay here, my own ambition stifled."

It was pure bullshit, of course. I didn't plan to stick around with the East Coast Pack, far from my home and friends. That was the sort of move that an ambitious manipulator like Cole would make, not me.

"You've barely even spent time with our pack," he said. "You don't understand us, wouldn't know how to run the place if you tried."

"Then I'll learn on the job. It'll be an interesting challenge."

And more importantly, I would only hold the job long enough to kick Cole out of the pack, making him a lone wolf. All sorts of things could happen to him once he lacked a pack's protection. Terrible, fatal things, with no political consequences for anyone. And once he was out, I could leave too, handing the pack over to its current Beta.

"This is just an excuse for you to hurt me."

"Oh no, it's more than that. And most importantly, it's something I have the right to do. You have a week to recover from your injuries, just like I did when you challenged me. Then it's time to see what the future holds."

The words were a smokescreen. No one in that room believed that I had an interest in running another pack. But the words were important, because if anyone from the other packs questioned what had happened, these words would prove that I had done everything by the rules, and they would show good intentions. Those just might not be the same as my real good intentions.

"You fucker," Cole rasped, his breath catching in his throat as he responded to the pain in his abdomen. His cheeks had gone red, despite the paleness of the rest of his face. He was furious, and there was nothing he could do about it.

I smiled at him, feeling pretty pleased with myself. I had turned the tables on Cole, and thanks to his own past actions, he couldn't even complain that it wasn't fair.

"I don't think we both need to be here," Winter said to Gavin. "I should go check on the cleanup in the sparring room."

Gavin raised an eyebrow, as aware as I was that what Winter really wanted was to tell people about the challenge. Her taste in television ran to trashy dramedies, and a gossip-worthy moment like this was as close to them as our real lives contained. Fortunately for her, Gavin didn't care much about other people—he would be happy so long as he got to stay here with Kelly. His grin said that he would also be happy to know that Winter was out there sharing Cole's misery around.

"You're right," he said. "I can handle any trouble."

Winter nodded and headed off.

"Are you done?" Kelly asked, stepping up to me.

"I am."

"Then would you mind leaving? It's easier to work without extra bodies crowding this space."

"I don't see any other patients for you to treat."

"Who do you think manages the stock, makes the beds, fills in the paperwork here? That sort of thing is never the doctor. Now out."

She ushered me to the doorway, where I stopped. Technically, she had the place to herself and Cole now, while I could linger around, keeping an eye on him, and soaking up the happy atmosphere of his discomfort. It was the first time in years that I had been genuinely happy to have Cole around, and it came from knowing that I would soon be rid of him.

Cole sat on the edge of the bed, glaring at me, while Kelly positioned herself between us, a human barrier to prevent violence from breaking out. Gavin slid into a corner of the room, more concerned with watching and protecting Kelly than with his duty to guard Cole. It was good to see that he had his priorities straight.

Sky approached down the corridor, looking at me in concern. I grinned proudly at her. She had created this opportunity when she lost her temper with Cole, and now I was seizing the moment. Between us, we would finish off a longstanding problem for the pack, and do it by the rules, making sure that there was no fallout from the Council.

"Ethan, you've made your challenge," Kelly said. "It's time for you to leave."

But I wasn't the only one she had to worry about; Cole was determined to provoke me again.

"Sky's skin is very soft," he said. "I enjoyed being on top of her today. It was only a matter of time before I'd have known what her lips tasted like."

An image of the two of them together flashed into my mind, of Cole lying on Sky, their bodies pressed together, his lips reaching for hers. I fought the urge to leap across the room and punch him in the face. I would get my chance to fight. I just had to hold on until then, had to resist letting him taunt me into doing something outside the rules, something I would regret.

Sky slipped her hand into mine and drew me away from Cole.

"She smells like me, doesn't she?" he said with a chuckle. "Me lying on top of her. Nestled between her legs—felt natural. Real. Right. It was where I should be."

He ran a lascivious gaze over Sky, as though he was

undressing her in his mind. My anger kept rising and I fought to keep myself still. It was all I could do not to launch myself at him, to finish him off in that moment and to hell with what the Council thought.

"Cole, that's enough!" Kelly snapped.

Sky moved around in front of me, trying and failing to push me away from Cole.

"Ethan," she whispered, her voice a soft plea for reason.

I looked down at her, then back at Cole. But in my mind, they were lying on top of each other, Cole pressing himself against Sky, running his hands across her body, marking her out as his.

"Ethan," Gavin said, the force of his voice drawing my attention. "If you attack him while he's injured, there will be consequences. You know the moment you attack him after issuing a challenge, he will request that you be restricted from challenging him. Don't do it. Seven days and you can challenge him."

Of course, he wasn't just trying to damage our reputation further, he was looking for a way to twist the rules against me, to protect himself from what was coming. I took a deep breath, suppressing the anger I couldn't release, and let Sky lead me out of the infirmary.

I threaded my fingers through hers, suddenly very aware of the warmth of her skin against mine, the smell of her body, the steady beat of her heart. All Cole's talk about lying with Sky had succeeded in its goal of making me angry, but it had drawn out something else as well. I longed to join with her, to remind us both of what we were to each other, and I was damned if I was going to wait until we got home.

I led Sky into a recovery room two doors down from the infirmary, closed the door behind us, and kissed her hard. She kissed me back, and my pulse quickened as my whole body stirred in excitement.

I took a step back and stood gazing into her clear green

eyes, then on down her body, taking in every curve of her, reminding myself of just how sexy she was. Then I was on her again, kissing her with a raw, uncontrollable hunger, our bodies pressing together as my lips ran over her jaw and on down her neck. I took a deep breath, and the only scent on her now was her own, mingling with mine as we leaned into each other.

"Today you were—" I didn't finish the sentence, as our lips locked in another deep, passionate kiss.

She panted as I peeled off her shirt and laid my lips on her skin. She moaned and pulled me close as I scattered kisses across her body. The need for her grew ever stronger within me, and I tore off my shirt, so that our skin touched as our bodies pressed against each other, glowing with the heat of passion. The burdens of civilization, of restraint, of consideration for the world around us fell away, our movements driven by something pure and primal.

I sank to my knees, hands running across Sky's body, unable to let go. She was a part of me and yet outside me, the embodiment of my desires, the focus of every nerve in my body. I tugged off her pants and underwear, then stood and cast off my own. We stood naked and panting, facing each other in a moment of desperate desire.

I seized hold of her legs and pulled them up around me as I thrust into her. We both gasped as our bodies joined in a moment of swift movement and searing pleasure. Then I was sliding in and out of her, the door at her back creaking beneath the power of our passion. My fingers twisted through her hair and hers dug into the skin of my back, pulling me in even deeper. Her scent was all around me, intoxicating, enthralling, energizing.

Sky licked at my neck and took a deep breath. I could sense her longing, as powerful as my lust, but for something more, and I had no desire to deny her. I tilted my head, exposing myself to her, and she sank her teeth into my neck, a brief moment of pain that set my skin tingling, making my pleasure all the more intense, and I groaned in joy.

The last vestige of restraint fell away. I grabbed her thighs and wrapped her tighter around me, slamming into her with feverish intensity. With one hunger sated, she pulled back from my neck, her head resting against the door, hair spilling across her shoulders, blood-reddened lips parted as we soared toward a climax. Her nails dug into my back and she tightened around me as, with one last swift stroke of my hips, we both reached our climax.

Sky moaned in delight as I pressed against her. I kissed her on the lips and then the cheeks, tasting the sweet salt of her skin, before lowering her down until her feet settled on the ground.

Panting softly from the exertion, we collected our scattered clothes and dressed. We paused by the door and she ran a finger along the bite mark on my neck. It was already healing but would be visible to the world for a while, a public sign of what we did in private, a reminder of the side of Sky that she preferred to conceal. It was a side of her, and of our love life, that I was getting used to, one whose meaning had changed from something unsettling to an added layer of intimacy. It was part of what made us unique.

"So, which one got you going," she asked, "what I did to Cole or the challenge?"

Just the mention of the strength she had shown in the sparring room made me lust for her again, an arousal I tried but failed to hide with my shirt. I looked at this fabulous woman, sweat-slicked from our encounter, and licked my lips, wondering if we had time for another round.

"That's a very disturbing kink, you know," she said. "Very weird."

"It's not a kink," I said with a grin, uncomfortably aware that I was blushing. "I just think you're very sexy."

"It seems like my sexy is only noticeable after I beat up or nearly slay someone."

I moved toward her, but she held me at arm's length, watching me with a mixture of amusement and curiosity. I was ready to repeat what we had just done, but she was straightening her shirt, preparing to face the world.

"It just heightens it," I said, smiling despite my disappointment. There would be time for more later.

"Sounds like a weird kink to me." She opened the door and backed out into the corridor. "Come on, we should get out of here."

"*Now* you all want to leave," Winter said. She stood a few yards from the door, a mocking grin on her face. "I am traumatized by hearing you two and it will be etched in my mind forever. So, you decide to go home *after* the damage is done. I can't unhear any of it."

She rolled her eyes and gave an exaggerated shudder. I almost laughed out loud—Winter was no more discreet than the rest of us when passion overtook her. I'd caught her in compromising positions with more than one woman around the retreat. But that was just part of pack life, the way things went when you lived in line with your animal instincts.

A real grimace appeared as she noticed the marks on my neck.

"I guess I should just go home and wait for the night terrors," she muttered, before heading off up the corridor.

Sky went so red with embarrassment I thought she might burst into flames. I just grinned. Sure, the blood drinking wasn't to everybody's taste, but why be ashamed of who we were? If this gave us pleasure, and no one got hurt, then I didn't care what anyone thought. I hoped that Sky could find that same place of peace with who she was.

By the next day, Cole was well enough to leave, as Jeremy made very clear after checking his wounds. Cole tried to protest, but Jeremy was insistent, and as we all knew, he made the rules in his infirmary.

None of us were going to disagree. Word had quickly gotten around the pack about what Cole had done, blowing away all the goodwill he had accrued through his previous charm offensives. If he wanted to stay nearby, there was the hotel where he had stayed before being picked up by the hunters. He wasn't welcome at the retreat.

Sky, Sebastian, Winter, and I stood by the entrance to the pack's home, watching as Cole left. After Sky's attack, the Council had sent three burly Canadian weres to watch over him, keeping him safe from our supposedly murderous intentions. I couldn't blame them, given that one of us had stuck a sword through his guts, but it still felt like an attack, a clear signal that we couldn't be trusted to live by the rules. The only thing in our favor was that I had then challenged Cole, rather than outright murdering him while he was down.

Standing by his rental car, Cole pressed his hand against the wound Sky had given him, which we knew full well had already healed past the need for such gestures.

"That thing with you and Ethan was a nice little trick," he said, looking at Sky. "You were like an animancer—calming the raging beast. You do realize that is what you are to Ethan —a tool to use at his disposal. Your purpose in his life has been reduced to nothing more than a caretaker. One that he sleeps with."

Here it was again. No matter what happened, Cole couldn't resist goading us, trying to force a reaction, to control our behavior. I growled and glared at him, but kept my distance. Anything more would risk putting us on the Council's bad side forever.

"Do you ever wonder what becomes of a man who is

driven by instinct only?" Cole asked, his tone low, as if he was worried for Sky, not trying to wind her up. Another display for the outsiders, but with barbs for the rest of us. "It has to cross your mind whether those instincts—those primal urges that he has very little control over—will lead him to someone else." He scoffed and shook his head. "I'm sure he's shown you what he is, and yet still you care for him. Noble of you, but selfish of him."

"So, it's a bad thing that Ethan lives by his instincts, which drive him to protect those he loves selflessly?" Sky said, her frosty gaze unwavering as she faced him. "I'm not naive about how intense Ethan is, and if I were to be honest with myself, it's one of the things I'm drawn to the most. Tell me, should I be drawn to a man whose thirst for power is so all-consuming that there isn't a life he won't compromise to obtain it?"

"You think Sebastian doesn't thirst for power? Do you for one moment think his alliances, pack friends, and positioning in the otherworld aren't about power?"

"Perhaps, but he's never aligned himself with anyone who would hurt another were-animal to improve his standing."

I watched the watchers, wondering what effect this was having on them. Would they assume that our outrage at Cole was all grounded in lies and bluster, or were they open to the possibility that he might be in the wrong? Were we changing their minds or simply reinforcing what they thought they already knew? Their faces were impassive, leaving it impossible to tell, and in a way I didn't care. Soon, I would fight Cole, and then all of this would be over. No more tricks, no more schemes, just one moment of violence before we put it behind us.

"I will not do a submission fight with Ethan," Cole said, his voice sinking to a whisper. "I will protect my position in the pack with my life."

"As you should. I don't want your betrayal to be punished

with a slap on your wrist. I want you humiliated from your loss of position and then penalized with death. A fitting ending for you."

Cole took a sharp breath and seemed on the verge of some retort. Whatever it was, it was something he didn't want to say in front of outsiders, because he bit back the words. Still glowering, he opened the car door.

Something stopped him, one hand on the door, halfway to climbing in. His gaze ran over the sprawling buildings of the Midwest Pack's retreat with the same slow, longing look he might give to a beautiful woman. Then that gaze settled on Sky, his expression still heavy with desire. At last I realized what lay behind it: more than anything, Cole wanted what he couldn't have. Refusal proved that it was desirable, and that proved that it should be his. He already wanted the power that running this pack brought, and being refused inflamed his ambition. It was the same with Sky.

"The witches, the elves, and the vampires are allies of the Midwest Pack," he said. "Do you think that's just to protect the pack or to stroke Sebastian's ego?"

He raised his eyebrow and looked expectantly at Sky. When no one answered, he nodded and gave a small, smug smile, as if his point had been proven. But none of this was agreement—it was simply a refusal to play his games.

Again I glanced at the hulking Canadian weres and wondered what they would report back to Niimi.

"You have adopted some of Ethan's arrogance by supporting him in this challenge," Cole said coldly. He looked at me. "You will lose"—he looked back at Sky—"and you will lose your mate. Are you prepared for that? Don't let my past performance be an indicator of what is to come. I am fighting for more than just my rightful position. No matter how you paint a picture of me, you know I only do what's best for the pack."

I held back my derision. We knew that there was only one

thing Cole cared about, and that was his own self-interest. If the Council couldn't see that yet, then no speeches by us would make a difference. Let his lie sit there, festering in the air. Let the visitors wonder why he was so insistent on these things. Let Cole's own words begin his undoing.

And then, in six days' time, I would tear him apart.

"I will not be reduced to a lone wolf," he muttered.

But his fate wasn't in his hands anymore, and I felt like he knew it. A fight between us would be close, but I had won before, and I could win again. It wasn't calm that made Cole's words seem icy cold. It was fear.

He dropped into the car, slammed the door shut, and drove away. As I watched him go, a smile flickered at the corners of my mouth. Our home was clean of his taint again.

CHAPTER 14

Winter raised her fists and stared at me across the sparring room. We were both already coated with sweat and dotted with bruises, signs of a good session, but I was far from done. If I was going to face Cole in four days, then I needed to be in peak fighting form. I had been preparing for it from the moment he left the retreat, and I wasn't going to let up until I was sure I was ready to face him.

"Come on then," Winter said, a glint in her eyes. "Time is wasting."

I advanced on her, my own fists raised, moving cautiously across the mat. She had already punished me several times for rushing my attack or signaling too obviously what I had planned. I wasn't going to let her taunt me into making another mistake, but I was glad that she was trying those tactics—it was exactly what Cole would do.

"I should have picked somebody taller to fight," I said. "There's only half as much of you as there is of him."

"But can he do this?"

With a sudden, fluid movement, Winter flowed past me, reaching inside my guard as she went, delivering a punch to my chest. I staggered sideways and turned to face her, only to run into her foot, which slammed into my stomach, nearly doubling me over.

"Seriously, Ethan." She shook her head. "You're better than this. What's gotten into you?"

It was a good question, and not one to which I had a good answer. I should have been laser focused on the upcoming challenge against Cole, but something about it was distracting me. Perhaps it was the politics that now hung like a sickly miasma around the whole business, this sense that we were being scrutinized by the rest of the were-animals. Or perhaps it was just the strangeness of imagining a world cleared of Cole, one in which I didn't have to worry about what scheme he would level against us next. Regardless of the cause, my mind wasn't in the fight, and when it came to the real thing, that could be fatal.

I took a deep breath to center myself and faced up against Winter again. This time I attacked her, going in with a high kick that forced her back and gave me a moment's advantage while she found her footing. There was a flurry of fists as we punched at each other, both dodging and weaving, blocking and counterattacking, shifting around the room in swift bursts of action. She caught me with a punch to the shoulder, but then I knocked her legs out from under her. She hit the ground rolling, but I was already following up, knocking her back once more before she was on her feet, sending her sprawling against the wall. If I was fighting to win, I would have dived in to capitalize on her vulnerability, but I would gain more from practicing against a capable opponent than a vulnerable one.

Winter pushed herself upright, grinning.

"That's better," she said. "I want you to make that bastard hurt, to take him down once and for all."

"That's the plan," I said, grinning back.

It felt like simpler times, sparring with Winter in the

basement of the retreat. Over the past few months, everything had been so busy, there had been little time for this. I had been tackling court cases, hunting down enemies, or recovering from the ensuing fights. Everything had been bound up in the tensions of threats to the pack or challenges in my personal life. This was the first time in forever that I had fought just for the fun of it, and it was a joy to sink into the uncomplicated thrill of the fight.

"Hold up," I said as Winter prepared to attack again.

I could hear Josh's footsteps and smell his scent coming down the stairs, and I figured that he was probably coming to see me. We hadn't had a chance to talk since I made the challenge to Cole, and judging by the tone of his messages, my brother was anxious about what that challenge might mean.

He emerged into the sparring room, dressed in jeans and a t-shirt with a strange, angular logo I didn't know—the symbol of either an old television show or a new and obscure house DJ, based on past precedent. His hands were stuffed in his pockets, but the tattoos on his arms rippled subtly as he twitched his fingers in agitation.

"Hey, Ethan," he said. "Winter."

"Hi, Josh." Winter grinned a predatory grin. "Come to spar with me at last?"

Josh smiled back. "Maybe another day."

This was a running joke between them, the pretense that Josh was ever going to take his place on the floor of the sparring room. As a witch, his power came from his magic, not his physical strength, and it was that magic he relied on in battle. He wasn't in bad shape, but Winter would thrash him within seconds if he ever took her up on the offer.

He turned his gaze to me.

"How are you doing?" he asked, looking concerned.

"Great." I flexed my biceps. "Getting ready to deal with our Cole problem."

"And you're sure you're up for that?" He raised his eyebrows.

"It's not going to be easy," I admitted, "but I've beaten him before and I can do it again."

I tried to sound as confident as I could, to boost my own morale as much as to put Josh's mind at ease. But the truth was that this would be a tough fight against a strong, skilled opponent, and there were no guarantees on how it would end.

"It hasn't been that long since you were badly hurt, remember?" Josh said. "The hunters, and then the big fight before that. Have you given yourself enough time to rest before taking this on?"

"Cole's been through those things too, and he had that silver slug inside him."

"Which he probably put there. Which means that he knew it was safe. That was a flashy way to make himself look vulnerable, but it doesn't mean he was in real danger, or that there will be any lasting damage. Whereas you were—"

"I was out of bed long before him, and there's barely a sign left of what happened to me." I pulled off my shirt, revealing the faint trace of a scar that was all that remained from where an arrow had pierced my shoulder. "See, good as new."

I was starting to get annoyed. I didn't need this sort of nagging from the people around me. I was mostly recovered, just a few lingering aches left. That was more than good enough to take on Cole.

"Dammit, Ethan!" Josh flung his hands in the air. "Can't you take just one moment to acknowledge that you've been hurt? That you nearly died? That you're putting yourself at risk again before you've completely recovered?"

"Can't you back me up on this?" I glared at him, my voice rising in anger just as his had. "I'm doing what's needed, for the good of the pack."

"You're rushing straight into danger, to a fight we can't help you with, and now you don't even want me to express doubts? I'm sorry, but I'm not heartless, Ethan. I'm your brother and I'm going to worry about you."

He deflated, eyes downcast, arms hanging by his sides, as if all that had been holding him up was those words, and now they were gone. I stared at him, stunned. I was so used to just throwing myself into the challenges life offered, I didn't think about how Josh might feel. Hell, until Sky came along I hadn't thought about how anyone would feel about how I lived.

Winter shuffled her feet, and I turned to look at her.

"What about you?" I asked. "Are you worried for me?"

She opened her mouth as if to give an answer, closed it, opened it again, and let out a sigh.

"The situation's not perfect," she admitted. "You should be able to beat Cole, but there's a risk. Any worries I've got, I can channel them into getting you ready for the fight. I guess maybe it's harder for people who can't do that."

Josh was looking at me again, his expression sad and resigned.

"Exactly," he said.

The indignation that had stiffened my body fell away. I strode across the room and wrapped Josh in my arms. For a moment he stiffened, caught by surprise, but then he hugged me back.

"I'm sorry," I said. "I didn't mean to be an asshole."

"And I'm sorry. I do believe in you. You're gonna kick his ass."

We took a step back and stood uncomfortably, both looking down at the floor. The closeness we had found recently was still a fragile thing, and neither of us was quite used to expressing our emotions to each other.

"Don't get too comfortable out east," Winter said. "I said I'd take your place as Beta while you sort this out, but I don't want to be stuck with that responsibility for a minute more than I have to."

Josh laughed. "I thought you'd love the chance to boss people around?"

"And have to listen to their worries, care about their well-being, plan for their futures in the pack?" Winter pulled a disgusted face. "I'd rather spend my day with Demetrius and his pack of posers than have to deal with that."

"I thought you worked in HR," Josh said.

"I manage HR." Winter's predatory grin returned. "That means I can do hirings and firings, and leave this soft stuff to the underlings."

"We all appreciate your sacrifice," I said with mock seriousness. "And don't worry, I'll be back just as fast as I can."

"Good, because the Worgen are already looking at me like stray kittens who think I might feed them, and there's no way I'm dealing with another dispute over who spilled cola on a Star Trek action figure."

We laughed as she rolled her eyes. I could understand where she was coming from, but the older I got, the more I enjoyed dealing with the little issues that came up between members of the pack. Playing peacemaker, calming worries, helping people to grow into their place in the pack, it was all part of the Beta's job, and it was satisfying in a very different way from beating up Cole.

"Come on then," I said, raising my fists. "Let's get back to training. The better shape I'm in, the quicker I can leave Cole in the dirt and save you from the horrors of human interaction."

For the first time in over a week, I walked through the glass doors of Wendell, Harper, and Holmes, and into the bustle of the busy law office. Officially, I had been working from home, as I often did, and I had used what spare moments I could find to respond to emails and keep up the pretense that I was focused on my job. But sooner or later, a return to the office had been inevitable, and I needed to get things in order before I took even more time out to deal with Cole.

"Good morning, Mr. Charleston." The receptionist smiled at me from behind his desk.

"Morning," I replied, stalking past.

More people than usual seemed to be smiling at me as I walked through the office, or taking the time to greet me. I felt as though I was missing something, but the problem with that feeling was that you never knew what the something might be. And the problem with everybody wanting to ask how I was doing was that they were slowing me down on my way to get work done.

Stacy was sitting at her desk outside my office. Always the good assistant, she snatched up a folder and a tablet as I passed, then followed me into my office, closing the door behind us. The bustle of the business was still visible through the glass partition, but the chatter was mercifully cut off.

"Where are we on Maxwell?" I asked, taking a seat behind my desk. Stacy sat opposite, scrolling down the tablet.

"All done bar the admin," she said. "You were right, using the local press put on some extra pressure. Big businesses don't like to be seen as bullies, especially in markets where they're trying to expand. We've got a settlement everyone can live with."

"Good, good." I switched on my computer and waited for it to power up. "What about Wadritsky?"

"Grinding on. The opposing lawyers still haven't released all the paperwork we asked for."

"Okay, write me an email to the judge. I've got a template for times like this and you can use it to get started on the wording. Send it to me for approval before it goes."

"On it."

"What else?" My email program had opened, revealing the horrifying sight of two hundred unanswered messages, a third of them flagged as urgent. One man's urgent was another's waste of time, but I was still going to have to work my way through it all. I would have preferred to spend the time training with Winter, but maintaining the secrecy around pack life meant keeping up the charade of my mundane existence. This was one plate I had to keep spinning no matter what.

"Knew cases coming in." She slid a file across the desk. "I thought you might want a break from the screen later, so the details are all in there. The partners want to know how many of these you can fit in."

I opened the folder and looked at a thick pile of case summaries. On my best day, with no distractions from the pack, I couldn't have taken on half this work.

"Why push so many my way?" I asked. "Is somebody else sick?"

"We've had an influx of new clients, and a lot of them want to work with you."

That made me blink in surprise. I hadn't exactly been setting the legal world alight with my presence over the past year. If anything, I'd been worrying that I was becoming too low profile, at risk of undermining the reputation I had built over the years.

"Steven's case did it," Stacy said, and I couldn't help noticing a small smile as she said his name. "You faced a storm of wild stories in the press, backed up by a hostile DA, and turned it into something that discreetly disappeared. A lot of people want that sort of service: celebrities, CEOs, politicians. You're the new golden goose of Wendell, Harper, and Holmes."

"Celebrities?" I looked down the list at the front of the pile of case summaries. Half the names were meaningless to me, the sorts of people who mattered to gossip magazines and talk show hosts, but there were some famous enough to have penetrated even my consciousness. Josh would have killed to get some of these people to visit his club, and already I was wondering what other advantages I could gain through working with them. This could be good for the pack, not just my legal career.

"How's Steven doing?" Stacy asked with forced casualness.

"Fine," I replied. "He's been busy."

The truth was that, while Stacy knew about the supernatural world, I was wary of anything that might entangle her further with it, including her crush on Steven. Keeping some distance between my two lives was useful.

Except that I'd just been considering crossing those streams, to the benefit of the pack. Maybe it was time to let go of a double standard.

"I'll tell him you were asking after him."

She blushed and turned her attention back to the tablet. "There have been some other inquiries about you too."

"Other inquiries?" The way she said it let me know that something wasn't right.

"People calling or visiting in person, asking questions that seemed to be more about you than your work, if you know what I mean. Mikey thought they were press, and he nearly called security on a couple of them, but I persuaded him not to make a fuss."

This sort of thing was why I worked so hard to separate the aspects of my life: even the low-level parts of pack business could be very disruptive to life as a topflight lawyer.

At least this time I had a good idea who was behind it. Sonja and Bethany had been gathering intelligence on their targets before they captured us, and investigating my professional routines would have been a good way to find out where I went and when I might be vulnerable.

"Was any of this in the past week?" I asked.

"One, maybe, though that guy said something about a legal case." Stacy waggled a hand in the air, signaling her uncertainty as to what that visit had represented. "The rest were before that."

"Then we don't need to worry about it. Some people were taking an interest in me, but they're not around anymore."

"Okay." Stacy tapped her tablet screen. "That's everything I had, so I'll leave you to your reading."

"One more thing," I said, halting her with a hand on the door. "The annual reviews have been approved, and that means it's time to decide on bonuses. After some persuading from me, the partners have agreed to double your bonus from last year."

Stacy's eyes widened. She was already the best paid paralegal in the firm, and rightly so.

"Double?" she whispered.

"You've earned it." I grinned. "Thanks for all your great work. And just a heads-up, I'm going out of town tomorrow, so you might need to cover for me again..."

CHAPTER 15

Once, decades ago, the East Coast Pack had tried working out of a base in New York. It made sense in theory, planting them in the heart of the region's power and population, arguably the cultural and political capital of the world. But what worked for human corporations didn't go so smoothly for a pack of weres. Without countryside to run around in, they had started going stir crazy, tensions mounting in the pack. Every full moon, most of them had needed to leave the city behind and find somewhere else to let out their inner beast. Within a couple of years, the plan had been abandoned, that building turned into a rental. The incident became a story passed down to Alphas and Betas, a lesson in the importance of understanding who we were.

Instead, the pack had made their home in a large, dark brick building out in Maryland. It wasn't the sprawling complex that the Midwest retreat had become, extensions piling on to fit in a powerful and growing pack, but it was a more elegant building, with poplars surrounding it, bushes lining the path to the door, and a wide balcony stretching out from the upper floor. It was the perfect place for Cole, a refined front hiding the darker rooms within.

I approached the front door, flanked by Sebastian and Sky. He had come along as Elite and Alpha of the Midwest Pack, to provide a witness to what happened. Sky didn't need to be there, but I doubted that anything could have dissuaded her from accompanying me. I was doing my best to stay calm and relaxed, but her heart raced, so I reached out my hand to give hers a squeeze. The attempt at reassurance failed: Sky remained as tense as ever.

I would have been tense too if the roles were reversed and I was watching her walk into a deadly fight. I wasn't entirely sure which was worse, being the fighter or the loved one waiting for them. At least I could do something in the challenge; all she could do was wait outside the room where the challenge was taking place, banned from watching and hoping for the best.

Fallon, the East Coast Beta, opened the door to us. She looked solemn and her voice sounded rough. Was she mourning for the potential loss of Cole, or fearful for the future of her pack? I had always assumed that he was well liked by his own people, but if any of them had the brains to see through him then things could be more complex, and that added to the challenge of the transition if—no, not if, when—I beat him.

"He's downstairs waiting," she said.

She started leading us toward the stairs, her footsteps soft on the tiled floor, but then she stopped, long brown hair swaying as she turned to look at me.

"You don't plan on remaining Alpha, do you?" she asked.

I shook my head. "This is your home. You deserve an Alpha who—"

"Ethan," Sebastian said, cutting me off.

I gritted my teeth. If I'd had my way, we would have been honest with Fallon, letting her know my full intentions and the reasons behind them, explaining Cole's part in the kidnappings that preceded Sonja and Bethany's hunt. But, as sometimes happened, Sebastian took a broader perspective than I did. He had pointed out that, if I lost, Fallon would still have Cole as her Alpha and would need to be able to work with him, at least until she had the skill as a fighter and the strength of will to challenge for supremacy. Fallon was good, but she wasn't good enough for that, not with her own life at stake. Even I was taking a risk, confronting an opponent as strong and swift as Cole. For all that Josh and I had joked about this being a sure thing before I left, fear sat like a lead weight in my belly. If I didn't win today, then I would die.

"I think you will make a good Alpha," I said.

Fallon frowned.

"Cole is a good Alpha," she said without conviction. At least now I knew where she stood.

The basement gym and sparring room had green walls, textured to hide the repeated repairs, and a thickly padded floor dark enough to hide a host of stains. It smelled a lot like our own sparring room, a mixture of blood, sweat, and industrial cleaner. No matter how hard anyone tried, chemical agents could never entirely clear away the stink of violence and death.

Cole sat bare-chested in a corner of the room, his muscles revealed. The scars where Sky had stabbed him were gone, leaving a body with every sign of being fighting fit. If he was nervous about the outcome of the fight, then it didn't show. He offered a thin smile as he stood up, gazing coolly in my direction.

"Ethan," he said, then greeted Sebastian with a small nod. The respect with which he usually treated the Elite Alpha was gone, and though nothing had changed, I suspected that Cole's perception had shifted. On some level, he had always believed that Sebastian would end up working with him, but Sebastian had made clear that would never be the case, turning himself from the promise of a future ally into the certainty of a current foe.

"We should get this over with," he said. "Shall we?"

I just stared at him, caught by the shocking strength of my own hate. I had despised Cole for so long, had been consumed by anger at him, but now the feelings had coalesced into something hard and dark, a certainty that I needed to destroy him, for the good of everyone I knew.

"Your Beta is here to bear witness, and so am I," Sebastian said, his tone steady and professional. "Ethan, the Beta of the Midwest Pack, has issued a challenge to your position as Alpha of the East Coast Pack. Cole Masterson, do you accept this challenge?"

Cole nodded.

"Do you still hold to the same terms with which the first challenge was made?" Sebastian continued. "Will this challenge be to the death?"

Cole smiled at me, a serpent's expression, devoid of warmth.

"The challenge will be to Ethan's death."

Of course he was confident. Cole always believed that he was better than everyone else in the room.

"Sky," Sebastian said and gave a pointed look toward the door.

Normally, a challenge like this would have drawn a crowd of pack members, but apparently Cole hadn't wanted his followers here. Instead, there were just the two of us, Sebastian and Fallon as witnesses, and Hannibal, the East Coast Pack's physician. Sky's presence was an anomaly, not just because she was unnecessary to the fight, but because mates weren't usually allowed to watch a challenge.

"I'm fine with Ethan's mate being here," Cole said, grinning darkly. At least he wasn't hitting on Sky, for once; perhaps he was waiting to do that over my corpse.

I took a deep breath and looked at Sky, considering how to handle this. On the one hand, I didn't want her to see me get badly injured or possibly even killed. On the other hand,

I could see a stubborn moment coming on, and I didn't want to have a fight with her moments before the real fight with Cole.

"The rules are there for a reason," Sebastian said, glaring at Cole.

"My pack, my rules," Cole replied. "I don't mind Sky being here with Ethan to the very end. I find it cruel to offer anything less. She should offer comfort at the end." He looked at me. "If you don't want her to see you in your final moments, I understand. She looks like she wants to stay, but you rarely take into consideration what she wants, do you?"

I laughed. The jibe was so crude, it was hard to believe that I had once thought of Cole as a subtle schemer. If he wanted to drive a wedge between me and my mate, he was going to have to try a lot harder than that.

Of course, there was more to Cole's words than just toying with our relationship. He knew that Sky hated fights to the death and would struggle to stand by and watch while I was hurt. It was a way of punishing her for rejecting him. It was also a way to manipulate the outcome of a fight he didn't want to have: If Sky felt the need to jump in and protect me, then I would forfeit the fight and Cole's position would be secure. He could go back to waiting until I was vulnerable to challenge me. Cole claimed to be protecting Sky from cruelty, but really he was the one inflicting it to serve his own agenda.

At least his words had helped me make up my mind: I would do whatever seemed furthest from the reaction he was trying to provoke. He wanted me to argue against him, and I wasn't going to give him the satisfaction.

"It's not that I don't want her here," I said. "I don't want her to see the brutality I plan to inflict on you, but it is her call. Sky, sweetheart, do you want to stay or leave?"

For a moment, I thought that I might have laid it on too thickly myself: That "sweetheart" was a step beyond how we normally talked. But Cole didn't know that, and his eyes narrowed in malevolent frustration.

"I want to stay," Sky said.

"Very well." Sebastian nodded, then frowned. This situation required a little delicacy. "Sky, you are here as an observer to the challenge. At no point can you intervene. Do you understand?"

Sky nodded, though she didn't look happy. Whatever happened to me, she would have to stand by and watch, unable to help. That she could even consider it showed the strength of her character. In her position, I could never have done the same. Seeing her in pain and danger would have driven me insane, and now she would go through the same torment. I didn't want to even think about the emotional suffering she would go through if I was to die.

"I will need two iridium cuffs, one for Ethan and one for Skylar," Sebastian said to Fallon.

Her eyes widened and Cole chuckled.

"You didn't realize that they are both wolves who are able to perform magic, did you?" he said, with the shocked tone of a veteran gossip. "It is something they don't advertise. Both of their mothers were witches, and they both host Faerie spirit shades." He smiled slyly as he warmed to his subject, taking one last chance to poison people's minds against us before the confrontation came. "Sky is more peculiar than anyone you will ever meet. Ah, today she doesn't have it, but if you ever encounter her again, study her eyes. She gets a *terait* like a vampire. She doesn't have a natural immunity to vampires entering her home, nor an aversion to silver like the rest of us."

Fallon headed for the door, but stopped halfway out, looking over her shoulder at Sky. Fear and fascination warred with each other in her expression. Would this make a difference to how she viewed this fight, knowing that my victory would put such a strange combination as Sky near the leadership of her pack?

"Fallon, no need for the iridium cuffs," Cole said. "I'd like to defend my position in animal form."

Sebastian and I exchanged a look. It was common to use animal forms as part of the fight, but announcing it like that, laying out that we should stay that way, it seemed an odd approach. Presumably Cole thought he could gain some advantage, but I had no idea what it would be. Ultimately, this was his pack, and that gave him some power to set the rules. Unless I wanted to dispute that power, then he would get the challenge the way he wanted.

I nodded, then started stripping off my clothes. Cole did the same, then the two of us shifted into our wolf forms, mine a little larger and more muscled, his longer, sleeker, faster. We faced each other, teeth bared, claws extended, eyes gleaming.

"The challenge begins," Sebastian said.

And just like that, a new tension took hold of me; not the taut wires of expectation but the coiled spring of aggression, waiting to be unleashed.

We slowly circled the room, facing each other. I watched Cole's movements for any sign of weakness, but if his injuries held him back then it didn't show. Neither did his intent—he stood back defensively, waiting for me to make the first move. For once, I was happy to do as he wished.

I leapt right, trying to get hold of Cole's neck, but he darted back. As I landed, he snapped out with his teeth, tearing a wound down my flank. Adrenaline beat back the pain as I clawed at his side and legs, slicing through skin and surface tissue, exposing the muscle beneath.

Cole staggered, keeping the weight off his injured leg, his eyes wide in shock. He had thought that he had the advantage, and I had proven him wrong. The pain he would be feeling was accompanied by another, unfamiliar sensation: the possibility that he might lose.

We both reared back, then charged at each other. The room became a blur of movement as we became partners in a violent dance, one with death at its end. He was faster, lunging in and out, slashing with his claws and snapping with his teeth, inflicting a score of wounds on me. But when I hit, the blows counted for more. Each thud of my claws against his side was accompanied by the rending of flesh and a fresh gout of blood.

We stepped back, evaluating our injuries. Cole's ear was a ragged mess while blood was seeping down my cheek. Both of us were limping. The floor was sticky with blood and littered with chunks of fur. But neither of us was the clear victor yet. No one was near the point of collapse.

My heart pounded in my chest. The smell of my enemy's blood filled my senses, urging me on. The longing for victory was stronger than the cruelty of pain. This was my moment, do or die, save the pack I loved or leave it all behind.

We both charged again, paws pounding the floor, slamming into each other with an almighty thud. Cole stumbled back and I followed through, but he was twisting around, turning the movement to his advantage. Our bodies tangled, limbs thrashing, teeth crashing, rolling over and over as we both sought an opening that could finish the fight.

At last, I got Cole pinned to the floor. I bit and clawed at him, trying to get at his throat, but he fended me off. Then his head slammed into mine, the shock of the blow knocking me back. I gasped at the unexpected jolt of pain, and in my moment of vulnerability, Cole shoved me off. His teeth closed on my neck, but I sprung clear, taking only a shallow cut.

Heads lowered, feet pawing the ground, we stared at each other. Rage made my heart beat faster and the pulse race in my veins. Blood ran from between my teeth, and my own dribbled from between Cole's jaws.

We were both battered, but it was clear that Cole was losing. I had torn ragged chunks from his flanks and his legs trembled with every step. The challenge wasn't over, but the outcome was clear. Unless he could manage something desperate and unexpected, Cole was a dead man.

He took a few steps back, then started running. I braced myself to receive the charge, but instead of hitting me, he swerved right, darting around me. Before I realized what had happened, he was leaping through the air, straight at Sky.

She flung up her hand to protect her neck, and Cole's teeth sank into her forearm. He clawed at her and she hammered at his face, her free hand pounding at him, trying to drive him off before he could sink his teeth into her throat and rip it open.

For a fraction of a second, I stared in blank incomprehension, unable to understand what was happening, why the focus of the fight had moved, the challenge abandoned. Then it hit me. Cole knew just as well as I did that he was going to lose, but if he was going down, then he was going to make me as miserable as he could on the way. He was going to kill the person who brought happiness to my life. It was vicious and petty, a dagger driven through the heart of his enemy's desires. It was the embodiment of Cole, trying to tear Sky away from me, and fury blazed through me in that moment as reality sank in.

I leapt across the room in a blind rage and grabbed hold of his leg, sinking my teeth through skin and muscle until I gripped hold of him by the very bone. I could feel his shudder of pain and it urged me on; he deserved every moment of misery I could inflict. Then I pulled with all my strength, wrenching him off of Sky, dragging him across the dark floor. Blood pattered onto the matting—his, hers, mine —as he howled in pain and frustration.

With a renewed strength powered by my anger, I pounced on him, biting and tearing as I worked my way up his back, ripping him to bloody shreds. Every hurt he had inflicted on Sky, every scratch and bite in those seconds he had been on her, every twist of the emotional knife down through the years, I poured those memories into my attacks, doing to him what he had done to her, and worse. At last he sank to the ground, all attempts at resistance spent, blood running down his face and flanks.

I had played by Cole's rules, fighting in animal form and with Sky watching, against the normal conventions of a challenge. But he had broken the rules when he attacked Sky. Now I was going to finish this my way. I shifted. Pain jolted through torn and battered muscles as they contorted into new shapes, but I didn't care. At last I stood over Cole, panting and weary, dripping with blood but triumphant. I planted a hand firmly on each side of his head, felt all the rage and hate he had stirred in me down the years, and poured it into a single, sharp twist. Bone snapped and his body went limp.

My leg, torn and bleeding, gave way under me and I collapsed next to the corpse.

"Can you change?" Sebastian asked as he, Sky, and Hannibal hurried over to me.

I nodded and, with one last burst of energy, shifted back to animal form before sinking to the ground. I was distantly aware of Sky lying down next to me. As she nestled into my neck, I growled and moved my head closer, then weariness overtook me and I sank into unconsciousness.

CHAPTER 16

I woke up in a strange bed, lying next to Sky. My mind still weary from the previous day's exertions, it took me a moment to overcome my befuddlement and remember where I was: a hotel room in Maryland, not far from the East Coast Pack's retreat. It was the day after my victory over Cole. The world didn't just feel strange because of the battering I had taken. It felt strange because a burden that had weighed me down for months was finally gone.

Smiling, I gazed at Sky, still sleeping next to me. Her face was a mess of scars from where Cole had attacked her in his frenzied attempt to have one last taste of revenge. I couldn't help feeling like those injuries were my fault. If I had been paying more attention, then I could have stopped Cole. If I had insisted on maintaining the rule that mates were excluded, instead of trying to weave around Cole's mind games, then he wouldn't have been able to make the attack. Hell, if it wasn't for the long-running animosity between me and Cole, Sky never would have been in danger.

But I couldn't let that feeling of guilt win. Attacking Sky had been Cole's choice, just like turning his desire for my position into a personal vendetta. And yes, I had been slow to react, caught off guard by an attack that did nothing to win the challenge, or even to protect his life. But in the end, I had done the best I could with a lousy situation. Thanks to my intervention and Sky's own strength, she was safe.

To my relief, Sky's injuries were fading already, just as mine were, through our were-animal healing and Hannibal's help. He wasn't as good a doctor as Jeremy, but he had cleaned the wounds, applied dressings, and made sure that there would be no permanent harm. We were in good enough hands with the physician of the East Coast Pack.

Of my pack now.

That was a burden waiting to be dealt with. After everything she had seen and heard yesterday, I didn't know what Fallon was thinking or feeling, and so had no idea of how smoothly my planned transition of power would go. I had no other plan, of course, and facing some wrinkles was an inevitable part of life. But I didn't know Fallon well enough to judge how big a complication learning the truth about me and Sky would be for her, especially when it had come minutes before seeing her Alpha die.

All of that could wait. For now, I had earned some time with Sky. I ran a finger along the marks on her face, these temporary mementos of a terrible moment. As far as I was concerned, they did nothing to mar her beauty; she would always be gorgeous to me.

Sky's eyes slowly opened and she smiled sleepily. The movement of her face accentuated the scars, and I flashed back to the day before, remembering her cries of pain and desperate struggle for survival as Cole clawed at her.

"I can't believe he attacked you," I said, angry at Cole for his underhanded ways, ashamed of myself for not seeing it coming. I had been the one fighting, the one watching his every move, the one waiting to spring at him. I should have noticed his shift of direction and lunged in to stop him before he could hurt Sky.

"No one could have anticipated it," she said, laying her hand on mine.

But the anger was still there inside me, and I had no one to turn it against. Cole was gone forever. He had been the target of so much of my rage that now I didn't know what to do with it. Logically, it should have died with him, poured into that last moment in which I snapped his neck and ended our bitter rivalry. But the feelings lingered, too familiar to vanish in a single night. They were something that I would have to either let go or learn to live with.

I was left with a strange mix of feelings, the sense of lightness that came with a burden being lifted, but also an absence, the void that came when something familiar was suddenly gone. Though we had hated each other, Cole had been in my life for a long time. He was someone I had worked with, someone I had fought alongside more often than I had directly fought against him. I had done the right thing in ripping him out of our lives, but it would take time to adjust to a world without him.

I got out of bed, my leg aching as I put my weight on it. I wouldn't be limping today, but I would feel every footstep. It was like the hunters' arrows all over again.

"So when do you turn the pack over to Fallon?" Sky asked. It was a distraction and I knew it, but any distraction from the darkness of my thoughts was welcome.

"Tomorrow. Technically, Fallon will request to challenge me for the position and I will give it up rather than accept it. The rest is a series of obligatory paperwork and requests for me to return to the Midwest Pack."

"You won't have a rank," she whispered.

"Does it bother you?" I hadn't expected this to concern her, but maybe she was becoming more invested in the pack hierarchy than I thought. After all, she had been one of us for a while now.

"Not at all."

"I'll have it back in a week or so, and things will return to normal."

I thought about Winter and her desperate desire to get rid of the Beta's responsibilities. For her, normal couldn't come soon enough.

Sky winced as she sat up, and I went to sit beside her, looking over her wounds for any sign that something might not heal.

"What is normal?" she asked. "Will we ever have normal?"

She bit her lip as she gazed at her engagement ring, lost in thought.

"Sometimes I want normal," she said. "The real normal and not pack normal. Life without the pack stuff. House, children, waking up with a schedule that doesn't include fighting Faeries, vampires, magic, elves, the dark forest or dealing with fringe packs, otherworld politics, challenges, and people kidnapping us to hunt us."

Those words clawed at my soul as surely as Cole had clawed at my body. It seemed that the previous day had been too much for Sky. In the early days, her connection to the pack had been tenuous, her willingness to accept our ways uncertain. Raised around mundane humans, she had struggled to live with people whose lives were soaked in magic and violence like ours were. And now it seemed that she wanted out again.

What did that mean for us? We could hardly stay together if she rejected this life while I stayed in it, and I couldn't imagine leaving it behind. My friends, my family, my sense of purpose as a person, they were all tied to the pack. But my love for Sky ran deep. If she left and tried to hide from the supernatural world, would I leave with her?

I felt as though I was being torn in two, but I couldn't make this about me. I had to let Sky process her feelings, however much they hurt.

"Sky." I lifted her chin, forcing her to meet my gaze. "Do you really want to leave the pack?"

She closed her eyes, shutting the question out—shutting me out. Confusion mixed with the hurt. She was the one who wanted me to talk about what I thought and felt, but now she wasn't doing it. The ground was shifting under me, the rules of our relationship being wrenched away.

Unable to sit silent while I waited, I stood, but forced myself to stay beside her. At last, she wrapped her arms around my waist and laid her cheek against my skin.

"I was just being hypothetical," she said softly. "I didn't mean it."

I ran my fingers through her hair. I could hear the beating of her heart, could tell where the truth lay. I drew out of her embrace, knelt down, and kissed her deeply. If this led to letting go, then I wanted to feel that she was mine one last time.

"You meant it," I said. "I heard it. All your signs were normal and your voice was level. You meant it, so we need to talk about it."

She shifted back on the bed, away from me, and I felt my heart break as that space opened between us.

"Okay," she whispered. "Let's talk about it."

I sat down next to her and took hold of her hand, clinging to whatever connection I could find.

"Yesterday, I watched you prepare to fight someone to the death, so that you could get him out of the pack," she said. "I spent days before that functioning because I had to, with my heart broken and feeling like the world was crashing down around me, because you were missing and probably going to be killed. I've been attacked and injured so many times that wounds don't even faze me anymore. That should bother me —it used to.

"I've been pulled out of this world, magically hijacked, prepared to perform a forbidden spell to save my pack, killed someone, and watched someone that I cared about be killed in front of me. *Normal* just seems so far from my grasp that it hurts sometimes. I don't need it to always be calm walks in the park and boring days. But I'd like the boring days to outnumber the ones where I'm fighting for either my life, yours, or someone else's I care about."

I nodded, absorbing her words, considering what they meant. It wasn't just that she had become part of the pack, it was everything that had followed. Since she joined us, we had been through the most tumultuous events I could ever remember, perhaps the most brutal and chaotic in a pack history stretching back hundreds of years. It was understandable for that to feel overwhelming, but what was the alternative?

"You think if we leave this, we'll have a normal life?" I asked.

She looked down at our clasped hands.

"I was about to have Cole assassinated," she whispered.

Those words, so softly spoken, left me speechless. The indignant, innocent woman I had first met would never have made that cold-blooded decision. She had abhorred the violence in our lives, had done her best to escape it. Now Sky was inviting it in, and in a way that would have shocked any were-animal, choosing assassination over the honest combat of a challenge.

Except that she had stepped back from the brink.

"Chris?" I asked. Who else could she have gone to for such a mission?

"It was a challenge and we knew it was going to be to death," she said. "Cole betrayed the pack, turned the Council against us, was trying to get you pushed out of the pack, and was orchestrating a coup of my pack, and he was going to get away with it."

She looked at me uncertainly, as though she was afraid of how I would react. Even I wasn't sure how to deal with this unexpected moment. I rubbed my chin, stubble rasping across my fingers, and moved closer to her once more.

"You didn't go through with it," I said.

"I couldn't."

I leaned in and kissed her on the cheek. "Because that's who you are. Parts of you are adapting, but the real Sky is there at the core."

I was so relieved at that revelation that I didn't know what to say. For a long moment we sat silent while I let the feeling sink in.

"Sky, you're a were-animal who hosts a powerful spirit shade and has the ability to perform magic that most haven't seen. You wouldn't have stayed invisible for long. You're right, we've been through a lot of things, but you can't believe a person like you can have a normal life. It's unrealistic." I ran my fingers softly across her cheek, then kissed it. "Some things might not have happened, but without this pack, I suspect things would be worse."

Silence hung between us, but a settled silence now. The storm of emotions had threatened to overtake us, but we were through it. Our relationship would survive this. We would survive this.

"I'm not leaving the pack," I said. "*We* aren't leaving the pack."

"I don't want to leave. I love it, but sometimes—"

"You want normal. I get it." I toyed with her engagement ring. "A wedding is normal."

"There's nothing normal about me getting dressed in a big white gown that makes me look like a fairy-tale princess or mermaid and parading down an aisle to a wedding march while people gawk at me and my overpriced party dress that I will only wear once."

"Overpriced party dress?" I laughed out loud, then lowered my voice, wary of hurting her through my mockery. "Sky at the core."

She hit me playfully on the shoulder, and I winced as the blow caught on the wounds that Cole had left there.

"Okay, no fairy-tale wedding." I grinned. "A honeymoon is normal."

"I'd like that." At last, she smiled, and my heart melted.

"Maryland's nice. We should stay here for a while. Sightsee or whatever. Do normal stuff."

"Don't you have a pack to run?" Now there was a glint of mischief in her eyes. I could have laughed again I was so relieved.

"Not after I sign the paperwork. It's up to Fallon and however the chain will fall. She'll oversee whoever vies for the position of fifth. We'll stay here for a couple days—see what normal is like." Another thought crossed my mind, and this time I did laugh. "And ignore Winter's calls. She will not be happy with taking on the role of Beta, and I'm sure she'll feel the need to express those feelings with a lot of choice, colorful words."

I crawled back into bed and drew Sky toward me.

"I love you," I whispered, my lips brushing her ear.

"I love you too."

I felt odd, swinging open the doors of the East Coast Pack retreat and striding in like I owned the place, but the fact was, for the next few minutes, I did. Weres stared at me uncertainly, some of them people I knew, others unfamiliar, all waiting to see what sort of Alpha I would be.

"Office?" I demanded.

Hannibal, standing near the back of the entrance hall, pointed up the stairs. "Top floor, first door on the right."

Without a word, I headed up the stairs, taking them two at a time. I could have been gentler with this pack, to try to ease them through a difficult transition, could have shown them that I was a leader who could be trusted, unlike Cole. But in the end, that would have done more harm than good. In a few minutes, they would be Fallon's pack, and it was her they needed to think fondly of. The last thing she needed was people wondering if they would have been better off under my leadership. Better to make me a threat hanging over them, a terrible alternative to the leader they had.

Fallon was waiting for me, standing on a balcony that extended from the study to the front of the house. I joined her there, looking out across the grounds of the house and the Maryland countryside beyond. This could have been a fine place to live, if circumstances had been different. A quieter place, perhaps, a more normal setting for me and Sky. But it wasn't our pack.

"You're sure about this?" Fallon asked, looking at me.

I nodded. I had done what I needed to. It was time to move on.

"Okay."

She walked over to an antique desk, on which the paper-work associated with a transfer of power was set out. A few signatures, and it would be done. She patted her pockets, then blushed, embarrassed.

"You don't have a pen, do you?" she asked. "I didn't think of it."

"I'm sure Cole had something."

I tugged at the handle of one of the desk drawers. When it didn't move, I became more determined to find out what was inside. Planting one foot against the base of the desk, I wrenched at the drawer. There was a crunch of splintering wood and it flew open.

There were no pens inside, but there were the pack's account books, bank cards, a couple of passports, and a box of gold Krugerrands—portable currency for the man who thought he might have to go on the run. Cole had been prepared for a number of eventualities, but in the end he had chosen to face me. Overconfidence really had been his weakness.

Behind the Krugerrands was another object—a small cloth bag that rustled at my touch. A label on the outside said that it was wolfsbane, but when that bag was opened it revealed a plastic bag inside, and within that a collection of dried leaves in an odd mixture of teal, gold, and pink. That was no wolfsbane I'd ever seen, either in person or in my books. I didn't recognize the leaves, but if Cole had valued them enough to keep them in this drawer, then they were clearly worth paying attention to.

"I might take this," I said, holding up the bag.

"You're the Alpha," Fallon said with a shrug.

"Only for a few more minutes."

"Long enough. And honestly, Cole has given me enough surprises over the past two days. Whatever mysteries he's left behind, I think it's best for the pack if someone else deals with them."

I slipped the pouch into my jacket pocket, then opened another drawer. This time, I found a gold-plated fountain pen.

"Ready," I said, holding it up.

Fallon whistled sharply. Hannibal appeared in the doorway, along with one of the hulking men Niimi had sent to guard Cole at our retreat, and a slender Latina woman I recognized from Mateo's pack.

"I thought the witnesses should be outsiders," Fallon explained.

"Good thinking."

"Ethan, I challenge you for the role of Alpha," she said, a tremble in her voice.

"And I concede. Let's get this over with so that your pack can move on."

As a lawyer, I knew better than to sign anything I hadn't read. I went through each document carefully, then set my signature to them. Fallon did the same, followed by our witnesses.

And just like that, I wasn't an Alpha anymore.

When I got back to our hotel room, Sky was sitting on the bed, watching television while she worked her way through a fat stack of pancakes. Empty plates lay scattered around her, along with a coffee cup. She was already looking revitalized compared with that morning and the scars were fading from her face.

"I take it you enjoyed breakfast," I said.

"I'd visit this hotel for the breakfast alone. I've never had red velvet pancakes. I didn't know that was a thing."

"It is. Not one that this hotel typically makes, and it wasn't on the menu, but I was able to work out something." I smiled at her. It was worth these extra efforts to see Sky happy. "I think I have to give the chef our firstborn."

"Deal."

She took another bite. I leaned forward with my mouth open, waiting for a taste as a reward for my efforts, but instead she kept shoveling them into her own face.

"If I'm giving my first child for this meal, do I have to share?" she asked, smiling up at me sweetly.

"That was supposed to be for both of us," I said, looking at the scattered plates.

"It was going to get cold." She held the last forkful of pancakes out for me.

"A whole forkful. I must be special."

"Don't you forget it."

It could have been a chance to make another kind of special memories, but I had something else on my mind. I pulled out the bag of dried leaves I had found in Cole's study and held it up for Sky to see. This time I leaned in closer and took a sniff of the faint scent escaping through plastic. The strange, musty fragrance made me shudder.

"What is it?" Sky asked, peering with curiosity from the leaves to me, distracted even from the thought of red velvet pancakes.

"I have no idea. We found it in Cole's office. It was in another bag labeled wolfsbane, but this isn't wolfsbane."

"It's usually purple, right?"

I nodded. "And poisonous to humans, not us. The myth is that it prevents shifters from changing. It doesn't. At worse, the noxious scent annoys us. This is different."

But perhaps that wolfsbane label hinted at something. I stepped away from Sky and opened the bag, even as she objected, then took a deep breath of its unsettling scent. There was something in it that stirred a familiar feeling in the back of my mind, like a memory I couldn't quite recall. Urged on by that feeling and impatient to find the cause, I took out a few leaves and rubbed them between my fingers. Particles flew up, creating a small cloud around my face.

My nose twitched, then my whole upper body. Alarmed, I dropped the bag and the loose leaves, but my body kept shifting, spasms running through me. Muscles strained and twisted, bones stretched, and my skin tingled as though something was trying to break through.

My body was changing against my will.

I fought to retain my human form, to hang onto who I was. But my body was turning despite me, transforming into my animal form. Sweat broke out and muscles strained as I fought back, but it was no good. With a drawn-out groan and a ripping of clothes, I fell to the floor as a wolf.

Sky stared at me, so I gave her the most reassuring look I could, trying to let her know that all was well. I had been transformed against my will, and though I tried, I couldn't change back, but nothing else seemed to be wrong. If I had chosen to change, this would just have been a normal moment.

I relaxed and waited, testing my body every minute or so, pushing at those instincts to see if I could change. After several failed attempts, I finally felt what I had expected. Muscles twisted, bones shifted, fur retracted, and I became human again. Exhausted from the unexpected exertion, shaken by the experience of changing against my will, I lay on the floor for a few minutes, surrounded by my torn clothes, before I stood.

"You couldn't change back, could you?" Sky asked.

I shook my head. "It's just like it was when we awoke in the room. No one was able to change back."

I grabbed my computer from out of my luggage and settled down with it in my lap. It took only a moment to fire up a video conferencing app and find Josh's name in my contact list.

"You want to put on some clothes before you do that?" Sky asked.

I shrugged. Being dressed was a much bigger deal for her than for most people associated with the pack.

"We've seen each other naked before."

Josh popped up on the screen, shirtless, waving a bagel and a cup of coffee.

"You're alive," he said, and then, with a heavy shot of sarcasm, "Thanks for letting me know."

"Sebastian called you as soon as the challenge was over."

"But *you* didn't! Seriously, how hard would it be to text me, pick up the phone and say, 'hey bro, I'm alive,' or whatever? I bet you let Sky know within minutes."

I waited with growing impatience while he worked his way through a whole indignant younger brother routine.

"Are you finished?" I said, cutting him off.

"Yep."

"I'm alive, bro. Happy?"

"No, I'm not happy. My brother's an ass."

"Betahole. He's a Betahole," Sky called out from across the room, before coming to sit next to me. "I guess for the time being he's an Alphahole."

I frowned at her. I hadn't called Josh for a lecture on my behavior, but now it seemed I would be receiving a double-barreled dressing down.

"You're right, Josh," Sky continued, "he should have called. Accept my apology on his behalf."

"Sweet. As a couple you make my brother less of an Alphahole."

I'd already had more of this than I was willing to put up with. It was time to get down to business. I held up the bag for Josh to see.

"I need you to come to town and get this. I don't feel comfortable mailing it, and Sebastian's left."

Josh leaned in to peer at the bag, and his smile broadened in excitement.

"Nice. Have you tried it yet?"

"Yeah."

"You think it will make a good edible?"

"What? I'm not going to eat it. It forces me to change to my wolf."

Josh's brows furrowed as he realized that this wasn't what he'd thought.

"What? It stopped you from changing? That's some weird stuff."

I growled in exasperation. I didn't need Josh to tell me the obvious.

"It's not *that*. I found it in Cole's office and it was marked as wolfsbane ..."

"That's not wolfsbane—"

"I know that," I snapped. Apparently today really was speak the obvious day. "It's what they used to make us change when they had us. I don't know what it is. I'm staying here with Sky for a couple of days."

"Pack business?"

I hesitated, trying to find the words for what I was doing. Did this count as a holiday? Some kind of special couple's thing for me and Sky? A medically needed rest?

"No, we're going to stay for a while and sightsee," I admitted.

"Mmmm." Josh turned his attention to Sky, his voice growing low and serious. "So, the brain injury—is it severe? I know there are different levels. Which one is he?"

"It's not a brain injury," I snapped, done with his mockery. "I just want to spend time with Sky for a few days. Get your ass here by tomorrow."

I shut off the connection before he could finish his response. Sky sat grinning at me, but I wasn't going to be goaded by her either. If she wanted normal, then she shouldn't mock me when I offered it.

Sky had come out to Maryland to support me, so I figured that the least she deserved was a day to suit her tastes. I scheduled a guided tour of the city, trips to a couple of museums, and a concert in a park to finish it off. Some of what we saw was to my tastes, some of it wasn't, but I enjoyed every moment of being with Sky, seeing her pleasure at doing ordinary human things.

The ordinary humans themselves were something I could have done without. The clumsy, unobservant way that they navigated their space meant that they almost bumped into me several times, and others unwittingly got in the way of our view at the museums. Strangers interrupted our day, asking us to take photos of them with their cameras, as if the only way that they could give depth to their shallow existence was by flattening it into a pixelated image. Fortunately, Sky was more tolerant of all of this, to the extent of taking those pictures for people, and as long as she kept enjoying her day, so did I.

To cap off a Sky-centered outing, I let her pick the restaurant where we had dinner in the evening. Almost immediately, I wished that I'd set some limits. I'd expected her to pick somewhere high end, where she could enjoy an exquisite meal before her inevitable dive into the dessert menu, but that wouldn't have been a Sky sort of choice. Instead, she took us to a tacky family style restaurant, with cheap prints of old photos on the walls and inanely smiling staff in bright matching uniforms. Trapped at a table in the middle of the restaurant, surrounded by inane chatter and bad background music, I felt like I had been sucked down into some circle of Hell.

We were halfway through our starters when a hand settled on my shoulder. I looked up, expecting to see a member of the local pack, and instead saw a woman from the next table over smiling down at me.

"Sorry," she said in a low voice. "Almost lost my balance, and I needed something strong to stabilize myself."

She gave me a lingering smile while her hand rested just a little longer than necessary on my shoulder. Behind her, her friend blushed and looked down at her food.

"No problem." I turned back to Sky and caught a glint of anger in her eyes. Apparently her tolerance for ordinary human antics didn't extend to humans flirting with me. I grinned. It seemed that her animal instincts were getting stronger, including the possessiveness over her mate that would come naturally to any were.

We were just finishing our main course, and I was wondering how long I would have to linger in this place for the sake of dessert, when that hand settled on my shoulder again. The woman might be persistent, but she sure wasn't subtle.

This time, her touch was followed by a quick burst of magic from Sky. A chair shot out, knocking the woman off balance, and I grabbed both her and the chair to keep her from hitting the floor. Another thrust of magic hit my arm, trying to make me drop her, but I returned a jab of my own, and nudged Sky's foot beneath the table.

"Play nice," I mouthed. It was good to feel wanted, for Sky's possessive side to reach out protectively around me, but I didn't want to cause a scene, especially not one involving magic.

After that, Sky's relaxed mood seemed to evaporate. She hunched over her dessert, swiftly demolishing a large slice of red velvet cake, and I was able to get us out of the restaurant before the woman at the next table could make a third attempt at grabbing my attention. I couldn't help smiling a little at it all. Sky, who normally railed against the petty jealousies of others, was feeling her own pangs of envy.

We walked back from the restaurant hand in hand, enjoying the cool late evening air. I was still amused by Sky's magical display of temper, but after a while, the fun novelty of the situation started to wear off. There was a serious issue we needed to address, one brought up by the scene at the restaurant. My love life had been busy before Sky came along, not stable but seldom quiet. She, on the other hand, had never had an adult relationship before me. The difference in experience could have been designed to engender mistrust.

"You worry about me in this relationship, don't you?" I said, stopping in my tracks and turning to her, trying to keep my expression blank. There was a long pause, and I started to worry at what she might be about to say.

At last, Sky shook her head. "No. But I'm not used to feeling… any of it. Women looked at you before, now it bothers me. It irritates me that women fawn over you. And I feel the irritation intensely. I'm not used to feeling that way. I don't like it."

"You're not used to feeling jealous." I grinned in relief to find that there was nothing deeper. Holding up my hand, I ran a finger along my engagement ring. "I guess the wedding band isn't the attention repellent I thought it would be. Jealous Sky is kind of cute... scarier and an abuser of magic, but cute."

We walked on in silence, while I thought about how our relationship had developed, how we had both changed with it. My own past jealousies over Sky came to the forefront of my mind, along with the passions that had driven that insecurity. I stopped and stared at Sky, who looked back up at me with concern.

"It was like having a craving that couldn't be satisfied," I explained, thinking back to the time before her. We started walking again, and I talked as we went. "You know you want something but you don't know what. And you keep searching for that one person who fits—who satisfies completely. There are women who come close, but it's not exactly what your body is craving."

It was hard for me to talk about these things. For so long, they had been the side of me that I concealed, out of habit as much as self-preservation. But Sky's hand gripping mine tight reminded me that it was okay to be open about my feelings now, that with her, I had someone who would listen and not judge, with whom I could share everything that I was.

"Then you find the perfect fit," I continued, "that one person who satisfies a longing you've had so long you accepted that it would be part of your life forever. Like a curse that can't be lifted." I sighed. "The person is like a decadent food that you know you shouldn't indulge in because there are consequences. Maybe it will lead to high cholesterol and be your physical undoing—a tragic death from an embolism."

"In this story, I'm the embolism-causing treat?" Sky frowned, unimpressed. "I do not come off good in that story."

I laughed deeply, not at her this time but at how familiar and comforting her reactions had become.

"Sort of. You make me vulnerable. It's difficult feeling this way. Superficial relationships are easy. I didn't try hard and didn't care." I shrugged. "I need you to trust me and know that I'd never do anything to hurt you."

Sky nodded. "For the record, I was annoyed that she saw that you arrived with me, wore a ring, was talking to me, and didn't care. It's a little uncomfortable that women are so drawn to you."

"I'm a very attractive man," I said. Why hide from the truth? It was something I had always known, something I took pride in.

"Oh, I forgot, I'm dealing with the arrogant brother," she said with a mocking scowl.

I stroked her hand and smiled at her, amused.

"I have a mirror, Sky."

"You're absolutely right. You're breathtaking, and people are going to look when you walk in a room. It's such a horrid burden you must bear. How have you lived your life like this? Causing eruptions of swoons when you walk into a room. Your life must be tragic. You're right, you *are* too pretty. We're going to have to disfigure you. Since we heal so fast, it's going to be brutal. Sorry, buddy, but that pretty face is going to have to go. How are we going to do it? Sledge-hammer to the face?"

"We aren't disfiguring my face. You'll have to deal with it the same way I deal with advances toward you." I thought back to the restaurant and realized that there was something more serious beneath all of this, a part of that encounter that we hadn't addressed. "But I need you to make a promise to me."

"What's that?"

"Magic. Let's never use it against each other, okay?"

"Why?"

I wished that I could explain it, to myself as well as to her. As weres, we might grapple with each other in our animal forms, using our supernatural nature as part of our interactions, giving in to what came through instinct. But that moment when we had pushed at each other with magical power, though only so briefly, had unsettled me.

"I don't know," I said. "It seems wrong for us to use it against each other. It made me feel disconnected from you."

"We're were-animals first," she replied thoughtfully. "We share that commonality, with more depth and similarities. It's our bond and what joins us. Our magic, I know it's a part of us, but somehow it still seems foreign and unnatural."

I grinned in relief at hearing her pin down what had bothered me.

"Yes," I said with a nod, "I guess that's it."

"Okay, I promise never to use magic against you. Just women who seem to forget what a damn wedding ring means. She was all over you. You couldn't have been more obvious showing her the ring."

"I know," I said in a mock-serious tone. "She deserved to fall flat on her face. You showed her."

"Your sarcasm is neither warranted nor appreciated."

"Of course, dear."

It felt good to slip back into being us, to have settled an important issue and so easily slid from there into the gentle mockery that gave light to our relationship.

I looked around as we walked into the lobby of the hotel, an instinctive assessment of potential threats, like I would make on coming into any building. There were no dangers here, but Josh and London sat at the bar, each with a glass in hand.

"I'm proud of you," Sky said as we walked over to them.

"For what?"

"Going out and just hanging out with people."

"You realize I deal with people regularly and don't have some odd aversion to them."

"You deal with people on your terms and are actually paid to be stubborn, cantankerous, and… well, let's just say 'confident.' It's your wheelhouse. But relaxing, hanging around with strangers, and not having a schedule and just taking it easy isn't your thing."

"And he's not fond of humans either," Josh said, turning to face us with a grin. A colorful image swirled up his neck, a new addition to his already excessive collection of tattoos.

I glared at him, not enjoying the feeling of judgment. "I'm not very fond of you right now."

"Of course not. The hierarchy is: were-animals, people who can use magic … and way down here"—he lowered his hand to a few inches above the ground—"humans."

"They don't bother me," I snapped back. This was a ridiculous conversation. I worked fine with humans all the time—just ask my legal colleagues—and I disliked this inaccurate image that he was painting of me. It was time to change the subject and get to grips with why Josh was here. "Have you found anything?"

The bartender handed the check to Josh, who in turn gave it to me.

"You got this, right?"

"Of course."

I frowned at the ink marks rising along my little brother's neck, the skin still red where they had been added. I didn't like seeing him disfigure himself in this way, and he knew it.

"Claudia said no more," I pointed out.

"She released me from it," Josh said brightly.

I looked across his tattooed arms, pierced ears, and the way the ink crept down toward more images hidden beneath his shirt. If he had intended to wind me and our godmother up, he couldn't have found a better way to do it.

We had other business to deal with. At a gesture from me, Josh and London finished their drinks and followed us to the elevator.

"No more," I said, once the elevator doors had closed us in.

Josh scoffed, then glowered, and I could see him readying himself for a burst of defiance.

"Whatever." Magic sparked from his fingertips.

I watched that erratic dance of power, the air crackling with raw magic, then looked up to Josh's face. I had to remind myself that we were both adults and that, as Sky had taught me, this bickering and commanding wasn't a healthy way to behave. Talking openly about our lives, and how I had protected him from a curse, had brought us closer together. I didn't want to lose that.

"It's just a suggestion." I shrugged, looking for a way to deescalate this. "You like getting them; I don't want you to run out of places to display them. If you slow down, that's less likely."

"Okay," Josh said, reluctantly acknowledging the point.

We looked at each other, neither of us sure how to continue from there. I could feel myself tensing to defend against his next verbal barb, and he looked like he was doing the same. Were we trapped in this dynamic, despite everything that had happened?

Behind us, there was a sound of stifled laughter from Sky and London. Josh and I turned to look at them, my eyes narrowing in suspicion. Sky had turned a shade of red, but London looked at us with a steady gaze and raised eyebrows, as if to ask why we were looking her way.

At last we reached the hotel room.

"Let me see it," Josh said.

I retrieved the bag of mysterious herbs from my luggage and held it out for him.

"You couldn't stop the change?" he asked.

I shook my head.

Josh let out a worried hiss. "This is bad, really bad."

"I know. I have no idea what it is."

London joined us, peering intently at the contents of the bag.

"It was in Cole's office, right?" she asked.

"Yes," I replied.

"What's the relationship with the elves here?"

"Why?" Sky asked.

There was an awkward moment, London looking at us like we were a bomb that might go off if touched in the wrong way.

"Just say it," I urged her. We were increasingly close to the witches, and dancing tactfully around a topic would just waste everyone's time.

"I don't want to be indelicate, but the were-animals are the weakest link in the otherworld." London smiled apologetically. "If someone sees one of us perform magic, it's easy to dismiss it as their eyes playing tricks on them. They see a person shift to an animal, there's no question about that. The Red Blood want to expose you all. But have they mentioned anyone else? They aren't even worried about vampires—who can live for an eternity. It's shifting to animals that seems to defy nature so much they seek to destroy those who do it. And if you all are outed, the otherworld could be rid of you."

She held up her hands, as if to distance herself from everything she had said, before continuing in the same vein.

"There are many who don't feel that way, but with the situation with Steven and everything that has occurred that has been linked to you all, there is unrest." She sighed. "Even the witches are being pressured to distance ourselves." She looked pointedly at me and Sky. "And your mating has caused an uproar like I've never seen before."

I had some sense of why those words came in such an apocalyptic tone. Many in the supernatural world knew that there was more to me and Sky than just a pair of weres. If I had heard about a couple with extraordinary powers in another pack, and then they had become mates, I would have had concerns too. The supernatural world was built on a delicate balance of power, and on the ability to hide that power from the mundane world. Bringing together unprecedented new abilities threatened to turn that on its head.

London tapped the bag.

"If this was something that could be easily found in nature, don't you think it would have been stumbled upon?" She ran her fingers through her hair, and pastel colors appeared before vanishing again beneath dark brown. "The Red Blood have been working diligently to out you all. Following you, waiting to catch you changing. You think Dexter wouldn't have discovered this stuff? The only explanation is that it has been created. We haven't seen anything like this, but who has been known to create harmful things and tuck them away until they need them?"

I sighed, then cursed. Cole had to have gotten this from the elves. We needed to know which ones and who else they had shared it with, so that we could cut this abomination off in its tracks. That meant relying on the pack I had just decapitated and then abandoned.

I pulled out my phone and called Fallon. This could be an awkward conversation.

CHAPTER 17

We strode up the walkway to a large brick house, Fallon leading the way past carefully sculpted bushes and exotic flowers, as well as a pair of gleaming bronze statues, capturing the elegant form of a pair of elves. I had expected a certain level of pompous grandeur from a pair of Makellos, the self-proclaimed elven elite, and these ones had outdone themselves. Josh nudged London, and both she and Sky laughed as he pointed out a distinctive bulge on one of the statues, but the laughter didn't last long. There was nothing funny about why we were there.

I tensed as we approached the front door. Fallon had arranged this meeting within a few hours of my call, but the level of cooperation that showed wouldn't necessarily last once our hosts, Dalia and Gregoire, saw what sort of people they were dealing with. In my experience, interactions with the Makellos were always a minefield; a few wrong words could see the whole thing explode in your face.

A servant opened the door seconds before we reached it and led us silently into an old-fashioned receiving room. Antique furniture was matched with a sturdy but fading rug and shelves of old books alongside oil paintings. Our hosts clearly had specific tastes and the wealth to enjoy them.

After a few moments of waiting, carefully used to put us in our place, Gregoire entered the room, gently escorting Dalia. I wasn't surprised to see that they looked like the statues on the lawn; what could be more Makellos than having yourself immortalized in high art?

Gregoire was just short of six feet tall, broadly built, with square features that gave a menacing twist to his forced smile. Dressed in a pearl-gray tailored suit, he looked like a man on his way to a wedding, though judging by the house, this was probably what he wore every day. Dalia was diminutively built, only five feet tall, dressed in burgundy slacks and a lace-trimmed silk shirt, but her striking features made her seem like a larger than life presence in the room. Her sepia, heart-shaped face framed an angular nose, full lips, and bright, wide eyes that flickered with inner energy. Braids held back her auburn hair, the better to show off her beauty.

As they entered the room, Dalia and Gregoire left the doors open, allowing us a view to another room, and with it a not so subtle threat. Three women and three men, wearing matching military-style uniforms and matching serious expressions, stood stiffly side my side. They radiated magic, an unmistakable concentration of deadly force.

Silence stretched out between us while I tried to work out what to say. Were those guards merely a precaution, or were our hosts looking for an excuse to set them on us? So much depended upon what they had heard about us and how they viewed Cole, and frustratingly, I knew nothing on either topic.

"You called this meeting, Ethan," Gregoire said with a note of annoyance. "I assume it's not to introduce yourself as the new Alpha, so I'd prefer if we get on with it."

Josh, looking through the doors at the guardian magicians, narrowed his eyes and flexed his hands by his sides, ready for action. Dalia watched him and smiled.

If the elves weren't going to be subtle, then neither was I.

"Do you know what this is?" I asked, holding out the bag of herbs.

"*Mond*," Gregoire replied. "It's a wonderful little plant that we've been dabbling with for years. It's taken a lot of trial and error but I'm quite happy with the result. I'd like it to be stronger, but it serves its purpose. Is there anything else I can help you with, Alpha?"

I stared at him, shocked by the casual tone with which he talked about such a powerful weapon. I had expected him to be evasive, to obfuscate or outright lie when faced with a were-animal asking about a drug designed purely to hurt us.

"Do you have more of it?" I asked.

"Of course we do."

"Darling, we *had* more of it," Dalia said softly, her lips forming an amused smile. "It's been dispersed among the masses."

"Who did you *disperse* it to?" I asked, struggling to keep my anger in check. These people had made the tool used to turn me into the victim of a hunt. They had unleashed a weapon that could see every were-animal on the planet revealed, leaving our whole species as prey to people who didn't understand us. He talked about it as if it was just one more painting on his wall.

Gregoire paced the room, tapping his chin in thought.

"There was a very enthusiastic witch," he said, "I believe his name was Sean, Sand …"

"Samuel, dear. His name was Samuel."

"Oh, yes. How could I forget him? He was quite enthusiastic in his agenda. He despises magic in this world, but he seems to find 'beasts who present themselves as men' even more offensive. Rumor has it that you've thwarted his plans." He smiled, apparently amused by others' suffering. "He was not at all happy with that and quite vocal about you siccing the new witches on him. Who, in turn, unleashed a rogue fae on him. He was livid just retelling the course of events."

"The 'beasts' do manage to rub people the wrong way, don't they?" Dalia said, toying with the lace at the end of her sleeve. The smile faded from her face as she noticed Sky looking at her with teeth bared and an expression of pure fury.

I kept my own feelings buried, as I had done so often before. There would be a time to settle this score, but first I had to know how far the damage went, how many people were wandering the world with bags of Mond, just waiting to bring us down.

"There was another witch, Rayna," Gregoire continued. "I remember her because I haven't seen fiery rage like that in years. It was white hot, vengeful, and oddly not directed at the were-animals, who tend to have their little snouts in everyone's business. If only someone took a rolled-up paper and whacked them to remind them where they belong." He let out a dramatic sigh. "Alas, it never happened. Oddly, Rayna's anger was directed at the were-animals' little witch. What a plot twist." His smile widened, teeth bared, and he shifted his gaze to Josh. "You killed the members of the Creed and it went unpunished."

"It went unpunished because it was justified," Josh shot back.

Gregoire laughed darkly as he ran an evaluating gaze across Josh. He knew enough to stand back from a witch of Josh's power, especially one whose temper he was provoking.

Josh's eyes clouded over as magic radiated from him. In the other room, the magician guards tensed.

"Ah, you have adopted the ways of the were-animals,"

Gregoire said. "Jury and executioner. Well, it seems as if Rayna is seeking her own justice."

"Mond won't affect me," Josh said, his voice as cold as his expression.

"Hurt the brother, hurt the witch," Dalia whispered, pressing herself back against the wall.

Muscles shifted in Josh's arms as he fought to stay calm.

"Then the humans found out about us," Gregoire continued with a self-satisfied chuckle. "Well, they didn't so much find out about us as much as we contacted them and told them of our little plant and that the very thing that could force were-animals to change could be theirs for free. Oh, they were elated."

"You are hurting yourself," I said. "When we are outed, then people will believe in the impossible. If humans can shift to animals, what's to prevent the masses from believing in those who can perform magic? As usual the elves are shortsighted and foolish."

"Are we? If the rumors are correct, you and your peculiar mate are responsible for the vampires' ability to blend seamlessly with humans. No more aversion to light. If they manage their appetites, no one will discover what they are. And as for those of us who possess magic, we will use self-control. We will never be discovered while they are dealing with the abominations that are you all. 'The beasts who present themselves as men.'" Gregoire turned a wide, self-satisfied smile on Dalia. "I rather like that description. What about you, love?"

"It's quite fitting," she said in a mocking tone.

Their snide, condescending tone was wearing away my patience. I had come here with the aim of making the supernatural world safer, but found the usual elven arrogance standing in my way. I moved closer to Gregoire, a reminder of the strength that could be turned against him if he kept this up. In response, the guards in the other room shifted, still out of reach but pointedly closer to us, hands at the ready by their sides.

"You know a great deal about us—which is good," I said. "At least you aren't going into this war unaware of what you've gotten yourself and the people who aid you into. I will be merciless in my retribution."

"Are you ever merciful?" Gregoire sneered. "That animalistic behavior is what got you into this."

He gave a small wave of his hand. One of the guards picked up a laptop from a side table, opened it, and turned the screen for us to see. A video started playing, but I didn't need to look to know what it was. I knew every second of the video that had gotten Steven arrested, the few minutes of violence that had almost exposed weres to the world. I had fought hard in court to keep it from destroying our lives, and hearing it now brought back all the frustration it had raised before.

"Perhaps if you all had practiced some mercy and discretion this wouldn't be happening," Gregoire said.

"We had handled it," I growled. "You've exacerbated the situation!"

"No, you didn't handle it. The humans, the Red Blood, aren't handled. You will be the sacrifice to keep the others hidden. Once they can prove Steven is a were-animal, that video demonstrates how dangerous you can be. There are so many were-animals that we will continue to go unnoticed. Resources and time will be directed at containing the beasts who hide behind a human shell."

Gregoire spoke about the Red Blood, but it was clear that he took as much pleasure in our exposure as they would. This was his doing, a direct attack on the safety of all were-animals. I growled, barely able to contain my anger at the betrayal.

"How did Cole get it?"

"He helped us test it. A sample of it was all he requested."

"I doubt he knew your plans," Fallon said, her tone low and measured despite the bitterness in her face. "There's no way he would have helped."

I wasn't going to disabuse her of her naivety, but I couldn't share her view. It was true that using the Mond could have exposed Cole along with the rest of us, but he wasn't a man to draw the line where others did. He had become a man obsessed with taking control of the Midwest Pack, and with it the position of Elite. If he had to expose us all to human scrutiny, force us to live our lives in fear and on the run, then I could believe he would consider that a price worth paying to achieve his goals. He hadn't cared about the good of the people around him, just his ability to manipulate and control them.

He had shown that when he chose to work with Sonja and Bethany. They had clearly had access to Mond, which Frayn had used to make the transforming drug, and which must have come from Cole. That also explained why Sonja and Bethany had both ended up dead, before we had a chance to ask them questions about their drug or their contacts. Cole had gone out of his way to kill off the loose ends that could have incriminated him.

In the end, all I needed to know was that he had been willing to unleash Mond against his own people. I remembered the crack of his neck breaking beneath my hands, and I knew more than ever that it had been an act of justice.

"Cole had proven to be of no use to us," Gregoire said. "He never used it. Such a shame; he seemed like he had been determined to do so. I was curious as to what he'd planned to do. Since you are the Alpha now … it doesn't matter."

I had heard enough. Gregoire couldn't be reasoned with. He was too wrapped up in his own cruelty and self-satisfaction to care about others, or about the consequences of his actions. But it was my job to care, to protect the people around me, and the willful way he had cast them into danger caused a storm of fury in my soul.

I wanted to leap on him, to beat him almost senseless and then force out the information I needed to know. But that wasn't the smart play, and I had long ago learned the power of perfectly channeled anger.

I shot a look at Josh, the smallest of nods, but enough to let him know that his moment had come.

Josh's fingers twitched and a blast of magic shot from him into the next room. The guards were flung against the walls, pinned in place by the power of his spell. All six struggled, trying to free their hands, to break out and leap to the defense of their master, but Josh was too strong. His eyes turned black as he let deep tides of power flow through him, pressing the guards against the wall so hard they were almost crushed, their attempts at invocations stifled as they fought to breathe. Josh strained, twisting the magic out, and the windows shattered, glass flying in bright slivers across the room. Instead of falling to the floor, those shining shards hung in front of the guards, deadly points inches from their faces. Eyes widened with terror as they realized how badly they were outmatched.

Josh wasn't the only one on the offensive. In the moment the windows shattered, Fallon sprung across the room, grabbed Dalia, and pinned her to the wall. London leapt in beside her, grabbing the elf with one hand while the other crackled with bright, menacing magic an inch from Dalia's face. Dalia gaped in shock, seemingly unable to comprehend the possibility that anyone would act like this in her home, or that crude beasts and their witch friends could get the better of her. But she and Gregoire had pushed us to a place where there could be no backing down.

"You are going to take me to the garden," I said, cool and commanding.

"Were you not listening to me?" Gregoire hissed. "There's nothing there."

"I'd like to see for myself."

"Let her go!" Gregoire looked at Dalia, and fear for her battled with fury in his face.

"She will be let go and unharmed, along with the others, as long as you take me to the garden."

"I will not take you anywhere until—"

I slammed my hand into his chest, pushing him up against the wall. He struggled to break free, pushing back against the wall and then against me, battering at my arm and then my chest with a flurry of feeble blows. But all his struggles achieved was to use up what strength he had. Unlike me, he wasn't built for fighting. He flailed and flapped around, glaring at me in frustration and indignation, but I had him pinned and he knew it.

Then his expression shifted. Anger gave way to resignation and he let his body go limp. He wasn't going to keep up his feeble struggle, but he wasn't going to acquiesce to my demands either. His coldly determined expression told me that he had decided his own fate, and he would rather die than let a beast like me get its way.

"Your death will mean nothing," Sky whispered into the tense silence. "I know you believe it will be an epic stance that will lead to you being hailed as a hero in historical accounts. It won't. This is foolish and without merit. Though you see us as the enemy, everyone else doesn't. The story will be framed by the ones who live to tell it. You will not fare well in it."

Gregoire's will faltered, a flicker of doubt crossing his face. He glanced at Dalia, who gave him a tiny nod of acceptance.

"Very well," he muttered. "The garden is in Elysian. I will take you there."

I let Gregoire down from the wall. While our companions

restrained Dalia and the guards, Sky and I followed him out of the house and into the front garden. He walked stiffly down the walkway, his shame all the clearer beneath the remorseless stare of his own statue, and down to the driveway. We got into our car and, following his directions, headed for the local entrance to Elysian.

"Hold on," I said as we got out of the car in front of a dense wall of foliage.

I had to do something more than pull up plants if I was going to prevent us from facing the same threat again. I needed to do something grander, something darker, something that would tap into the magic within me. And for what I had planned, I needed a tool.

I grabbed a cardboard coffee cup from the car, tipped out the cold remains of cappuccino, and handed the cup to Sky. It wasn't the most impressive or dignified tool ever wielded in the magical arts, but it would do.

Gregoire stood at the edge of Elysian, where trailing strands of red and white roses met. He raised his hands, parted them, and the earth split open. We strode through the gap and into the hidden forest.

Even having been there before, the bewildering beauty of the elves' secret land caught me off guard. The deep and peaceful pools, the trees whose leaves gleamed like emeralds in golden sunlight, the strange beasts roaming around us, garishly furred and feathered over bodies barely comprehensible to the human eye. Sky and I gaped at it all, and for a moment Gregoire smiled to see our response. Then his frown returned, focused on these intruders in his land.

A distinctive, musty scent caught my attention, my muscles twitching at the faintest hint of it, caught in the memory of my forced transformation in the hotel room. I followed that smell to a small patch of disturbed dirt, my heart beating faster as I approached. Forcing myself to stay calm, I ran my fingers through the dark, rich soil and sniffed at them, before holding them out to Sky. The stink of Mond was unmistakable. This was where the abomination had been grown.

"Do you have more?" I asked.

"No, it's served its purpose," Gregoire said. "It is out of our hands."

"How did you make it?"

Gregoire pressed his lips together, stiffly silent despite the hate burning in his eyes. It seemed that we had reached the limits of how far he would go to preserve his own life.

"Cup, please," I said, and Sky handed it to me. I scooped a handful of dirt into the cup, then set my free hand on the disturbed ground. I could feel the power of this place, a form of magic that tapped into life itself, encouraging it but warping it, so that what grew was nothing natural, only malformed beasts and twisted plants.

This place was soaked in the magic of life, but I carried the magic of death within me, a power whose nature was to bring such things to an end, a power that had let me kill the Faeries when they came for us. This wouldn't be the same magic I had used against them, but it would draw upon the same source, the darkness that lay inside me. Today, I would turn it to a different sort of destruction.

Shaping my thoughts around the cup of dirt in my hand, I started chanting, following some instinct from inside. The magic wanted to be used, and it was showing me how. It seeped out into the air, a softly humming nimbus of power that hung for a moment around us before seeping into the ground.

As my magic flowed, the dirt around me changed, its rich, moist loam turning into something gray, grainy, and dried out, like the parched ground that announced the arrival of a famine. The change spread out from my hand in an ever-widening circle, grass shriveling at its touch, bushes wither-ing, trees creaking as their fruits and leaves dried out and then fell, blackened husks replacing the verdant foliage that had stunned us when we arrived.

Gloom fell across the dead forest. All that remained of the lush soil that had been here was the small sample in a cheap coffee cup.

I had destroyed a place of wonder, and I had no regrets. Gregoire and Dalia had brought this on themselves. They had shown that no one could be trusted with ground that could grow something like Mond. All that had remained was to make the Elysian ground infertile, to cut the threat off at its source. My magic had killed this place, but Gregoire's actions had brought us here, his decisions had drawn down this doom.

Gregoire stared around him, mouth hanging open, struck dumb by grief. He had chosen martyrdom over helping us to keep our people safe. Now he saw that he wasn't the one who would die for his crimes. His forest had instead.

I hoped that he never stopped regretting his choice.

We left Gregoire standing alone in the dead ground of Elysian. Call it cruelty to leave him standing amid his loss, or a mercy that we gave him time to mourn; either way I didn't care. We were done with him, and as soon as we picked up the others from his house, we would be done with this whole sorry mess.

Sky kept glancing at me as I drove. I could understand that she would want to ask about what had just happened, but I was in no mood to discuss it. I had unleashed the full power of the darkness that lay inside me, and while it had been the right thing to do, it left me feeling cold and queasy.

"We will have to return home," I said, looking for a distraction. "We're going to miss the play."

"What play?"

"*The Lion King*. I got us tickets to see it Friday in New York."

Sky pulled a confused face. "Why did you pick *The Lion King*? I've mentioned *Hamilton* a dozen times."

"You keep singing the soundtrack to *The Lion King*. I've heard you hum 'The Circle of Life' at least seven times."

I looked at her in confusion. This had seemed like the perfect choice, but she looked disappointed. Then there was a moment of realization, and her cheeks flushed red with embarrassment.

"The Presentation," she mumbled.

"Chris's Presentation?" I asked, confused. I knew that Chris was due to be presented as Mistress of the Northern Seethe, formally taking her place at Demetrius's right hand, a big moment for the Seethe, and one the pack would be expected to show its face at, if only to keep the peace politically. But how did that connect to a Disney film? "You hear that the most powerful vampire in the world will be presenting a new Mistress to the otherworld. His partner, the woman who will wield as much power and influence as he does and could change the dynamics of the world we know, and 'The Circle of Life' plays in your head and you imagine him a lion—"

"Mufasa," Sky cut in.

I swallowed, still struggling to make sense of this nonsense.

"Mufasa is Demetrius, and I'm assuming Chris is the lion cub—"

"Simba."

I squeezed the bridge of my nose. Was this really how Sky made sense of supernatural politics, through the filter of Disney films? What next, me as Aladdin and Cole as Jafar? Or maybe Claudia as a fairy, seeing as she was my godmother?

"Okay," I said, imagining the moment. "Chris is Simba

and she's being lifted up and presented to the other denizens like the cub? That's what comes to your mind when you think of the Presentation?"

I fell silent, struggling not to laugh at Sky's skewed perspective of our world. It was at once both endearingly sweet and a little worrying. The Presentation was a serious affair, with important implications for everyone sharing territory with the Northern Seethe. I hoped that she had at least given it some serious thought alongside this absurdity.

"Oh, come on," she said. "You want me to believe it didn't cross your mind once?"

I gave in and laughed out loud. "Sky, you are a *very* unique woman."

That uniqueness was one of the things I loved about her; the ability to see the world through a lens I never could, to present a perspective outside anything I would have heard from the rest of the pack. For all that I gently mocked her about it, I would never have changed that.

"Why do I have a feeling you're not using *unique* in a flattering way?"

"How should I describe a woman whose mind goes to *The Lion King* and Mufasa presenting his offspring, Simba, to the animal kingdom to describe a vampire ceremony?"

"Of course it sounds silly when you put that tone with it!" she said indignantly. "Everything sounds silly with that level of condescension in it."

"You're right, love, it's very much the same thing. I can definitely see why you think of *The Lion King* when you hear 'Presentation.' That's a reasonable thing to think of. It's practically the same thing."

"Your sarcasm is neither needed nor appreciated."

Maybe Sky didn't need it, but I did. Sometimes it was the only coping mechanism I had for dealing with the madness of her mind.

I took my eyes off the road again to glance at her, offering a soft smile. Our holiday was at an end, and I was sad to see it over. This time alone with Sky had felt so precious amid the whirlwind of events around the pack, a moment of calm at the eye of the storm. Now we had to step back into the maelstrom.

CHAPTER 18

Seeing Winter kneel in front of me in Sebastian's office, her head tilted to one side to expose her neck, wasn't the strangest thing I had encountered in the past few months, but it felt deeply and instinctively wrong. Winter wasn't a woman to bow before others, and there was no bad blood between us. But the rules of pack life were grounded in tradition, and our lives depended upon maintaining those rules. Some other packs were big on ceremony —Niimi loved to drag her pack out into the Canadian wilderness for a big ritual in the snow—but in the Midwest, we liked to keep things more low key.

"I acknowledge your strength and concede the rights and power of Beta to you," Winter said in a deadpan tone. "May we thrive under your guidance." She rolled her eyes, glanced at Sebastian, and her usual lively spirit returned to her voice. "There, done. Can I get up off the carpet now?"

"You might have to check with your Beta first," I said, with a mocking grin.

"So that's a yes." Winter got to her feet, then punched me on the arm. "Congratulations, you've got your job back. Don't ever make me go through this bullshit again."

"The ceremony or the part where you were acting Beta?"

"All of it." She groaned and sank into a seat. "Do you know how many people came to me with moans about their pack duties?"

I laughed. "It was the same when I took over, everyone pushing their luck, seeing how the new boss would respond."

"Are you two done moaning about the horrors of being my second in command?" Sebastian asked with a mocking smile. "Because we have real business to discuss."

I took a seat and waited for Sebastian to continue. There would be time to catch up with each other later. With the pack, duty always came first.

"Jeremy and Kelly have been running tests, using that sample of Mond you brought back. They've even roped in Eddy from the Southern Pack."

"Little Eddy or Big Eddy?" Winter asked.

"The biochemist or the boxer? Which do you think?"

"I don't have to think anymore, I'm not the Beta."

Sebastian rolled his eyes.

"The point is, they've made no progress so far. It's taking a long time to even start understanding how the Mond works, and until that happens, there's almost no chance of countering it, whether by magic or by mundane means."

I leaned forward, frowning. This wasn't unexpected, but it was still worrying. Gregoire and Dalia had put a weapon out into the world against which we had no defense. We couldn't even be sure who had it anymore, and if we couldn't come up with a countermeasure, then we would be in a world of trouble when it was used.

"Do they have any leads?" I asked. "Any possibilities?"

"No, and before you ask, they haven't learned anything from that cup of dirt you brought back either, though Eddy tells me it's fascinating stuff." Sebastian sighed and rubbed at his weary eyes. "The truth is, we'd need a whole lab full of bio scientists to get a quick grasp on this thing, and there are barely a handful in all the North American packs. We're just going to have to be patient."

I could see that concern about the Mond was weighing down on him just as much as it was on me. It wasn't something Sebastian would show outside this room, but behind closed doors, he had given himself a moment with his defenses down, a brief minute of vulnerability.

He tapped his pen against the desk, then turned to the next item on his list.

"We need a strategy for the Faeries," he said. "They're out there now, and they've attacked us once. How do we respond to that?"

"Kick their asses," Winter said, her eyes flashing with anger. "Show them that no one messes with the Midwest Pack."

"I think we made that point already," I said, "when we kicked their asses before."

"That was defensive. Now we need to punish them for making the attack."

"Normally I would agree," Sebastian said. "But they're not an ordinary opponent. They have so much power, we were lucky to survive their previous attack, and that mostly came down to Ethan. Even if we could find them, launching an attack would be risky, especially if we only have one guy who can really hurt them."

I pondered the options before us, and the threat we faced. The attack by the Faeries had been brutal and unexpected, but we had survived it. They hadn't gotten what they were after, so there was a risk they might return, but we had shown them that we were a real threat, and maybe that was enough of a deterrent. Given how close I'd come to dying, and how much damage they had done to the pack, I wasn't keen on stirring up that trouble again.

"Sky thinks that we should leave them alone," I said, "and on balance, I agree. They're leaving us alone, and that's as close to a win as we can get with creatures that powerful. Better to accept what we've got than to risk picking another fight."

"They already picked the fight," Winter snarled. "How will it look to the other supernaturals if we don't fight back?"

Sebastian sat with his fingers steepled and a distant expression on his face, as he contemplated what we were saying. Pick a fight or accept an imperfect peace: The two options would take us down very different paths. As our Alpha, he was responsible for the consequences of a decision that could cost the lives of people under him. The pressure of that decision showed in the furrowing of his brow.

"It's not an urgent problem," he said at last. "The Faeries stayed in the shadows for years before attacking us. As far as we can tell, they've gone back to that. Even if we wanted to attack them, we wouldn't have to do it now."

"If?" Winter asked.

"If." Sebastian rubbed his temple. "They're not an imminent threat, and other things are. There's no point in kicking a hornets' nest when we're already being chased by a bull."

"If we sit back and wait, then they can just attack us again," Winter said. "We might not get so lucky if they surprise us a second time."

"That's why we won't just sit back and wait. We'll do research, craft spells, do all the preparation we need to defend ourselves if they attack again. We'll make sure that the Midwest Pack are the last people the Faeries want to mess with. We beat them once, and we'll beat them harder next time."

"And what about the others? Won't they see us as week for letting the Faeries get away with this?"

"They'll see that we survived the Faeries, a power that could have destroyed any of them." Sebastian nodded decisively. "That's good enough for me.

"Moving on…"

One of the tasks of a Beta was managing the other ranked weres. In my case, that meant giving Winter a chance to vent when she was frustrated with Sebastian. Deep down, she knew that he had made the right call in not attacking the Faeries, but that didn't leave her any less annoyed. So we hopped in my car and headed out to a roadside diner not far from the retreat, where we could drink bitter black coffee and eat thick slabs of apple pie while Winter ranted away her feelings.

"The worst part is that it makes us look weak," she snarled, waving her fork in the air. I'd finished my pie and was onto a refill of coffee, while Winter had barely touched hers, being too preoccupied with her opinions on the decision. "What if other packs decide that we're vulnerable now and start encroaching on our territory, or the Seethe decide to have a go at us? What if the elves think they can stir up trouble again?"

I made a noncommittal noise, just enough to show that I was listening, and took a sip of my coffee.

"No, you know what the real worst thing is?" Winter exclaimed, stabbing her fork down into the pie like she was stabbing one of the Faeries. "It's that we don't get to balance the books. They trashed the retreat, nearly killed half our people, but there's no counterattack. There's no..."

She waved her fork in the air, trying to summon some concept that was eluding her.

"No revenge?" I asked.

"Exactly, no revenge!" She frowned. "No, wait, that doesn't sound right. That makes it sound petty or spiteful."

I shrugged and made another noncommittal noise.

"Dammit, I know what I mean." Winter sank back in her seat, finally running out of words.

"But you're going to accept this, right?" I said. "You're not going to charge off and attack them singlehanded?"

"I'll accept it," Winter muttered, petulantly. "Just don't expect me to like it."

The list of things and people Winter liked was a pretty short one, so I could live with that. I took a sip of my coffee and watched her stab her fork through her pie, waiting in case there was more to come on this subject.

"I suppose I should fill you in on what you missed," she said at last. "All the stuff I had to deal with while you were gone."

"I guess," I said. "But could I ask you about something else first?"

Winter must have caught the note of uncertainty in my voice, because she looked up from devouring her pie with an eyebrow raised.

"Sounds serious," she said.

"Not serious, more personal."

"Well." She pushed her plate aside and leaned forward, grinning. "Now I'm intrigued."

I sighed. This wasn't the sort of conversation I was comfortable with, but I needed to talk about it with someone, and Winter, who had been a good friend of mine for years, seemed like she might understand. It was also a way of reassuring her that I still trusted her judgment, despite our disagreement over the Faeries. Managing ranked weres could be a delicate process.

"I'm trying to work out what's going on with Sky and Chris," I said. "I mean, they've got nothing in common, they used to hate each other, but now they've started talking, going out for drinks, even…" I almost said that Sky had lined up Chris to assassinate Cole, but that was something that was probably best left unsaid. "I mean, what's going on?"

"Your ex and your mate getting chatty, I could see how that would make you uncomfortable." Winter grinned, then her face twisted up in puzzlement. "I've got to admit, I don't get it either. It's like they've formed this friendship out of nothing. Have you asked Sky about it?"

I gave a bitter laugh. "What am I going to say, 'I'm worried about who you hang out with'? That's not going to go down well with any woman, never mind Sky."

"Fair. I've lost at least one girlfriend that way, though if her friends are biker junkies, you're probably better off without."

"How does a hunter turned vampire compare with biker junkies?"

Winter waved a hand back and forth in the air. "Tough call, but go on."

"I mean, if they want to be friends, I can hardly stop them, but relations between the pack and the Seethe can get tense. Should I be worrying that this might lead to ugly complications?"

It wasn't just that, and I knew it. I was also worried about what growing closer to a vampire meant for Sky. Was she giving in to that side of her nature, becoming something dark and twisted? I wanted to trust her, but I couldn't help being cautious, especially now that blood drinking had become a regular part of our sex life. Had we found a peace with her vampirism, or was all of this urging it on?

There were limits to what I felt I could say to Winter, but by the glance she shot at my neck, I figured that she had guessed a good part of it.

"It's a weird relationship," she said. "And I'm not going to pretend to understand it. But ultimately, I've got no idea what to do about it. Do you?"

"No." I shook my head.

"Then I guess we both have to trust Sky's judgment, if not her taste in friends."

My laugh was bitter, but at least it was there. I felt better for having talked with someone, which I would never have done before knowing Sky. She had made me into a better person, and I had to trust the fact that she was a good person too, one who could keep her darkness under control.

"Now," Winter said, "let me tell you about Tabby, Eric, and the great Worgen war over the new server stack. It's an epic tale of technology and pettiness, and if you can work out how to solve it, then you're a better Beta than I was…"

The problem with extracting information from the elves was that most of them were scared of me, after what I'd done in Elysian. In some ways, that was a good thing: Fear was a powerful motivator in getting people to talk. But it was also a powerful motivator in getting them to hide. I couldn't question people I couldn't find, and I couldn't force my way into Elysian or into one of their leaders' fortified houses to start shaking down the servants; things were tense enough already politically. So instead, I had to resort to tracking down the loners, or those sent out on missions, to see what information I could squeeze out of them about Liam and Mond.

I crisscrossed Chicago and the surrounding area, following leads from informants and members of the pack. I talked to disillusioned elven exiles in seedy bars, cornered pointy-eared couriers in back alleys, dragged a shame-faced Makellos gambling addict out of a poker game to find out what she knew. At last, fragments of rumors fit together, leading me to an elf hiding out in the open, in the most obvious place for an expert on plants.

I pulled up into the parking lot of the plant nursery. Behind the shop and office buildings, long rows of growers' tunnels stretched out across the site, clear plastic sheeting pulled across hooped frames. Cheap, simple greenhouses for mass production.

I walked into the main office like I owned the place and waved to the receptionist.

"I'm here to see Joan," I said. "Legal thing, I don't know if she mentioned it...?"

The receptionist shook her head.

"She didn't, but she can be a bit forgetful at times." She smiled fondly and pointed to a door that led out to the tunnels. "She's working in number three, near the back. You can't miss her, she's always wearing those bright head scarfs."

The air in the tunnels was humid, almost oppressively so. The banks of lush plants reminded me of Elysian, but without its warped twist on the natural world. I could easily see how an elf had ended up working here.

"Joan" was actually Joavari, who the other elves had told me was an expert on growing things. If Liam was trying to grow Mond, then she would know about it. Hell, she would probably be the one doing it.

Joavari was working near the back of one of the tunnels, well away from the rest of the facility's staff. The place was owned by the elves, one of Liam's smaller investments, but that didn't mean that they could work on strange plants where everyone was watching. There had to be spots like this reserved for Joavari's work.

As the receptionist had said, Joavari was wearing a brightly striped headscarf, which kept her hair out of her face and covered the tips of her ears. It was enough to pass as human to humans, though anyone else would know what she was.

"Growing anything interesting?" I asked as I walked up.

"Always," she said. "Who could get bored of plants?"

She finished pressing compost in around a seedling, then looked up at me.

"Do I know you?"

"My name is Ethan Charleston." I let the words sit

between us, heavy and menacing. She had to know who I was by now.

"Ah." Joavari brushed the dirt from her hands, then stood and looked me up and down. "Apparently Liam is sending some guards to protect me from you. Should I be scared?"

"You tell me." As I stepped closer, my hands shifted into claws. I bared canine teeth and let the wolf show in my eyes. For all I knew, this woman was growing a threat to my pack. That alone made her my enemy.

"Did you know that studies indicate torture is ineffective as a method of questioning?" Joavari turned her back on me, picked up a tray of seedlings, and returned to her work, transferring them into pots. This wasn't the reaction I had expected. "People will say anything to make the pain end, so they say whatever comes into their heads. It leads to more lies than truths."

"I'm not going to torture you."

"Really? You're not going to threaten me with violence?"

"Only if you don't talk."

"That sounds a lot like torture to me." She patted the dirt down around another of the seedlings.

"I'm not here to play word games. You're going to tell me what I need to know."

I clenched my fist, frustration rising. If there were guards on the way, then I needed to get this over with. I needed to know if Liam had grown Mond for himself, in imitation of his East Coast cousins. If he had, then he would be more of a threat to the pack than ever.

"I don't like people like you, Ethan," Joavari said. "People who use violence and intimidation to take what they want from others. You're the sort of people who destroy the world."

"Sounds a lot like your boss, Liam."

"I don't like him either. He's as short-sighted as he is pompous. But he paid for all this, so that I could grow living things, whereas you, I hear, make plants die and soil go barren. Isn't it enough that we're losing the rain forests, without you scouring Elysian as well?"

"Some things deserve to be scoured away. Mond's only purpose is to expose and hurt my people."

"A plant does not need a purpose in our eyes for it to have value." She sighed. "You're like him, so reductive of the value of life. But I don't intend to waste mine talking to you, so let's get this over with. Follow me."

She led me through a doorway at the end of the tunnel, into a dome made from the same clear plastic sheeting. The plants here were different, the sorts of wild and wonderful things that grew in Elysian; bright flowers, intricate leaves, spiked and snapping jaws. Joavari walked to a bench at the back, on which were rows of pots holding rich, sweet-smelling soil.

"Understand that I'm telling you this purely out of practicality," she said. "Not because I'm scared, not because I think you deserve the truth, but because it's the easiest way to get some peace and quiet."

"I don't care why. Just tell me, can Liam's people grow Mond?"

"What do you think?"

She gestured at the pots. Now that I looked more closely, I saw that every one held the beginnings of a plant, like the ones I had seen in Elysian. Every one had wilted and died.

"These were Mond?" I asked, feeling angry just at the sight of them.

"Attempts to graft it onto other root stock, after everything else failed. Trust me, I have tried every measure I could, and this plant is not coming back. The ground in Elysian cannot sustain it any longer, and as it turns out, the mundane soil of this poor, beautiful planet cannot either. You have wiped out a part of nature's beauty. I hope you one day find the good grace to regret it."

She stared at me with as much anger as I felt for her. She wanted to paint me as the bad guy, but she was the one who had tried to grow a weapon Liam could use against my people. I didn't care if she liked him or not, she had been doing his dirty work. She deserved to fail.

"Why would I regret any of this?" I asked. "I won."

<hr>

When I got home, there was an unexpected car sitting in the driveway. It looked familiar, but it took me a moment to realize where from; it was David and Trent's.

I sighed and readied myself to face them. David and Trent weren't bad people, they were just a little vacuous and too ready to talk at length about nothing. The behavior that made Sky so fond of them grated on my nerves, and I would have preferred a long night dealing with the pack's accounts and its petty squabbles to a single hour hanging out with them. But they made Sky happy, and that was all the reason I needed to accept them in my life.

I opened the front door quietly and slipped into the house. Part of me wanted to creep into my study and hide away until the visitors were gone, to enjoy some peace and quiet with my books. But I hadn't seen Sky in hours, which left me longing for her presence, and the sound of conversation from our bedroom made me nervous at what her friends might be up to in there. I approached warily.

"Please," Trent said, whining like a spoiled child.

"We already decided against a wedding," Sky replied, and though she said it in a firm, matter-of-fact way, I caught a hint of sadness in her voice.

David and Trent were right. This was something Sky wanted, and that meant it was something I was going to give her, because she made my life brighter, and she deserved every happiness in the world.

"I think it's a good idea," I said quietly as I walked into the room.

The three of them stared at me in surprise for a moment. Then Trent leapt across the room, trying to block my view of Sky, who was wearing a pearl-white wedding dress decorated with intricate embroidery and frosted lace, with layers of satin and lace pooling at the bottom. She looked both excited and nervous as she watched for my reaction, but there was also a slight redness to her eyes that made me wonder if she had been crying. Had she been that upset by the thought of not getting married?

"Trent," I said, making his name into a low, warning growl.

He stood taller and puffed out his chest, a skinny sentinel standing between his friend and… what, some thin shred of tradition? Even if we were going to get married, there was no reason to think that this would be the dress, even if I accepted that I shouldn't see the bride in it beforehand. The absurdity of his blocking my way to Sky only made me more annoyed.

Trent must have seen the steely resolve in my eyes, because his own will trembled and then collapsed. He stood aside, allowing me a full view of Sky.

Even by her standards, she looked spectacular. The dress clung to her, accentuating every curve of her beautiful body. Her shoulders lay exposed, a stretch of nakedness that hinted at what else lay underneath. Even her uncertain smile and the way her hair spilled across one shoulder added to the gorgeous vision.

I walked up to her and ran a finger over her shoulder, then across the lace of one sleeve, tracing its delicate pattern. One of my hands ran on down her arm, while I wrapped the other around her waist, pulling her close. I ran a line of kisses along her jaw, down her neck, and across her shoulder, tasting the warmth of her skin. Then our lips met and I pressed her against me, while we lost ourselves in a passionate kiss. My body stirred at her touch, and as stunning as she looked in that dress, I wanted to rip it off her there and then, to join together in a perfect moment.

A movement in the corner of my vision caught my attention, and I was surprised to see Trent standing only inches from us, an expectant look on his face.

I stepped back from Sky, putting some distance between me and Trent's intrusion.

"So, wedding or no wedding?" Trent asked, eyes fixed on me.

"Do you want to do this?" I asked Sky. "Because I do."

It was strange to say that out loud. Brought up around were-animals, with our own codes of family and mating, I had never expected that a wedding would be part of my life. But the seeds that David and Trent had planted in my head had been growing in my subconscious over the past few days, and the sight of Sky in a wedding dress had given them fresh life.

David watched us with a calm composure to match my own, but it was Trent who came closer to my inner feelings, as he practically buzzed with eagerness to hear an answer.

Sky ushered me into the hall, then chased away Trent, who had tried to follow us. Once we were out of earshot, she turned to look at me, her voice soft and uncertain.

"Are you sure?" she asked.

I stepped back to compose myself, and as I did so, took the time to look her over again, drinking in the sight of her body wrapped in that dress, the bare skin of her neck and shoulders, the blush of her cheeks.

I nodded. "I'm sure I want to marry you."

"That's sweet. But are you *sure* you want to give Trent and David full rein in our lives as they plan a wedding? I don't think we are prepared for this—for *them*."

"I'm prepared to marry you," I said, then pulled her to me,

kissing her hungrily as I clawed at the fabric of the dress, dragging it up her leg until I felt her skin again beneath my fingers.

She nipped at my lips, and my passion grew.

"There are people behind us," she said.

"So," I purred, my lips hovering over hers, my hands pressing against her body. "They'll leave."

With a shudder, she took a step back. "No, they won't."

I closed the gap between us and tried to kiss her again. It was almost impossible to resist Sky in that dress, its clinging cloth perfectly accentuating her body. I wanted to hold her against me, to feel our bodies join. But as I stepped closer, she backed away.

"Stop it," she said. "What's with you?"

"You look gorgeous." It seemed like a perfectly sensible answer. How did she expect me to react to seeing her like this?

She looked down at herself, then back at me.

"Is it the dress? Please don't tell me this is a *thing* too."

I licked my lips. "It's not a 'thing.' I love the way you look in it."

Sky looked over her shoulder, down the hallway to where David and Trent were peering out expectantly from the bedroom.

"So, what's the answer?" Trent shouted, then immediately decided that he couldn't wait to hear, and started walking toward us.

"Stop," I said sharply. I'd had enough of their intervention. I needed to talk to Sky. "Leave us alone."

"Broody and rude," Trent said, dramatically turning away. "You got yourself a good one, Sky. Being gorgeous can only get you so far, you have to have a personality too, you know."

He stopped by the doorway and leaned against the wall, arms folded, glaring at me. I missed the days when he had found me intimidating.

"What do you want to do?" I asked Sky.

"They agreed to do everything so it would be simple for us. But you know how it is. They might plan it, but they are a lot. At times over the top. It'll be beautiful—"

"But it will be intense for a while working with them."

She nodded, a thoughtful look on her face. After a few moments of quiet consideration, she looked back at them, waiting eagerly for an answer. Her soft smile told me what her decision would be.

"You have a month," I said. "That's it."

"We only need twenty-one days," Trent said boldly.

"No, thirty days is good," David said, glaring at his partner.

A moment later, the two of them were beaming, caught up in the excitement of whatever plans were unfolding in their heads. Sky and I walked slowly toward them, my hand resting on her waist. The feelings that dress had stirred in me would have to wait until later. For now, we had our wedding planners to manage.

I was getting married, and that thought made me happier than I could ever have expected. Only Trent's look of smug satisfaction kept me from a face-splitting grin.

Trent's hand whipped out, smacking my own hand away from Sky. After a shocked moment to process the attack, I growled at him, happiness turning to annoyance.

"Paws off the dress," Trent said. "We have to return this one."

He was right, and now I was caught in the trap of having given him authority, if only over this one part of my life. He nudged me aside so that he and David could close in on Sky, both chattering excitedly as they pulled at the dress. I stepped back, smiling in amusement at the state they were already working themselves into.

"You can't wear this one, it's already been seen," David announced. "But don't worry, Kitten, we'll get something just as striking. In a couple days we'll have more specifics. Fitting, dresses, venue and all that, and menu."

They started talking about different styles of wedding dress, about music, food, and venues. Sky stood between them, her face reflecting a state of increasing bewilderment, nodding along like a doll being waved around by overexcited children. Now that I was out from under their attention, they were actually quite entertaining to watch. Maybe the next thirty days wouldn't be so bad.

"Don't go too far, mister," Trent said, rounding on me. "We want to discuss colors and tuxedos with you too. I don't see you in just a typical tuxedo; we'll need to go over some options. I'm assuming Josh will be the best man. Well, set up things with him. And you'll have to tell us what plan to give the wedding party."

Now Sky was the one grinning in amusement at my growing discomfort. Josh had said that I could leave the decisions on these things to other people. Why was I suddenly being bombarded with questions? I backed away, taking one last good look at the dress and at the two men who had somehow taken over a key part of my future. Then I turned and stalked away, heading for the safety of my study. Behind me, the excited chatter continued.

Somehow, David and Trent had embedded themselves in our lives. Fine, I accepted that. I was even willing to use their expertise for the sake of the wedding. But I had to draw a line somewhere, and right now, I needed to be alone, to feel like my house was still my own, even if nothing else was.

CHAPTER 19

An hour later, there was a knock at the study door. I looked up from my book and took a deep breath. I could mostly smell Sky, but David and Trent's presence mingled with hers. Were they still there, lurking behind her in the hallway, waiting to jump in and harass me with questions? Or did their scents linger because they had spent so much time standing close to her, adjusting her dress, battering her with ideas for the wedding?

"Are you alone?" I called out.

"Yes, they went home. It's hard to feel welcome when someone, in no uncertain terms, tells them to go away."

It was good to hear that, even if they couldn't take a hint, David and Trent could accept something more blatant. I set my book aside, unlocked the door, and opened it to reveal Sky, back in her ordinary outfit of jeans and a shirt.

"You were right," I said, "they are going to be a handful, and I'd answered their questions already."

"You came here to hide from them?"

"I'm not hiding, but they're your friends…"

I stepped aside to let Sky into the study, and with it the concerns that had been playing on my mind, making it harder to care about the minutiae of dresses, cakes, and flowers, or to tolerate the intrusive antics of David and Trent. My desk was scattered with books and papers, a tablet open on one corner so that I could reread emails and messages. I had sunk back into the pack's most pressing issue, and I didn't like what I had found.

"Liam hasn't been able to make the Mond, but it's not for lack of trying," I said, settling back into my seat. It had taken quite an effort to squeeze that piece of information out of the elves, and it was perhaps the only thing working in our favor, knowing that supplies of the herb remained limited. "Sebastian thinks we should just come out."

"And you don't?"

I shook my head. "Gregoire said Samuel, another witch, and humans were given the Mond. I'm going to assume the humans are the Red Blood. The witch, Rayna, one of Marcia's acolytes."

Sky scowled, and I could understand why. As head of the Creed, Marcia had been a cruel leader who clung to outdated beliefs, a purist trying to trap the world in a form that suited her. Most of the Creed had moved on since she was deposed, but there would always be fanatics clinging to an imaginary version of a golden past, willing to follow a monster to preserve it.

"She had followers who mourned her," I said.

I went to the shelves, looked over the spines of my books, and pulled out some grimoires that might be relevant. They joined the others in my growing heap of research. Looking over it all, I should have felt some sense of progress, but all I could find was frustration. How could we defend ourselves against an unprecedented threat when we didn't even know who held the weapon?

"There's no way we'll be able to get a hold of all the Mond," I confessed, feeling a wave of despair rise through me.

"You're looking for a spell?"

"One that will nullify it."

While Sky studied the books lined up on my shelves, I flicked through the ones I had retrieved. There had to be something here that we could use, something designed to manage were-animals' transformations or to protect against drugs and toxins. But everything I had found so far was either too weak, too specialized, or too vague in its effects. Centuries of research had done nothing, leaving us as vulnerable as if they had never happened. I hated to feel vulnerable, hated even more to see my pack that way.

"Have you found a spell?" Sky asked.

I shook my head, frustrated. "Josh is better at creating spells than I am."

What was the point of having all this magic inside me, the power of a spirit shade, if I couldn't use it when I needed it? Despite years living like this, I had never managed to master its subtleties, and I felt embarrassed at my failure.

"They seem complex," Sky said. "It took nine witches working together to come up with one to remove Josh's curse."

"I think we're going to need those nine witches again."

I turned a page, no longer expecting anything of use, and that expectation was met. Perhaps we really would have to turn to the Creed for help, but I was loath to do it. Some of them were already wary, even angry, about our use of magical power. If we asked them to help us unleash some experimental new spell to fight back against the Mond, we could expect criticism and suspicion before we got anywhere near help.

"What's in here?" Sky asked, tugging at the locked door of the dark wood cabinet in which I kept my most precious papers.

"Nothing," I said, deliberately not looking up at her. I grabbed a notebook I had been scribbling in and held it out for her to see. "Do you mind looking over these spells and telling me what you think?"

"I will," she said, "once I see what's in the cabinet."

I sighed. The day had already been draining enough, I wasn't in the mood for another round of the boundary-pushing game.

"It's nothing of importance to you."

"If it's important to you, it's important to me."

"Sky," I said, putting all the primal, commanding power of a Beta were into my voice. "It's really nothing."

It was a tone that would have bent any other member of the pack to my will, but Sky stood unmoved. Whether it was her vampire blood, the spirit shade, being Beta as my mate, or just strength of personality, something stopped me from moving her in that way.

I was almost relieved. Even as I'd done it, I had known that I shouldn't use that commanding presence on her. This wasn't pack business, and when it came to our relationship, the pack hierarchy didn't apply. Trying to bend Sky to my will had been a bad move.

"Then you won't mind showing me nothing," she said breezily. "I'm sure I'd lose interest in nothing."

It was the witches all over again, prying into the personal space of my study, demanding access to the things I held close. But while they had wanted to pry into my spell books and notes on the supernatural, Sky was asking for something more, something I was reluctant to release.

"It's personal," I said, my voice tight as I struggled to get the words out. "My personal things."

"We can't have secrets, Ethan. I know that's how you survived and what you had to do. But I'm your mate. We are as one and you can't keep things from me. I tell you every-thing about me."

"Eventually," I said pointedly. She hadn't told me she had tried to hire Chris to kill Cole, not until the decision had been made not to follow through, and that was an action that could have thrown pack politics into turmoil.

"You're right." She smiled. "I don't want any secrets between us. I'd like to know what's in there but if you're not ready, I understand."

That smile, those words, they made my heart melt. And then she came to sit beside me, looking over my books and notes, intent on helping. I knew how much it bothered her not to know what was happening, especially when it involved the people close to her. It must have taken a huge effort to let go and let me keep my privacy; either a great effort or a change in how she dealt with me, a lightening of the pressure to open up that she had long exerted. Either way, it was a remarkable moment from Sky.

I gazed fondly at her, and after a moment she looked up to meet my eyes.

"I love you," I said, the words a simple truth and yet so powerful that they could reshape my entire life.

"I love you too."

She deserved better from me, and just like the wedding, if I could give it to her, then I must. With heavy movements, I got out of my seat, made my way to that private cabinet, pulled out a small key, and unlocked it. I withdrew my mother's spell book, feeling the comforting familiarity of its worn binding, then a small box, and with it my old iridium chain bracelet, the metal cold and heavy.

I handed the bracelet to Sky, who started at the weight of it.

"I wore it instead of the iridium injections," I explained. How else was the wild magic inside me to be controlled, before I was old enough to manage it?

I laid out more mementos on the table, reminders of who I was and where I had come from. Each one was a piece of my heart, and though I felt vulnerable exposing them to another person, I also felt a sense of pleasure at sharing them with Sky, revealing my childhood to her. Next came a photo album, full of family moments from when I was more innocent; one of my mother's old notebooks; and the medallion of a member of the Creed.

"Are these your family things?" Sky asked.

I nodded and picked up the medallion. "This was my mother's, before they cursed her."

I could feel my bitterness creeping back in as I remembered what had happened. My mother had been cast out by the people who mattered most to her, struck by a curse that would afflict not just her but her children, and which would have killed Josh if not for the costly magic with which we had countered it.

That magic had shaped my life, transforming it for the worse. Still only a child myself, I had become my brother's keeper, my body filled with the most powerful and evil sort of magic for the sake of keeping him alive. Any chance at normality, even by the standards of were-animals, had vanished for me, my childhood sacrificed to save my brother. If I had to make the choice again, it would be the same, but I resented the burden that had been placed on me. How might my life have been different if not for that crushing responsibility? Might I have found the lightness and joy with which Josh approached the world?

My eyes fell upon the photo album. I flicked it open and fonder memories returned.

"I like having actual pictures," I said, smiling at a photo of my mother, her honey-colored hair pulled back to reveal the brightness of her eyes and the warmth of her smile. This was how she would always be to me, preserved as a figure of love and compassion.

On the next page was a picture of my mother and a younger-looking Claudia, the two of them smiling at some shared joke. Claudia's spirit had been lighter then, despite the darkness of her magic. My mother had brought out her playful side, and I had seen her through the lens of their friendship, as a lively, carefree woman.

All that had ended, of course, with the curse. Our lives had plunged into darkness as we raced to save Josh, and my mother and Claudia had never been the same afterward. Their feelings changed them, the guilt at putting me and Josh in danger becoming a cloud that darkened both their hearts.

"She changed after the curse," I said, seeing Sky's bewilderment at this vision of Claudia.

"What happened?"

I hadn't meant to discuss this; it wasn't just my story to tell. But the cabinet stood open, and there were no more locked doors to hide behind.

"Claudia made a vampire," I said.

"She can make vampires!" Sky looked stunned. "Is that why Demetrius shows her such reverence? Because she's a Messor, a combination of Faerie and vampire?"

"He's unaware of what she is. His 'reverence' isn't because he knows what she is, it's because he doesn't. It's equivalent to us sensing an Alpha among us. You might not be able to put your finger on it, but you know there is power." I smiled at her, half proud, half mocking. "You're the only one I know who senses it and ignores it."

"I sensed it when I met you and Sebastian."

"Really, and that's how you responded?" I said, thinking back to my first troubled encounters with Sky.

"Meh, you weren't so special."

I laughed, as much in relief at the lighter subject as at Sky's flippant response.

"Claudia created a vampire?" she asked, dragging me back to the past.

I shook my head. "Based on what my mother said, it wasn't a vampire. Not like the ones we were used to. Claudia didn't know that was going to happen. She found a nearly dead man who'd been drained and discarded. She knew what she was and thought she could save his life by changing him. Making a vampire is easier than making a were-animal. The transition is easier too. Claudia waited until the heart slowed and fed him her blood. She did everything she was supposed to do."

Just thinking about those events made me restless. I paced across the room, running my fingers through my hair, trying to shake loose some of my agitation.

"It wasn't like a regular vampire, was it?" Sky asked.

"No. It was ravenous like a new vampire, but even they can be reasoned with and controlled by their creator. He behaved as if he wasn't linked to her. A savage animal that ran rabid throughout the city. Leaving a trail of bodies.

"She's part Faerie, and they are difficult to kill. A stake through the heart wouldn't work, and this thing moved so fast that they couldn't contain him—or kill him. Magic didn't work against him. She'd created something that should be feared. She didn't have a lot of options and couldn't go to the Creed."

I scowled. The Creed were so judgmental about how we used our powers, but their own attitudes caused as much trouble as anyone. Their prejudices against hybrids and unfamiliar magic sometimes made it impossible to approach them with problems that they were best equipped to solve. Things were getting better under Ariel, but our history was littered with incidents that would have been less dangerous if the rest of us could have trusted the witches on the magic they held so dear.

"The only way to stop him was to do the *rever tempore?*" Sky asked.

"Yes, and my mother never told Marcia and the others why she did it. And for that reason, she was punished. She couldn't say what Claudia had created, because it would have been their mission to find a way to destroy her because of it."

And so a curse had been laid on my mother, one meant to

punish her by killing one of her sons when he reached his eighteenth birthday. Putting the curse on Josh had given us time to find a solution, because he was the youngest, and Claudia and I had eventually found magic to keep him safe, by trapping a spirit shade. But it just showed how counter-productive the Creed's policies were; in punishing renegade magic, they had forced me to use more of it.

"Who found the shade for you?"

"Claudia. She knew we'd need magic stronger than the group of witches that performed it, and my mother's magic had been restricted as part of her punishment."

"That was extreme."

"Marcia and the others were always looking for a reason to restrict my mother's magic," I said bitterly, remembering the triumphant look on Marcia's face as she had announced the punishment. "Her skills and abilities surpassed theirs tenfold, and they had a problem with that."

"Your mother wasn't able to help you with the spell?"

"She did; she made the spell that we used. But I had to perform it. It was a witch's spell, so it was a combination of her magic and the Faerie's that made me strong enough to perform it."

Sky opened my mother's spell book and carefully turned the pages, revealing both the printed spells and the hand-written ones in the back, each one written in both Latin and English. This was where Josh got his gift for crafting new magic from. He took after our mother, a link to what we had lost, and nothing could have made me prouder of him.

"Your mother found a way around a curse. Do you think maybe there's a spell in here to nullify the effect of the Mond on us? Something that can act as a workaround?"

I was so used to thinking of my mother's spell book as a memento, not a practical thing, that the thought had never crossed my mind, but it made perfect sense. Who better to help us through this crisis?

Excited at the thought of collaborating with my mother one last time, I sat down next to Sky and started leafing through the book. The warmth of my mate so close beside me made me smile, happy to share these memories with her.

If there was a solution to our problem in that book, then Sky and I couldn't find it. We pored over healing spells, shifting spells, touches of necromancy, and even three potential spells to help circumvent Josh's curse, but nothing that provided an answer to the problem of Mond.

I knew full well that there were minds better trained to parse spells than me and Sky, so the next day we took the book to Josh and London, explaining what Sky had suggested and what we had found. By the time they had finished with their own detailed dive into the notes my mother left, they were both brimming with excitement for other magic they might weave using her ideas, but even they hadn't found the answer we were looking for.

What that spell book did achieve was to motivate a new burst of magical research, as the witches found fresh enthusiasm for their work. Josh brought London and Nia to the retreat, to make use of our library and see what progress they could make.

Nia gazed across the library, not for the first time since she had arrived. I stood off to one side with Sky, impatiently waiting to see what they would come up with, while Sebastian stepped in from time to time, clearly hoping that Ariel would turn up.

"You all have far more books than we have," Nia said in a slow drawl. "Books that we thought were lost."

There was a judgment behind those words, as there so often was when dealing with the Creed. We weren't witches, so by their definition we shouldn't be doing magic, and we certainly shouldn't have resources about it that they lacked.

"It seems odd that we have to come here to research it instead of our own library. After all, we are witches."

"Josh is a witch," I pointed out.

"True. But since we are here, perhaps—" She hesitated, looking carefully at me and Josh as she considered her words. "The Midwest Pack seems to be in need of skills beyond his personal reach. I am confident he will obtain them with our assistance. Providing that assistance would be easier if he'd accept our mark."

This was delicate territory, politically for the pack as well as personally for Josh. He had discarded his Creed medallion during Marcia's rule, casting it down at her feet in protest at her leadership. Ariel had offered it back to him twice since her ascension, and he had rejected it both times, preferring to stay outside of the Creed's control. But just as the Midwest Pack couldn't allow rogue were-animals to run loose in its territory, the Creed couldn't allow a rogue witch to live on their turf indefinitely. It was placing a strain on our relations with them, at a time when we needed allies.

I glanced at Josh, who kept his face under control, his feelings on the subject carefully guarded. While I hoped for all our sakes that he would rebuild his ties to the Creed, I resented the pressure Nia was trying to put on him. It wasn't some junior witch's place to push my brother around.

"Perhaps you are right," Sebastian said. "About the books. I can't make Josh's decision for him, but maybe we can work out a deal with the books. I'll have to discuss it with Ariel and Josh."

"I'm sure Ariel would appreciate it," Nia said, her face brightening. "Perhaps I'll take these two as an act of good faith. If you find two others that are more suited for us, we can work out a trade."

"Nia," London said in a warning tone. "Rude."

"I'm not trying to be rude. I enjoy working with you all. The dilemmas you get yourself into definitely stretch our magical muscles, and you're sleeping with Josh, good for you." She looked pointedly at London. "It's fine that you want to help your boyfriend—so be it. But us being called in to help you all so often makes this alliance seem very one-sided. It just seems like it would be a nice sign of appreciation to at least offer us something. After all, how does finding an inoculation from whatever you all were poisoned with affect us?"

London's eyes went wide, but whatever she thought of Nia's opinion, she kept it to herself.

Personally, I valued Nia's direct approach. We needed to know where we stood with the witches, and whether or not her view was shared by Ariel, it clearly held some sway among them.

"Let me think about it," Sebastian said with a firmness calculated to shut down the conversation.

"Well, I really hope you can do that within the hour," Nia said, either oblivious to or ignoring his tone. "I'm getting tired, and I think a shot of knowledge from books with spells over a hundred years old might be the little perk I need."

Sebastian smiled. Like many of us, he enjoyed the challenge of a strong personality, even if that person was disagreeing with him. It explained a lot of the pack members' relationships, not least my own attraction to Sky.

"Point noted," Sebastian said, then left the room.

A moment later, Sky hurried after him, leaving me alone with the witches.

"I could do with coffee," Josh said, stretching his arms above his head. "You want one?"

London and Nia both answered in the affirmative.

"I'll come with you," I said. "That way you won't have to juggle three cups with two hands."

We got to the kitchen before I brought up the issue on my mind, the real reason I was helping my brother fetch coffee.

"What Nia was saying about you rejoining the Creed," I said, "have you given it much thought?"

Josh shrugged and reached for the coffee pot.

"Not much," he said. "I like where I'm at right now, doing my own thing. Being in the Creed brings work and responsibilities, on top of my duties to the pack. Plus I don't want to tie myself to another Marcia if Ariel goes off the tracks."

That last point seemed unlikely, but I wasn't going to get distracted by it. I needed to find a way to discuss the topic with Josh, without getting into pushy older brother territory. That way lay the arguments we were struggling to put behind us.

"Do you think it might be good for you?" I asked. "Having a magical support network and access to their resources?"

Josh looked at me with narrowed eyes. "You mean you think it would be good for me."

"Yes, but that's not the point. It's your life, your choice. I just want to be sure that you're thinking it through."

I wanted to be sure because I was worried. Talking about our mother with Sky had reminded me of how vulnerable a witch could be when they were excluded from the Creed, and how brutally that organization could turn against outsiders. I didn't want to see that happen to Josh.

Saying any of that out loud would only add to his sense that I was pressuring him, and I could see him tensing already, preparing to defend himself against my views.

"By thinking it through, you mean agreeing with you?" he asked, glaring at me.

"Josh." I bit back an angry response about his ungrateful attitude. If I was going to avoid us spiraling back down into old patterns, I had to pick my words carefully. "Honestly, I'm not trying to pressure you. If you don't want to rejoin the Creed, I'll drop it. I just wanted to know where you were at on the subject."

Josh took a deep breath. He turned to a cupboard, pulled out four mugs, and started pouring the coffee.

"Sorry," he said, still not looking me in the eye. "It's just hard not to hear the old Ethan when you say something like that."

I gritted my teeth. Never mind the old Ethan, what about the old, reckless Josh?

He looked up with an apologetic smile and handed me two steaming mugs.

"I'll think about it, okay?"

<hr>

I'd almost gotten used to the barrage of warm welcomes and polite smiles that now greeted me when I got into work. Most days, I could make it as far as my office without getting annoyed at anyone, which was better than I'd managed before Steven's court case. I was even getting used to the benefits of being one of the firm's star lawyers, though I could have done without the endless emails asking for my help or advice.

Stacy was sitting at her desk outside my office. A slender woman with short dark hair stood next to her, gesticulating as she talked. Stacy smiled up at her, unmoving, and for a moment I took it for a polite, attentive expression, but then I realized that something was wrong. There was a blankness in her gaze that was at odds with the bright, intelligent woman I knew.

Now that I was on alert, I caught the tingle of magic in the air. The woman talking to Stacy was a witch, and she was putting her under a spell.

I glanced around. If any of my colleagues had seen that something was amiss, they had decided that it was none of their business. That was something, at least. I needed to resolve this discreetly, if I was to prevent my pack life from spilling over into this place.

"Can I help you?" I asked, striding up to them.

The woman kept weaving her magic for a moment, but then she looked at me, and recognition dawned. She took a step back as I bared my teeth, and the spell broke.

"This lady was asking…" Stacy said slowly, her words trailing off. Then she blinked, and the distant, sleepy look vanished from her eyes. She frowned. "She was asking a lot of questions about you."

"Was she really?" I raised an eyebrow. "Why don't you come into my office, miss, and you can ask me your questions directly."

I gestured toward the glass door. The woman's eyes narrowed as she took in my barely concealed anger, the isolated office, and then the people surrounding us out in the open.

"We can talk out here," she said.

"I can call security," I said in a low rumble. "Would you prefer that to a private chat?"

The woman forced a smile, then led the way into my office. I closed the door firmly behind us, shutting out the sounds of the rest of the firm.

"Who the hell are you?" I snarled. "Apart from a witch, that is."

"I'm a harbinger," she said, glaring at me. "A representative of the people who understand what danger you represent, and the steps that need to be taken to keep you in check."

"You mean me personally, or my pack?"

"Either. Both. You choose."

I was seething with anger. This woman had brought the supernatural world into my office, threatening to expose my double life. She had cast spells on my assistant in an attempt to spy on me. If we'd been in private, I would have made her pay for that by now.

"What are you going to do, wolf, tear me apart in front of your colleagues?"

She gestured through the glass to where Stacy and a couple of paralegals were trying not to look like they were watching us.

"What are you going to do?" I asked. "Blast me with magic while people are watching?"

"Oh, we're watching you, Ethan Charleston, and we'll make sure that abominations like you can't threaten the safety of our world."

Of course, a magic purist, intent on keeping witches as witches, weres as weres, each type of being in its own little container. Someone convinced of their own righteousness and dead set on revenge. In better circumstances, I would have taken her prisoner and squeezed her for information, but right now, the best I could do was to keep my colleagues safe. A magical fight in this office could have tragic consequences for the vulnerable humans, never mind blowing my secrets wide open.

"Get out," I hissed. "And if I ever see you here again, I won't just send you away, I'll hunt you down and make you regret the day you ever set foot in this building."

She took hold of the door handle, but stood for a moment longer, looking at me, like she was fixing every detail of my face in her memory. As she tilted her head, I caught a glimpse of a medallion hanging from a silver chain around her neck, the symbol of the Creed.

"This changes nothing," she said with cold finality. "The people who matter know what carnage you bring, and we have an eye on you."

Then she opened the door and strode away.

CHAPTER 20

Ariel lived in a luxury apartment on the top floor of a modern high rise, near the center of Chicago. Through the windows outside the elevator, I could see halfway across the city, a teeming mass of people and traffic scurrying like ants between the buildings that walled them in on every side. It was quite a view, but not one I was interested in taking the time to appreciate.

I hammered on her door, pounding my anger into the inanimate wood. After a few moments, her voice sounded from inside.

"Ethan, what are you doing here?"

"We need to talk," I growled, trying hard not to make "talk" sound like code for "fight." I was happy to stick with words if they got my point across, I just wasn't sure that my inner wolf believed in them.

Ariel opened the door and then took a step back, letting me in. She was dressed in jogging pants and a loose t-shirt, both white like the rest of her wardrobe, and a yoga mat was rolled out in the middle of the living room. As I strode in, a small gray cat strolled casually over, took one sniff at my ankles, hissed, and scurried away.

"What brings you here?" Ariel asked as she closed the door. She was trying to keep her tone polite, but my fury was there for anyone to see, and she had tensed the moment I stepped past her into her home.

"That witch you sent to spy on me," I said. "Assuming there was only one."

"I didn't send anyone to spy on you," Ariel said. "And frankly, I'm offended that you would even suggest it. I thought that the pack and the Creed were allies."

I turned to face her, treating her to the full strength of my stare. The cat, now sitting on the kitchen counter, watched me with its teeth bared and claws exposed, like it was ready to attack at any second. Maybe it was: I had read stories of witches with familiars, tame animals they used to carry messages, channel magic, and sometimes even fight for them.

"Cut the bullshit, Ariel. I've been in this game longer than you have, I know how it's played. We all gather information on each other—pack, Creed, Seethe, the whole ugly bunch of us. It's the only way to stay safe in a world of magic and secret politics. But when you send your people to my office, casting spells on my assistant, almost getting seen by outsiders—"

"Someone cast a spell on your assistant?"

"So now you're pretending you don't know about it?"

"I'm not pretending!" Her voice rose as she stood facing me, hands on hips, her face increasingly flushed. "Why would I pull a stunt like that? If I want to learn about you, I could ask London or Nia or any of the other witches who have been working with the pack. I could ask Sebastian—or had you forgotten that I'm sleeping with your Alpha? Hell, I could cast a divination spell, which is a whole lot more powerful and less risky than setting foot where you work."

She walked up to me, her voice growing quiet but no less stern.

"But you know what I would actually do, if I wanted to

know something about you? I would ask you myself, because, in case you've forgotten, we're on the same side."

I glared down at her, and she stared unwaveringly back up at me, not in the least intimidated by my presence. There was a reason she had risen to the top of the Creed, and it wasn't an intensely practical taste in clothing.

"Fine," I said. Her heartbeat was elevated, her body tense, but nothing about her said that she was lying. "Maybe you didn't send her, but someone from your Creed has crossed a line."

She sighed and rubbed her eyes. "Not again."

Her bare feet silent on the soft carpet, she walked over to the kitchen, stroking the agitated cat as she passed. She peered at a coffee pot, took a couple of mugs off the draining board, and held one up.

"You want one?"

My first reaction was to demand that she cut the crap and focus on the issue at hand, but I could tell when it was time to rein my instincts in. I had lost my temper, storming up here like this to throw accusations at an ally of the pack. Bridges needed to be mended, and Ariel was holding out a hand across the gap.

"Black," I said. "No sugar. Thanks."

We sat facing each other across the counter, coffee in hand. The cat still glared at me, but its claws at least receded as Ariel stroked it softly with her free hand.

"Do you have a picture of the witch who came to your office?" she asked.

I took out my phone and pulled up an image captured by the office security cameras, showing the witch in the moment when she had arrived in our lobby. The security team were used to receiving requests for photos like this. Lawyers have a knack for attracting criminals, cranks, and private eyes, and it's a rare month when we're not tracking down some would-be intruder in our office.

Ariel took one look at the photo and muttered a low curse. "I thought she was on my side."

"Your side?" I asked.

Ariel took a slow swig of coffee and scratched the cat behind its ears while she considered her best response. She looked tense, despite her best effort to hide it.

"There are power struggles within and between Creeds, just like there are with packs," she said. "And just like you keep yours private until the East Coast Alpha winds up dead, we mostly keep ours to ourselves. Your brother blasting a bloody swathe through our leadership brought our issues into the open, but there's still a lot going on behind the scenes."

The cat, apparently contented, stretched out on the counter and rolled onto its back, exposing the soft fur of its belly. It looked at me with big blue eyes, and I reached out to stroke that belly, only for clawed paws to clamp around my forearm. I jerked my hand back, a little scratched, while Ariel laughed and tickled the cat's chin.

"Oh, Ethan, can't you spot a trap by now?"

I frowned at the cat, but it seemed to have lost interest in me already and was licking its own fur. I almost envied the simplicity of its life, getting to live as a pure beast.

"You recognized this woman," I said, tapping the phone.

"Hannah. She's been part of the Creed for a few years, after moving here from Philadelphia. She arrived under Marcia's rule, but I thought that she had accepted my leadership. She certainly made all the right noises."

"The noises she made to me were purist politics, with a side order of hate."

"Well, now I know. I'll try to bring her in for a conversation, but if she knows that she's been caught then she's probably in the wind."

"Where will she go?"

Ariel shrugged. "Wherever the rest of Marcia's old loyalists are hiding out. Josh took out the leadership, but witches don't live in a tight group like weres, it's not so easy to hunt them down."

"Are there many of them, Marcia's old faction?"

Ariel shrugged. She looked uncomfortable, like the ground was shifting underneath her.

"More than I thought, apparently, but hopefully still far fewer than there are of us. We'll find out when they make their move."

I gritted my teeth and set down the empty mug. I shouldn't be surprised to see one more complication in the mix, I just hoped that this wasn't one we ended up having to deal with.

"Thanks for the coffee," I said. "And sorry about…"

I let the words trail off, embarrassed at how I had started this.

"You were protecting your people," Ariel said. "I understand. But remember, witches do that too. Push too hard and it could end very differently next time." She glanced at the scratches on my arm, a small memento of her furry friend. "Consider today's punishment a gentle reminder."

I smiled. Things with the witches weren't straightforward, but of all the allies we could have found to face the struggles of the supernatural world, I couldn't think of anyone better.

I was working in the living room, examining a list of spells, when my phone rang. I'd settled there while waiting for Sky to come home from an evening out with Steven. The two of them took so long over dinner that I could cook, eat, wash up, and get a good chunk of work done in the time it took them to pick their starters. Now it looked like a conversation with Sebastian would be added to my achievements while they ate.

I hesitated for a moment before answering. Since Ariel took over the Creed, all our relations with them had been managed by Sebastian. Today, I had gone around that informal arrangement, going directly to confront his lover over an apparent conflict between us. I didn't know how he would respond to that, an infringement on his territory both politically and personally. Looking back on it, I should have spoken to him first, but I'd been too angry about the witch intruding on my workplace. I'd been driven by the need to vent my anger at someone.

Staring at my phone wasn't going to give me any answers. I picked it up and answered.

"Sebastian, how are you?"

"Ariel tells me you visited her."

I hesitated. His tone was controlled, but that didn't mean that he wasn't angry. Sebastian was always one of the hardest people to judge, and that got worse when I wasn't in the room with him. Years of working together meant I knew him better than most people, but in dealing with his new relationship with Ariel, I was up against my limit.

"There have been witches at my office," I said. "I thought that I should discuss it with her."

I braced myself for a lecture of hierarchy and obedience to my Alpha.

"Good." That word caught me by surprise. "We can't have every interaction with the Creed be about me and Ariel. As long as it's like that, everyone will be worrying about how my relationship is affecting pack politics."

I wasn't worried; I trusted Sebastian's judgment too much for that. But this wasn't just about me, I could see the wisdom in what Sebastian was saying, and I was relieved that it meant I hadn't crossed a line.

"So why were there witches at your office?"

"It looks like our opponents, the rogue witches, were trying to gather information on me. Probably information on the pack as well, given that I handle our legal issues."

"Do you think they learned anything?"

I hesitated. On the one hand, without interrogating one of those witches, I couldn't be sure how effective they had been. On the other hand, I had a lot of faith in Stacy and my colleagues, and in their ability to be discreet.

"If they'd learned anything important, I think they would have acted on it by now. They certainly won't be learning any more."

"Good," Sebastian said. "Hopefully this will improve our relationship with the Creed, if we show them that we can deal capably with rogue witches."

"It certainly can't do any harm."

"That's not the main reason I called, though," Sebastian continued. "I want to talk about what happens if we can't counter the Mond."

I stiffened. This problem had been on my mind too. We were working hard to find a solution to the plant's effect on us, but I would have been failing as a Beta if I didn't at least acknowledge the possibility of failure.

"Going public won't be good for us," I said, "but there are some ways we can limit the damage. Hiring a PR firm will be an important start, and there are a couple I know about through work. Then we can—"

"There's another option, before we get to that," Sebastian said.

I stopped, confused. If we couldn't stop the Mond from affecting us, then surely we would be revealed sooner or later: there were just too many opportunities for our opponents to use it against us.

"Ariel found references to a series of ancient spells," Sebastian said. "Ones that would mean weres only changed under the full moon, Mercury, an eclipse, or whichever part of the astronomical calendar affects them. We wouldn't be able to choose to change anymore, to use our powers when we come under attack or want to run as a pack. But because we couldn't change out of cycle, we would also be protected from the Mond."

A terrible chill ran through me. Taking on my wolf form was how I protected myself and those around me, it was how I bonded with my pack. If I lost that, I wouldn't feel like myself anymore. It would be as if a critical part of me was ripped away.

And what Sebastian was saying wouldn't just happen to us. For a spell to ensure safety from Mond, it would have to affect every single were-animal. From the people we loved to strangers on the far side of the world, we would be robbing them all of a part of their essence.

"Are you saying we should do that?" I had to force the words out. The possibility was too terrible.

"I really don't want to," Sebastian said. "But it's an option we have to consider in theory, at least."

"Well, in theory, it might be better than exposing us all to the world. In practice, I don't know how many were-animals could stand the consequences. Hell, I don't know if I could. It feels like chopping off a limb to escape a trap, not knowing if we might just end up bleeding to death."

"Fortunately, we don't have to decide yet. But I needed you to know what the possibilities are, and what we're up against if this doesn't work."

We hung up and I returned to what I'd been working on, but it was impossible to concentrate while in the back of my mind I was imagining a life in which I could never choose to change, only accept the transformation when the full moon forced it on me. Was that an existence I could live with? It didn't feel like much of a life at all.

The sound of Sky's car dragged me out of the dark thoughts into which I'd descended. Just knowing that I was about to see her made me grin, and the darkness sped away as she walked in, bearing takeout bags and a contented smile. Thoughts about a world without my wolf could wait for another day.

"Dinner for me?" I asked.

"Of course," she said with a nod, though she knew my habits too well to think that I would still be sitting here hungry. She went through to the kitchen and put the food away, then settled in the seat next to me.

I took a deep breath, wanting to enjoy the scent of her, but too much of Steven clung about her for my tastes.

"Tell me, when you and Steven are together are you engaged in some weird Tantric hug-fest? You smell like him. It's like you two are one."

I tried to make the comment lighthearted, but it was hard to conceal a note of jealousy. I had been hoping to spend some of the evening with Sky, and five hours was a long time to spend over dinner.

She stroked my cheek. "It was just a hug. He won't come near me. You all have successfully indoctrinated him in all the pack's rules and heightened his sensitivity to impropriety. We don't sit on the same side of the booth anymore."

"That's good, because that's just odd for anyone to do if there's a seat available across from each other." I smiled. "Winter's right, you two are pretty peculiar."

"What's weird is me having to get a crown, because apparently I'm the pack's 'princess' and you can't bear for me to feel any form of discomfort, pain, or denial in any way," she said in a loud aristocratic voice. "Interesting. That's going to be a full-time job, protecting me from life."

I frowned. "What?"

"You told Steven he needed to tell me what was going on with Taylor's transfer."

I laughed. Hearing that Steven was transferring his new bedtime buddy up from the south had come as a relief. As well as taking up some of the time he spent with Sky, Taylor should be enough for him to resist Stacy's interest, keeping the lines of my life from crossing.

"I live for the day that you feel some discomfort from Steven and my brother. The day when you ask them to do something and they actually say no. I'd like a front-row seat for that monumental event. Sky denied. Priceless. But it will never happen because they can't bear to see the face. Steven hadn't made a decision and it bothered you. You didn't know if he was coming back and that's where your anxiety was coming from. It wasn't fair to you or the pack. He'd hold off and try to never tell you because he didn't want to see the face. If he wasn't coming back, you needed to know so you could deal with it. Steven leaving would trigger a grieving process for you."

We sat looking at each other in silence for a long time, while I tried to work out what was really bothering her. Sky was okay with change, she'd been the catalyst for plenty of it in our pack, but there were some adjustments that she might not be ready to make.

"Steven may eventually leave this pack—you know that, right?" I said. "He'll be an Alpha one day, and I don't want him to be reluctant to do what he needs to because he can't bear to see the face. It's not fair."

"The face—my face."

She scowled as if this whole conversation was some sort of attack on her, as if the world was changing just to ruin the parts she wanted to keep. Was it too much all at once, or was this about losing the attention of one of her best friends? I leaned in and kissed her on the tip of the nose. I could try to offer some comfort at least, even as I delivered the hard truth she needed to hear.

"The face: doe eyes that look like someone just kicked a puppy, demolished a world, broke your heart a thousand times over. Then there's the little puffs you make with your lips. When you finish, a small pout remains, making you look like you'll never know happiness again. I took a vaccine; it doesn't affect me. For a while, I was convinced that you had the power to compel."

"You couldn't have thought that, because it didn't work on you," she said, reminding me of our early, less than friendly interactions.

"Exactly." I shrugged. "Then I realized it's just Josh and Steven." I laughed wryly. "They are Sky weak, or maybe they don't know how to deal with a person like you. It is quite complex. How do you deal with Sky? You never know what supernatural miscreant she'll bring home to fix. A person whose filter is so broken, it doesn't stop her from telling her Alpha to put his 'big-boy Alpha pants on.'"

Sebastian had told me about Sky confronting him and his behavior. I almost wished that I had been there to see the look on his face as a member of the pack tried to put him in his place.

"You heard about that?" Sky asked with an innocent smile.

"Yeah, I heard about it. And I heard about your inquiry regarding his relationship with Joan."

"So there was a relationship. Do tell?"

She turned to face me, eager for more details, but she was talking to the wrong were-animal if she wanted a good gossip; that was what Winter and Steven were for. I turned my attention back to my notes.

"What did Sebastian tell you about it?" I asked.

"He told me to get out of his office, and he wasn't very polite about it."

"Did your superpower fail you?"

Sky glanced down at the list of spells, all of which we had run unsuccessful tests on, trying to find a way to beat the Mond.

"I think Ariel and the other witches need to get involved," she said. "This can't be handled lightly."

Despite myself, my thoughts were still on Sky and Sebastian.

"I didn't say you were wrong about telling Sebastian what he needed to do, I just can't believe you said it that way." I couldn't quite suppress my laughter at the thought of it.

"Sometimes you just have to shoot from the hip." Grinning, she drew imaginary guns and shot pretend holes in the wall. The confidence and excitement flowing from her drew my attention away from any thoughts of work.

"Nice." I set the notebook aside and kissed her on the cheek, relishing the softness of her skin under my lips, then trailed on down her neck.

I turned around on the sofa, so that my legs were outstretched and her back leaned against my chest, our bodies pressing together. I scattered kisses across her neck and then nibbled on her ear, drawing a low moan from her.

"The listing realtor that I recommend is named Megan Franks," I said, speaking softly between kisses. "She'll be e-mailing you the contract. Let me know if you'd like to use someone else. The movers are scheduled next week Friday. Plenty of time for us to pack up your things." I paused to lay a kiss where her neck joined her shoulder blade. "Take a look around the house and see where you'd like to put some of your things."

Sky jerked away from me and spun around, a look of confusion on her face. Yet again, by doing the obvious, I had caught her completely off guard. I imitated her air guns, taking a few exaggerated shots at the ceiling.

"Movers?" she exclaimed in alarm. "Realtors? What's going on?"

"Yes, movers. Realtors. We're mated and will be married in less than a month. What exactly are your plans? Do you plan to live here and your place?"

Sky gazed silently around the room, as if she was seeing it for the first time and determined to take in every detail. There was a solemnity to her expression that unsettled me. Was she unhappy with my house? Was she having second thoughts about living here?

I looked around, trying to see it as she did. It was far more spacious than the place she had been calling home, and far less crowded. It was also very different in style, refined and understated, the way I liked my space. But what I saw as an ideal place to live lacked the homely clutter that Sky seemed to enjoy—the throw pillows, framed pictures, and knickknacks. To me, they seemed like unnecessary clutter, but now I realized that to Sky they might be what made a house a home.

I liked my house the way it was, but I loved being with Sky, and if some changes to the decor were needed for her to feel comfortable, that was a price I was more than happy to pay.

"We can redecorate, and it can be a combination of our styles," I said.

"I love your home."

"*Our* home. Then what's the problem, Sky?"

I looked at her, struggling to hide the anxiety I was feeling as I saw my vision of the future start to unravel over something as small as interior decoration.

"I have a chair, I want it," she said. "I usually read on it. And I need to bring all my blankets because"—she grabbed the blanket lying over the back of the sofa—"these are so nice and luxurious I'd feel terrible if I spilled something on them and damaged them. Mine already have stains."

A wave of relief flowed through me. A block had appeared on our way to happiness, and Sky had flung it aside. The addition of her tatty chair and stained blankets would take some getting used to, but I could live with that. What mattered was that we were in this together, and we could work through anything if we set our minds to it. There were adjustments to be made, but they would be worth it.

She kissed me on the lips, then rested her forehead against mine.

"I adore our home," she said, "and the fact you are a neat freak so I don't have to lift a finger. It has nothing to do with you. It's another chapter in my life. I seem to be zooming past them all so fast, I find myself digging my heels in, trying to slow things down. I want to live here, with you. I'll have all my things moved in by next week, and I'll contact Megan tomorrow."

I kissed her lightly across the lips and the cheeks. "Please tell me all your sexy nightwear is still at your house. Because I saw footed pj's yesterday."

"I have so many more of them to bring here. So. Many. More. You've seen my sexy clothes. I wore them for you last night."

"The pink tank top with the unicorn and glitter and lime-green shorts?" I asked, unable to work out if I was being wound up or if this was really what Sky considered alluring.

"It was hot, right?" she asked, her eyes shining with stifled laughter.

"So hot," I replied in a sarcastic voice.

But the truth was, anything draped over Sky would look sexy to me.

CHAPTER 21

I was working in my study, going over the magical ideas we were experimenting with to counter the Mond, when I heard a light, energetic tapping at my front door. I frowned, confused about who might be there. I wasn't expecting any deliveries, Sky had her own key, and everyone in the pack knew better than to disturb me at home without an invitation. My house was far enough off the beaten track to deter most salesmen and door-to-door evangelists, but maybe the Pentecostalists or Mormons were getting extra diligent again. The local evangelicals liked nothing more than to add a wealthy new worshiper to their congregations, and a house like mine wasn't exactly subtle in what it said about the owner's bank account.

At first, I tried to ignore the knocking, but it persisted. Reluctantly, I set my notes aside and headed for the door. I was halfway there when I heard a voice calling out.

"Hello, grumpy pup! We're here to talk tuxedos."

I gritted my teeth. Would it be wrong to turn away Trent and David, when they had agreed to plan our wedding for us? Not that they were really doing it for us; this was about their pleasure in showing Sky off and getting to be the center of attention. But I was aware that I was benefiting from David's substantial skills as a professional event planner, not to mention Trent's experience in putting on a PR show. Grinning and bearing the antics was the price I paid for doing this thing right.

At the door, I stopped for a moment to take a deep breath and prepare myself, then let them in.

"We have design options," David said, holding up a bulging ring binder.

"And fabric samples," Trent said, holding up a bag that ran over with pieces of black cloth.

"Come in," I said, a moment after Trent had swept past me. "Do you want a coffee?"

Nothing was going to stop them from making themselves comfortable, or sticking around for far longer than I wanted, but at least making coffee would give me a few minutes to get used to their presence, while they burned through the worst of whatever manic energy had driven them here. And once they finished their coffees, I could use that as an excuse to get them out.

"Do you have anything herbal?" Trent asked as he started spreading identical-looking swatches across my sofa.

"Does he look like a man with herbal tea?" David asked, shaking his head. "Coffee would be lovely. No milk for either of us, we're on a pre-wedding-suit diet."

I wondered if that diet ran as far as cutting back on their copious consumption of red wine. I suspected that alcohol would be an exception.

I expected the two of them to stay in the living room, arranging their evidence, ready to interrogate me, but instead they followed me through to the kitchen, gazing around them as they went. Clearly wedding planning wasn't the only reason they had come here. They'd had little chance to look around my house, and they had to be burning with curiosity.

"Well, this is splendid," David said, looking around the kitchen. "So much more stylish than Sky's place. She is one lucky lady."

I got the coffee pot going while they nosed around the room.

"Do you choose your own crockery, or do you have someone to choose it for you?" Trent asked, looking enviously at the mug I had put down in front of him.

"I like to make my own choices." Including choices about who to spend time with, but apparently that was out of my hands right now. My life had stopped working that way the moment Sky stepped into it, and if I didn't like everything that came from that, it was still a win for me.

"Then you have excellent taste, grumpy pup," David said with a wide smile.

I turned on him with a glare. Even Sky didn't get to bestow cutesy nicknames on me, and she knew me infinitely better than these jokers. "Don't call me that again."

"What, grumpy pup? I think it's rather sweet, and it suits you down to the ground."

Against most opponents, I would have used the threat of violence, whether stated or implied, but David was too confident in his friendship with Sky to believe that I would do him any harm. So while I glared at him with the full force of my annoyance, I chose a different sort of threat.

"Do you want to attend this wedding you're planning?" I growled with all the menace I had.

David stood frozen, eyes wide, caught off guard by my tone. After a moment, he gathered his thoughts enough to nod his head.

"Then don't ever call me that again." I handed him a cup of coffee. "And in case you're thinking that will only stop you for the next few weeks, remember that I own this house, and I could make your visits to Sky very uncomfortable."

David flung back his head with a snort.

"I suppose you don't want to see our tuxedo ideas, then?" he asked, his voice rising with indignation.

"Not really," I said. "I've got more urgent work I need to deal with, so if you want to storm out, then feel free."

"Ethan!" Trent exclaimed in outrage. "How could you? You're ruining Sky's wedding!"

"It's my wedding too."

"Yes, yes, of course, but really…"

He let the words trail off. He had me. While I was looking forward to the wedding, the real reason it mattered to me was Sky. This was about making her happy, and I would do whatever it took to achieve that.

"Fine," I said with a sigh. "Tell me about your tuxedo ideas."

"We've found some exceedingly stylish examples to work from," David said, taking my arm to steer me back toward the living room, his indignation of moments before forgotten. "We don't need you to make decisions today, but you should at least start thinking through the options."

"Are you ready?" Josh asked, a notebook in one hand and a channeling crystal in the other. As he had explained it, the crystal wasn't necessary for the spell, but it would help the witches to get it right at this early, experimental stage. I was willing to take his word for it, willing enough that the pack had splashed out for several of the crystals, to give our newly assembled team every possible advantage in their work.

"Ready as I'll ever be," Steven replied.

He stood in the middle of the library, all the chairs and desks cleared away from around him, stark naked and with his hair a ruffled mess. Off to one side, Taylor watched him with more than a little interest, while I sat by the door, a video camera running beside me, ready to record the results.

Unlike Steven's previous appearance on camera, this wouldn't be shared with the world. Once the witches had watched back as many times as they needed to, the memory card would be formatted, wiped with a magnet, and then burned. We couldn't be too careful.

Josh nodded and I hit record.

"Anti-Mond spell version three, fifth iteration," Josh said. "Starting the process now."

Then he, London, and Nia spread out around Steven, crystals raised, channeling their magic as they chanted. I could feel it filling the room, trails of power tickling at my mind. A sheen of multicolored light filled the air, like the glistening of oil on water, as the spell wound its way around the test subject. That magical glow closed in and settled on Steven, seeming to sink into his skin.

"How does it feel?" I asked.

"Like touching ice," Steven replied, goosebumps covering his skin.

I didn't know whether that was a good sign, a bad sign, or just a sign that we should turn the air conditioning down, but Josh had said that it would be good to get the test subjects' statements on what they were experiencing, and that was what Steven had become for the day, a test subject like a rat in a lab. Yesterday had been Winter's turn, and tomorrow would be Quinn's, unless we had a breakthrough today. I was exempted because of the unknown effect my spirit shade might have on the results, so instead I sat by the camera, trying to make myself feel useful rather than swimming in the frustration of a magic user faced with a problem beyond his skills.

"All done," Josh said, stepping back.

Taylor walked up to Steven, holding a Ziploc plastic bag full of a fine dust, which Jeremy made by grinding up one of the Mond leaves. She had insisted on being the one to do this part of the testing, but she still held the bag out at arm's length before she opened it, holding it up so that Steven could take a deep breath of the contents. Then she stepped back, carefully closing the seal on the bag.

Almost immediately, Steven grimaced and his shoulders hunched. His arms trembled as the Mond battled his mind for control of his physical form.

"That's it," I called out. "Fight back. You can do it."

Those words hadn't been true even once yet that day, but I kept saying them anyway. We needed him to resist with all his will, so that if he did change, we knew it was all down to the Mond.

Shaking, he sank to the floor, hands clawing at the carpet, back arched as he resisted the change. But it was useless. A spasm ran through him, fur burst through his skin, and moments later we were faced not with a naked man but with a grumpy-looking coyote.

He stalked over to Taylor, who patted his head and rubbed the fur of his flanks, soothing him. His bushy tail swished from side to side and he sank to the floor at her feet.

"Remember, keep trying to change back," Josh said to him. "We need to know how long it lasts." He turned to me. "You can switch off the camera for now. We won't learn anything from this part."

Josh, Nia, and London compared notes on how the spell had gone, while I leafed through one of the books Nia had pulled out from our collection. It was a grimoire of spells connected to the cycles of time, and particularly the movements of the sun and moon, not a book I would have thought to look at, but one that was surprisingly relevant, given the way were-animals' transformations normally worked. Though I didn't like Nia's pointed questions about how we had amassed our collection, I couldn't argue with the benefits of having her and London around to help Josh. With them, we were working through more ideas for countering the Mond than we ever could have on our own. We were incredibly lucky to have the Creed on our side.

Particularly lucky given that I could have smashed that alliance apart by confronting Ariel. However tough things got over the next few weeks, I had to keep my temper in check, to make sure we kept the allies we had. Expressing my feelings was all well and good with Sky, but there was a limit.

It didn't help that my worries about the Mond were growing. Our attempts to track down the humans who got it from Gregoire had led nowhere, meaning that it could be anywhere out there in the world, a threat hovering over us for months or even years to come. If it was used to transform a large number of weres, then it could blow open the secrecy that was our greatest protection, and our most fragile one. I had already been hunted once, turned into a wild beast to satisfy some people's cruel concept of entertainment. Could this awful elven herb lead to my whole pack facing the same fate?

Steven let out a growl, then started to shake. His legs and arms twisted, his head tipped down, and his tail shrank up toward his spine. Fur retreated through his skin and his large, pointed ears shrank back against the sides of his head. At last he lay there human, his head in Taylor's lap, sweating and panting from the exertion.

The simple act of changing shouldn't have put such a strain on a healthy were, but he had been through the process eight times now in the course of a few hours, fighting the forced transformation in one direction and struggling against the aftereffects of the Mond when he wanted to change back. This was more than anyone could have simply put up with, and it was starting to show.

"Twenty seconds more than last time," Josh said, looking at his watch.

"Not enough to be statistically significant," Nia said, shaking her head.

"It could feel pretty significant, if he's trying to hide from hunters," I pointed out.

"That's not how this works," Nia said, frowning. She was one of those witches who liked to combine magic with a rigorous scientific process, which meant that she got very picky about how much we read into the results.

"Is it going to work at all?" Taylor asked, looking worried. "I mean, this is taking a lot out of him."

"I'm fine," Steven said, forcing himself to his feet. He stood for a moment, swaying slightly, then walked back to the middle of the room. "Let's get on with the next test."

"Taylor's right," I said, noticing Steven's flushed and sweaty skin, his uneven movements and the rapid beat of his heart. "You've pushed him as far as he can go for now."

"I'm fine," Steven snapped. "I can—"

"No," I snarled back, glaring at him. "This is about saving lives in the pack, not putting them at risk. If this breaks you, then I'm failing in my duty as Beta. And if we miss something about these spells because our test subject is so exhausted that he warps the results, then we're all failing the others."

"I'll be fine," Steven insisted. "Just give me a chance to rest."

"Maybe." I got up out of my seat and headed for the door. "Put some clothes on, get some food, sleep if your body tells you to. I'm going to go and find a new test subject."

Steven looked disappointed, but Taylor was clearly relieved as she led him out of the room. While the witches went to watch the video recording, I headed through the retreat, in search of someone to take Steven's place. As I walked, tension knotted my stomach, and I could feel the muscles tightening in my neck.

This had to work, because if it didn't, what other option did we have? For the second time in only a handful of months, the pack was in serious danger of being exposed.

CHAPTER 22

Sky and I sat to one side of the bar, sipping at our drinks. I was making faster progress on my Scotch than she was on her martini, which she only sipped at briefly between talking in an agitated fashion about the invitation she had received to Chris's Presentation and how David and Trent now wanted to go along.

"And then they made me feel like I was being unreasonable for not wanting them to hang out with vampires. Like they couldn't understand that dressing in fancy gowns and nice menswear doesn't change the fact that they are vampires!"

I had heard the story at least four times in the past few days, and the part that surprised me wasn't that David and Trent wanted to put themselves in danger for the sake of a party. The novelty of the event would have been enough to draw their attention, even without the air of glamour that mundane people inaccurately attached to vampires. David and Trent were doubtless expecting something fabulous and exotic, and they would keep wanting it no matter how often Sky pointed out that the hosts were murderous bloodsuckers

265

more interested in seeing humans as hors d'oeuvres than as guests.

What had caught me off guard was the fact that Chris had personally invited Sky to the presentation. My invitation as Beta of the Northwest Pack extended to my mate, and I had been assuming that Sky would come along, but it had never occurred to me that Chris might give her a personal invitation. It was a testament to the growing strength of a friendship that still baffled and unsettled me.

Out on the dance floor, the witches were dancing up a storm, London throwing herself around with wild abandon as she worked off her frustrations from days of working on ineffective spells. Nia presumably had her own way of dealing with those setbacks, as she hadn't come along. Given the greedy way she had looked at the two books we had let her borrow from the pack library, I suspected that they would play a significant part in her night, though she had been flicking through a dating app during breaks between the spells, so I doubted that she would be spending the whole night alone.

Josh watched London from the edge of the dance floor, where he was drowning his sorrows in bourbon. Steven, exhausted by another afternoon as a test subject, stood off to one side, gazing wearily into the distance. I made a mental note to check in with him tomorrow and make sure that the repeated forced transformations weren't doing him permanent harm. Not far from him, in the corner of the room, Winter was drinking alone, often her favorite way to drink, though a succession of optimistic men seemed determined to change that. I hoped that they enjoyed the swift rejections she gave out to each of them in turn, because she certainly wasn't enjoying their attention.

Sky seemed to have run out of steam on the topic of David and Trent's dangerous desire to attend the Presentation. I turned to look at her, saw the frustration screwing up her face, and planted a kiss on her forehead.

"It has to be hard to have someone want to go into danger while you try desperately to stop them," I said quietly, kissing her on the temple, the cheek, and then the lips. I took her by the waist and pulled her close, enjoying the feeling of her hip beneath my hand and then the pressure of our bodies pressing together. "I can only imagine the challenge of seeing the potential for danger and having that person totally ignore it."

I kissed her again, trying to balance the pointed words with a gesture of affection, but Sky was unimpressed. She stepped back and glared at me through narrowed eyes.

"It's not the same thing," she said, jutting out her chin.

"Really," I said, preparing myself for another heated debate. "Please, Sky, tell me how different it is?"

But the message had already struck home. Stuck for a response, Sky growled and rolled her eyes.

I bent in close to her, nipped at her ear, and whispered, "Did I just win?"

"No," she snapped. "I'm right because I am."

"Ah, yes. The 'I'm right because I am' argument. It's one of your most insurmountable defenses."

"You're neither funny nor clever," she announced, though apparently I was smart enough to leave her without a coherent response.

She turned her attention back to the dance floor, and I followed her gaze. Across the floor from London, Kelly was drawing the attention of everyone around her, moving with all the fluid grace and perfect precision that her training as a dancer gave her. It was the same artful control that a really good fighter showed, her body completely under her command, each movement flowing into the next, in perfect sync with the music. Those movements were all the more striking by comparison with Gavin, who she had dragged, reluctantly, onto the dance floor, and who danced with all the stiff, lumbering gracelessness of an elephant having a heart attack. He still grinned with pleasure whenever he looked Kelly's way, but he was completely out of his element.

"I believe Kelly can get people to do anything," Sky said, sipping at her drink.

"I wonder if Kelly can get David and Trent to leave me alone?" I asked, looking down at my buzzing phone. It wasn't the first time that the wedding planners from Hell had tried to get hold of me this evening. I doubted it would be the last.

"What do they want now?"

"I told them I owned a tux," I explained. That was the cleaned-up version of what I had said after an interminable hour of looking at styles and samples, with the two of them unable to just let me accept anything as good enough. "But apparently since one person in this damn city has seen me in it, one who won't be at the wedding, I can't possibly wear it again." I polished off my Scotch and signaled the bartender for another. "You think they're being a pain to you? They're pains in my ass."

"The polite thing to say is they are enthusiastic and determined."

I shrugged. "They are enthusiastic and determined to be pains in the ass."

My phone buzzed again, yet another picture of a tux flashing up on the screen. It was as if my phone had been taken over by the Instagram account of a suit hire company. I growled at the thought of sitting through weeks more of this.

Sky looked at my phone with interest, then pointed to one of the photos.

"I like this one. It'll look good on you."

I gave her a grin.

"If you say 'everything looks good on me,' I won't run interference and you will be dealing with Trent and David yourself," she said.

I forced the smile away and leaned back so that Sky could see me in all my glory.

"I don't really think I need to say it, now do I?"

Sky rolled her eyes, but I knew full well what she thought. After all, we were together. But somewhere in the conversation she had got hold of my phone, and was now messaging our wedding planners on my behalf.

"You have to have it fitted," she said. "He said he'll text you the time and day."

"Of course he will," I said wearily. "And then he'll keep texting until I reply."

By that point, I was starting to wonder whether picking the tux with David and Trent's help was really such a good idea. This was one small part of the wedding that I could make mine, and if I let Sky and her friends take control of it, then there would be nothing left of me in the event. It was one thing to accept outside help, another to lose all choice. But I had my own opinions—it would be hard not to, after seeing so many pictures of near-identical suits—and my own tailor who I'd trusted for years. Perhaps it was time to approach this differently.

I glanced at Sky. Judging by the seriousness of her expression, her mind had wandered to other issues, like the Mond and how it might be used against us. Until we worked out a defense against it, that plant was our most serious threat, and we still didn't even know how long it would take to find a solution. I was worried for the future of the whole pack, but I was also worried for Sky and how she might struggle if those dark thoughts came to dominate our lives forever. Whatever issues I had with the wedding, it was something she was excited about, and for a night out, that seemed like a much better topic of conversation.

"They already have a location for the wedding," I said.

Sky didn't respond, her brow furrowing as she sank deeper into the darkness of dwelling on our dangers.

"They also have the flowers and a caterer," I said.

"David texted me about it already."

"Based on the invoice, I'm assuming each person involved is a graduate of Le Cordon Bleu," I added, sipping at my Scotch. The tone of disapproval that slipped into my voice was far more about having to deal with David and Trent than it was about the expense. If I was going to celebrate my life with Sky, then I was going to do it in style. Between my job and my investments, I had the money to make this spectacular, so why wouldn't I? Judging by Trent's and David's expressions when they realized how far they could go with the budget, they were enjoying being let loose almost as much as I intended to enjoy the end results.

"I can't believe they got so much done in such a short time."

In some ways, I couldn't believe that David and Trent ever got anything done, they seemed so flighty. But it seemed that the energy they put into idle chatter and celebrity gossip could be a powerful force when channeled into a project that inspired them.

I let my attention drift away from Sky, who seemed lost in her own thoughts, and took the time to survey the room. Watchfulness wasn't a habit I ever intended to break, not where the security of my pack was concerned. I couldn't remember the last time we had been free of threats, and vigilance was our best armor against being caught unaware.

"Where are we going to honeymoon?" I asked as I scanned the dance floor, trying to keep the conversation going.

Even as I said it, something else was falling into place in my mind. Our bar wasn't just restricted to were-animals, or even to the supernatural, but it wasn't the sort of place that drew a lot of casual customers either. Josh had worked hard to craft a venue that attracted people by word of mouth and kept them coming back through its lively yet relaxing atmosphere, with the additional thrill of the occasional discreet celebrity guest. I knew most of the regulars' faces, and had a feel for the style of the people who came less often. And right now, I was seeing a lot of people who seemed out of place, the faces unfamiliar, outfits just a little off, some of them holding themselves stiffly or looking around uncertainly, certainly not relaxing into a casual night out.

I set my glass aside and sat up straighter in my seat.

"What's the matter?" Sky asked.

I frowned and looked around the room, spotting more of them, trying to work out when they had started drawing the attention of my subconscious.

"In the past eight minutes there has been an influx of people that I don't recognize," I said. "Something's off. They don't really fit in here. Do you smell it?"

The air was heavy with all the usual smells of this place— alcohol, sweat, cologne, the distinctive pheromones of humans out having a wild night or looking for a potential mate. But there was something else as well, a trace of something unfamiliar that seemed to mix the scents of metal, grapefruit, and juniper.

In a corner to the left of where we were sitting, a group of unfamiliar people had clustered. We had a new band in, and normally I would have taken these people for their friends or fans, but they held themselves wrong, not enjoying the music but standing expectantly, waiting for something to arrive.

"New faces," I said.

"I don't think that's a big—"

Suddenly, the group of strangers started to move, splitting up so that they could head for the were-animals spread around the bar. Several of them held a small package in their hands, and I didn't think they were about to hand out gifts or try to sell us drugs. Others were pulling out their phones.

Sky and I leapt from our seats a moment too late, as the packages were torn open. Dust swirled into the air, thick with the familiar, musty smell of Mond. Sky grabbed a handful of napkins and I did the same, covering my nose and mouth to try to keep the Mond particles out. We couldn't transform here, in such a public place.

Except that was obviously what the strangers wanted.

People screamed as some of the weres started to convulse and fall to the floor, while other weres ran, their faces twisted with pain, toward the back exit and the office beyond.

Steven led the rush for the office, but others weren't fast enough. Gavin fell on the dance floor, writhing as he fought to keep from a forced transformation. A man stopped only feet away from him and instead of offering help held up a phone to film what was happening. This was more than just the casual gawking of a bystander seeing something worth sharing. There was a thrill of anticipation in the guy's eyes, even as Kelly dragged Gavin to his feet and followed the others making their escape.

My pulse raced as the fight or flight instinct took over, but who was I going to fight? The people with phones were getting in the way, but how would it look if I was caught on camera punching someone just for that? Chaos had descended as panic spread to some of the regular customers, but no one knew what to do. There was noise and movement but no order to any of it.

I was about to shout for everyone to get out when London got ahead of me. She gave a flick of her hand and a pile of napkins burst into flames. Even as a bartender grabbed an extinguisher and rushed to put out the fire, Josh followed London's example and set some of the wooden chairs ablaze. Magic filled the air, all of it familiar, though I didn't think it all came from my friends.

Now people really were panicking, rushing away from the fires and toward the exit. Sprinklers kicked in moments before sirens blared outside the building.

The streaming water sucked the dust out of the air, even as it extinguished the fires and drenched the carpets. It soaked through my shirt and pants, sticking them to my body. I wanted to rush out into the street and deal with the PR problem that was heading our way, to try to control the crowds and the reports they gave of what people had seen. But first I needed to check on the pack.

While Josh and London covered the door, Sky and I headed for the exit at the rear of the bar, toward Josh's office. Bodies swirled around and between us, panicked weres heading for the safety of the office, hunched and twitching as they fought for control; panicked humans rushing out the door, screaming "fire!" and shoving each other aside as they raced for safety. I was caught up in the moment, ushering people out, trying to hide my pack while keeping others from getting hurt.

Then I was in the rear of the building, glancing into an office filled with fear as the weres hit by Mond struggled to keep control, before losing the battle and transforming into their animal forms. I glanced around, but there was no one else to keep an eye on them, and I needed to get out into the street. I would just have to trust the weres, exhausted as they were, to protect themselves until I got back.

I dashed back through the bar, joining the last of the fleeing customers, while the sprinklers soaked us all. The whole time, a single thought dominated my thoughts, one laden with dread: this could be it, the moment we were all exposed.

Outside the bar, the chaos was even worse. A couple of stressed-looking cops were trying to herd the crowd away from the building, while firefighters pushed their way through the mass of moving bodies. Drinkers were streaming out of other nearby bars to see what the fuss was about, while our customers, now safely away from whatever they thought had caused the panic, were stopping to compare notes, shouting excitedly about what they had seen, and generally getting in the way.

I emerged from the building, pushing the last few customers ahead of me, as the first firefighter made it through the door.

"It was in the main bar," I said, hoping to deter them from investigating the back room where the transformed weres were hiding. "I think the sprinklers have put it out."

"Thanks," he said. "Now you go get to safety."

I wasn't sure anywhere was safe right now, with people carrying Mond nearby, but it seemed best to comply with the emergency services. I didn't want to make this situation any worse than it already was.

Stepping away from the building, I glanced around the

crowd. Most of those suspicious faces from earlier were gone, presumably having fled with whatever evidence they thought they had captured on their phones. I saw a couple lurking near the fringes, cameras still out, but I also saw friendly witches heading toward them with determined looks and the flicker of magic in their eyes. They should be able to deal with the phones discreetly, while I tried to manage the brewing PR nightmare. The last thing we wanted was some lurid story about a disaster in a bar drawing unwanted attention to the pack.

More vehicles were pulling up, some with the lights of emergency services flashing, others the ordinary vehicles of gawkers or journalists. I headed to the north corner of the crowd, where a burly police sergeant was addressing a small group armed with cameras, microphones, and notebooks. On the way, I pulled out my phone and ran a hasty search for a few obscure facts. We were going to need a cover story, and one was already forming in my head.

"We don't yet know what happened in there," the cop was saying. "We probably won't know anything tonight, so why don't you all go report on some real news, and wait for a report in the morning?"

I could tell by the tone of his voice that it was a familiar speech, and one he knew was doomed to fail. But if he had the journalists corralled, perhaps I could make the most of the opportunity.

"Excuse me, sergeant," I said. "I'm the lawyer for the management of this bar, and I was inside when this happened. Perhaps I can help?"

I handed him a damp business card. The journalists eagerly shifted the attention of their cameras and microphones to take us both in. The sergeant narrowed his eyes and flicked a glance at the cameras, but there was no easy way out of this for him.

"All right, mister lawyer," he said. "What did you see?"

"It looked like a small fire started in a trash can," I said. "Probably someone putting out a cigarette they shouldn't have been smoking in the bar. It happens more often than you'd think." I started reeling off statistics about fines for breaking smoking bans, both in Chicago and across the US, then when into a spiel about nicotine addiction, fatality rates from lung cancer, and the amount that tobacco companies spent on lobbying. As I talked, I could practically hear the attention of the journalists collapsing in front of me. They had wanted a juicy story about a dangerous situation in a bar, and instead they were getting a lecture from what looked like a crusading lawyer with an anti-tobacco agenda.

Eventually, the cop cut me off.

"Okay, I get it," he said, one hand unconsciously reaching for a pocket that bulged in the shape of a cigarette packet. "I reckon we've heard all we need to, right folks?"

The journalists who hadn't already turned away took their chance to head back to their cars and the hunt for a better late-night scoop.

"A trash fire, huh?" said a familiar voice behind me.

I turned to see a tall black woman in a loose, practical suit, and a short, bald guy with a mustard stain on his lapel. Both wore detective's badges.

"Detective Rankin, Detective Flynn." I forced a smile. "I thought you two worked homicides, not bar fires."

Rankin wore her impassivity like a shield, but I could sense the hostility underneath.

"We were in the neighborhood when the call went out," she said. "Everybody has to do a bit of crowd control from time to time."

"Of course." I looked pointedly at the crowd still swirling behind her, some of the customers starting to disperse now that the excitement was over.

"Plus this place sounded familiar," Flynn said with a smile. "Came up when we were looking into your pal Steven, and we figured it must be worth seeing if he liked it that much. He's not here, is he?"

"Steven?" I kept my forced smile in place. "Not that I'm aware of. Besides, he doesn't smoke, so if you're looking for someone to pin things on, then you'll have to try elsewhere this time."

"We're not looking to blame anyone for anything," Rankin said. "Just looking for the truth, and we already got that for Steven, right?"

If looks could have killed, hers would have drilled a hole through my skull and turned my brain to paste.

"Of course, detectives. Why else would the DA have dropped the murder charges?"

"Of course," she said coldly.

"Come on," Flynn said, tugging at his partner's sleeve. "We should go get these people moving so the fire crew can do their work."

I watched as they marched off to deal with the crowd. I wasn't surprised to hear that someone from Steven's case still had an eye on us, aside from DA Price and his Red Blood connections; after all, the evidence against Steven had looked strong to some people, and there had never been a trial to prove his guilt or innocence. The danger of Mond wasn't just that people would know who we were, it was that they would evaluate us in a whole different light. Past criminal cases could easily rear their heads again if we didn't get this under control.

Already stretched tight with stress, I looked around and realized that Sky was nowhere to be seen. I could feel her presence, but not in the back of the bar like I had expected. She was farther away, and I felt her trembling with the proximity of danger. She could have been grabbed by our enemies in the confusion in the club, or been turned by the Mond and now be desperately trying to hide. Fear for her replaced every other thought and feeling. I cursed myself for having somehow forgotten the most important person in my life.

I pushed my way past the people at the edge of the crowd, hurried a dozen yards down the street, and got into my car. I was just starting up the engine when my phone buzzed.

"I'm fine," Sky said as soon as the call connected.

"Good." I let out a ragged breath and pulled away from the curb, heading slowly down the street, following my instinct for her presence.

"I guess I'll see you in a little while."

"Don't hang up," I said quickly. "Just stay on."

Now that the rush of action had passed and the immediate danger was over, I needed something to bring me back to a place of comfort and safety. I needed to hear Sky's voice.

"Okay," she whispered. "Ethan, are you okay?"

"No," I confessed. My fingers were trembling on the wheel, my heart racing in shock at what I'd seen and everything it represented. "We were almost exposed today. The witches aren't able to find a spell to inoculate us, and it's just a matter of time before we are publicly outed. We were lucky today; London thought quickly, but I'm just waiting to see if anyone got enough for it to make people speculate. And—"

"You know Samuel is involved?"

I had assumed it was Red Blood, based on all the ordinary humans releasing Mond in the club. They'd been following a similar play book to when their leaders had kidnapped Sky and tried to film her changing under the full moon. But it made sense for our enemies to band together, and who better than Red Blood and the rogue witch who wanted to remove all magic from the world?

"Of course he's involved," I snarled. "We have to fix this some way. We can't let them win."

I saw Sky standing by the side of the road ahead of me and pulled up to the curb. As she got into the car, I felt a desperate yearning to feel her skin against mine. I kissed her on the lips, then on the forehead, seeking the stability of her presence, then rested my head against hers. For a moment, I had been facing the threat of losing her again. I needed her touch to give me the certainty that she was safe.

"You're okay," I breathed.

"They're more afraid of me than I'll ever be of them."

I turned the car around and headed back toward the bar. As I drove, Sky explained how a trail of magic had led her to Samuel, and with him Rayna, the witch Gregoire had mentioned. It was an unlikely alliance, apparently held together purely by hatred of us.

"They want me to use the Clostra to cast some sort of magic," Sky said. "To stop all the were-animals from changing."

I snorted. "Good luck to them with that."

"But there's a creepy bit too. They're kind of obsessed with you and me mating, and with that representing something bad." She looked at me with concern. "Are these people even going to let us marry in peace?"

I squeezed her leg and put on my most reassuring voice, countering all the doubts and fears I felt.

"It doesn't matter what they do and don't allow. Nothing in the world is going to stop us from being together."

Josh's office looked like a picture of the inside of Noah's Ark, every available surface covered in animals. A pair of panthers lay in one corner, Gavin and Kelly wrapped protectively around each other; near them lay two wolves, muzzles pressed together as they sought the comfort of contact; Steven was curled up near the door in coyote form; a leopard, an ocelot, and a hyena filled up the remaining space. Beyond them, Josh sat at his computer, searching the internet to see what accounts of the night had already slipped out.

The animals looked exhausted, hardly surprising after what they had been through. I knew how it felt to fight against the forced transformation that Mond brought on, and they had held their human forms long enough to get out of sight and safely back here.

"Can you change back?" I asked.

The animals looked up, some with more energy than others. It was Steven, who after all the experiments was more experienced with Mond than anyone else in the pack, who got up on four legs and tried to shift. Muscles strained, his body twitched, and he let out a low, frustrated growl, but nothing changed. At last he sank back down.

I started heading toward him, planning to see if I could help, but Sky stopped me with a touch to my arm.

"Let's see if they can," she said.

She was right, this was a useful opportunity, a chance to learn more about the impact of Mond. One by one, each were-animal tried to adopt their human form, without luck. It was distressing to watch, seeing them forced into shapes they hadn't chosen, a reminder of how horrifying that had felt.

According to Josh, there had been three phones filming people in the bar. The witches had retrieved two of them, but the third was unaccounted for, and we had little idea what it had captured. We had gotten everyone out before they changed, but was that enough, or would the sight of people writhing in response to Mond somehow be enough to serve Red Blood, Samuel, and Rayna's aims?

"Quinn has a list and pictures of the Red Blood," Josh said as he alternated between his phone and the computer. "Hopefully we can identify them."

Identifying them was a start, but nothing more. The real challenge would be stopping them, especially now that they had magical allies. It couldn't be the easiest alliance to hold together, but it was enough to make life difficult for us, and the magic might be used for concealment as well as to fight back. Our enemies were combining, and that could make things very uncomfortable.

It was nearly forty minutes before the first transformation took place, Gavin easing back into his human form, and Kelly following along a moment later. Steven, seeing Gavin's success, took his turn, and soon everyone was back in human form, whispering reassuring words to each other as they came to terms with what they had been through.

London peered in from the corridor, saw the mass of naked people, and waved her hands. Clothes appeared one by one on the sad and weary weres. Then she settled in a seat at one of the desks, and Josh moved to sit opposite her. He looked up at me with an anxious expression.

"We need to figure out a way to inoculate you all against it," he said.

I nodded. What else was there to say? We had gotten lucky this time and kept the public spectacle to a minimum. If we didn't find some sort of protection, we might not be so lucky next time.

CHAPTER 24

"So you two are half-brothers, huh?" Detective Rankin raised a cynical eyebrow as she walked into the bar. "I didn't realize until our last call that this bar was a family business."

Josh reached out a hand to Detectives Rankin and Flynn, offering them his most winning smile. I followed his lead. The less confrontational we could make this, the better. It was about calming the authorities' fears, not stoking them.

"You're a fan of family businesses?" I asked, carefully couching the question as a positive rather than a negative. I shook the detectives' hands before taking a seat across the booth from them. The bar was quiet, only the four of us and Tabby present. The contractors couldn't start work on repairs for another two days, and until then we were stuck with an unusable business that smelled of ashes and damp carpet.

"Not every family business is a mob cover or a tax scam," Rankin said, as if she was still deciding which of those two we were.

I braced myself. If the cops had already decided that we were trouble, then they could make things difficult for a business that had been the site of a public disturbance, and which relied on its liquor license to turn a profit.

"You guys serving lunch?" Flynn asked, looking around with an amiable smile. "I could kill for a plate of wings right now."

"Sorry, detective," Josh said, "but we're not that kind of bar even when things are going well."

"Wait, did you bring me here under false pretenses?" Flynn turned his attention to Rankin, who rolled her eyes. But I wasn't buying this amiable old slacker act Flynn was putting on. There was a spark of brightness in his eyes that made me wary of what lay behind the smile.

"And who is this?" Rankin asked, nodding at Tabby. "Another lawyer?"

"Tabitha Creel," I said. "She's an IT consultant who maintains our security system here."

Every word of that was true. It just happened to miss the bigger picture, where Tabby was also a hacker and part of our were-animal pack, and had spent the previous twenty-four hours carefully adjusting the security recordings from the Mond incident.

"Here." Tabby slid a USB stick across the table.

"And this is?" Rankin picked the device up between the tips of her fingers, like it was a piece of trash she'd found lying on her lawn.

"All our footage from the night of the fire," I said. "I know you didn't ask, but you seemed to have concerns about what happened, so we thought we should help."

"Hm." Rankin looked straight at me, her gaze unwavering. "Let me guess. I'm going to see someone having a fit, just like witnesses described, and if I interview that guy, he'll say that he has epilepsy. Then I'll see a fire start in a trash can, but I won't be able to work out who chucked their cigarette into it. After that, a bit of chaos, before the sprinklers come on and the water shorts out the cameras. All perfectly timestamped to the events as you've described them, of course."

"Of course." My smile was as fake as hers. "Why would we have lied about what happened?"

Rankin tapped the USB stick against the table for a moment, her brow furrowed in thought.

My phone buzzed.

"You need to take that?" Flynn asked. "Cause we're not in a rush, if you want to just…"

"It can wait," I said, glancing down at David's name on the phone screen. "Just my wedding planners."

"Congratulations!" Flynn smiled widely. "There's nothing better in the world than getting married, am I right?"

"So I'm told. Now, you were asking about—"

My phone started buzzing again. I glared down at the same number as before.

"Are you sure you don't need to deal with that?" Rankin asked. "It seems urgent."

I glanced from her to my companions. I wouldn't have dared leave Tabby alone with a couple of cops. Between her poor social skills and her inability to read people, she would have said something suspicious at best, and probably gotten herself all the way to arrested. But with Josh to supervise her, I could probably risk a minute away, and it would be easier than having to keep rejecting calls through the rest of the interview.

"If you don't mind." I got up from the booth and walked to the back of the bar, where I could talk discreetly while watching the others.

"This had better be urgent," I snapped into the phone.

"Of course it's urgent!" David declared. "You haven't told us your opinion on the wines."

My fingers clenched around the phone so hard I was at risk of breaking it.

"You called me in the middle of the working day for that?" I growled angrily.

"We told you we needed answers this week. Now, for the red, I think the cheeky—"

"Enough! The wine can wait. I have important things to deal with."

"More important than your wedding?"

"More important than picking the right damn wine."

I looked across the room. Flynn looked like he was telling a joke to Tabby, who seemed deeply unimpressed, while Rankin leaned forward, elbows planted on the table, talking earnestly to a worried-looking Josh. I needed to get back there.

"Ethan, I can't believe you'd say a thing like that! You only get to do this once, one chance to make a perfect moment for you and Sky. Every little detail counts. What could possibly be more important than that?"

"Many things," I growled as Tabby pulled a face at Flynn, then leaned forward angrily, waving her finger in his face. Had he offered a wrong opinion on which was the best Marvel movie, or had he said something that insulted her computer skills? That look of fury from her could mean either thing, but only one of those conversations could lead to her saying something that caused suspicion about the security recordings.

David snorted. "This may not be important to you, but it's important to Sky, and you need to start treating it that way."

I sighed. He was right, the wedding was important to Sky, and that made it doubly important to me. I couldn't let David and Trent take over my every waking moment, but I needed to start taking some of their huge pile of queries seriously.

"I'll set some time aside this evening," I said. "Put a list of all the answers you still need from me in one email, and I'll deal with it."

"Just one email?"

"One. Email."

"Well, all right, but it's going to be a very long email, you've been ignoring far too many of our—"

I hung up. I'd done enough to appease the wedding planners, and now I needed to make sure we were all out of jail for the big day.

"...who is exactly nothing like Captain Kirk!" Tabby was saying as I returned to the table, her arms waving in the air. All three of the others were looking at her, Josh with concern, Rankin in annoyance, Flynn looking like he was about to burst out laughing. "I mean, how can you even mix those two up? I thought you had to be smart to be a cop, but even Jar Jar Binks wouldn't make such a basic mistake. Do you have to go through some sort of re-certification, because I really think that—"

"Tabby." I planted a hand firmly on her shoulder. "Not the time."

"But—"

"No."

She slid down her seat, arms crossed, scowling but at least subdued.

"Where were we?" I asked, taking a seat across from Rankin.

She looked at me, then down at the USB stick, before sliding the device into the pocket of her suit.

"I don't know what's really going on here, Mr. Charleston," she said, looking across the three of us. "But there's no sign that you're dealing drugs, and no bodies have dropped. If it's some sort of insurance fraud, well, your provider will have their own investigators, and good luck to them if they're hoping to get anything out of you."

"And if we're all innocent?" I asked.

She shrugged and stood. "Then you may never see us again." She glanced at Tabby. "And I'm okay with that. Come on, Flynn, we should get back to the precinct."

Flynn clambered out of the booth, still smiling amiably.

"Seriously, you should serve wings," he said to Josh. "People love that stuff."

Then the two of them were gone.

Josh and I let out a simultaneous sigh of relief.

"Those guys were jerks," Tabby said, glaring after the detectives.

"Probably," Josh said, grinning. "But so is Ethan, and he's much better at it than them. That's how I know that everything is going to be okay."

"So, Ariel and Sebastian," Winter said as we walked up from the sparring room into the main corridor of the retreat, both bruised and sweaty from a good hour of practicing new moves and working out our frustrations with our fists. "They're a couple now, right?"

I hesitated to answer. Ariel had flat out told me that she and Sebastian were sleeping with each other, but they hadn't exactly been announcing it around the pack, and things clearly weren't straightforward. How could they be when the leaders of two powerful factions started spending time together?

"I don't know what they'd call it," I said, trying to avoid giving anything away.

"But there's an it to be labeled?" Winter grinned. "I knew it."

"I didn't say—" A thud from the living room made us both stop in our tracks. It was followed a moment later by the sound of frantic panting.

By unspoken agreement, we both rushed to the sound. Sebastian lay in the middle of the living room, his body racked by spasms, his forehead wet with sweat. I could hear his heartbeat racing as his muscles writhed and twitched.

The musty smell of Mond hung around him like a noxious cloud. Ariel and Sky stood to one side, next to a table on which a bowl sat holding a trickle of blood, a knife lying next to it. They watched him, neither showing any sign of moving to help. There was an unmistakable tingle of magic in the air.

"Stop it," Winter demanded sternly. Her body was rigid with anger, and I could see her preparing to leap in.

"There's nothing for me to stop," Ariel replied calmly.

Winter started moving toward the witch, violent intent written across her face, but I grabbed her by the arm and held her back.

"You need to stop it now," she snapped.

"Winter, if I could do something, I would," Ariel said. "I can't stop his change."

And it was undoubtedly a change we were seeing, though a painful, forced one. Bones cracked and twisted, muscles spasmed, and hair burst through Sebastian's skin in irregular clumps. He howled in pain, and more weres came running from across the retreat. I hastily closed the door, keeping the rest of them out in the corridor. We didn't need everybody to see our Alpha in this state.

At last, Sebastian settled on the ground, fully transformed into a large wolf. His fur was matted with sweat and his chest rose and fell as he fought to get his breath back.

Winter sat down beside him, gently stroking his flank, offering reassurance to the injured beast that was our leader. Ariel walked toward them, but Winter's intense, steely gaze stopped her in her tracks. The witch flung up her hands and a defensive field of magic sprung up around her, an under-standable response to the intense hostility radiating from Winter.

"I didn't do this to him," Ariel said, still calm and composed.

"I know," Winter whispered.

But what Ariel didn't know, what she might never fully

understand, was the intense feeling of protectiveness that seeing Sebastian like this drew out of not only Winter but myself. It was taking all of my willpower to hold myself back instead of leaping to Sebastian's side and standing guard over him like a watchdog. In that moment, I didn't want to let an outsider like Ariel anywhere near him. I even understood why Winter hissed at Sky when she came near, associating her with what had been done to our Alpha. Protecting our leader was one of the deepest, most natural feelings in any were-animal, and seeing him like this, we couldn't help but respond.

We waited for half an hour in expectant silence, watching while Winter stroked Sebastian's fur and the rest of the pack whispered to each other outside the door. At last, his body started to jerk and twitch again, limbs contorting and back arching, fur receding a patch at a time as he went through the most graceless, uncomfortable change I had ever seen, forcing the wolf back to let him retake his human form. At last he lay naked in the middle of the room, looking up at us with a pained expression.

Ariel took a step forward and waved her hand, starting the spell that I had seen London use to summon clothes onto naked weres. But Sebastian held up a hand, stopping her.

"I'm fine," he said.

I approached, ready to help him to his feet, but he shook his head at me, then pushed himself upright, standing as if weighed down by a great weight.

And then I realized what was at stake. This had been a last attempt, one final spell that might protect weres from the Mond. If it didn't work, then we would have to take more extreme steps, finding a way to stop us from transforming at all except when the moon, Mercury, or an eclipse called for it. We would lose a part of what we were, to protect the rest. That was a terrible possibility for any were-animal to consider.

And now the responsibility for deciding on it lay with Sebastian. We had discussed it before, just a theory, and he had rejected it. We would be crippling ourselves, like a desperate beast gnawing off its own leg to get out of a trap. It was a dreadful option, an ultimate backstop for if other plans failed, one we had never thought that we would have to accept. Except that we had tried the other plans, and they had failed. Now we needed to think the unthinkable, and it was Sebastian's duty to face that decision.

I didn't envy him.

A decision this monumental could not be made alone. At Sebastian's call, the Alphas and Betas of the other packs came to the retreat, summoned not just by the command of the Elite, but by the deathly serious tone in which he had spoken to each of them. One by one or in small groups, they came into the living room, while Sebastian and I stood waiting with Sky.

Everyone knew what challenges we had been facing, and they had to have some idea of what was to come. They seemed pensive, concern visible behind their stoic expressions. The emotional tone of the room was as close to a funeral as to a grand council.

My own feelings matched those around me. If we went ahead with what Sebastian had planned, then I would only be able to change when the full moon called me to. For the rest of the month, I would be trapped in my human body, unable to break free and run as the animal that lay inside. I would lose all the advantages that came with that transformation, not just the strength and speed but the joy of being myself. Its only advantage would be that we couldn't be changed by the Mond. It was a terrible choice that we had to make, but if it was that or be exposed by the plotting of our enemies, we were left with little choice.

Standing next to me while the room filled, Sky blinked away tears. As was so often the case, her uncontrolled emotions were taking a grip on the weres around her, and most of the room was staring at her.

"Sky," I said, leaning in to whisper to her, "do you need to take a moment?"

This was enough of a problem when it affected our own pack, but now it could be crippling. Sky's emotions were spilling out, overriding the thoughts and feelings of the people around her, threatening to swamp any discussion we might have with the overwhelming weight of her sorrow.

Then three more guests walked in, and all attention turned away from Sky. London, Josh, and Ariel entered the room, outsiders in a gathering of weres. The response to them wasn't exactly hostile, but it was far from welcoming. They were a symbol of how horribly wrong things had gone, and how much was at stake.

Slowly, calmly, keeping his own emotions concealed, Sebastian explained to the gathered weres what had been happening with the Mond and everything around it. Fury, frustration, even horror crossed their faces as he talked it through. While the Midwest Pack had been the target of this activity, it was an attack on the secrecy of all weres.

"Why can't we just find the Mond and destroy it?" asked Kyle, the new West Coast Alpha. I had been too wrapped up in Mond and wedding planning to follow the details of his challenge against Mateo. That in itself was a sign of the strain we were under, that something so politically important hadn't been at the top of my list.

"It's not possible," Sebastian said, his voice tight. "There was too much distributed among Samuel, Rayna, and the Red Blood. There's no way of guaranteeing we'll get it all."

It was a tense moment. Kyle's question wasn't just a

request for information. There was an implied challenge there to Sebastian's decision-making and to his authority. Any meeting of ranking weres was shot through with these political considerations, but it was particularly prominent in that moment, where a challenge for Elite might be the answer for someone who disliked Sebastian's plan.

"The options we have are either to come out or give up our ability to change on our own," Joan said, her tone part weariness at the whole business, part her usual attempt to calm tempers and keep the peace.

Last time these leaders had gathered, it had been for a similarly difficult decision, about whether to reveal ourselves to the world. That had also been triggered by an attack on the Midwest Pack, a fact that I was painfully aware of. This new decision would be decided as much by the limits of everyone's patience with our pack as it would by what was best for all the weres.

"Will coming out be so bad?" Fallon stepped out into the middle of the room, her eyes shining with an optimism that no one else shared, an optimism she clearly hoped to spread. "We are the unknown to most people; but there are some humans who are aware of our existence. Those people will come forward on our behalf. We've all dealt with humans and they lived, so they know we aren't monsters."

Kyle scoffed and gave a flick of his hand, dismissing Fallon's arguments like he was brushing off a fly.

"That's not helpful, Kyle," Joan said, her tone carrying just the slightest hard edge of rebuke.

Kyle looked steadily at her, then at Sebastian, who was letting his displeasure show. The West Coast Alpha was new to his authority, riding high on the status it gave him, on the thrill of being in charge. Now he had been placed in a room with the only man who outranked him, the only person with the power to put him in his place, and his desire to fight back against that was only just suppressed.

"That was rude and unnecessary, Kyle," Sebastian said. "But it is being foolishly optimistic to think humans will come forward on our behalf. That people won't fear us."

"Or that you won't cause strife in the otherworld," Ariel said. Hostile glares shifted onto her, this outsider speaking up in a meeting of weres, but she ignored them. "Coming out is a terrible decision if you have other options, and you do have other options. It's not ideal but your anonymity will be preserved."

A flicker of confusion crossed Sebastian's face, only visible for a fraction of a second, but Ariel caught it.

"I'm with you, Sebastian," she said, her gaze shifting briefly to Joan before settling back on him. "I told you last night that I will support any decision."

Just what we needed, one more petty complication to derail the discussion, as Sebastian's new romantic entanglement marked her territory in front of his ex.

"We appreciate your help and your role in helping us deal with this matter," Joan said with quiet firmness, "but it is still a pack concern. I'd appreciate it if you would take that into consideration."

"It is your business, but contrary to what Rayna believes, the humans won't stop," Ariel said. "Once you expose yourselves, their imaginations will go rampant. All the stories they speculated about or marked off as fantasy will have merit. They will pursue those things. Logic won't rule their actions, paranoia will. People who aren't of the otherworld will be accused, and life will change and turn upside-down." She had started out relaxed and confident, despite the hostility around her, but her words gained urgency as she spoke. She paused to catch her breath, then continued. "I understand your hesitation to do this because it can't be reversed, but being able to control your animal in the manner that you do now is fairly new. You all will adapt." She looked directly at Joan. "To save your son, I think it was an option. And I agreed, but honestly, I was confident that a way to protect him without having to expose your existence would be found." She turned back to Sebastian. "I agreed in front of the others because it needed to be done. I know how the were-animals are seen, and your enemies are just waiting for a reason to turn against the pack. Honestly, you've made it hard not to hate you."

The gathered weres fell silent, stunned by the blunt force of Ariel's words. It was easy to shrug off the opinions of outsiders when they were opponents, but Ariel was an ally, speaking directly about how the rest of the world viewed us, and we didn't come across well. It made the pressure to make the right decision even more intense. After all, if we got this wrong, we could face the wrath of the whole supernatural world.

"The elves created the Mond," Kyle said, "so it only exists because of their magic, right?"

"Yes," Josh answered, "and in order to make it ineffective, the elves associated with Gregoire and his bloodline would have to die. Like witches', elven magic doesn't die with the person, but is passed down to their descendant. Innocents would be paying for the sins of another. Being penalized for something that they probably wouldn't have done. Not all of the elves are against us. I know you would never suggest genocide or containment for the actions of a few, right?"

Kyle flushed, but he didn't deny it. The fear that filled the room could push any of us to extremes if we let it take hold.

"Can their magic be stopped?" Fallon asked. "If you are able to take away their magic, can't that nullify the Mond?"

Ariel opened her mouth to respond, then hesitated. For the first time, I felt a flicker of hope. Maybe there was another way out of this.

"I don't know." Ariel exchanged a thoughtful look with London and Josh. "We had been trying to inoculate against it; we never considered removing the magic from it."

I struggled to keep my expression blank, not to give away my desperate desire for this to work. I didn't want to give up the power to change at will, but I couldn't give in to false hope, not when so many people were relying on me and Sebastian for leadership. Still, something in the room had shifted, and now all eyes were on the witches, not with the hostility that had previously prevailed but with a sense of yearning.

"We don't know if it will work," Ariel said. "If it doesn't…"

"We know," Sebastian said, the words heavy as lead. "We use the final resort."

His posture had changed, just as the tone of the room had. He wasn't a receptive leader gathering the opinions of his advisers anymore; he was a decisive one taking charge.

"To counter elf magic, we'll need an elf."

"I can do it," Sky said. "I can mirror their magic. I've done it before."

"Mirroring their magic isn't the same," London replied. "We will need the blood and magic of an elf. A Makellos elf. The stronger the better. Gregoire was a Makellos?"

Her fingers darted through the air, starting to sketch the outline of a spell. Green and orange script glowed in the air, its components dancing to the rhythm laid out by her hands, shifting and reforming as she sought the shape she needed. Josh stepped back to watch, and I could tell by his face that this was work worthy of admiration.

London froze in her spell weaving and looked around at the rest of us.

"Are you all going to watch me or find an elf? I have the easy part—you getting an elf to agree to help is going to be the difficult part."

Ariel went pale, and London's eyes went wide as she realized that she'd said something she shouldn't. Immediately, she turned her whole focus back to the spell, ignoring our inquisitive looks.

"Why will I have a hard time getting a Makellos elf?" Sebastian asked. "Gideon is one."

"Then go get him," Ariel said in a flat voice.

"You seem to think I'll have a problem doing that."

She sighed. "It's not my information to tell."

"Can I have a moment?" Sebastian nodded toward his office.

Ariel turned away from the spell to face him, her expression stern, arms folded.

"No. We are working, and there's nothing we can discuss in your office that can't be said here." She straightened her shoulders as she met Sebastian's gaze. "Being allies with this pack is hard. Period. It puts a target on us and taints our reputation. I've accepted it as the consequences. Not only do I see the value of an alliance with you all, I respect and admire the dedication that you all have for the safety and health of the pack."

The two leaders squared off against each other, only a sliver of space between them. The warmth was gone from Ariel's voice, as was the fondness I had seen in Sebastian's face when he looked at her before. This was purely professional, their private lives carefully set aside. Part of me wished that I could manage this with Sky, but another part was glad that I couldn't. The thought of cutting off our closeness, however briefly, was just too sad.

"But make no mistake, I see you," Ariel continued. "I see all of you. And sometimes the pack is just as reckless and cruel as the other races. I don't think it's just about power but self-preservation as well. And with all your posturing and power plays, at the core of it, you are the most vulnerable. The easiest to be found out. But I don't agree with all your tactics. Let me be very clear about that. I didn't agree with the elves' rule to contain dark elves, although I understood the fear. I didn't agree with the witches' fear and the cruelty with which they dealt with were-animals who showed magical ability. And I definitely don't agree with some of the things that were suggested here today, by your Alphas."

She shot a deeply judgmental look at Kyle. "I have responsibilities to my witches, as you do to your people. So, if you want to find out if something has changed between you and Gideon, I suggest you ask him. I will not get between you and him on that. If you can get an elf, you need to do it quickly. Each moment that passes increases the likelihood of you being exposed." She turned her back on Sebastian, bringing her focus to the spell that London was still weaving in the air. "If it can't be achieved today, I expect the other option to be performed immediately."

"The witches' help in this matter has been appreciated," Sebastian said coldly, "but it is a good practice to know where you stand when making commands about what we do. You don't have that power."

"You're right. But I've made my opinion known. This is a last-ditch effort and I hope it works—I do—but if you decide not to pick the other option, you've made your choice. A reckless choice that will put us in danger as well." She looked over her shoulder at him with narrowed eyes. "I will remember that selfishness."

A deathly silence fell. It wasn't Sky's uncontrolled emotions that filled the space now, but the terrible tension between Sebastian and Ariel. Who broke it and how could decide whether the fragile peace between Pack and Creed even survived this moment. I saw Kyle preparing to speak, and dreaded what would come next, but I didn't know what I could say to make things better or to move us on from here.

"If we have limited time, it's probably best that you get Gideon," Joan said quietly, looking at Sebastian.

He dragged his gaze away from Ariel. "You're right. I need to handle this."

"Yeah, she's right," Ariel muttered.

"I'm sorry, I missed that," Sebastian said, but with a softer tone than before, a hint of humor shining through.

"No, you didn't," she replied.

Sebastian gestured to me, Sky, Winter, and Josh, then headed for the door. We followed him, drawn along without question in the wake of our Alpha. Behind us, the tension restraining everyone in the room finally unraveled, and a chatter of conversation started up. I sighed in relief. We hadn't burned all our political bridges yet.

Rain poured as we got out of the car in the parking area outside Gideon's home. It pelted down with growing ferocity while the wind battered at us and thunder rumbled over-head. This wasn't just a chance downpour. This was the disapproval of the elves, expressed through their elemental magic.

Drenched within a few paces, we strode up the sidewalk, and then up the steps to the door of the residence. I half expected to be kept standing in the rain, but the door opened immediately and we were allowed inside.

Uniformed guards stood to attention at either side of the entrance hall, the brass buttons on their tunics gleaming, while we stood between them, shivering and dripping on the tiled floor. Gideon's way of running the elves had clearly grown more formal since we were last there, more like Liam, the Makellos with whom he had vied for dominance of elven politics. Liam lacked Gideon's large power base, but the fervor of his followers and their commitment to the pure elven cause gave him disproportionate strength, a strength Gideon had apparently decided to mimic.

A guard stepped out of the line and, with a curl of his finger, gestured for us to follow. Leaving a trail of sodden footprints in our wake, we headed past the living room, a series of offices, and a trophy room full of portraits and historical documents. At last, we reached a massive room at the back of the building, with floor-to-ceiling windows. Through these, a spectacular garden was visible, filled with exotic plants and strange trees, a small slice of Elysian brought into the mundane world. The room itself contained a long desk at the far end, its wood as elaborately carved as the arms and legs of the high-backed, patterned-silk chairs behind it. This room had been set up to impress and intimidate, every bit as much as the guards in the entrance hall.

Sky was shivering so I stepped closer to her, offering the warmth of my body to help counteract the cold from the storm.

"That was a hell of a welcome," she said quietly.

"Yeah," Sebastian said. "I don't think we're welcome here anymore."

We waited in silence for fifteen minutes, expecting Gideon to appear at any moment. After letting us in promptly, this was clearly unnecessary, just a way to put us in our place. Perhaps it would have impressed elves, but to a bunch of weres it was just irritating. At last, Sebastian looked at his watch, exhaled irritably, and made for the door.

A clicking of heels on floorboards stopped him.

Abigail walked in, her platinum-blond hair hanging in a French braid over the shoulder of her clingy red dress. The way Winter's gaze followed her across the room, I suspected that Winter was thinking about when the two of them had been together, before Abigail's arrogance and scheming had put an end to that relationship. Perhaps Abigail was aware of the effect she was having or perhaps she just took it for granted, because she walked with an unshakable swagger.

She took a seat behind the desk and looked up, waiting for us to come and pay court to her. But we were there for her brother, not the woman who had failed to become the power behind the throne. None of us budged.

"I need to speak with Gideon," Sebastian said.

"I know you feel that the world is at your beck and call," Abigail replied. "I'm here to ensure you that it is not. My brother is coming eventually. He's handling other problems that have arisen."

She shot me an angry look, then returned her attention to Sebastian, and then on to Winter. For a moment, her cold hostility faltered into something like desire, but Winter responded with clear animosity, her eyes flashing into the slitted pupils of a snake, and Abigail's affection gave way to her usual calculated poise. We continued to stand in silence while she drummed her lacquered nails against the desk.

More footsteps preceded Gideon's arrival. He strode in wearing tight pants and a tailcoat, like he was playing dress-up as a founding father, and went to sit beside his sister. It was uncanny to see them together, those aquiline faces so akin that they could almost have been twins.

"Unexpected guests," he said, looking at us with violet eyes that carried the cold menace of storm clouds.

"You made that painfully clear," Sebastian said. The debate at the retreat had already drained him of patience, and he had little left for petty power plays.

"I'm sorry I can't be more accommodating to the very people who destroyed Elysian," Gideon said. "Are you here to apologize?"

Sebastian laughed. An elven courtier would have responded with more subtlety and finesse, but we weren't here to make the elven lord feel big. We still all stood exactly where we had stopped when we came in, not shifting an inch toward where our hosts sat waiting for us.

"We need to borrow your magic," Sebastian said.

Gideon snorted and his mouth settled into a cruel sneer.

"I've repaid my debt to you tenfold. We are no longer able to provide unconditional assistance. You ensured that when you allowed your Beta to destroy our land. And instead of an apology, you have the audacity to request more favors. Your arrogance is showing."

"And so is yours," Sebastian replied. "I'm not here to ask for a favor, I'm here to give you the opportunity to right a wrong."

Gideon leapt to his feet and leaned over the table, fists planted on the ancient wood, staring at Sebastian.

"Right a wrong! Are you serious? You destroyed Elysian. The grounds are fallow, and it will be years before anything can be grown from the soil. Ethan made sure of that, and you feel that I have something to right?"

"Yes." Now Sebastian moved, stalking over to face the twin elves across their desk. Instead of a supplicant coming to ask a favor, he stood like a parent looking down on a pair of misbehaving children, offering only judgment. "Your land being destroyed was the doing of your people. Before you even ask, if the situation was reversed, would I be obligated to right a wrong? The answer is yes. But here is where we are quite different. Everyone judges us for our perceived carelessness and lack of respect for magic and the rules. Where is your judgment? The sole purpose of the Mond is to force us to change. What purpose does that serve other than to have control over us?"

Gideon frowned and his righteous anger faltered. Had he been caught by surprise, or was this guilt catching up with him? Over the years, I had learned to see the deepest problem of the elves, that their lack of empathy meant that they often failed to recognize how things looked from the other side. Gideon's greatest strength was that he could overcome this, but that didn't mean it came naturally to him.

While something in Sebastian's words had gotten through to Gideon, his sister sat unmoved, indifferent to their role in an attack on us. No, not indifferent, complicit. She had known what was happening, she had approved, and now Sebastian could see it in her response.

"Gideon, you might not have known of this, but your sister did," he said. "There has to be some accountability for this."

Gideon closed his eyes and pressed his fingers to the bridge of his nose, trying to release the tension that had been building in his face.

"I didn't agree with its creation," he said. The words were a defense, the tone a confession.

"I know you wouldn't have, but as the leader of the elves you have an obligation to help me fix it. I will not mince words; I would not be here if I didn't need you. I realize I've come to you for a debt that has been satisfied. But as I am culpable for the actions of those under my rule and even of lone were-animals—because I pride myself in making sure they aren't causing trouble—I hold you to the same standard."

Gideon sank back into his seat, taking his place beside Abigail. She leaned in and whispered in his ear, malice turning up the corners of her lips. Gideon frowned and clasped his hands in front of him, resting his chin on them. As Abigail spoke, his eyes drifted from Sebastian to me and Sky, looking at us with terrible seriousness.

Abigail sat back, smiling smugly.

"It is my understanding that there have been failings in an effort to contain Ethan's and Sky's magic?" Gideon said. "They are quite the force, don't you think? Magic so strong that it's summoned the Faeries. So virulent and uncontrollable that it can't be contained by powerful witches—or so the rumors have suggested. I'm inclined to believe them. People are concerned with the level of power and destruction you will have at your fingertips with a pair of weres who can do great damage. Ethan and Sky's union has caused a lot of concern, and I'm sure you are aware of that."

My hand curled into a fist as I bit back a response. This wasn't about me and Sky, it was about the poisonous plants the elves had created. Abigail was just using us to shift responsibility, to avoid dealing with the consequences of her own actions. I would have been angry if this had just been about me, but they were lashing out at Sky as well, and that made me seethe with outrage.

"And yet whatever goes on between them has nothing to do with you," Sebastian said sharply.

"It does," Abigail said, apparently forgetting that she was meant to be the power behind the throne, not the one speaking from it. "Unfortunately, as much as we like to believe we can live independent of one another without the actions of others affecting us, it isn't true, now is it? You all doing forbidden magic affected us all because it awakened the Faeries. How many years had they been dormant? Then Sky joins your pack—the world as we know it changes. We deal with people like Samuel … rumors swirl about the mad witch who wants to get rid of magic. And if we map it back— his actions, the fervency of them, the potential for his scheme to be made possible—who do we find entangled in it? Your little wolf! Shall I go on with my list? Because it is quite extensive."

"You can read from whatever goddamn list you'd like," I said, as calmly as I could, just a hint of my rage creeping into the words. "It doesn't change a thing. Whatever goes on with me and Sky isn't your business, nor will it ever be."

"Fine, then we have no more business with you," Gideon said.

He sat back in his chair, his sister leaning in toward him with a proud smile on her face. Booted feet marched in sync down the hallway, coming to escort us out.

Josh's hands shot up. There was a flicker of magic and the door slammed shut. A translucent barrier fell, closing Gideon and Abigail in with four angry were-animals and their friendly witch.

"We need your magic to undo the Mond," Sebastian said,

his voice dropping into the growl of a feral beast, his restraint almost exhausted. "I'm not asking. Don't make me force you. I won't list your number of transgressions. Gregoire put us in this situation and you will get us out of it or so help me—"

"Enough with your threats," Gideon snarled.

"If only it were." Sebastian glanced at his watch. "We are running out of time. Send your guards away and come with us."

Their movements as perfectly matched as their faces, Gideon and Abigail stood and crossed their arms defiantly. If they thought that they could face us down after everything that had happened, then they badly misjudged the anger of the pack.

"What do you want from us?" Sky asked, her voice little more than a whisper.

Hard as it was to admit it, she had found the smart play, one that the rest of us had missed. Abigail always wanted something, and if we knew what, we would at least have some kind of leverage.

"You all have the protected objects in your possession," she said. "They have been the source of a great deal of problems, and it has been proven that you cannot be trusted with them. In exchange for our help, we want them. All of them."

"No," Sebastian said. "You penalizing us with that is equivalent to me wanting retribution for the sleeper that we found on your brother that eventually infected Kelly. Or making you continue to pay for our help in recovering your creatures that escaped from the dark forest, or for Mason putting together a group of mercenaries to put us down like rabid animals. *Or* the fact that I believe you had something to do with my abduction." That last was an angry hiss, a hint at the other side of the Mond issue, that it had been given to people whose sole aim was to hurt weres. "I'm feeling really fucking vengeful about that. No, you don't get any protective objects. You will get one thing and one thing only, the promise that I won't hold you accountable for those things. End our alliance, fine. But know that if you ever need us, we will not be available to you. Ever."

A flash of panic crossed Abigail's face as Sebastian drew the dots from her to a range of crimes, including an attack on her own brother. But it was too late now for her to undo what had been said, and Gideon's expression was shifting, looking at her with fresh suspicion as previously separate pieces fell into place. Perhaps for the first time, he was seeing how she manipulated not just their opponents but him.

"You know how it works," Sebastian continued. "We can't stop the change when exposed to the Mond. Eventually we will be discovered by humans. Before when this was a possibility, I promised to protect everyone from it, and I accepted it was our actions that caused it. Now it's the elves' actions that have put us in this predicament—do you think that protection still stands? We will be at a disadvantage if you decline to help us, but I will ensure that it is indeed a Pyrrhic victory for you."

Gideon swallowed, struggling to keep his expression neutral, to hide what he was thinking. But it was clear that Sebastian had made his point, the unspoken part as well as the open one. Whatever the rights or wrongs of the situation, picking a fight with the Midwest Pack would put Gideon and his people in danger, while remaining our allies would grant him powerful support. That mattered far more than whatever poison his sister had been dripping in his ear, words which he himself was finally starting to doubt.

He waved a hand toward the exit.

"We'll follow you out," he said, surrendering to the inevitable.

Abigail rose and headed in the opposite direction.

"Where are you going?" Sebastian asked, taking command.

"I need a jacket," Abigail announced haughtily. "Or have we been stripped of all our autonomy and have to get your permission to address our basic needs?"

She was responding to Sebastian, but her angry glare settled on her brother, punishment for his surrender.

"We'll wait for you in the car," Sebastian said.

Out in the street, we waited by Sebastian's car while Gideon took his seat in the back of a limousine, chauffeured by one of his uniformed guards. The rainstorm was over, and around us puddles were evaporating in the sunshine.

"Abigail's taking her time," Sky said, glancing back at the door of the house.

"You know how it is, women and clothes," I said with a wry grin.

"Hey, I'm not that bad!" she said, then looked at me in concern. "Am I?"

I shook my head, laughing. "Hardly ever, and it's always worth the wait. This, though, is going to be different; someone is making a point the only way she still can."

"Trust me," Winter said bitterly, "Abigail has turned the wardrobe-based delay into an art form."

After twenty minutes, Sebastian stopped glancing at his watch and made to stride over to Gideon's car, ready to demand that he drag out his sister. And in that moment, as if by magic, Abigail appeared, not just in a jacket but in a completely different outfit, a dark shirt and slacks replacing the red dress for a dramatic, brooding look. She stared at Sebastian, as if daring him to complain, but he just shrugged. He had won, and none of her petty games could change that.

"Come on," he said, getting into the car. "We've got magic to do."

CHAPTER 25

We gathered once again in the living room of the pack, ready for the witches to perform their new spell. To ensure that we all benefited from the protective magic, Sebastian had summoned members of every family of were-animals; not just the wolves who were the most plentiful weres, or the coyotes, panthers, and other hunting beasts that ran with them. There was Winter, whose animal form was a snake; Cheyenne of the equidae, the elusive weres who turned into horses; and last to arrive, the towering form of Dakota of the ursidae, who looked a lot like a bear even when he wasn't transformed into one. Representatives of different families and packs crowded the room, waiting for the work to begin, while Gideon and Abigail pressed themselves into the wall, as out of the way as they could be.

It was good to see everyone gathered like this, and to see an end to the threat of Mond in sight, though I wasn't ready to relax about it yet. The spell was new and untested, so things could easily go wrong. It didn't help that our fate wasn't in our own hands but in that of the witches. That left me feeling nervous, the loss of control like a claw clenching my innards. But I felt hope too, seeing the possibility that we might break free from the threat of the Mond. This was the light at the end of a dark tunnel.

The witches had taken over the middle of the room, lining up their ingredients on a low table. Herbs, bowls, crystals, knives, the full regalia of modern magic. Notes about the spell hovered in the air around them, reminders that they dismissed one by one as the pieces were put in place. Their expressions were serious, yet there was a sense of excitement to their movements as they prepared to face an unprecedented challenge.

Ariel, her usually calm, controlled movements now stiff with tension, picked up a pair of knives, each with an elaborately decorated handle and a simple, razor-sharp blade. Just as there had been a terrible burden on Sebastian earlier, deciding what our fate would be, now that weight fell upon her, in carrying out his decision and ensuring the future of all weres.

I was glad to see that she was taking this seriously. I would rather have our future decided by someone who was nervous from feeling the consequences than by someone who didn't understand or didn't care. This moment was significant for Ariel as well as us.

Sebastian took the knife offered to him, but Abigail held back, looking at the offered blade like it was muck on the bottom of her shoe. She stayed pressed against the wall, as if hoping that she might fall through it and escape all of our company.

Gideon looked at his sister sharply. His whole attitude toward her seemed to have changed, his reserves of patience running out fast. The sibling bond that had given her such power over him was fraying, threatening to unravel entirely, and I was pleased to think that we had played a part in freeing him from her influence. When she only glared back at him, he took the knife himself.

"Let's just get this over with and then we go home," he said.

He ran the knife across the back of his arm and let blood flow into a small brass bowl, the patter of liquid against metal the only sound in the room. Abigail did the same, her blood mingling with her brother's. Sebastian followed, his blood running into a larger bowl engraved with images of nature. Then Ariel took the knife from him and handed it to Dakota. One by one, the representatives of the different families stepped forward and added a little of their lives to the larger bowl, until it held a pool of crimson liquid given by every kind of were.

The witches, Josh and seven of the Creed, set the bowls down on the table and chanted an incantation. As the words spilled from their lips, magic pulsed through the room. Inside me, the spirit shade reached out, its curiosity stirred by this sudden welling up of power, and I sucked in a deep breath as I summoned the strength to hold it in. But something about this magic wasn't to the spirit's tastes. It touched a tendril, turned away, and receded into the dark.

Magic swirled around us, natural and unnatural combining. The witches' eyes turned as black as the void and they clutched at each other, seeking support as their bodies trembled with power.

The blood rose from the bowls and formed two scarlet lines that hovered, rippling, in the air. They hung parallel to each other for a moment before moving together at a gesture from the witches. But something in those lines of blood resisted being combined. They pushed away from each other, like magnets forced apart by the power of their poles. The blood drew close at each push from the witches, only to fly apart. The witches chanted ever louder, their expressions growing more intense, and the whole room seemed to hold its breath. But something was broken. The blood would not mix.

My hope withered away. We had put all our faith in an untested spell, and it had failed. We would have to fall back on the other plan, to give up the chance to change when we wanted to. We were going to have to give away a part of ourselves. I could already feel myself grieving at the thought of that loss.

Suddenly, Ariel looked up, as if she had heard a gunshot or a cry of alarm. Her hand shot out and Abigail slammed into the wall so hard that the plaster cracked around her. The elf's small, smug smile turned into a sneer as she struggled to break free of the magic pinning her in place, while her brother watched with narrowed eyes.

"Keep the spell going," Ariel said as she stepped away from the group. "Don't break it, or we'll have to start over."

The lines of blood shivered, shifted closer, then rebounded again.

Ariel ran her hands up Abigail's legs and across her body, searching for something. When she reached the left arm, she stopped and yanked back Abigail's sleeve, revealing a bracelet that coiled all the way up the arm, small spikes on its inner surface burying themselves in the elf's flesh. Her brow furrowing in concentration, Ariel studied the bracelet, running her fingers down its length. Then she pressed on it near the middle, the spikes unclamped, and the whole thing tumbled to the floor. She kicked it away, then stepped back, releasing her power so that Abigail fell to the ground, her face full of loathing.

I didn't know what I was looking at, but the implication was clear. Abigail had tried to sabotage the spell, to leave us exposed to attacks by Mond. Even when Gideon agreed to help, she couldn't be trusted not to betray us. Anger curdled to hate in my stomach as I glared at her.

As smoothly as if she had never left, Ariel stepped back into the circle of witches and rejoined the chanting. The lines of blood inched together, each starting to unravel, and for a moment I feared that the whole spell was about to fall apart. But the threads of blood combined, meshing, mingling, reforming, until they took the spiral shape of a double helix. The chanting changed, the magic shifted, and the blood vanished, leaving only a lingering red haze and a distant tingle of magic.

The blackness faded from the witches' eyes as they turned to each other, some looking pleased, others uncertain.

London picked up a bag of Mond from the table and pulled out a handful.

"Who do we test?" she asked.

"Probably best to check us all," Sebastian said, gesturing to the representatives of the different were-animal families.

London took a deep breath, then blew a handful of the dust into his face. He blinked as it got in his eyes, then tensed, waiting for the spasms of transformation to take hold.

Nothing happened.

I smiled widely as my feelings finally caught up with reality. It had worked. We were going to be safe.

All at once, everyone in the room seemed to be grinning, apart from Abigail.

London moved on to test the other weres, all of whom resisted the power of the Mond. As she did it, Abigail walked quietly toward the door, Gideon trailing behind her. We hadn't fully broken her hold over him, at least not yet.

"What was that?" Sebastian asked, looking from them to the discarded bracelet, which lay inches from Abigail's feet.

She stopped, glancing from him to the door, and then at the hostile weres between her and freedom.

"Spitze," she said defiantly, and stood waiting for some response. When none came, she stooped and picked up the bracelet.

As the elves continued toward the door, Joan made a move to intercept them. She wasn't easily riled, but when someone tried to harm her family or her pack, she took it extremely seriously.

"Joan," Sebastian said, his soft voice a warning. We had gotten what we wanted, and any violence now would only cause problems later. Reluctantly, she stepped back and let them leave.

Joan turned to the witches, looking for an explanation of what Abigail had been doing with the bracelet.

"It neutralizes blood," Ariel said stiffly. "It makes it undetectable as elven, which is why the spell wasn't working."

Joan clearly had more questions, but she held them back, as aware as any of us of the awkward atmosphere between her and Ariel.

As the weres and witches set to celebrating their victory, I watched the elves' limousine drive away. I felt a huge sense of relief. Their people had almost destroyed us, and even at the last minute, Abigail had tried to thwart our plans. But now the problem of Mond was dealt with, a threat against the pack neutralized, and the united front between Abigail and Gideon shaken. Things were going our way.

***

I sat on the sofa in my living room, a book propped up on my knees. Only three days on from the ritual to protect us from the Mond, and I was already mired in other issues, looking at improvements to pack security while trying to finish preparations for an upcoming court case, shifting between the book and my laptop as I tried to balance the different issues running through my mind. These included an email from Quinn with a video message attached, which I hadn't had time to watch yet.

"You are going to love what I sent you," the email announced, but I ignored it. Last time Quinn had told me I would love something, it had been a trailer for a film about

Sherlock Holmes's sister. It was safe to say that Quinn and I had very different tastes, and that he still hadn't accepted it.

Sky emerged from the kitchen. In one hand she held an apple, in the other a bowl of ice cream topped with cookies, caramel, and fudge.

"We had dinner half an hour ago," I said with a frown.

She stopped and looked around the room in an overdramatic fashion.

"What's the matter?" I asked, making space so she could sit next to me.

"I was just looking for the judgment-free zone. Is it over there?" She jerked her head at the chair she had brought from her place, its synthetic red fabric woefully out of place amid my leather sofas and mahogany tables. It was the ugliest thing in our whole house, made worse by the multicolored comforter Sky had flung over it and the disorderly heap of battered books that sat in a stack on the adjacent table. I wanted to get used to it, to accept its presence as a happy sign of the fact that she had fully moved in with me, but I could barely bring myself to look at it. Years of work refining the tasteful decor of this place had been undone by a single tacky chair.

Perhaps we could redecorate. There must be some version of our home where that red monstrosity would fit in, or at least not be so obtrusive. Was buying a whole new home going too far to solve this problem?

"We can move," I said, looking from the chair to Sky.

She licked the melting top of the heap of ice cream. "I just moved in here. I'm not moving again."

"Fine. The house can be decorated again."

Sky looked slowly around the room, taking in the sculptures and canvases, the tasteful, comfortable furniture and the safely neutral walls. I dreaded to think what alternatives she was considering. Would I end up living in some nightmare of bright bubblegum colors for the sake of love?

"What are we going to love?" she asked, licking her spoon as she looked at my screen.

"Don't know yet."

Based on past precedent, Sky was more likely to appreciate any offering from Quinn than I was, so I opened the email and hit play on the attachment.

This didn't look like any movie trailer I had ever seen, and a moment later I realized why. The camera was following Alexandria, a were-jackal loner who we allowed to live in the territory of the Midwest Pack. She didn't want the complications that came from pack life, which I could just about understand, and she had shown that she could be trusted when left to her own devices. Judging by her leggings, loose sweater, and sensible shoes, she was probably on her way to or from one of the dance classes she attended with Kelly, and she was clearly oblivious to the presence of the camera. Now that I knew who was involved, I had a good idea of what I was about to see. I smiled in anticipation.

Something had grabbed Alexandria's attention. Her gaze sharpened and she looked around, took a deep breath, and frowned. Suddenly, a passerby brought up a hand and flung herbs in Alexandria's face. Leaves in the familiar autumnal colors of Mond drifted down around her.

Alexandria cried out as if she had been hit. Her acting lessons were clearly paying off, and I grinned as I saw the effect. Even as the camera zoomed in closer, people were rushing to her side, while others tried to grab the guy who had thrown the herbs.

"What did you do to her?" a woman asked angrily.

"Don't let him get away," a man demanded.

Concerned people crowded around Alexandria, asking if she was okay, helping her wipe away the dust. Whoever was holding the camera, they had chosen their spot well, and managed to keep Alexandria in sight even as the crowd gathered. She sneezed violently a couple of times and looked around with a convincing expression of fear.

"Why would they do this?" she asked, her lower lip trembling.

The camera stayed on her, but by now its owner had to be getting frustrated. Someone had probably promised them the chance to see a were-animal transform, and instead all they had was a woman sneezing and looking tearful while others swirled indignantly around her.

"Was it a prank?" someone asked.

"Not much of a prank if it was," another pointed out irately.

"I'm okay," Alexandria said, brushing dust and herbs from her clothes. "It just startled me. It came out of nowhere."

Her voice stayed soft, her body and face radiating vulnerability. And then, just for a moment, she looked straight at the camera, and animal fury blazed in her eyes. At that moment, the video cut off.

I had to give credit to Alexandria, it was possible she might make it as a star after all. It was just a shame that she couldn't use this performance as part of her audition reel; after all, she couldn't tell the world that this was just acting.

We'd laid out bait for Red Blood, and they had taken it. They had wasted their time, made fools of themselves again, and probably shaken the faith of some of their supporters. I closed the laptop, feeling very satisfied.

"Why would they keep that when it only makes them look bad?" Sky asked. "Reinforcing that they are nut cases. They believe a magical dust will change humans to animals or that people who shift to animals exist."

"I'm sure Quinn acquired it before they could delete it," I said, knowing full well that he had been poised and waiting for his chance for two days.

"How did he get it?"

"I don't know, and I like it that way."

"Good, plausible deniability," Sky said in a half-mocking tone. "That's exactly what you need. When the federal officers come for you, the lie detector won't snitch on you."

"I can beat it," I said smugly.

"Don't be proud of that!"

I laughed, set the laptop aside, and turned on the sofa so that Sky could lean back against my chest.

"Sure, I'll remember not to be proud of it."

"The woman in the video—who is she?"

"Her name's Alexandria, and she's a jackal."

"You saw how well she handled it. Very in control of her other half."

That was one of the other reasons we had asked for her help with this little project: no risk of her getting stressed out by aggressive Red Blood agents and changing without the influence of Mond.

"Yes, Sebastian noticed that about her a few years ago. She's been living as a loner for nearly five years."

"Have you all approached her to join the pack?" Sky's enthusiasm surprised me. It wasn't like she lacked for female company in the pack. Was there something else about Alexandria that had caught her attention, or was she just worried about rogue weres? "Who asked her? You or Sebastian? Did you use your subtle threats that, believe it or not, are more of a deterrent? You know, the whole 'if you become a threat to the pack, we'll treat you like all threats'?"

"We do know how to behave," I said indignantly, "and can be quite charming when we need to be."

"I didn't see any of that charm when you were recruiting me."

"You weren't going to get any from me—I didn't want you in the pack."

Looking back on it, I could see that I had been wrong, but at the time, it had seemed like the right approach. I had seen that Sky would be trouble and wanted to avoid bringing that into our lives. I had been trying to protect the pack, and to preserve my own sanity, in the face of a woman who resisted everything that defined our lives. But now I knew that she was exactly the sort of trouble I needed, someone who could challenge me to become better than I was, who would stand by me no matter how tough life became. It was amazing to think that the willful woman I had struggled with back then had eventually stolen my heart.

Sky offered me a spoonful of ice cream, and I declined. This was becoming a nightly ritual, and I enjoyed the rhythm of it, the sense of stability that came from having something familiar in my life. But even by Sky's standards, this was a lot of dessert to be getting through. Was she working out more than I realized, and in need of the food to fuel that? Was this just a comfort thing, given the stresses we were facing? Or was something else going on?

I leaned in, pushed her hair back, and kissed her appreciatively on the neck, then wrapped my arms around her, placing my hands on her belly. The only sound was the clatter of her spoon against the bowl. I had no good reason to think that this was more than just Sky indulging her sweet tooth, but a small hope stirred inside me.

The relaxing silence was broken by the buzzing of my phone, a nightly ritual I was less pleased with. I ignored it at first, but it just buzzed again, and kept on going. I growled in annoyance.

"You're going to have to answer it eventually, or they're going to come over," Sky said.

I grabbed the phone. "What!"

"Good evening to you too, Mr. Broody," David said. "You didn't respond to my calendar invite."

There was a silence, less comfortable than the previous one. If he wanted an answer from me, then he could ask a damn question.

"Fine. You will be there tomorrow at three?"

"Yes," I said through clenched teeth. I could have done without David and Trent breathing down my neck about the wedding, but it was too late to protest that now.

"I've sent over the invoices for the violinist, rental of the arboretum, and the photographer."

"They've been handled," I said, trying my best not to let my irritation out. Even I could tell it wasn't working. "I didn't realize you got Annie Leibovitz to take pictures. I'm impressed."

"You know it's not Annie, and if you have a problem with the cost, take it up with Claudia. She recommended the photographer, and after seeing her portfolio, I see why. She's fabulous. Once all those invoices are taken care of, just send me screen grabs or copies."

"If I say I'm going to do something, no need to worry—it will be done."

"Then say you'll send the screenshots or copies and the conversation can end." His tone turned cloyingly sweet. If he thought that would make me more cooperative, then he had badly misjudged the situation.

"I'll send them over," I said, while Sky set determinedly to eating her ice cream.

"That's settled then. See you tomorrow."

"Goodbye." I hung up and set the phone down. I just had to remember, all of this was going to be worthwhile once I was married to Sky.

"Ethan," she said softly, putting down her bowl and settling more snugly against me. I pulled her close, fingers clasped across her stomach, trying to focus on the comfort of her presence and not my annoyance at David's attempts to control every last detail.

"We should have just gone to a justice of the peace," I said. I didn't mean it. Sky had warned me about the risks of working with David and Trent, and I had accepted them with my eyes wide open. It would be worth it to give her the wedding she deserved, and to celebrate my life with her.

"In three weeks it will be over. You won't have to hear anything about flowers, food, photographers, or any of it." She stroked my hand and my tension started to ease. "Really, all we are doing is either rejecting or accepting their decisions. We have it easy."

"Really? Easy. They contact us at least five times a day. My e-mail is full of pictures and invoices and invites. When did we agree to a reception?"

Of course, I knew the answer to that, which was that I hadn't. David and Trent had just kept going on about how lovely the arboretum at the venue was, how it would be a shame to waste it, how it wasn't even a proper wedding without a reception, and eventually I had stopped arguing back. I hated how badly I had lost control of this situation, every decision being snatched from my hands, but at least I could hang on to one thing. I was going to sort out my own tux, regardless of all their pictures and cloth samples and opinions about how I would look. One damn thing was going to be mine, a lifeline to cling to through this storm.

Sky turned to face me. "It's just two hours. And then—"

"We leave," I said, relieved. Knowing I could get out would make the whole thing more bearable.

She smiled. "We leave."

I kissed her lightly on the bottom lip.

"Where are we going for a honeymoon?" I asked. "You haven't committed to anything."

"Portugal is out of the question."

"We can go," I said. I understood that she was trying to minimize the disruption, to avoid tearing me away from pack business, but what was the point of a honeymoon if not to leave that all behind for a while?

"Ethan, the Presentation ceremony is five days after the wedding. We can't leave the country. You have to go—it's your responsibility." She pulled a mocking frown. "Besides your prickly personality, I knew what I was getting with your role as the Beta."

That made me frown for real. I didn't like to feel as though my responsibilities were limiting Sky's life, but there was no avoiding the impact that they had.

Sky turned back to her apple and her bowl of ice cream.

"*And*, I promised Chris I'd go," she said, leaning against me again. She took a bite of the apple and followed it with a spoonful of ice cream, as if she was trying to wash away the taste of healthy living.

"I really don't like this burgeoning friendship between you and my ex," I said. It wasn't just the fact that Chris and I had once been an item that bothered me. It had been bad enough when Sky was friends with Quell, now she was entangling her life with that of the woman who was about to become Mistress of the Seethe. All this closeness to vampires was bound to cause trouble.

"We aren't friends," Sky said. "She asked me."

"And you could have said no."

"But I didn't." There was a long, awkward silence, and then Sky spoke quietly. "I couldn't."

That wasn't the "couldn't" that came from some sort of obligation or political consideration. It was a personal thing, Sky's unwillingness to hurt someone, even if that someone was a murderous vampire. If this wasn't a friendship, then what was?

By comparison with this, David and Trent didn't seem so bad. Sure, they were vacuous and annoying, and far more interested in the contents of my wardrobe than anyone else I knew, but at least they weren't going to kill anyone.

Of course, given their interest in supernatural life, they might end up getting themselves killed, particularly if they insisted on coming to the Presentation.

"Then you'll be there to babysit Trent and David," I said.

Sky twisted around to face me, then reared up onto her feet.

"There is no way in hell they are going to that vampire prom."

I clasped my fingers behind my head and leaned back, enjoying the display of futile anger. Surely even Sky knew how this one would play out? After all, she was the one who had brought David and Trent into our lives.

"Do they know the day of the Presentation?" I asked. She nodded. "I'm assuming they know the time and location as well, correct?"

"They saw the invitation."

"Hmmm," I said, smiling. "And you are under some illusion that they won't show up?"

"If I tell them they can't—then they won't," she said with confidence completely detached from reality.

"Ah, yes. You would think people would respond when you request that they not do something for their own good. After all, you're just trying to protect them, and they should accept it and follow your directions…"

Her scowl only urged me on. "I once knew this woman; she was so tenacious and spirited. I would tell her to stay away from Tre'ases, and guess what? She didn't. She'd been warned no less than five times to stop playing with vampires, and I swear she set up weekly playdates with them. She was a very rare wolf who could do wondrous things with magic, so she was advised to use it sparingly, so she practiced it daily with a tattooed renegade witch who had an aversion to following basic rules. I seem to remember telling the precocious, beautiful, doe-eyed brunette not to go to Logan's. I'm sure if I searched my phone, I can find the old texts. Hmmm. I can't remember if she listened, but my gut is telling me she didn't."

"She sounds terrible. What ever happened to that troublemaker?"

"She's still around. Now she's on the opposite side of a similar situation. Karma is a joyous thing. The naïveté with which she's handling things is quite entertaining. She's so cute." I pitched my voice high, a terrible impersonation of Sky, but as good as I was ever going to manage. "'If I tell them they can't—they won't.'"

"You think they'll show up even if I ask them not to?"

"Definitely." It was satisfying to see Sky face the same frustrations she had caused me, to watch her grapple with the responsibility of this challenge. "You aren't thinking about locking them in a room on the night of it, are you?"

Sebastian had done that to her the first time she fed Quell, so it wasn't the wildest solution she could come up with.

"Yeah," she mumbled, red-faced.

"Let them go," I said softly, realizing that I had pushed things too far. No more mockery now, just a solution to help Sky feel better about it all. "David was right. There's no way Demetrius or Chris will allow them to be harmed. Not because Demetrius has any code of honor to protect them, but hurting them would surely cause chaos at this absurd event."

She rolled her eyes. "This vampire prom is going to be obscenely over the top."

"Agreed." And that was why it was so perfect for David and Trent. But now it was time for a distraction, so I grabbed my computer. "We have to find a honeymoon destination."

<hr>

It felt strange to meet up with Josh for drinks somewhere other than our own bar. For years, it had been the default drinking place for most of the pack, and so when, after our difficult conversation about his curse, we had started hanging out together again, the bar had been the natural choice. It was easy for me to get to, and even easier for Josh, who could keep an eye on business while we chatted.

That option had gone out of the window with the Mond attack. Though work had started on repairing the place, stripping out damaged carpets and painting over soot stains, it would be weeks before they could open for business again. So instead, I wound up at a bar down the street, sipping on a whiskey in a window seat while I waited for my brother to turn up.

It was one of those days when the rain pummeled the city, a ceaseless downpour that tumbled from slate-gray skies, a dark and brooding evening. The bar, by contrast, was warm and comfortably lit, just lively enough to create a positive atmosphere without becoming intrusive. The selection of Scotch was good and the jazz quartet playing in a corner helped to set a relaxing tone. As I sank back in my padded seat, I started wondering if I should be drinking in other bars more.

The door swung open and Josh came in, shaking off rainwater with a toss of his head. He took off his coat, grabbed a beer, and came to join me, sinking into a seat across the low table.

"Nice place," he said, looking around. "How did you find it?"

I shrugged. "Closest place to you."

Josh laughed. "So luck then? Well, I can live with that."

He ran his fingers through his hair, dragging it up from where it had plastered to his forehead.

"How's the repair work?" I asked.

"Faster than I expected. Marion knows some really good contractors."

"That's why I use her any time my place gets wrecked. That and her discretion. You pay a bit extra but..."

"But it'll be worth it to get the place up and running

already. Do you know how much we're losing every night we're shut?"

As one of the people who read the pack's accounts, I had a pretty good idea, but that wasn't a detail worth getting into. The important thing was that some semblance of normality was on the way.

"How are you doing?" Josh asked. "Pre-wedding jitters getting to you yet?"

I raised an eyebrow. "Why would I get the jitters? I love Sky, I want to spend the rest of my life with her. I've never met anyone like her, somebody who makes me better the way she does, someone I want to spend every waking moment with. That's what marriage is supposed to mean, right? And that's what I have."

"But everybody's supposed to have some doubts before a wedding, worrying about whether things will work out, whether they'll be a good spouse, all those things the ceremony brings into focus."

I shrugged. It hadn't even occurred to me to worry. Sky and I loved each other, we wanted to spend our lives together, so why would I start getting anxious now?

"We're already committed. If I was going to get the jitters, I should have done that before we mated, and that's already done."

"Not even a little knot of anxiety, that mix of excitement and tension that comes with getting the details of the big day right?"

"You know me, I get very excited about dresses and flowers," I said, my voice heavy with sarcasm.

Josh laughed out loud. "That's the Betahole we're all used to, dismissing the things that bring other people joy."

"I can take joy in this, I'm just not going to give in to some cliche of getting wound up about having the flowers just right. I have people doing that for me.

"Speaking of which, I was wondering, would you be my best man?"

Josh grinned. "I'd be honored. Though I have to admit, I assumed you'd pick Sebastian."

"You're my brother, you've always been an important part of my life. It would feel weird for you not to be an important part of my wedding."

"Cool. Will I have to do much?"

"Not unless David and Trent are hiding something from me. Just hold the rings and maybe give a speech at the reception."

"That I can do, on one condition. If I ever go through this, I want you there by my side in return. Your relentless calm will help keep me steady."

I studied him over the top of my drink. The thought of Josh settling down and getting married wasn't one I'd ever considered, but then I hadn't seen it for me before Sky came along. A lot could change when the right woman turned up in your life. The question was, had that happened for Josh too? How serious were things between him and London?

"You think you ever will?" I asked. "Get married, I mean?"

"Jeez, we're straight into the big topics tonight, huh?" Josh laughed. "No chat about the latest hot record or who won the big game."

"Who did win the game?"

Josh shrugged. "I don't know, who has time for sports?"

Outside, lightning flashed above the streets of Chicago, followed a moment later by the low rumble of thunder.

"I have to admit, it's not all been easy," I said, swirling the Scotch around my glass. "Sky's fine, but David and Trent are using up all my patience."

"You shock me." Josh grinned and leaned forward. "Go on, tell me about it."

I went through the whole business, from the first disturbance of my working day to the endless late-night calls and the insistent texts wanting to know if I'd looked at a Pinterest board. It felt good to get it off my chest, something I could do with Josh in a way I couldn't with Sky. After all, she was caught up in this too, while he was an outsider, not a friend of our wedding planners, someone who was happy to sit back and laugh and commiserate at my misfortunes, as long as I kept the drinks coming.

"What do you even need a violinist for?" he asked as I finally started to run out of steam. "Surely the venue has speakers you can stream music through?"

"That part at least I can understand," I admitted. "If we're doing this, I want to do it in style, and a live musician adds to that feeling."

"I guess," Josh said. "If it was me, it would just be a quick ceremony then down to the bar for drinks."

"Such a romantic."

"I can be romantic! Just ask London."

"I've seen what you two consider romantic." I looked pointedly at a tattoo on his forearm, which exactly matched one in the same spot on London.

"Hey, this is art." He flexed his arm and half a dozen different images shifted on his skin. There was more ink visible than there was of his original coloring. "Just because you're too scared to face a bunch of needles doesn't mean that the rest of us have to live our lives looking boring."

"I can live without your definition of exciting, especially if it's going to leave me looking like a comic strip."

"So now that Claudia's laid off the criticism, you're stepping up to take her place?"

The tone had been playful up to now, but I could hear real antagonism slipping like an old habit back into both our voices. This wasn't a path I should keep walking down. I took a sip of my drink and considered where else to take the conversation. Backward seemed like the best option.

"This business with David and Trent is all going to be

worth it," I said. "At the start, I thought I was going through with the wedding to make Sky happy, but it's more than that. It's something I really want, a way of marking how special she is to me, how much we've grown together, you know?"

"I think so." Josh smiled gently. "You've gotten happier since she came along, more relaxing to be around. You're far less of an asshole than you used to be."

"Sorry to hear that my standards are slipping. I'll have to fix that."

We both laughed.

"But seriously," he said. "I'm glad Sky came along, and not just because she's fun to hang out with. She's been good for you."

I smiled. He was right. I was loath to admit that I'd ever needed to change, but my moods were a lot less dark than they had been, my connections with other people in the pack better. Sky was the light to my darkness, and while I wouldn't want to throw away who I was, that contrast lifted me up.

"Almost worth putting up with David and Trent for, huh?" Josh asked.

"Almost," I said, rolling my eyes. "But let me tell you about the latest drama with the cake…"

CHAPTER 26

I sat behind my desk at the law firm, reading through a file Stacy had brought me. It was for one of the new clients who had come to us thanks to my success with Steven, and it was a corporate lawyer's dream. An international tech firm, with the budget to match, but not one of the high-profile ones that would mean the courtroom was crawling with journalists. There were questions of intellectual property, contractual obligation, and even land ownership on an area claimed as a reservation, all tied into a set of mergers stretching back twenty years. The client's biggest concern was that the other sides of their various legal claims might realize that they had a common cause, and so band together to fight them. Discretion was needed, as well as a quick resolution to the parts that could be wrapped up, and so here we were.

I could already see the billable hours stretching out ahead of us, and the happy emails I'd be receiving from the finance department once we got this one rolling. Best of all, it was genuinely interesting, a puzzle I could enjoy pulling apart to find a strategy that worked for us.

My phone buzzed; not the office one on my desk, but the

personal mobile in my pocket. I pulled it out and frowned as I saw Trent's name on the screen. I thought I'd gotten them to stop calling me during the working day.

"What now?" I snapped as I answered the phone. Refusing to answer had never worked, so I tried to get these things over and done with.

"Why haven't we seen your tux yet?" Trent asked, his voice shrill.

"Because it hasn't been made yet."

"What?" I could hear David as well as Trent practically shrieking down the phone line.

"I said it's not made yet."

"But you picked a style you liked, remember, and we booked you a fitting, and—"

"Sky picked a style she liked, but I want to make up my own mind."

There was a moment of deathly silence.

"And your fitting?"

"I canceled it. I'm going to use my regular tailor."

I felt a little rude, not having told them about my change of plans when they were running the wedding, but I'd tried to tell them I had it covered, and they just wouldn't listen. This was the one thing I got to control, and I wasn't letting go.

"Of all the ungrateful, hurtful, inconsiderate..." Trent's voice trailed off. "If this ends up ruining Sky's big day, we will never forgive you, will we, David?"

"Too far, Trent," I growled. "I'm not going to do anything to upset Sky, but this is my thing, and you need to leave me to it. Got that?"

Incomprehensible muttering emerged from the line.

"I said have you got that?"

"Yes," Trent said sullenly.

"Good." Now that I'd tamed the wild wedding planner, I

could at least give him something to ease his pain. "If it helps, I'm going to see my tailor today."

"You haven't even started on this yet?" His voice went shrill again. I thought I was the one who was meant to be stressing out. Whatever happened to the professional approach to wedding planning?

"I've been going to Rimbisi for years, he knows my style, he's quick when I pay for quick, and he's never let me down."

"Madness," Trent muttered. "Utter madness."

"Anything else?" I asked.

"No."

"Then I'm getting back to work."

I set the phone down and picked up the file again, trying to find the train of thought that had derailed when Trent called. Before I could do that, there was a knock at the door, and I waved Stacy in.

"What's up?" I asked.

She closed the door carefully behind her, set a device down on my desk, and pressed a button at one end. I'd seen a lot of security hardware while I was setting up protection for the pack, and I knew an anti-listening device when I saw one.

"I did a sweep this morning," Stacy said quietly, her expression drawn, "but you can never be too careful. This should mean that most bugs only pick up static."

Now she had me worried. I had hired her in part because of her technology skills, but if she needed to worry about my workplace security, then something was seriously wrong.

"Tell me," I said, gesturing to a seat.

"I think we're being spied on," she said, straightening her skirt as she sat down.

"We the firm, or the we that's you and me?"

"You and me. I've seen people following me at lunchtime and on the way home, and one of them turned up again just after you this morning. Then I found these."

She laid out half a dozen small devices on my desk. They looked like nothing more than black boxes half an inch long, some with wires or antennae trailing from the ends. I didn't need to recognize the exact models to know what they represented. We had been bugged.

"You think it's to do with this?"

I tapped the folder in front of me. It was the sort of case where it would be worth breaking the law to win, and this wasn't the first time we had seen these sorts of tactics. It was always hard to prove who was behind it, but knowing could give you an edge, and unwittingly giving away your strategy and intelligence was the surest way to lose a case. I felt angry but also intrigued, an itching in the back of my brain like the first hit of adrenaline at the start of a chase.

"I think this is from your other life," Stacy said.

Now I really felt angry. It was one thing dealing with vampires, elves, and witches when I was on pack business, but this was crossing a line, breaking the barrier I carefully maintained between my different lives.

"Tell me," I hissed.

"Whoever it is, they managed to get malware onto both of our computers. I took a copy before I wiped it off, and tracked down where it came from. I'd been expecting Silicon Valley or Hong Kong, given the contents of that file, but instead it led to a shop in Chicago, one that specializes in crystal healing and occult books."

A local hacker, and the only local connection in the new file was our client. Of course, they might have enemies nearby, but a more likely option was emerging. New age shops were often fronts for real witches, imaginary magic hiding the real stuff.

"Witches," I said.

Stacy nodded. "It makes sense, after that woman came here the other week..."

First they had tried to spy on me in person, now they

were doing it through viruses and listening devices. After all the effort Ariel had gone to in dealing with the Mond, I was sure that she was on our side, but as she had pointed out, there were other witches out there, ones who didn't share her views. It seemed that Hannah's visit had only been the start.

"Thank you, Stacy," I said. "I'll give this some thought. If you spot anything else, let me know straight away."

"Of course."

Once she had gone back to her desk, I sat brooding behind mine. I was furious at the rogue witches for meddling in this side of my life, but there was little I could do about it. Even proving they were responsible would be difficult; the connection to the shop would fall apart if they simply claimed that someone else had used their Wi-Fi. Identifying which of them had done this would be virtually impossible.

I needed to do something, but my mind was already rammed full of legal cases and wedding planning. I needed time to think this one through, but until then, this crossover between my lives increased the risk that someone at the law firm would notice something unusual. Never mind Mond or full moon videos, lawyers could easily crack open our defenses if they set their minds to it.

Until things calmed down, my ties to the law firm presented a risk to the pack. What was I meant to do about a problem like that?

My phone buzzed, not a message from David or Trent this time but a reminder that I was due to meet with Claudia for lunch and suit shopping. I locked the file away in my desk and headed out of the office, leaving those concerns behind for a few hours.

David and Trent might have an eye for style, but when it came to judging aesthetics, no one I knew could match Claudia. Perhaps running an art gallery had given my godmother a fine eye for the look of things, or perhaps that fine eye had led her into the world of art. Either way, she was the perfect choice of company to help pick out a suit, not least because she would stay calm and reasonable about it.

"This cloth will hang better, dear," she said, weighing up the two samples in her hands. "Don't you agree, Mr. Rimbisi?"

The tailor nodded and smiled. Seeing them together took me back to when Claudia had first brought me here, to have my very first suit fitted.

"It's worth paying extra," she had said, "to own something tailored for you. Nothing conveys power and confidence like a good suit."

Those were words I had lived by ever since, and Rimbisi continued to supply me with the finest suits I had ever seen, now made in collaboration with his daughter Theresa.

"Absolutely," Rimbisi said. "But that shade of gray, that I'm not so sure about."

"It's an outdoor ceremony," Claudia said. "Imagine him in sunlight, surrounded by trees, not in a church."

"Ah." Rimbisi smiled. "In that case…" He took out another sample. "Perhaps this?"

Claudia weighed the cloth in her hand and ran a finger over it, feeling the smoothness. She smiled as she handed it to me.

"It seems ideal. What do you think, Ethan?"

I just nodded. Every sample I'd been shown was excellent. This was what happened when you told a tailor of Rimbisi's quality that money was no object.

"If you're happy with that, then we have everything we need," Theresa said with a smile, setting aside the tablet on which she had recorded my measurements and the details of what I wanted. "Come back in three days, and we'll check for any adjustments."

The Rimbisis hadn't needed to adjust anything on a suit they'd made for me in the past ten years, but I wasn't going to protest. Their professionalism was part of why I was there.

"Let me pay you up front," I said, taking out my wallet.

"No no no!" The elder Rimbisi waved his hands in the air. "Not until we are done! Never until we are done!"

"I insist. It's the least I can do, given the service I receive here."

"No no no no—"

"Thank you," Theresa said, taking my card. "In these difficult economic times, up-front payment is always appreciated."

Her father scowled at having his ritual of protest and eventual acceptance interrupted, but he didn't say anymore.

"What next, dear?" Claudia asked, taking my arm as we left the shop.

"Cuff links," I said.

"Ah," Claudia said with a small smile. "And where would you like to go for that?"

"You know full well where we're going. After all, you're the one who took me there."

"I try to be a good influence."

She said it with a smile, but then a look of sadness crossed her face. She had to be thinking about my mother, about the vampire and *rever tempore*, about how her own mistake had brought a terrible curse into our lives. Just thinking about it brought out a sadness that would never entirely leave me, but despite her part in those events, I could never have blamed it on Claudia. She had always done the best she could for us.

"You've always been a good influence," I said. "And a huge help to me and Josh."

"Without me, your lives would have been infinitely easier."

"No." I stopped and turned, forcing her to look me in the eye. "What happened was an accident, something you couldn't possibly have predicted. I've seen how the Creed used to act, and sooner or later, they were going to turn on my mother. Without you to help us after that happened, we would have been lost."

"But still…" Tears welled at the corners of her eyes.

"Don't ever blame yourself. Nobody else does."

I pulled her into a hug and we stood like that, letting the world pass us by, until she finally relaxed.

"Thank you, Ethan," she whispered. "I needed to hear that."

"And I've needed you there," I said. "Every step of my life, from keeping Josh safe to helping me balance my two lives to hunting down the Tre'ase who created my spirit shade. You've done so much, I wouldn't be the man I am today without you. Hell, I probably wouldn't even be alive."

She wiped away a tear. "That's very sweet, but it's utter nonsense, you would have been fine without me. You are one of the strongest people I know. You have been since you were a child."

"And where do you think I got that strength from? I can never repay you for everything you've done for me and Josh, but at least I can say it out loud. Thank you for being there."

"Oh, Ethan." She placed a hand on my chest. "You've made an old lady very happy."

"You're not old yet," I said with a mocking frown.

"I'm certainly not young. But there's something I want you to remember. We can never repay the generations that come before us, but we can pass it on by taking the best possible care of the generations that follow. Some day, that will be your job. Make sure that you do it well."

"I will. I'll do it just like you."

"Perhaps try to include slightly fewer curses."

We both laughed, and the heavy atmosphere evaporated, freeing us to move on.

A few minutes later, we approached a jeweler's with fine rings, necklaces, and watches gleaming in the window display. The smartly suited security guard smiled at Claudia and nodded respectfully to me.

"Good to see you, ma'am," he said.

"Fernando." Claudia beamed. "Is Ms. Tanaka available?"

"For you, ma'am? Always."

Fernando opened the door wide and let us in.

The shop was quiet, no other customers standing between the rows of waist-high glass cases. I took a moment to appreciate the quality of the abstract art pieces stationed between them, which I now realized had probably been picked out by Claudia. Many of her best customers were also friends, and vice versa.

"Claudia." A short woman in a simple black dress emerged from the back of the shop, smiling serenely. "And Ethan. I hope you haven't broken your ring again?"

"You broke your ring?" Claudia looked at me, appalled.

"Not me, Sky. It was during that business with…" I hesitated, not sure what I should say. There was something magical about this shop, beyond its hypnotic power, but I didn't know how connected its owner was to the supernatural world. Fighting with Faeries wasn't something you talked about in public.

"It is all fine," Etsuko said. "What is worth having is also worth mending. And what are you looking for today?"

"Cuff links," I said. "To go with a tuxedo."

"Ah. The wedding is imminent?"

"So the planners tell me."

"Well then…"

She led the way to a corner cabinet, in which pairs of cuff links were laid out together. There were none of the amusing novelty designs that some shops pushed, just simple, elegant styles.

"What takes your interest?" Etsuko asked.

I looked over the cuff links, trying to make up my mind. Then I remembered whose company I was in, and how the hunt for the right ring had ended. I could keep control of selecting my outfit while still leaning on the guidance of others.

"What would you recommend?" I asked.

"Do you have a color scheme?"

I pulled out my phone and hit a link in one of the seventeen emails David had sent me that day.

"You do Pinterest now?" Claudia asked, looking at the screen, a hint of mockery in her voice.

"David and Trent do Pinterest, what I mostly do is ignore their emails."

Etsuko looked at the phone, then at me, then down at the display case, even those small shifts of her head slow and graceful.

"These, I think," she said, taking a pair of cuff links from the display. Their color matched the wedding scheme, and their simple shape subtly fit with the flower arrangements. But what really caught my attention was the flattened oval in the center of each one, gleaming like the eye of a wolf.

"Perfect," I said.

***

"Now that that's all under control, how are you feeling about the wedding?" Claudia asked.

With our trips to the tailor and the jeweler done, we were finally sitting down to a late lunch in a quiet corner of one of her favorite restaurants: a large rare steak with a salad for me, pasta in a mushroom sauce for Claudia. Like drinks with Josh, it was a chance to leave the worries of the world behind, except that our conversation inevitably came back to the things that were occupying my mind. That day, they weren't all bad.

"I feel good," I said, beaming. "No, better than that. I feel great. Sky makes me the happiest I've ever been, and this is a chance to share that with the world."

"I'm so glad that you and Sky found each other," Claudia said. "She's a perfect fit for you, and it's wonderful to see you both happy. I just wish your mother could be here to see this."

She sighed.

"Me too." I reached across the table to take her gloved hand. "At least you'll be there, and Josh."

"He'll be far too busy chasing bridesmaids to sit and talk with an old woman."

"First, you're not that old, and second, hasn't he told you about him and London? That's looking pretty serious now."

Claudia shook her head and tutted. "I thought you were the one who didn't tell me anything, but now it's your brother's turn to disappoint me." She smiled. "Though if he's going to disappoint me with anyone, London is a good choice."

My phone buzzed. For once it wasn't David and Trent, but someone from the office wanting to know when I would be back, so that they could discuss an upcoming court hearing.

"Sorry," I said, putting the phone away. "It can wait."

"More trouble with the flowers?"

"More trouble at the office." I tapped my fork against my plate, wanting to say more but not sure how.

"Go on, dear," Claudia said. "You can trust my discretion."

"It's not this," I said, tapping the phone. "It's the bigger picture. For years, I've balanced my work against my pack duties, kept them both rolling along. It was like my human and wolf sides, two separate but compatible pieces, working in harmony. Recently, that's changed. Pack life has gotten busier, and I don't see that changing. It's the same with work, especially since Steven's case. Even clients I'm not working with want to meet me, to get some sort of reassurance from what I represent, or perhaps just for the celebrity part. I'm being given really high-profile cases, which is great for my career and my bank balance, but terrible for time."

"So you're struggling to balance the two parts."

"Not just those two. I want time to spend with Sky. She means so much to me, I want to spend every waking minute I can with her. But even the evenings we set aside to spend alone get interrupted by work or pack business. I'm not giving her the time and attention she deserves."

"The time she deserves, or the time you want to share?"

"Both."

A thoughtful look occupied Claudia's face. Her hand drifted to the pearls she was wearing, which I knew were one of her favorite sets, and her fingertips traced the shape of those tiny, precious orbs. For a minute, it didn't seem like she was even in the same room with me. Then she looked up wistfully.

"If you find someone who means the world to you, then you should find a way to hold onto them," she said. "Because there's nothing in the world more precious than that connection, nothing more vital to our existence. I don't know what happens after we die, even though my very life is tied to it. But if anything can endure past death, then it's love.

"So when you find the person who makes you complete, who makes your heart soar and your life feel complete, then it's worth making sacrifices to preserve what you have. And if that means giving up something else, then maybe that's what you have to do. Because some things are easily replaced, but love isn't one of them."

Listening to Claudia talk like that, I realized how little I knew about her life before the curse on Josh, about who she had been when I was a child and couldn't understand that adults had feelings of their own, who she had been before I even knew her. The look on her face didn't invite deeper inquiry, but there was a melancholy there I had never seen before. Maybe one day, I would understand who my godmother was, or maybe she was too much of a parent figure to ever cross that gap.

Either way, Claudia had given me the wisdom I needed, as she often did. Sky meant the world to me, and the pack was the foundation of my life. They deserved my full attention, and that couldn't help interfering with my legal work. Whether it was missed meetings, rescheduled hearings, or witches snooping around the office, my supernatural life was bound to interfere. Sooner or later, something had to give, and I would rather make that choice than have it forced on me.

I would miss my career, but thanks to my investments, I could cope without it. Sky and the pack, them I could never leave behind.

As soon as I got back to the offices of Wendell, Harper, and Holmes, I headed to Eileen Harper's office. Of the named partners, she was the one I had the best relationship with, and so the natural person to break my news to first. But as I approached the office, I saw that all three partners were present, the others just rising from their seats at the end of a conversation. It seemed like chance had given me an opportunity, and I might as well take it.

"Sorry to interrupt," I said as Harper's assistant led me in, then shut the door on her way out. "Do the three of you have a moment?"

"I think so," Harper said, locking her steely gaze onto me, and Wendell and Holmes nodded in agreement.

"I'll make it quick," I said. "Some issues have come up in

my personal life, and I don't think that I can continue to commit the effort that you expect of me. I'm going to quit now, rather than wait until it becomes a problem. You'll have my resignation letter by the end of the day."

The partners looked at each other, and something passed between them. To my surprise, they settled into their seats, their attention still on me.

"Naomi," Harper said into her intercom, "please reschedule my next meeting, and hold any calls for the next half hour."

"Yes, Ms. Harper."

"Ethan, take a seat." Most people would have made it a question or an offer, but from Eileen Harper it was an order. I sank into a chair, doing my best to face all three partners at once.

"If this is a bad time—" I began.

"There's never a good time," Harper said. "But that's no excuse to ignore the inevitable. Ethan, we know that there's something odd about you. If we weren't smart enough to work that out, then we couldn't do the jobs we do."

"Might as well retire us," Wendell said.

"Or send us to serve on the bench," Holmes said with a chuckle.

I stared at them in shock. I knew that there had been moments when the mask of my life slipped, or when the supernatural tried to intrude on this place, but I had worked hard to cover my tracks. Clearly I hadn't worked hard enough. I could only hope that they hadn't worked out the truth, and that no one else had noticed as much as they had.

"We don't know what's going on," Harper continued, "and after careful consideration, we've chosen to ignore it, rather than find out anything we might not want to know. There aren't many lawyers I like—hell, there aren't many people I like—but you're one of them. You take your job seriously, you get the work done, and you use your intelligence instead of just taking the obvious path. Even before your friend's curious criminal case, you brought a lot of value to the firm. You set an example to the others, and your own work pays off in impressive profits. If we had ten more like you, we'd be the best fucking law firm in the country."

"Hey, we already are!" Holmes said, grinning.

"Save it for the boardroom, Bob." Harper kept her gaze on me. "The point is, we would be loath to lose you."

In its own weird way, it was a touching speech. Nothing spoke to corporate lawyers quite like cold hard cash, and apparently I had earned enough to gain allies I didn't know I had. It would make leaving harder, but it didn't change the calculus of my life. Given a choice between Sky, the pack, and my career, this was the part that would have to give.

"I'm sorry," I said, "but other parts of my life are really busy right now. I want to make time for them, and to keep them from getting in the way here."

"Those parts would include the people spying in our offices?" Wendell asked, her tone sharp. "The ones who somehow managed to make half the staff forget them?"

Witches. Again. This was well past the point of tolerance.

"I'm sorry about that," I said. "And it just goes to show why I have to leave."

"Far from it." A small smile crept up Wendell's face. "We haven't had to deal with competent corporate espionage since McCluskey left his firm in oh-three. I've missed the fun and games."

I blinked, bewildered. This was the last thing I'd expected to hear.

"The point we're making," Harper said, "is that we can help you too. We would like you to stay, on the understanding that we keep not asking questions, even when that means cutting you a little more leeway than most. If anyone else comes around asking questions, then we'll find ways to put them off."

It was an increasingly tempting offer, one that seemed almost too good to be true.

"That's very kind," I said, "but for what you pay me…"

"Well, we might want to renegotiate that," Holmes said, rubbing his hands together.

"Bob, seriously," Harper said, flashing him a warning look, and in that moment I learned who really ran the firm. "We talked about this." She turned her attention back to me. "Your bonus will still depend on performance, so that sorts itself out. As for your salary, I'm confident that you'll make up for any lost time at the first chance you get. You've done it before, every single time, and there's a reason why we trust you now. Isn't there, Bob?"

She flashed a look at Holmes again.

"Sure." He smiled at me as broadly as if he'd just gotten his way. "We don't want to lose the golden goose."

"It's not the goose that's golden," Wendell said.

"I know that, but sometimes the phrase matters more than the facts."

"Try telling that to Judge Pattison."

All three laughed, and I laughed along, not knowing what the joke was, but happy to be sat in on it. I was appreciated enough not just to keep my job on favorable terms, but to be let in on a moment like this, when the partners showed their conflicts and their human side. What I had here wasn't quite friends, but it was good, and as Eileen Harper looked at me, I understood that I had meaningful relationships beyond the pack, even if I hadn't noticed them until now.

"Well?" she asked. "What do you say?"

"Thanks," I said, smiling at them. "Guess I'll stick around." Then I remembered what the next few weeks held, and I laughed for real. "After my honeymoon, that is."

CHAPTER 27

I paced back and forth in the parking lot outside the arboretum, glancing at my watch every thirty seconds. No matter how many times I did that, things didn't seem to change. Still no Josh, and the time for the ceremony was getting close.

"He'll be here soon, dear," Claudia said, laying a hand on my arm. Even by her standards, she was smartly dressed, an elegant gray dress set off with a fascinator and a silk scarf in shades of mauve and cream, all of it in tune with the wedding's color scheme. On anyone else, I would have assumed that this was David and Trent's handiwork, but Claudia was quite capable of achieving elegance all by herself.

"I don't want him to be here soon," I growled. "I want him to be here now."

I knew I sounded childish and petty, but if there was ever a day when I was allowed to let my emotions show, then it was my wedding day. What was the point in dressing up in a dove-gray tuxedo if you weren't also allowed to vent at the unreliability of family?

I wouldn't have minded so much, but I didn't have any of

my close pack members to keep me company. Sebastian was busy preparing for the ceremony; Steven was giving Sky away; Winter was, against her repeated objections, a bridesmaid; and Gavin was accompanying Kelly, bridesmaid number two. Unless I wanted to spend my last unmarried moments playing some weird card game with Quinn and the Worgen, Josh and Claudia were the only ones available to keep me sane, and half that sanity was running late.

It was possible, I finally admitted to myself, that I was stressed about getting married. Not about the part where Sky and I bound ourselves together, that felt as natural as anything in the world could be. What had me stressed was the need to get through a ceremony and a structured celebration, with so many people's expectations pressing in on me. I would be happy when the whole thing was over.

At last, a taxi pulled up and Josh and London climbed out, each of them a surprisingly formal figure of elegance. London had even picked out a dress that matched the pastel streaks of her hair while still looking smart enough for the most stylish occasion.

"What time do you call this?" I snapped.

"Uh, within ten minutes of what we said, which by my reckoning counts as on time." Josh grinned at me. "Why, do you have somewhere else you need to be?"

"We're not going by your reckoning today," I said. "We're going by David and Trent's ridiculous, overcrowded schedule. Oh, and by my need to get married, in case you forgot that part."

"Never," Josh said.

Then he flung his arms around me, catching me completely by surprise. Apparently we were a hugging family now.

While my first response was to sneer, after a moment I felt my tension fading away, and I hugged him back. I couldn't remember a time I'd been happier to see him.

"I love you, bro," Josh said quietly. "And I'm so glad to see you happy. This is the best day ever."

"I love you too," I said, slapping him on the back.

"I wish Mom was here."

"Me too." That almost brought tears to my eyes. Her absence was all the more noticeable on a day like this, a day for celebrating family and everything it represented. I would always miss her, but her memory helped me cling more strongly to what I had. "I have you though. Thanks for being here for me."

"Hey, a chance to dress up and party." He took a step back, brushed away a tear, and grinned. "I wouldn't miss it for the world."

A large taxi pulled up and Quinn leapt out, followed by more of the Worgen. Apparently someone understood the meaning of "on time."

"Hi, Ethan," he said, waving. "You missed a great game."

"He missed borderline cheating, more like." Tabby glared. "I can't believe that deck was tournament legal."

"And yet it was." Quinn shrugged.

"You guys are early," I said, looking at my watch again.

"Didn't want to be late. That would have been rude."

"Wouldn't it?" I looked pointedly at Josh, who laughed.

"Come on," he said. "Better get inside, before more of your guests turn up. It's time to tie you down for life."

"You know I'm already mated, right?"

"Sure, but that's just the important version; this is the one with a party!"

<hr>

I could say this much for David and Trent as wedding planners: They had found the perfect venue to marry two weres. Surrounded by oaks and poplars, as well as the flowers growing there and the ones brought in for the wedding, I almost felt like I was out in the wild. With my pack gathered in front of me and Sebastian standing ready to perform the ceremony, it was like being at home, but with an extra buzz of excitement.

Then the violinist and the cellist changed their tune, shifting from soft classical sounds to a heartfelt rendition of the Wedding March, and my heart skipped a beat.

Sky emerged from a tent that had been set up beyond the trees, her arm through Steven's as they walked toward me. She wore a floor-length dress of champagne-colored silk and lace, drifting layers giving it the look of something from a fairy tale. It was a long way from the clinging dress that I had seen her try on at our house, and somehow it made her look even more gorgeous. I watched, enchanted, as she made her way past our guests, every eye on her, the radiant smile on her face matching the happiness that beamed from my heart.

Sky stopped in front of me and it was all I could do to drag my gaze away from her and turn to face Sebastian as he gave a speech on joining together two people in love. In one sense, we were already joined, having followed the ways of the pack by becoming mates. But this was something else, an acknowledgment of the human side of both our lives, the fact that we were more than the beasts that ran wild beneath the trees. Each of us was two parts, and so was our life together. When we combined, those halves became a perfect whole.

When it came time for our vows, I found my breath catching, the words frozen, unable to draw them out past the wonder of staring at Sky. She was my whole world, and everything else seemed unimportant by comparison.

I cleared my throat and looked past her while I composed myself, then looked back at her.

"I never thought I'd be here," I said softly. "Not here and especially not with you." The world around us seemed to recede—the trees, the guests, the flowers all fading to nothing—until there was just us. "I didn't think I'd be here, and I didn't think it would be with you, but I'm happy it is. I can't imagine anyone else I'd rather spend the rest of my life with. Our life together won't be easy." I drew closer to her and dropped my voice to a whisper, a moment no one else needed to hear. "And we'll never have the normal that you want, but we'll have each other and we'll create our normal. I can't think of anything better than experiencing life with someone who makes it infinitely better. I love you, Skylar Brooks, in a way that I never thought I could. In a way I never thought I could love anyone. I plan to do so until I take my last breath. To make our normal the best it can be, for us."

Overwhelmed with emotion, I leaned in, pressing my forehead against hers.

"It was a bumpy ride getting here, but I am here—with you. And there isn't any place I'd rather be—ever." The breath catching in my throat, my words faded almost to nothing. "You are my forever."

The whole world was us, and we were the whole world. Sky, smiling at me, blinked back tears, but one slipped out and I kissed it away.

"I guess I can't just say 'ditto,'" she said shakily.

I chuckled. Out of the two of us, she was the one I had been sure would take this seriously.

"I love you, Ethan, and everything about us—even the things that drive me crazy. You're right, it took us a while to get here, but it was the journey that made us what we are. It grounded it into something that is real—that is truly us—and nothing else compares. I am so happy to have my forever start now with you. Until I take my last breath, I love you."

"I love you too, Sky."

There was a long moment of quiet, in which all I could hear was our two hearts beating in unison. Then Sebastian cleared his throat, reminding us that we weren't the only people in the world. We stepped back from each other, and with a smile he started speaking again, bringing the ceremony to a close. Every word would be perfectly chosen, but I didn't hear a single one of them. All I could think about was Sky.

The reception was also taking place on the grounds of the arboretum. As the ceremony ended and the congratulations began, Steven, Gavin, and Winter ushered our guests in that direction, with the promise of a party to lure them away. But there was no chance that Sky and I would ever be left in peace today, unless we made that peace for ourselves. So I grabbed Sky's hand and led her, our fingers tangled together, to where our car was parked, near a large oak tree.

The car was a new addition to my collection, a Spyker C8 Preliator that I'd bought to reward myself for getting through the wedding. It was a fantastic vehicle, but its curves weren't the ones I was interested in.

I helped Sky to climb into the car, folding her voluminous dress in, then joined her. In the rearview mirror, I could see our friends trailing toward the party, full of excitement and sociability. After everything it had taken to make this wedding happen, I was completely burned out on that last point.

"Let's leave," I said, looking at Sky in all her stunning beauty. We had done our public duty, now we were entitled to celebrate being married the old-fashioned way, by getting naked and enjoying each other's bodies.

"And not go to the reception?" She stared at me in shock.

"It's just a party. Let them eat, drink, and have a great time."

"Without the bride and groom?"

I licked my lips, then moved in closer and kissed her, giving in to the passion I could no longer contain. I pulled her close, our bodies pressing together, and kissed her along the jaw, then down her neck, tasting the sweetness of her skin. I toyed with the edge of her corset, brushing lightly across the swell of her breasts, and she shivered in delight.

"We go to the hotel, order room service, spend the rest of the night there," I said, nipping at her bottom lip before kissing her, "leave the next morning for the honeymoon."

I ran my hand from the nape of her neck, through the layers of fabric that enveloped her body, down to the bottom of the dress, and then up again. My fingers caressed her thigh, feeling the lace of a stocking and the clip holding it up. I growled in excitement at the thought of what else lay underneath the dress.

To my disappointment, Sky pulled away, putting as much space between us as she could in the confines of the car.

"We go to the hotel and..."

I imagined that dress dropping away onto a hotel room floor, leaving only the stockings. In my mind, our hands ran over each other as our bodies pressed together, and I kissed every perfect inch of skin before losing myself in her.

"What do you have on under there?" I asked, drawn by the question of what else went with those stockings.

Sky's gaze grew distant, and I doubted that she was preoccupied with her own underwear. Maybe she would be willing to get away from all this after all, to have some time just for us after all the hard work that had brought us here.

"So, we're going to leave..." I asked.

"No," she said, with renewed resolution. "We go to the hotel and then what, spend the next three hours with Trent and David knocking at our door? Because they aren't going to go away. We go to the reception, make an appearance, eat food, toast, have wedding cake, and then escape."

It wasn't what I wanted, but it would have to do. Grueling as this bout of sociability might be, at least I would get to spend it with Sky.

The reception had ended up as a compromise, somewhere between what I could stand, what Sky wanted, and what David and Trent would let us get away with. The end result wasn't full on formality, but there were carefully decorated tables, with vases full of white flowers and images of wolves wrapped around their bases. A large dance floor, a DJ, and an open bar promised a spectacular party once everyone had eaten, and the size of the venue, far larger than was needed for the number of guests, meant that there was plenty of space for everyone to mingle, chat, and enjoy each other's company.

A certain amount of ceremony was unavoidable, and for me, it created a sort of comfort. As long as all eyes were on someone else, I didn't have to worry about the attention.

Josh was up first, doing his best man bit.

"Thank you all for coming," he said. "I know it's unusual for Ethan to stay quiet, he's usually so cheerful and chatty, but I thought I might make the most of this rare opportunity to talk."

Across the room, people laughed, then laughed harder when I scowled in response. I'd known what I was getting myself into, but I figured they'd be disappointed if I didn't respond in familiar Ethan form.

"When Sky first came into our lives, Ethan didn't seem to like her much. Of course, he's always had terrible taste—trust me, I saw his bedroom growing up—but at least this time, he realized in the end that he was wrong, and that he'd found a real treasure.

"Sky, on the other hand, has excellent taste, so goodness knows what she's doing today."

He paused to let that one get a good burst of laughter, and winked at me while he waited for quiet. One day, I promised myself, I would get my revenge, but for now I just had to keep listening.

"Seriously, I know that being with a Beta is prestigious, but is that really worth the price of waking up every morning to the pre-coffee version of this grouch? I can't help thinking that there's a reason it's taken so long for him to settle down.

"Mixing these two together has led to all sorts of drama. Shouting matches, angst, more shouting matches, angrily chasing each other through the woods, yet more shouting matches, and the times when it was just one of them shouting about the other. Everyone here has at some point thought it might be best to let them fight it out and just quietly bury the body of the loser.

"Despite all that, I think we're all glad they got together." He paused for a moment. "Or at least, that they got together before they ended up killing each other." There was laughter and applause. When it faded away, Josh's expression was less jovial, but still happy. "Seriously though, I'm glad that my brother has found someone to make him happy, and who he can make happy in return. May we all be lucky enough to find what they have. So please raise your glasses, to Sky and Ethan!"

"Sky and Ethan!" The whole place resounded with those words, and I smiled to see my bride blush.

Sebastian was up next, glass raised as he spoke in an earnest tone.

"You two were the bane of my existence." He looked at me, and I couldn't help smiling back, even though the whole reception had already run longer than I wanted. "Your differences complement each other despite the battles, the eye rolls, frustrations, and constant assertions that 'the brunette is going to be the downfall of this pack.' And here we are. I don't think I'm alone in saying that I didn't see this coming—but I'm glad it did. It's a completed circle."

I took Sky's hand and squeezed it. Seeing ourselves

through others' eyes didn't bring many surprises, but there was something satisfying about it, to know that they didn't think we were completely mad, and to share this moment of absolute happiness with them.

The toasts continued, getting further into mockery with each one, and I enjoyed the increasingly raucous atmosphere. It was good to see that the combative spirit of the pack could come through even at a time like this. If I didn't get to fight back now, I would at least make up for it later, when some twist of events put my friends at my mercy, and they knew it.

At last, the toasts and the dinner ended, and Sky and I were able to get up from our seats. We moved through the small crowd, greeting people we hadn't had a chance to talk with yet, thanking everyone for coming. It was great to see so many good friends together, but I had to admit to myself, I still wanted out. I felt like a caged beast, trapped behind the bars of everyone's attention.

"That looks sincere," Josh said, noting my smile.

"It's been a long day," I admitted, though the smile stayed.

"And we are going," Sky said, to my immense relief.

She clasped my hand and we hurried out the door, leaving the others to celebrate in our absence.

I opened the door to the hotel room and led Sky inside, our fingers intertwined. As the door closed behind us, I stepped back, letting go of her hand, and ran my gaze up and down her body. The fall of the skirt and the tightness of the corset showed off her curves while enhancing her natural poise and elegance, while her raised hair exposed her neck and shoulders, soft bare skin promising so much more.

"You look beautiful," I whispered.

She looked down at herself, taking in the luxury of the dress, with its layers of satin and silk, and she grinned.

"I feel like I should be in an amusement park, taking pictures with small kids."

"No, it's beautiful. You're beautiful. Mrs. Skylar Brooks-Charleston?"

I moved closer, the scent of her like a drug to my senses, making my heart race and my head fill with thoughts that had nothing to do with that dress. I removed her headband and released her hair, running my fingers through those dark tresses as I kissed her.

Cupping her face in my hand, I explored the taste of her, the softness of her lips against mine, the warmth of her breath. A hunger rose inside me, something fierce and desperate, a fire that longed to be quenched. The feel of her body next to mine was all I wanted in the world, and yet, until we tore away everything between us, it was not close enough. She ran her fingers through my hair, drawing me in, her own hunger clear in every touch.

I stepped back, my eyes on her, that gaze holding the connection between us. I cast off my tie, then my jacket, then my shirt, my body trembling with desire. Then I pressed myself against her again, sinking into the depths of passion and the rhythm of our hearts beating as one. She panted as I pulled away and looked down her body again.

"I'd like to see what you have under the dress," I whispered.

She smiled and nodded, then turned around. I pushed her hair away and kissed her lightly on the nape of the neck, then along its pale and perfect curve. My fingers ran across her shoulders, feeling her silken skin, and she shuddered at my touch.

I took hold of the zipper, a delicate thing amid the folds of cloth, and drew it down her spine. With the slightest of tugs, the dress fell off and pooled at her feet. Then she turned to face me, dressed in lace-trimmed stockings, a garter belt with a little bow, tiny panties, and a pearl-colored lace corset.

I took in a deep breath, practically drooling at the sight of her, then let the breath out in a deep, sensuous rumble

"This is a far cry from t-shirt and shorts."

I ran my fingers over the swell of her breasts, then followed that with the touch of my lips. She pressed herself against me and my urgency grew, a longing that filled my whole body. I wanted to stand back and admire her beauty, wanted to hold her so close that we became one, and it didn't matter that the two were incompatible, I wanted them both at once. Her breath, soft and rapid against my ear, urged me on.

I knelt in front of her and unfastened her stockings, then rolled them slowly down her legs, pressing my lips against her skin as I undid each one. Then I rose, running my hands across her, feeling the heat as she responded to my touch, until I reached the lacing of her corset. I unfastened the bow and loosened the corset until it came off, landing discarded with the rest on the floor.

Pressing our bodies together, I cupped her butt and lifted her up to carry her to the bed. She lay there, smiling up at me, as I tore off my remaining clothes, my desire for her fully visible in the soft light of late afternoon.

Still I held back, kissing and stroking every inch of her body, marking every part of her as mine. I wanted to relish this moment, to taste her and feel her, to know that soft skin, the curve of her breasts, the flat of her belly, the place between her legs so full of promise and of passion. She gasped, clawing at the sheets as my tongue darted across her body and her pleasure rose. Her skin grew flushed and she arched her back, then reached down with one hand, drawing me in.

I slid onto her and inside her, a shiver of excitement running through my flesh as she wrapped herself around me, arms and legs pulling me close. Our bodies joined at last, sending a shudder through both of us. I moved slowly, rhythmically, feeling our flesh combine, building momentum with each stroke. I scattered kisses across her chest and neck, relishing their sweet softness, then kissed her fervently on the lips, our tongues tangling as she urged me, wordlessly, to move faster and harder. My hands wrapped around her and held her tight, our flesh becoming one. I whispered her name, her new name that included mine, the two of us bound in human as well as in animal ways, as we marked the beginning of a new stage in our lives, burned it into our memories with passion. At last, I felt my body reaching a crescendo and Sky's fingers bit into my back as she cried out in ecstasy. Together, we reached a desperate, panting climax.

I looked down at her, grinning.

Skylar Brooks-Charleston.

My wife.

A relatively quick and comfortable flight took us to Hawaii, sharing our plane only with one other couple, who were as happy to be left alone as I was. Then it was a taxi straight to the hotel, and the most spectacular room I had been able to find, a suitable place to celebrate our honeymoon. The floor-length window gave us a fantastic view of the golden beach and clear blue sea beyond, with the palm trees and flowers of the hotel's gardens framing the sight.

A basket of fruit and chocolate had been left out for us, but I was more interested in exploring the bed. I walked up behind Sky as she gazed out of the window and wrapped my arms around her.

"This is amazing," she said, her smile wide.

"It's not Portugal," I said, "but we'll have a great time."

I wished that I could have given her the honeymoon she wanted, but the need to be back with the pack in a few days had limited our options. Sky kept saying that she was all right with that, but a little guilt still gnawed at me.

"It's beautiful, Ethan. A perfect beginning."

She turned to face me, still smiling earnestly. I listened to the beating of her heart and accepted what she was telling me. This was the truth. There was nothing she could want more. I smiled in relief.

"And we won't miss the vampire prom—" she began.

"Presentation, Sky."

"Whatever. They are going to be dressed in their finest attire—you saw the invitation, and it's going to be the most extravagant, ridiculous soiree I'll ever witness in my life. I am positive of that."

I laughed. When the time came, it would be my duty to treat the Presentation seriously, but Sky was right, it was a laughable moment of vampiric pomposity. Having her there with me would be the only way to get through it sane.

The sun was shining outside, and I could hear the waves lapping on the beach. Perhaps bed could wait for later. There was a chance now to get out into nature, if not the part of nature we were used to.

I fished the swim trunks out of my bag and changed. Sky followed suit, putting on a bikini that left very little to the imagination. I almost laughed as she added a crocheted cover-up that covered almost nothing at all.

"When we change with the pack, you spend most of your time crouched over, hiding your 'lady goods,' but you're okay with your barely there bikini."

"It's the beach. Of course, I'm fine with it. Standing in the middle of the forest naked is odd, and you can't convince me otherwise. You just like being naked. Oh, so I won't have to say it again, just because it is a semiprivate area doesn't mean you don't have to wear clothing. People can see you."

I grinned, thinking about how little anyone was likely to complain at seeing me naked.

"Just. Don't. Do. It," she said. "No one wants to see your ass, no matter how nice you think it is."

"You think it is."

She rolled her eyes and started stuffing things for the beach into a bag. I added my Kindle, figuring that we would be out there for a while. Then I switched off my phone and stashed it in a drawer beside the bed.

"Are you sure you want to do that?" Sky asked.

I nodded. For once, I was determined to leave my pack behind. "For five days—it's just the two of us. Winter can handle anything that happens. I'll just deal with her litany of complaints when I return. For years, I was concerned about her eventually challenging me—I'm not anymore. Apparently, I have to do too much." I put on my best impression of Winter. "'You know how I feel about Sebastian, but I don't need to talk to him every day. That's just weird.'"

Sky took her phone out of the bag, switched it off, and stowed it away next to mine.

"Okay, just the two of us."

And for five glorious days, it was.

CHAPTER 28

*S*ome time alone with Sky turned out to be the perfect break from everything that had been bothering me. Concerns about the pack and political events surrounding us faded into the background, while we enjoyed five days of sun, sand, and sea, as well as long, luxurious evenings exploring each other's bodies.

The moment I took my phone out of the bedside drawer and switched it on, that changed. It was like a cord tying me to our life back in Chicago, and the moment I touched it, I felt familiar concerns come flooding back. More than anything else, I worried about Josh. There were conflicts going on between the witches, conflicts connected to our pack, and if anything had happened, then he would have been caught up in the middle of it. I imagined assaults, kidnappings, spells gone badly wrong.

I needed to talk to my brother, but by the time we got on the plane, it was clear that he wasn't answering.

"Why aren't you picking up your video call?" I snapped when he finally answered.

"I answered your text," Josh said far too casually, as if he was hiding something. I tensed, leaning in close to the speaker.

"I texted you because you didn't answer the chat. I texted you to answer the damn call."

"I'm quite aware of what your texts said, Ethan. So, what's up, bro?"

The forced relaxation of his tone only wound me up more.

"Don't 'bro' me. We will be taking off in a few minutes. I need you to answer your video. I want to see your face."

"No."

"No?"

"No, that's weird and so random. What's wrong with you? You want to see my face? You see it all the time, it hasn't changed."

Except that I hadn't seen it for five days, and anything could have happened in that time. That was why I was calling. But if I let my paranoid fantasies out, then I would just be exposing myself to his mockery, and I certainly wouldn't get the answer I was after.

"Is everything okay?" I asked through gritted teeth.

"Yes. Everything is fine, just like I texted."

"I can hear it in your voice. I need to see your face. I can tell when you're not being honest with me."

"The world didn't fall apart because you left for five days. Have a safe flight."

He hung up, leaving me staring in disbelief at the silent phone. Sky pried it out of my hand and set it aside.

I sank back in the leather seat and stroked my chin, considering what Josh was hiding from me. Five days' worth of beard beneath my fingers reminded me of what a relaxing break I'd had away from my normal routines, and how easily the calm it produced had shattered now that I had to deal with my brother. I was back, and I needed to know what was going on, but apparently Josh didn't agree.

Sky laid a hand on my leg. "We'll stop by his house as soon as we land."

I nodded, as if I hadn't already made that decision. "You're damn right we will."

———

When we pulled into Josh's driveway, he was already standing in the doorway, looking expectant and more than a little smug. He grinned mischievously as we approached, and I had to dig my fingers into the palm of my hand to keep myself from shouting at him. I wasn't going to throw away the peace we had made, however annoying he got.

"Rayna has the Aufero," he said once we were all inside the house.

"That's not something you thought you should tell me?" I snapped. The most important thing to happen in weeks, and he had deliberately been keeping it from me. No wonder he hadn't wanted to answer my calls.

"What exactly could you have done about Rayna getting the Aufero?" His show of calm cracked a little now, concern showing through his flippant demeanor. "We've been looking for it for weeks. She got to it first. You couldn't have done anything about it while in Hawaii. You needed to enjoy your honeymoon."

I had to reluctantly admit that he had a point. As Claudia had said, when you found someone who made your life complete, you did whatever it took to keep them, and for me and Sky that included having a real honeymoon, away from all the concerns of the pack. It might not have been what I would naturally have chosen, but those five days of staying uninformed had been a perfect bonding experience, good for us and for me.

"Thanks," I said, conceding that he had done the right thing.

But now that that was over, it was time to get down to business.

"She's approached Ariel," Josh said, shoving his hands deep into his pockets.

"About what?"

"Their hand in helping you all, the were-animals. She expressed her concern that Ariel is doing a disservice to the witches' reputation."

Concerns that could act as excuses, reasons for Rayna to grab the reins of power from Ariel. I knew a political play when I saw it. Whether or not Rayna believed in her cause, she was seizing the opportunity it gave her.

"Is she strong enough to use the Aufero to strip them of their power?"

Josh took a sharp breath, and I could see a trace of fear in his face.

"Us," he said, the word a portent of trouble to come. "You know once she comes for them, I'll be next."

As if this wasn't enough of a threat already, now Josh's safety was at stake. If the magic was drained out of him, what would that mean for the careful balance of powers we had used to keep him alive? I thought that he was safe now from the curse that had been inflicted all those years ago, but what would happen if someone stripped away layers of magic and destabilized him? The thought of my brother powerless and in danger made me shake with anger.

"Does she have the other objects?"

"I think she has them all." Josh frowned. He had something more to say, but he didn't want to face it, and a long, strained silence stretched out before he spoke again. "She's not going to stop until she has everyone turned against us— the were-animals."

There it was, the pain of Josh's position clear for us all to see. His powers were those of a witch, but politically, he was bound to the pack. Our fate would be his, but it might be inflicted by his own kind.

Rayna had placed him in a terrible position. For that alone, I would have been determined to make her pay. But she was threatening the pack, and that made it even more personal.

<hr>

We sped through the streets of Chicago, Josh at the wheel of his jeep and Sky in the back, while I flicked through documents on a tablet, going through the dossier that Quinn and I had pulled together on Rayna. The information included Rayna's last four known addresses, but only one of those was in the city, so if we were going after her, then that was the logical starting place.

"What triggered it?" I asked, talking to myself as much as to the others.

There had to be a reason why Rayna had emerged now, to launch a fresh campaign against us. Marcia's legacy of hatred against weres ran deep among a certain sort of witch, but it took more than long-ingrained habits of thought to drive someone to action. Perhaps the Faeries attacking us had made her think that there was more going on than she realized, or had led her to the conclusion that we were vulnerable. Maybe someone else had stirred her up, just like Gregoire had fed into the schemes of Red Blood as well as Bethany and Sonja. The possibility that it was about Sky and I being together seemed absurd, yet people were clearly more worried about that than I had realized, and some people couldn't help turning their fear into hate.

When we reached Rayna's house, the lights were off, and there was no sound from inside. I pressed my shoulder against the door just hard enough to break the lock, and we stepped inside.

The place was empty, except for a single book lying open on the kitchen counter. It was a journal, opened to an account of what were-animals had once been, before the powers of magic, evolution, and civilization turned us into our modern form. It was all familiar to me, but no less unsettling for that, to imagine our roots as savage, scavenging beasts. Back then, we hadn't even had our divided form. Instead we were left in a state of half-man, half-animal, walking on two legs but covered in fur, with snouts, pointed teeth, and long, vicious claws. Instead of speaking in words, we were restricted to savage snarls. These weren't the weres that I knew, the ones that lived in the world today. They were terrifying abominations.

And that was Rayna's point in leaving this book here. It was a reminder of who we had been, who we still were, according to her and her followers. Through the lens of hate, she could only see us as monsters, a fearful threat that needed to be stopped. This was the vision she was sharing with the world, the one that she acted on, the one that had justified stealing the Aufero. That vision drew out my own anger, my determination to stop her and protect my people from this warped perspective and all the cruelty that followed it.

She must have thought that she was being smart, leaving just this book to taunt us, nothing else to give us a clue on where she could be found. But something else had been left behind, something that would have been undetectable to a witch but that was clear to the enhanced senses of weres like Sky and me. Beneath the smells of sulfur and burnt offerings that magic left behind, there was a familiar scent.

Liam. The leader of the pure blood elves and arch prince of arrogance had tied himself to the rogue witches' cause.

Taking the journal with us, we headed back out of the

city, to the entrance to Elysian. A magical barrier stood around the elven realm, but we had penetrated that protection before, and we could do it again. Together, we chanted the words of power that should make a doorway through the barrier and let us in, but the words didn't work. All three of us poured our magic into it, but still the barrier held. Though it rippled and pulsed, at times weakening almost to the point of breaking, something always seemed to hold it shut.

"They're stopping us," Josh said. "Fighting back against our efforts, closing any gap the moment we make it. We're never getting in this way."

I pressed my hands against the barrier and let my power flow. "I'm not giving up yet."

A threat to all of us could be hiding just on the other side of that magic, and I wasn't going to let her get away.

There was a pulsing in the barrier, a weakening of its strength a few feet away. I turned toward it just as Liam emerged, blocking the gap he had stepped through. He sneered at us, his aristocratic features haughtier than ever.

"Is there a reason you are here?" he asked, exuding boredom and disdain.

"We need to speak with Rayna," I said sharply.

"You think she's here?" Liam arched his eyebrows. "Go away. You're wasting my time. But for the sake of amusement, let's say she's here—what do you want with her?"

"She has something of ours that we want returned."

"Does she have something that is yours or something you think should be yours? Because possession is ownership. I can't imagine with your colorful retrieval tactics and ways that anyone would have anything that you considered rightfully yours."

"It's mine and I want it back." I squared up to Liam, ready for trouble. He had elemental magic on his side, along with the poise and precision elves brought to any fight. I had strength and the determination to use it. "In fact, I want them all back. They aren't rightfully hers."

"And yet she has them," Liam said, casting away any pretense that he wasn't sheltering Rayna.

"We need entry to speak to her," I said with a deep, menacing rumble.

Liam took that sound as a challenge. He stood straighter and kept glaring at me.

"I do not wish to be part of your battles, but whether or not she's here is not really of your concern. If she were, I'd not allow you entrance to speak with her. Nothing you have presented has warranted it.

"Unlike Gideon, I will not buckle under the demands of your pack, and I'm fully prepared to fight for the privacy of Elysian. Our guests will remain unharmed and unharassed. But I am not a man without a moral compass. If I believed you were missing an object you indeed owned, I'd ensure that it was returned to you. After all, I am a man who honors and respects the rules." That eyebrow arched again, a silent judgment on our attitude to the rules. "But until you have more evidence, I cannot be of help."

"She threatened me," Sky said. "We need to make sure that she's not in a position to follow through with it."

He dismissed her concerns with a snort and a wave of his hand. I tightened up inside, my desire to protect Sky adding to my mounting anger at Liam's arrogance and his unwillingness to cooperate.

"Posturing and threats among the denizens are so typical, they're essentially greetings," he said, waving his hand again as he took on a mocking tone. "'Hi, I plan to destroy you,' 'Good evening, tonight I will bathe in your blood,' 'I'm going to wear your head as a charm.' It's so"—he took a deep breath, then exhaled it as a single word—"exhausting. I'm going to suggest you file away her words as just that, words. She hasn't acted on them, and you of all people know how often threats are used and not enforced."

"We've never made one that we didn't follow through on," Sky said.

"Of course." He looked at us with disgust. "Well, most do it out of anger and frustration. More so when dealing with the likes of you. It does take a toll on a person, as it is doing with me now. To be honest, I'm quite bored with it all. I've been reduced to only responding to attempts. Has an attempt been made on your life, Skylar Brooks-Charleston?"

He managed to say her name like it was an insult, though whether it was targeted at me or Sky I wasn't sure. Either way, I took it personally.

"No," Sky said.

"If she acts on those words, then I won't offer her safety, but I will not stand by and allow you to steal from her. If it were indeed yours, you'd have it in your possession."

"Then know this," I said, "if one of the objects she has is used to hurt others, you allowed it to happen and will be held just as accountable as she is. These are not just words that I've spoken on a whim. I mean it."

"Well, of course." Liam's nostrils flared. "You are nothing if not consistent."

He looked over the three of us, his gaze lingering over me and Sky, his expression turning strangely thoughtful.

"I preferred what you were before to what you are now. Then we could see the were-animal. It's too far removed now." He turned his attention to Josh, a note of warning in his voice. "Were-animals and magic don't mix well. There was a reason you were made that way."

Then the wall around Elysian rippled and he stepped back through, before it sealed firmly shut.

Josh and Sky flexed their hands, preparing to take their magic to the barrier again, to tear it open at the weak spot where Liam had come through. Part of me wanted to join them, to prove how little his arrogance and his power meant when faced with our strength. Giving in to that desire would have been immensely satisfying.

"Just let it be for now," I said.

The others looked at me in surprise.

"The picture," I explained, imagining how the moment would look. "It gives her more credence and proof. If we tear open the barrier and she hasn't actually made an attack, she'll continue to win people over and make allies of those who otherwise would remain neutral. We take away that power and make her look like the aggressor by doing nothing. If she stays quiet, great. If not, then we respond with force."

CHAPTER 29

As we walked into the ballroom of Demetrius's mansion, I kept my hand pressed protectively against the small of Sky's back. She, in turn, kept glancing at David and Trent. It seemed that we were both feeling protective, and understandably so. Even before we walked through the double doors, we were wading through the graveyard stink of a huge gathering of vampires.

The ballroom was everything I expected it to be. Statues of oriental dancers in erotically charged poses flanked the entranceway, leading us out onto a polished marble floor. From there, pillars rose to a high ceiling, from which star-shaped chandeliers hung, their lights dimmed to create a more intimate, brooding atmosphere. It was the sort of grandiose display that took elements that might once have been tasteful and arranged them into something so pompously old-fashioned that it would have made a reenactment fair look like the height of modernity. The whole place was designed to impress someone, presumably Chris and possibly all the other vampires Demetrius dealt with, and perhaps it worked; after all, vampires had a particular view of their own lives, one rooted in blood and tradition. But to me, it was all so absurd I might have laughed if the stink of vampire wasn't making me so tense.

Sky, David, and Trent all seemed impressed. They gazed around at the opulent decor and elegantly dressed crowd, while I scanned the room for threats. This Presentation was a huge event, a shift of influence in the most powerful vampire Seethe, and there was every possibility that someone would take the opportunity to cause trouble.

In a corner of the room, a band played soft, bland music as background to the multitude of conversations filling the room. Like the people serving, the musicians were humans dressed in tailored suits, members of Demetrius's garden wheeled out to keep his supernatural guests entertained, and to sate the vampires' desire for blood. And as if they weren't enough, a pair of half-naked acrobats hung from aerial hoops in opposing corners of the room, twirling and twisting for the crowd's entertainment.

The one good thing about the evening was that it had led Sky to dress up. She wore a strapless silver gown, its dark embroidery running all the way to the floor, a perfect match for my own dark-gray suit. The dress had been a last-minute purchase, as Sky claimed to have put on weight through the relaxation of our honeymoon and not enough exercise around the wedding. But I couldn't help wondering, not for the first time, if something else was going on. Surely she would have realized before me if she was pregnant? Yet her scent had subtly changed, and I couldn't help hoping that meant something more, as well as worrying about the timing. With the threat from Rayna's witches and Liam, would now even be the right time to have a child?

"This is so over the top even for them," I said, forcing myself back into the moment. I took a sip of champagne as I gazed through the floor-length windows at the far side of the room, through which a light show could be seen playing across a selection of sculpted fountains.

"Look at that." Sky nodded to an ice sculpture of an angel emerging from a flower, her arms extended as if offering a gift, or perhaps holding up a newborn lion cub while *The Circle of Life* played in the background. We both chuckled at the image.

"This is amazing," Trent said. If they hadn't been human, he and David would have seemed like a good fit for this place. Their suits were impeccable and they held themselves with the casual grace of men used to grand events. But then they would look across the room and go wide-eyed, giving away just how much they didn't belong.

Normally, I considered David and Trent to be a burden, their naive interest in the supernatural a problem to be worked around. This evening was different. They were out of place, and their undisguised enthusiasm diminished the poised dignity of the affair. Anything that punctured the pomposity of the vampires suited me, and so, for once, I was glad to have them there. As long as they stayed in sight so we could protect them, everything would be fine.

The doors opened again and I tensed as I saw who had arrived. Alexander wore a navy suit with no tie and a brightly colored pocket square. He had lightened his hair, and together with the splash of color on his outfit, it made him standout amid a sea of black. The Master of the Southern Seethe had come with the intention of drawing attention, and he paused in the doorway long enough to make sure it all soaked in.

I hadn't seen him since Bethany and Sonja released us to be hunted through the woods, but I immediately remembered just how obnoxious he was. As his gaze drifted across the room, I caught a blast of his icy disdain, directed specifically at me and Sebastian.

Vampires had started hovering around us, not out of political interest in the Beta of the Midwest Pack, but out of a more primal interest in David and Trent. They looked at

Sky's friends like they were eyeing up a buffet, but David and Trent seemed oblivious, happy to have the attention of glamorous strangers, sucked in by the unmistakable allure that vampires held for any ordinary mortal. Sky's face fell as she saw what was happening.

"They'll be fine," I assured her. "I suspect more humans will show up for dinner and the entertainment."

Sky just kept staring, looking like she was going to be sick. She had gotten used to drinking my blood, a consensual activity between the two of us, but vampires preying on humans, even willing humans, was another matter. Something for which I had a long-standing but low-level dislike became a source of horror for her.

Mixed in among the vampires were a few other leaders of the supernatural world, here to bear witness and to acknowledge the power being bestowed on Chris. Sebastian stood at the far side of the room beside Ariel, he in a black suit, she in a flowing white dress, the slit up one side revealing a length of supple leg. While their outfits displayed their contrasting natures, those of Gideon and Abigail, who stood near the center of the room, seemed made to match. His wine-colored suit helped draw attention to her deep-taupe sweetheart ballgown, decorated with a layer of delicate embroidery. As was so often the case, brother and sister had come as if they were a couple, and were keeping their cruelty carefully concealed beneath their delighted smiles. If Abigail was still angry at how we had treated her, then she showed it indirectly, avoiding my gaze, while Gideon gave me a nod of greeting, not a gesture between equals, but at least an acknowledgment that I had a place in his world.

Claudia was one of the last to arrive, as seemed fitting for her place within supernatural society: not truly an insider to any of the parties present, but respected, deferred to, and of course invited to such a significant occasion. She kept her feelings on the event hidden as she crossed the room, wearing a modest tulle dress whose appliqué decorations matched her gloves. She greeted the four of us, then paused to look around the room, and it was noticeable that anyone who caught her eye bowed their head in acknowledgment of her power. It had long been rumored that she was a powerful fae, and though the truth was more complicated, she had acted as their representative, reinforcing an assumption she had no need to dispel.

It was good to have her there, but I could sense from the moment she arrived that she wouldn't be around for long. I knew her better than anyone else present, and could see the small signs that others might miss. I moved next to her, taking comfort for a moment in her reassuring presence.

"Enjoy yourselves," she said. "I'm here to make the obligatory appearance, but once I greet Chris and Demetrius, I will be leaving."

Then she was off to mingle with the other guests, to play politics, gather gossip, and probably sell art while she was at it.

David and Trent were several glasses of champagne down, and like them, the vampires were giving in to the temptation to indulge themselves. A woman in a silk dress walked over and flashed Trent a smile that revealed the tips of her fangs.

"Hello." Her voice was as soft and smooth as her dress, her dark eyes warm and inviting. "You may be the most beautiful person here. Please, you must dance with me."

Blushing, Trent reached for her outstretched hand, but Sky grabbed his arm, snatching him out of the vampire's reach.

"You do realize David's here," she hissed.

"Yes, Mother, I realize that. She asked me to dance, not to have sex with her in the middle of the room. And I promise if you let me go, I'll be a good boy."

He broke out of Sky's hold and let the vampire lead him

onto the dance floor. Meanwhile, David's laughter burst lightly from the other side of the room, where he was walking arm in arm with a couple of other vampires. Sky stared, aghast, at the sight of her friends relaxing into a party whose dangers she had repeatedly spelled out for them before we arrived. Her protective instincts, almost as strong as my own, reached out for them. Her fingers tightened around her champagne glass, so I took it out of her hand, afraid that she might shatter it.

"Calm down, they're fine," I said gently. She looked down, and for the first time seemed to notice that I'd taken her glass. "I was afraid you were going to break it. Then we'd have something to worry about." I kissed her on the cheek. "You don't have anything to worry about. Just enjoy the night."

"Give it to me!" she demanded, hands outstretched.

Confused, I held up the champagne glass, but that didn't seem to be what she meant. She patted my chest and pockets, frisking me for something I had missed.

"What?" I asked in confusion. "Give you what?"

"Drugs. Whatever you've taken, I want some too. And if you had some of those fun brownies your brother's so fond of and didn't share, I'm going to be really upset with you."

I laughed. She had a point. It wasn't at all normal for me to be the more relaxed one out of the two of us. But if I thought this moment of self-awareness might lead Sky to relax, I was very wrong. She continued to watch David and Trent with fierce intensity as the evening progressed, shooting looks like daggers at any vampire who seemed too set on holding their attention. I watched her out of the corner of my eye, wary in case she got carried away in her protectiveness and caused a confrontation, but also amused at how this contrasted with her usual mockery of me. I wasn't going to let her forget this night anytime soon, possibly ever.

"You don't have to worry, because any bad behavior would reflect on Demetrius and would be penalized harshly," I said. "Do you think he would prepare such an extravagant event only to have it ruined by a fight? You think the vampires aren't aware that they are our humans?"

"Our humans," she said, frowning.

I sighed. I understood her objection, but when in the vampires' lair, we had to think like vampires.

"Do you think they refer to them any other way? That means something to them. While they are friends to our pack, they are nothing more than 'our humans' to the vampires, which gives them just a slightly higher standing than other humans."

The band stopped playing and we all turned to watch as Demetrius and Chris entered the room, arms interlinked. Even by the standards of vampires, they had taken the goth look to new extremes. Demetrius wore a tailored tuxedo in midnight black, and his dark, oiled hair gleamed in the light of the chandeliers. Chris wore a clinging, deep-red gown, strapless and plunging at the front, held together with a web of thin straps at the back. Large diamonds in platinum settings shone on her finger, her ears, and a necklace that drew attention to the curve of her barely concealed cleavage.

While their outfits were striking, what caught me most was their demeanor. There was pride in Demetrius's face as he entered the room with Chris on his arm, showing off what he had obtained. But there was a tension as well, an unsated hunger that shone when he looked at her. He was desperate for her to want him in the way that he wanted her, and it was never going to happen. She had accepted him, in return for the power and security he represented, but she didn't return his look. Instead, she surveyed the room with an expression constantly on the verge of breaking into disdain. The new Mistress of the vampires had accepted what she had become; that didn't mean that she liked her fellow bloodsuckers.

The silence broke as they moved into the crowd and started talking with their guests. More buildup was still needed, more anticipation before Demetrius moved on to the main event. The vampires swirled around their rulers, paying court to them, and even Alexander was eventually drawn in. As he approached, I saw a flicker of interest from Chris, a focus on his movements that she was trying to hide, and I remembered that she had previously tried to take over the Southern Seethe. Surely she didn't still fear reprisals from its Master, now that she was under Demetrius's protection?

At last, after half an hour, Demetrius broke away from a conversation with Alexander and clapped his hands.

I had known from the beginning that there were new heights of extravagance still to be reached, that nothing about this evening could go any way but up in that regard. I wasn't disappointed.

A woman in a flowing gold dress emerged from each corner of the room, their heads adorned with crowns of flowers. They played a flowing melody on golden chimes, backed by the band, a light and dancing tune that cascaded through the air. As the music came to an end, Demetrius took Chris's hand and led her to the center of the room. At his nod, the band filed out, followed by the acrobats and some of the servers. Either they weren't members of the Seethe's garden, or they weren't yet being allowed the privilege of this grand moment.

"Thank you all," Demetrius said in a deep, smooth tone, "for joining me in this momentous event as I present to you Christina Rose Leigh, my partner, consort, and the new Mistress of the North. This marks a new era, one that I'm sure we will be proud to be a part of."

Alexander snorted. The whole crowd tensed. Demetrius

gave him an icy gaze, but instead of being intimidated into submission, Alexander advanced slowly into the heart of the room.

"It *is* a new era," Alexander said. "The one where the North will fall from greatness because you've decided to take a paramour that is so common and a very undiscerning choice. Even if you ignore that she attempted to kill me, should we ignore the fact that the new Mistress of the North used to warm the bed of the Beta of the Midwest Pack? Is this what you've been reduced to, taking the discards of a cur?"

He stood facing Chris, who looked back at him with apparent disinterest. While Alexander's attention seemed to settle on her, his words were still for Demetrius, and for the crowd.

"Have you no shame?" he continued. "Must your people be subjected to having"—he turned from Chris to shoot a look of disgust in my direction—"the were-animal's cast-off as a Mistress?"

I didn't care what Alexander thought of me, and I doubted he cared about my response. It was Chris who mattered and she responded with a smile as withering as his own.

"If he should have shame for anything, it should be for allowing a poorly controlled Neanderthal such as yourself to have control over the South," she said. "You shouldn't be responsible for the care of your own life, let alone hundreds.

"I make no secret of my past, because it is what has made me who I am today. But *you*? You have plenty of things you should be ashamed of because they have not made you a better person, just more abhorrent. I tried to kill you because, although minimal, we do have rules of engagement when it comes to those in our use. You had drugged that poor woman and were doing cruel things to her. If I had my way, I would have done even crueler things to you. But you are Demetrius's, and I will not fault him for the fondness he has for you. It does seem that he is blinded by the love he has for his imbecilic progeny. Where most fathers would harbor nothing but shame and regret, he still manages to show pride and adoration for someone who is clearly undeserving of it. While you cast aspersions in my direction, know that you can never think any less of me than I think of you."

I had never seen a confrontation like this. Matters of vampiric succession were normally settled well in advance. There was no room for confrontation and controversy when the Master and Mistress of a Seethe held such absolute control. Apparently today was different, and the stony silence of the other vampires said that they didn't know how to react. As for the rest of us, the best that we could do was to stay quiet, stay inconspicuous, and hope not to get caught up in whatever followed.

Alexander opened his mouth to respond to Chris, but Demetrius held up a hand, silencing him. He looked saddened and confused at this act of defiance, of betrayal, by a vampire he had sired.

"You have been in my city for days," he said, "have fed with me, been entertained by me, and have spoken with me about all the inane things you could think of, but it is *now* that you've chosen to express your concerns with my choice?"

"How should I have handled it?" Alexander spat the words. "You held no regard for us by choosing *this*! And I am to answer to her as my equal?"

"As your superior. I created you, and the South was a gift. One that you didn't earn or ascend to. And yet, this is how you reward my generosity?"

"Demetrius." Chris's voice was firm but gentle, like a mother helping discipline a child. "You can't be surprised by this behavior. He is handling this in the manner he's handled most things: without any reason, strategy, or propriety. I understand and respect the love you have for him. But do not expect him to be anything more than a disappointment. I've dealt with him only a fraction of the time you have, and because I am not blinded by emotions, I see him for the maladroit that he is. You continue to waste time trying to make him something I can assure you he will never be. Though created by you, he will never meet your expectations or your greatness. He is indeed a waste."

Her whole body tilted in toward Demetrius, showing him the affection he wanted, the support he needed. In that moment, she was the perfect mistress for him.

Oh, she was good, and she was playing these two off against one another. I wondered if she had gone out of her way in the preceding weeks to remind Alexander of his dislike for her, to stoke the fire of hate so that she could provoke him now.

Pale and fuming, Alexander stared at her with a terrible hate, while she poured all her concern and affection onto Demetrius. Alexander could see part of her game, could see her turning his creator against him, but he hadn't realized the other part of the trap, and he fell straight into it.

His hand shot out, backhanding Chris so hard that she stumbled back several feet. Except that Chris wouldn't stumble from a blow like that, wouldn't even have been touched by it if she hadn't wanted to. Alexander was fast, but she was faster, and she was choosing not to use it.

Before anyone could react, he leapt at Chris, slamming her against a wall. With one hand, he hauled her up by her throat, while his other hand slapped her again.

She whimpered and sagged, the image of a battered, broken creature, and Alexander's face filled with a cruel grin. But beneath the facade, Chris was scanning the room, watching how others responded.

Sky started moving toward them. I remembered, almost too late, that Chris was her friend now, and that she would risk herself to protect any of her friends. I grabbed her hand, but she broke free. I snatched at her again, wrapping my arms around her, holding her tight.

"This is not your concern," I hissed, trying not to draw attention. "Let it play out."

"'Let it play out,'" she replied through clenched teeth. "This isn't a childhood fight on a playground over a toy. He will kill her."

"Sky, I'm not going to let you go," I said, clinging on even as she struggled. "Let. It. Play. Out."

She stopped struggling and stood tense, ready to take any opportunity I gave her to break free. With the speed at which events were unfolding, I doubted it would matter.

Alexander bared his fangs and stretched up toward Chris's neck, ready to rip her throat open. But Demetrius was on him. He wrenched Alexander off of Chris and flung the younger vampire across the room. Alexander slid across the polished marble floor, a look of shock and betrayal on his face. Then Demetrius leapt, a swift, vicious movement driven by the fury that radiated from him. I didn't even see where the stake came from, but it was in his hand as he landed—and he plunged it through Alexander's chest. The marble cracked as the stake's tip pierced the floor, driven by Demetrius's pure fury.

Demetrius stood over his fallen son as reversion took hold. Starting around the stake, Alexander's body dried and shriveled, skin crinkling and then crumpling, fingers clenching into claws. His eyes rolled and then shriveled to nothing, while his lips cracked and peeled back, exposing needle-sharp teeth.

Demetrius, his face emotionless, looked around the room, daring anyone to intervene. No one moved. None of the vampires were going to feed the loser in this fight and save him from death. None of the humans would ever act without their Master's order.

As the last remnant of Alexander's body crumbled into dust, emotions shone through Demetrius's mask. Pain, regret, anger, grief, all fought for control for a moment, before settling into the despotic certainty of a dictator seeing his throne challenged, determined to cling on for all he was worth.

"Does anyone have anything else to say?" he asked, his voice tight.

Silence fell. For several minutes, no one even dared to move. Released from my arms, Sky stood perfectly still, staring at the pile of dust that had been Alexander.

"Very well," Demetrius said, as if the disturbance had been nothing more than a glass breaking, "let's continue with our celebration."

The ashes stirred, and for a moment I wondered if Alexander had set up some last trick, a trap to catch his sire with. Then I saw that Ariel's fingers were moving, using magic to sweep the ashes up into a champagne glass that levitated in front of Demetrius until he took hold of it, a look of appreciation and then of sorrow crossing his elegant features. It was a smart move on Ariel's part, building her rapport with the Master of the North, seeking to extend her alliances beyond the pack. Not for the first time, I was glad that we had such a sharp operator as a friend, not an enemy.

Uniformed members of the garden led in a new set of humans, or perhaps ones we had seen before but in different outfits. Their formal clothes were tailored to expose their necks, wrists, and thighs, providing easy access to their veins. Now we were in for the true darkness of a vampire party, and my stomach turned at the thought.

The formalities were over, and it was time for us to leave. I didn't know if the vampires would feel even slightly uncomfortable feeding with outsiders around, but as one of those outsiders, I didn't want to be there. Claudia was already halfway out the door, and Sebastian and Ariel were heading that way. While Sky went to find David and Trent, I followed my Alpha's lead.

I reached the door just as he and Ariel did, and they paused there.

"That was unexpected," Sebastian said, glancing at the glass of ashes being carried away from Demetrius on a silver tray.

"For us, yes," I said. "But I think Chris knew what she was doing."

"Really?" Ariel raised an eyebrow. "I didn't know that the new Mistress of the Seethe had such depths."

"She wouldn't be where she is without them," I said. "By all means work on your relationship with the Seethe, but don't ever make the mistake of trusting them. Not even Chris."

The words could easily have sounded bitter, especially when directed against an ex, but I couldn't prevent a note of admiration from coming into my voice. Chris had pulled off a great coup, capturing the heart of one vampire and using him to destroy another. Her power and influence in the Seethe was increasingly impressive.

Sebastian and Ariel headed out into the night, and a moment later Gideon and Abigail stalked past. Alone by the grand double doors, I looked back to see how Sky was getting on in retrieving "our" humans. They seemed to be caught in conversation with a pair of eager vampires, and David and Trent were resisting Sky's attempts to make them leave. Not quite able to hear the details, I read their lips, and saw the vampires' attempts to keep David and Trent around. Fortunately, Sky had a persuasive touch and managed to drag them away, but not before one of the vampires kissed her on the back of the hand. I gritted my teeth and fought back the deep disgust I felt at seeing a creature like him trying to win Sky around.

The vampires watched the departing humans with

hungry stares that set my teeth on edge. As Sky, David, and Trent approached the door, I picked out their conversation from the background chatter.

"I don't think I've ever met more intriguing people," David said, giddy with delight. "They are over a hundred years old. So many wonderful stories."

"Yes," Sky said, "but I can assure you that their interest in you was more than just another person to tell their entertaining stories to."

"Life has to be hard for you to be so cynical and on alert even during such a nice party," Trent said in a snippy tone.

"You are human," Sky said, blushing. "They see you as entertainment only. What you were being treated to was seduction into being just that. It is easy to be enthralled by it and not see it for what it is."

"Your relationship with Quell didn't happen by seduction."

I could have slapped Trent for that comment. The heartbreak at her friend's death, still fresh after several months, sank Sky's face into grief. There was no need for any slapping though, as Trent's own face fell, realizing what he had done.

"No, we were friends," Sky said, her voice quivering.

They were close enough now for me to intervene.

"I don't doubt that they were interesting and they were probably interested in you as well," I said, looking sternly at the two humans, "but that would not override their desire to feed from you. You two would present a challenge, far more exciting than the willing participants they traipsed in. Whether you realize it or not, you were being hunted. Their Master was just killed and they are in a new town. I doubt much care would be given. Not everyone respects your affiliation with our pack. Or perhaps they'd be willing to take the risk to have you. Flattering, but won't mean a thing if you are dead. Sky saved your lives."

The blood drained from their faces. At last, something had sunk in, and we headed in silence to the car.

<hr>

"You scared them," Sky said as we drove away from David and Trent's home.

Trent stood at the window, peering warily out into the darkness. He probably thought that he could protect them with the sword Winter had been teaching him how to use. Winter was a good teacher, but not good enough to make Trent a threat in a fight. If trouble came, that sword and his determination wouldn't help.

"They need to be afraid," I said. "Fear might motivate them to be safer. I don't want them to die."

I hated to admit it, but working with them on the wedding had given me a certain fondness for Sky's friends. I didn't want to hang out with them, but I definitely didn't want them drained dry by vampires. Once we were out of sight of the house, I pulled out my phone and called Winter.

"Are you busy?" I asked.

"What did Sky do and how bad is it?"

"I'm right here," Sky responded indignantly.

"I stand by my question." There was amusement in Winter's voice, and I laughed in response.

"It's not Sky, but it's Sky-adjacent."

"David and Trent?"

"Yeah. The Presentation didn't go as smoothly as expected and the Southern vampires no longer have a Master. He wasn't much, but his erratic behavior did help some. I have a feeling they are going to have a lot of fun in our city and leave a mess to clean up. I don't want David and Trent to get caught up in that. They piqued the interest of two old vampires. I don't think they are going to leave without having that interest satisfied."

"Okay, I'm going over there, but I'm going to kick Trent's ass if he tries to 'find the woman behind the scowl' and give me one of his dumbass makeovers. I don't like people touching my hair."

"Don't scowl, 'black swan,'" I joked.

Winter cursed me out, and I laughed again. Some days, I really needed someone smart enough and strong enough to push back against me. Somebody other than Sky, that is.

"Winter, things are a little fragile. If any vampires show up, please try diplomacy first."

"I will. I'm going to show them all types of diplomacy. Diplomacy will be seeping out of all the cuts on their body."

The phone went dead and I set it back down. David and Trent should be safe in Winter's hands, as long as they didn't push her over the edge. At least the end of their evening would be relaxing.

"I didn't see what happened today coming," I admitted. Sure, I could see Chris's manipulation once it was in front of me, but I'd had no idea that she was plotting anything, or that she would push it so far.

"I think Alexander was underestimated," Sky said, sounding annoyed, though I couldn't work out why. "You saw how quickly he overtook Chris. With all the rumors and things said about him, I didn't expect him to be so powerful."

"Powerful?" I frowned. "Why do you think that?"

"He overtook Chris so quickly." She turned to face me, and now I understood. She was still unhappy that I had held her back from helping Chris. She didn't understand that it would have been quite the opposite of helping. "Why did you stop me? He could have killed her."

"I stopped you because it needed to play out the way Chris intended. She goaded him into attacking her." I glanced from the road to Sky, trying to judge whether the words were sinking in. "Chris allowed him to overtake her. Alexander didn't stand much of a chance against her when she was human. Now that she's a vampire, he had no chance in hell.

"When he attacked her, she didn't look at him, she watched the crowd. The Northern vampires who moved to protect her are the ones who have accepted her position and can be trusted. Those who did nothing will be watched and are possibly enemies. In her position, I would have done the same thing." I chuckled, my admiration growing as I realized how deep Chris's plan had gone. "Most people would have missed that and will perceive her as weak. That will give her an advantage, because those who haven't accepted her position and want to remedy it will be surprised. It's an excellent strategy. People often dismissed her success as a Hunter as luck. It's always good to have those who might be opponents underestimate your abilities."

Sky frowned. "Is there a class about this or something? If so, I need to take it."

"Sweetheart, if there were a class, you would spend most of it looking at videos on YouTube," I said, reminding her of her own behavior in the pack acclimatization classes. "I can't imagine how many videos of cute animals there are on there to distract you."

"Do you think the visiting vampires are going to start trouble?"

"Some will, to test Demetrius. I'm sure there are some that cared deeply for Alexander and, although they would never directly challenge Demetrius, they will do things to make his life hell. One way is to visit and leave a mess in their wake for him to clean up."

I'd seen that sort of crap from vampires before, treating other people as nothing but cannon fodder in their own fights. Just thinking about it made my blood boil.

"The witches," Sky blurted out. "Sebastian took Ariel with him. I'm sure they know who you are and her display of magic revealed her ability."

"I don't think they would go after the witches. Vampires and witches have had an amiable relationship for many years. It's the relationship with vampires and were-animals that's strained and fragile…"

"Vincent and Ashton's interest in David and Trent is just to start trouble?"

"I'm not sure. Although Vincent claimed to be appreciative of your effort to save Chris, he didn't move to prevent Alexander from attacking her. There could be a number of reasons: fear of Alexander's retaliation if he'd lived, the desire for him to fail and die, making the Master's position open, or just indifference."

"You heard what he said from across the room."

"I read lips too," I said, thinking back to the sleazy vampires and the way they had treated not just David and Trent but Sky too. "And I wasn't happy with him kissing you."

"On the hand?"

"Still didn't like it."

My phone rang, and Winter's number flashed up. This couldn't be good news. I tapped the screen to take the call.

"This isn't going to be handled diplomatically," she said, sounding tense. "There are more than just two here. There are seven. Two of them came together. Two annoyingly fancy ones I suspect are the vampires you were worried about. There are others and they aren't formally dressed. Maybe visitors that just started trouble."

"No, it's doubtful," I said, trying to work out what I would have done in their position. "Alexander had been here several days. I suspect they are newly created by him and have heard of his death. They are going to try to start a war between us. With Alexander dead, control falls to Demetrius until another Master is appointed. Their behavior is a reflection on Demetrius. We'll be there in a few."

I slammed on the breaks, spun the car around, and raced

back in the direction we had come from. As we went, I dialed Josh's number. If the vampires wanted to provoke us, that was another soft point they could hit.

"What's up?" Josh asked, sounding confused. "I thought you were meant to be at the big bad vampire rave."

"Is anyone strange hanging around near your place?" I asked.

"Not that I've seen."

"Good. Keep an eye open. The Southern Seethe lost their Master tonight, and they're out to cause trouble."

Josh whistled long and low. "Okay, I'll keep my eyes peeled and my magic fingers ready."

I hung up and called the other ranking pack members, leaving Steven with the job of spreading the word. We needed everyone to be on the lookout in case this trouble spread.

We reached a junction and I hesitated, hands gripping the wheel tight. One way, the road led to David and Trent, who we knew were in danger. But the other way would take us to Josh. I had worked so hard my whole life keeping my brother safe, could I really leave him unprotected now, with hostile vampires roaming Chicago? Was I willing to take that risk when my kid brother's life was at stake?

Except that my kid brother was a powerful witch, while David and Trent were a pair of cartoonish corporate workers with all the magic and combat prowess of a dead beetle. Without me, Josh might end up in danger. David and Trent, on the other hand, would almost certainly end up dead.

I turned the wheel and headed for David's house.

CHAPTER 30

We pulled into David and Trent's driveway, and straight into a tense standoff. David stood in the doorway, a shotgun in his hands, aiming it at a group of vampires. Two of them were Ashton and Vincent, the impeccably dressed creatures who had been chatting to David and Trent at the party. The other five were scruffy looking, not proper inductees into vampire society but casual creations, probably made by the Southern Seethe with the aim of causing trouble for Demetrius. Winter stood to one side, a crossbow in her hand, muscles coiled tight and ready for action as she watched to see what the vampires would do.

Fortunately, it was late, and no lights were on in the windows of David and Trent's neighbors. For now at least, we didn't have an audience.

Despite what seemed to me like the obvious danger of the situation, David looked as much confused as scared. The gun seemed like a token effort, rather than a sign that he was ready for serious violence. That was fortunate, as I doubted that David was ever ready for that kind of action.

Sky got out of the car, took off her high-heeled shoes, and walked slowly up to the door.

"Get in the house," she said. "They can't pass the threshold without being invited."

Behind David, Trent pulled an embarrassed face.

"You invited them in already, didn't you?" Sky said in a tone of irritation.

"Just Ashton and Vincent," Trent replied. "They were here before the others came."

She cursed under her breath.

I climbed out of the car and shut the door quietly behind me. All attention was on the conversation at the doorway, and I crept closer to the nearest vampires, ready to intervene if trouble started.

Even with the shotgun out and Sky's warnings about the danger they were in, Trent couldn't contain his curiosity. He followed David across the threshold and out into the fresh air, where he stood watching the vampires. I didn't know what he'd heard from Sky about the realities of life in the supernatural world, but I could see the appeal for him. This was all something new, exotic and exciting, quite unlike the reality of his life, and after seeing the Presentation, it held a great aura of glamour, as well as a thrill of action and intrigue. What he didn't seem to understand, but David finally seemed to understand, was how easily that violence could turn on them. If he kept up the attitude of naive curiosity then he was going to get into a lot of trouble.

Whatever Vincent had planned to do here, it was spinning out of his control. Some of the other vampires were backing off at his command, but others leaned forward, eager for a taste of Trent and David's humanity. Meanwhile, Winter's patience was wearing thin, and she raised the crossbow, ready for trouble. She looked more than ready to kick off but was holding back, not knowing the details of how the Presentation had played out and so the politics behind this situation. She might be a woman of action by nature, but she hadn't reached the position of Third in the Midwest Pack without paying attention to what lay behind the violence.

The youngest vampire pounced, leaping past David so fast he didn't even have time to pull the trigger, and slammed into Trent. He bent back Trent's head and opened his mouth wide, exposing his fangs.

Sky grabbed hold of the vampire's hair and jerked, trying to wrench him off of Trent. He writhed and flailed, but she pulled him off, leaving Trent lying on the ground terrified, one hand clutching his own throat. The vampire swung around, Sky's hand still gripping his hair, and hissed at her.

I stayed back, my attention on the other vampires, ready to step in if they intervened. Sky had control of this. I needed to let her sort it out.

Trent started pushing himself to his feet, eyes wide. The tussle had left him exposed, as David looked wildly around at the other vampires and Sky grappled with the attacker.

Another vampire leapt at Trent. There was a twang, a thud, and a crossbow bolt pierced him through the heart, its tip protruding from his chest. He crumbled to ash, falling in dust across Trent, while Winter grinned in predatory satis-faction.

The other three newly made vampires stood staring at me and I stared at them, willing them to make their move, to give me the excuse I needed to rip them apart. But either they were wiser than that or they were too scared, because they stood back, each waiting for the others to act.

A bright flash of headlights made me avert my eyes for a moment. When I looked up, a bright-red Audi R8 convertible was skidding to a halt inches from the nearest vampires. Chris stepped out, her face carrying the glowering menace of a thunderstorm swelling on the horizon.

This wasn't the elegant, dressed-up Chris that we had seen a couple of hours before. She wore jeans, a t-shirt, and solid boots. The only trace of the gothic Mistress persona was her ring, whose huge diamond shone like a knife's edge in the headlights.

"We have this handled," Ashton said to her dismissively. "You should be with Demetrius, not here dealing with this."

"True. Yet *this* is now my responsibility." She looked across the assembled vampires, the terrified humans, Winter sliding another bolt into her crossbow, and me and Sky, both of us blazing with fury. "Which ones are yours?"

Ashton's lips tightened. "We had every intention of taking them with us. We weren't going to leave them behind."

"That's not the question I asked," Chris said in a voice of command. "Which ones are yours?"

"These three." Ashton pointed to the nervous vampires facing me.

"Neither one of you are strong enough to be creating vampires." She closed her eyes for a moment in thought, and when they opened again, she treated Ashton and Vincent to a severe look. "You will bring them to our house, where you will stay until they exhibit control that I am satisfied with."

"We were planning to leave tomorrow," Vincent said defiantly, facing her with his head raised and shoulders squared.

"Those *were* your plans before you decided to create vampires and let them loose in my city. There are new rules of engagement..." She let those words hang for a moment, let these disobedient vampires consider what had happened to their Master when he tried to attack her. "Your plans have changed. Alexander allowed things that won't be accepted any longer."

Vincent dropped all pretense of pleasantry as he prowled toward her, apparently trying to intimidate. "Alexander's way worked and we were happy to follow him."

The other side went unspoken; that many of the Southern Seethe had no intention of obeying Chris, no matter what. If he thought that would shock her, or that his presence would put her on edge, then he was a fool. Chris looked bored.

"Gather your newbie vamps," she said, "and the ones that Alexander created and left, and come to the house. I expect you to be there within the hour."

She turned her back on Vincent, dismissing any argument he might make, any threat he thought that he presented to her. This was his moment. If he wanted to take her out, he would never have a better chance. If he didn't take it, then he would prove his weakness to the rest.

He just watched, face furrowed with frustration, as she opened the door of the car.

"You can choose to ignore me," she said, "but I assure you it will be the biggest mistake in what will become your very short life."

She climbed into the car and drove away.

Vincent stared after her until the sound of the Audi's engine faded into the night, leaving silence except for the tapping of Winter's finger against the side of her crossbow.

He wheeled around, grabbed the vampire Sky had been restraining, and flung him into the back of a car. The others meekly followed, their dreams of vampire menace abandoned, and all six survivors sped away into the night.

I stared in incredulity at the four glasses of wine and the platter of cheese and chocolates that David and Trent had laid out on their coffee table. There was soft rock playing in the background and the lights were turned down comfortably low. This was a setup designed to make guests welcome, not to fend off the uninvited sort.

"You asked them over?" Sky growled, cutting through David and Trent's rambling mess of defiance, apology, and defensiveness. "What did I tell you?"

David crossed his arms. "Look, I know there are some bad vampires, just like there are horrible weres, but I don't appreciate being treated like a child. I can pick my friends just fine."

I took a deep breath to control the frustration bubbling up inside me. I was so rigid with tension I could have turned into a statue. Here we were, rushing back from our own evening to protect David and Trent. Winter sat outside with a crossbow and a sword, ready in case the southern vampires changed their minds and came back to cause more trouble. Yet these idiots, who minutes before had been attacked by a vampire, weren't ready to acknowledge their mistake.

"Handle this, Sky," I said through gritted teeth, pressing my fingers to the bridge of my nose, trying to squeeze away some of the tension.

Even Sky's patience was crumbling. I could feel her frustration as clearly as I could hear the music and smell the chocolates slowly melting on the platter. But she controlled herself, let out a long breath, and lowered her voice.

"Vampires are intriguing. The lure is undeniable—"

"It's not the lure of vampires," Trent butted in. "It's Vincent and Ashton. They are different."

Sky bit her lip, physically holding back the rebuke I could sense she wanted to unleash. The tables had turned and now she was the one holding back someone else's stupidity and impulsiveness, but I couldn't take any pleasure in the reversal. David and Trent hadn't just put their own lives in danger, they had nearly triggered an act of violence that could have unleashed a fresh war between the pack and the Seethe. They were foolish beyond belief, and I was too angry to even try to deal with them.

"Fine," Sky said, "they might be good—there are plenty of good vampires."

I scoffed, and she gave me a look that said she didn't appreciate my input.

"I told you guys to be careful," she said.

"We were careful," David said calmly, presenting his

words as if they were reasonable. "You saw them—they handled it and would have handled it just fine if you all hadn't intervened. Quell was a good person—not a vampire. And Chris doesn't seem that bad. Let's be honest, if we were staying away from scary supernaturals, you two wouldn't be in our lives."

Sky clammed up. I didn't know if it was her friendship with Chris, the memory of Quell, or just her relationship with these two, but something was stopping her from brushing off David's argument with the dismissal it deserved. A few good vampires didn't mean that the rest were safe, and treating weres as if we were the same was willfully ignorant. But apparently Sky didn't have it in her to fight that fight.

"Okay," she said, "but I need you two to be more careful."

David looked pointedly at the shotgun standing next to the door and the sword in the umbrella stand. "We are."

Sky gave up. Instead of trying to make them understand, she turned and walked out of the house. I followed her, incredulous that she had left it there.

"You handled that just great," I muttered as we approached my car.

Sky stopped walking, leaving me to stride on by myself. I stopped a few feet from the car and turned to see her glaring, channeling her anger at me. I had no time for it. She had introduced David and Trent to the world of the supernatural, had wound them into our lives, and now had failed to bring them safely into line when they acted like idiots. If she wanted to be mad at someone, she could be mad at herself.

"What did you say to me?" she snapped.

"You handled that just great," I said, irritated, directing the commanding gaze of a Beta at her.

She stomped up to me, red-faced. "You think that's the way I wanted it to end up? If you knew all the horrible things that went through my mind, what I was willing to do to keep them safe, you wouldn't dare talk to me that way."

She blinked back tears, and that sight shamed me. I was trying to protect Sky, not hurt her. How hard could it be for her to understand that? I looked away, taking deep breaths to bring my anger under control, and looked down at the rings on our fingers, a sign of our love for one another. That was what mattered. That was what I needed to cling onto.

I cupped her face in my hands, took a deep breath of her scent, and felt my racing heart rate slow. I pressed my lips to her forehead, feeling her warmth and softness.

"If something happens to them, it will devastate you," I said. "I don't want to see that happen."

"They're not as careless as we think they are," Sky replied quietly. "Things might not have happened the way you would have liked, but it was handled."

"Yeah."

Sky hadn't convinced me—hell, she hadn't even convinced herself—but it was time to let this one go. I stepped back and held out my hand, which she took in hers, squeezing it tight for the last few feet to my car.

As soon as we were on the road, I made a call.

"This can't be good," Josh said sleepily.

"Can you go to Trent and David's and put a ward around the house?"

"Does it have to be now?"

I considered that for a moment. Could I leave them for tonight, now that Ashton and Vincent were out of the picture? Not safely. Who knew what other vampires Sky's pet humans had been chatting to at the party, letting slip who they were, where they lived, and how fascinated they were by all things supernatural.

"Yes. I'd like one as soon as possible."

"Okay, give me half an hour."

"How about we go out for dinner tomorrow night?" I asked, leaning over the kitchen counter so I could soak up Sky's scent and feel the warmth of her skin inches from my own. Between us, the dinner plates lay empty, and Sky was scooping up the last of a big bowl of ice cream. "An interesting new fusion place just opened in town, and I feel like we're due some special time to ourselves."

The five days since the Presentation had been intense ones. In between working on a couple of court cases, I had been gathering every scrap of intelligence I could on the activities of the local vampires, watching for any sign of instability in the wake of Alexander's death, while down south, Joan had her people doing the same thing. It was proving difficult to track who was doing what where, with so many vampires moving around outside their territory and only so many weres available with any skill for covertly watching them. I was busy and frustrated, needing some distraction from it all. And with the bar's refurbishment well underway, Sky was likely to become busier over the next few weeks, meaning now might be our last good chance in months for a night out.

"Fusion food," Sky said, pulling a thoughtful face. "You mean like red velvet cake combined with an eclair?"

I laughed. Of course that was the part of the meal that interested her.

"Perhaps," I said. "I didn't look at the desserts."

"What kind of monster doesn't look at the desserts?"

"One without a sugar addiction."

She snorted. "It's not an addiction, just a habit I need to cut back on if I want to fit into my clothes."

"So no fusion food?" I asked, the corner of my mouth quirking up as I anticipated her response.

"Don't be ridiculous." She smiled and leaned forward to kiss me. "Maybe afterward we can—" Her phone buzzed in the next room. "I should get that."

She hurried through and I ambled slowly after her.

"Demetrius?" she said in surprise as she picked up the phone.

"You need to come get your humans." The Master vampire's voice emerged, cold and callous, from the phone. He gave an address, which I recognized as one of the places where the southern vampires had been lurking in town, one we hadn't yet had a chance to investigate. Then he hung up.

There were only two humans Demetrius might describe as Sky's, and I could see all too clearly how they might have stumbled into Demetrius's path. Her heart was racing, fear for David and Trent taking over.

I walked up behind Sky and wrapped my arms around her. I didn't think yet about what the wider implications of this call might be, just focused on staying calm, using the slow rhythm of my breath to soothe Sky and bring her heart rate down. She would need a clear head to deal with the vampires, no matter what terrible things we found when we arrived. Gradually, her breath slowed and her heart followed it. At last, she relaxed against me.

Twenty minutes later, I drove up the driveway of an abandoned-looking stone house, with Sky beside me. The garden of the place was overrun, weeds growing through the driveway, moss creeping up the dirty stone walls. Paint peeled from the door frame and one of the windows was boarded shut.

I parked behind Demetrius's car, a dark vision of tinted windows and black body work. Tall poplars obscured the moon, so that only fragments of its light dappled the path up to the front door.

The place stank of blood, almost obliterating the aromas of wine, perfume, and body spray. Vampire smells—decadence and death. Trickles of blood ran from the leaf-strewn path across the porch and through the splintered frame from which the open door hung, one of its hinges broken away.

I silently cursed myself for not having checked this place out sooner. If I had, then we might have caught whatever was going on here and dealt with it ourselves. We might have saved a lot of hurt for whoever the vampires had drawn here, including David and Trent. But I hadn't been focused enough.

Groans, whimpers, and the occasional thud emerged from darkened rooms as we made our way through the house. It was deceptively spacious, but poorly lit, light flickering from dusty bulbs through spider-webbed lampshades. Sky hesitated for a moment, but I pressed my hand against her back and urged her on—this wasn't somewhere I wanted to linger any longer than I needed to.

Demetrius stood, black-clad and menacing, in the center of what had once been a dining room. He was holding Ashton by the throat, suspending him in the air while the younger vampire gasped and clawed, trying to break free.

"Was this your plan?" Demetrius said angrily. He dropped the battered Ashton, then grabbed him by the scruff of his neck and turned him to face a small crowd of vampires, all of them wide-eyed with fear. "Did you and Vincent really think you could overtake me with these new vamps?" Ashton's head dropped and Demetrius yanked it back up to face his creations. "What the fuck were you thinking?"

So this was what Ashton and Vincent had been up to since the night of the Presentation: creating their own army of vampires, in preparation for a coup against Demetrius. I couldn't fault them for wanting rid of the bloodstained tyrant, but I didn't think that they would have been any better, or that their plan was likely to succeed when they were pitting new creations against a master of the unliving.

Despite the disparity in power, several of the new vampires seemed to be finding their courage, too ignorant perhaps to understand how badly they were outmatched. They squared their shoulders and fanned out, moving toward Demetrius, but he pinned each one of them in place with a stare of pure malice.

"He is your creator; I am your Master. Who do you fear the most?"

He exposed his fangs, sharp and bloodstained, ready to perpetuate more violence against anyone who defied him.

Sky sniffed, then ran off down a hallway, and I followed her, flinging doors open and looking through each one, pursuing David's and Trent's scents. Then I heard a sound, a distant sobbing, so faint it would be inaudible to almost anyone. Drawn by that sound, I rushed past Sky and headed left down a long hall, with her close behind me. I flung open the last door I found.

Inside, David sat on the floor, pale and with his head lolling to one side, revealing the bite marks on his neck. Trent lay cradled in his arms, his skin bone white, eyes closed, not even his chest moving. David stared up at us, his eyes red with tears, and clutched Trent tight as he sobbed with wild abandon.

The scene looked desolate, but I sensed hope: the slightest murmur of a sound, faint and erratic, coming from Trent.

"He still has a heartbeat," I said. "It's really weak, but it's there. We have to get him to Dr. Jeremy."

I snatched Trent from David's arms and ran for the front door, trusting the others to follow. Around me, the house was breaking down into violence. There was a thud of a body against a wall and a crash of breaking glass. We ran out the front door a moment before Ashton, who was fleeing for his life.

Demetrius followed, a dark streak of movement that collided with Ashton and slammed him to the ground. Before the Master could complete his victory, the other vampires came swarming out and flung themselves at him. The garden became a mass of flying bodies, as they hurled themselves at Demetrius and he tossed them aside.

A flash of headlights, the roar of an engine, and Chris's car pulled into the driveway, blocking us in. When she saw what I was carrying, she pulled back out, parked in the street, and leapt out, crossbow in hand.

"Is he alive?" she asked brusquely, her gaze flitting between Trent and the whirling melee around Demetrius. "Hurry up and get him out of here."

She leveled the crossbow and headed toward the fight.

As I was settling Trent in the back seat, Vincent appeared at the edge of the violence whirling through the overgrown garden. He darted in, stake in hand, and swung at Demetrius. The Master vampire turned too late, and instead of dodging the attack, he was penetrated by the stake. He sank to his knees as reversion took hold.

I climbed into the driver's seat, ready to go, but Sky's attention was fixed on the fight. Chris fired her crossbow, hitting Vincent through the heart, then reloaded fast enough to do the same for Ashton as he staggered, battered and bloody, to his feet. Both started to revert, their bodies crumpling faster than Demetrius.

With Sky in her seat, I started backing out of the driveway, even as Chris went to kneel beside Demetrius. Then Sky's door swung open and I slammed on the breaks, staring at her in alarm.

"Get them to Dr. Jeremy," she said, gesturing at David and Trent. "I'll meet you there."

"Sky, get back in the car," I called out in alarm. We needed to get away from this madness, to leave the vampires to their well-earned destruction. "Now!"

"Just go. Please."

She slammed the door shut and ran across the garden, to where Chris knelt sobbing over Demetrius.

I cursed. I could see where this was going already, Sky's compassion overriding her good sense, risking her life for these monsters just because Chris had decided she was a friend. I should go after her, to make sure she was okay.

In the back seat, David groaned, and Trent's heartbeat grew ever fainter.

Still cursing, I pulled out of the driveway and tore off down the road, driving hell for leather toward the retreat. I couldn't let these two idiots die, not after everything we had gone through to protect them. That would be a waste. Not only that, but it would break Sky's heart.

I raced through the night, running red lights and leaving speed limits far behind, intent on getting David and Trent to help. On a long straight stretch, I fished out my phone and called Jeremy.

"This had better be an emergency," he mumbled sleepily.

"David and Trent, sucked dry by vampires," I said. "Heading for the retreat now. Not sure they'll both make it."

"Crap." I heard a rustle and a thud of feet. "How far out are you?"

I glanced at a traffic sign. "Ten minutes."

"I'll start prepping the infirmary."

As I hung up, there was another groan from the back seat. The pain and misery of that sound made me squirm. I needed to get through. I needed these two to be okay.

"Hang in there," I called back to them.

I was glad that it was late enough for the streets to be nearly empty, but as I flashed past a speed limit, another worry crossed my mind. There were so many people with vendettas against us, and after Steven's trial I was in the public eye. How much harm could a speeding violation do us? It could become the latest weapon to turn the eyes of the world onto us and try to expose the weres.

I dialed another number as I swerved through the winding streets that led to the retreat.

"Ethan!" Quinn said excitedly. "What's up? You change your mind about joining us for Klingon night? We've got a wicked game of—"

"Speed cameras," I snapped. "Can you hack speed cameras?"

"Sure," Quinn said, his voice turning serious as he caught my tone. "What do you need?"

"I'm on my way to the retreat now, and I've probably left a trail of violations between here and the east side. Can you get in and scrub the evidence before anyone sees it?"

"Sure. Where did you start?"

I gave him the address. "And make it quick. I don't want to wake up in the morning to any more trouble than we already have."

"I'll make it so."

I flung the phone aside just as I drove into the driveway of the retreat, coming to a stop in a squeal of brakes and a stink of overheated rubber. Gavin and Kelly were at the doors of the retreat, standing on opposite sides of a gurney.

"Get Trent!" I shouted to them as I leapt out. "He's almost gone."

Just saying that felt like a spike being driven into my gut. These overeager idiots didn't deserve to die just because they were curious about the world, because our wild lives had fallen onto their doorsteps and they hadn't been able to resist. That would be stupid and unfair. It would be one pointless tragedy too far.

I scooped David out of the back seat.

"I can walk," he mumbled. "'S okay."

"It's not fucking okay," I growled, rushing into the retreat with him in my arms, following the gurney on which Kelly and Gavin pushed a prone Trent. His heartbeat was even fainter, a final glimmer of life's light that was on the verge of flickering out.

"Trent!" David wailed, delirious with blood loss. "Where's Trent?"

Jeremy stood in the doorway of the infirmary, a cannula in his hand attached to an IV bag full of blood. The moment the gurney stopped, he thrust the needle into Trent's arm. Only when that was done did he don his stethoscope and listen to Trent's heartbeat.

"Just in time," he said, wiping his brow. "Well done, Ethan."

I set David down on a bed. "He'll need one too."

Gavin and I stepped back, leaving the medical professionals to do their work.

"When did we become nursemaids to a bunch of humans?" Gavin asked, exasperated.

I shrugged. I wanted to say that it was all about Sky, that for me, looking after these two was a way of looking after her. But somewhere along the road from that rundown house to here, I had realized that was no longer true. I wanted to keep these two idiotic innocents safe for their own sake. They were… what, friends?

I had been using Sky to explain away my own emotional connections, to pretend that I didn't care about the world.

But faced with the real risk of losing people who mattered to me, I had to acknowledge their existence.

Sky had done it again, like she kept doing. She was turning me into—I shuddered at the thought—a better person.

CHAPTER 32

I paced the entrance hall of the retreat, waiting for Sky to return. David and Trent were resting, and the rest of us were under instructions from Jeremy to leave them in peace as much as possible. Now that their lives were secure, my biggest concern was Sky and what she might have done.

Demetrius had been dying when I left, and I was willing to say good riddance to the blood-drinking trash. But Trent had also been dying, and now the color was starting to return to his skin, thanks to Jeremy and the fact that he had been ready with their blood types on file. Just as an infusion of blood had saved Trent, a different sort of blood infusion could potentially have saved Demetrius and forced us to continue dealing with him.

In any sane world, Sky would have left the Master of the Northern Seethe to die. She could have offered Chris the consolation of a shoulder to cry on if she needed it, could have helped her mop up any survivors from Ashton and Vincent's improvised army, could have taken sensible measures to limit the damage from what had happened. But no world with Sky in it was entirely sane, and I suspected that, on this occasion, she had run fully mad.

She stalked through the door, surfing in on a vast rolling wave of emotions. As she looked at me, panic took hold: she clearly feared the worst.

"He should be fine," I said, doing my best to reassure her. "There was a significant amount of blood loss, but Dr. Jeremy is confident he'll be okay."

She let out a deep breath and I watched her face, looking for any sign of what had happened while we were apart.

"You Skyed it, didn't you?" I asked. When she didn't immediately answer, I moved closer, eyes fixed on her. "Demetrius is alive, isn't he?"

She nodded slowly.

"Skyed." I had to laugh, because the alternative would be to get mad, and there was no point in doing that. Sky had followed her instincts, had let compassion overcome common sense. Nothing I said would make her recognize that reality, but there was a grim amusement to be had from knowing that I had been right. Her mistakes were entirely predictable.

Demetrius was a powerful vampire, one who had repeatedly acted against us, who was responsible for countless deaths. Saving him was an act of madness, but it was a very Sky sort of insanity. She had chosen to let her feelings for Chris, an outsider to our pack, take precedence over the greater good. Her compassion was one of the things that I loved about her, but it could be bewildering to deal with, especially where the vampires were concerned. They were our natural enemies, self-centered killers with all the compassion of a corpse, but still she treated them like people. It was this kindness of spirit that led to so many of her worst mistakes, and the only way I could cope with it was to turn it into a joke: Sky Skying things up again.

"Did you see her face?" she whispered, sounding stunned.

"Yes, which is why I knew he'd be alive." I remembered the sight of Chris, her face a vision of grief, sorrow like nothing I'd ever seen on her before. Chris was a hunter turned vampire, a woman made hard by the scars life had inflicted. She didn't cry. And yet there they were, tears for a man I had been sure she was just manipulating, a show of misery for an audience that wasn't there. Whatever else was going on with Chris, she really did care about Demetrius.

She had become a mystery to me.

I took Sky's hand and led her to the hallway outside the infirmary, where David stood watching through the window. He already looked far better than he had, and was recovered enough for Jeremy to have booted him out rather than deal with his fussing while there was medical work to be done. Though red-eyed and weary, David managed a smile.

I put Sky between me and David. Part of it was a gesture of comfort toward him—Sky was the one he was close to, and a far better source of support than me right now. But there was also the anger bubbling away inside me, which had been manifesting since I learned that these two were safe. My frustration at how they had endangered themselves was coming to the surface, and I didn't want to unleash it here and now.

Through the window, Jeremy and Kelly were treating Trent. They had set him up with another IV and connected him to a monitor. Fearing that memories of the vampires might lead to panic when he woke up, they had also sedated him. He lay there placidly, pale still but better than before, on his slow way to recovery.

"They said they just wanted to talk," David said, shooting me a look. He stood tall, showing no sign of acknowledging what an idiot he had been, or that believing the vampires had almost gotten his partner killed.

"Don't talk," I replied. I wasn't going to sit through his

self-justifying bullshit, and he wasn't well enough to face my wrath.

"They were nice, I never—"

I wheeled on him. "What part of that fucking command did you not understand?"

"I am not part of this pack, you don't command me to do a damn thing," David said, glaring at me.

"Then don't take it as a command; it's a threat. Don't open your mouth again. Nice or not, the damn ward was put in place for a reason. To protect you two. The only way it could be dropped is with the keyword that we have and you all had. You let them in." I pointed at the infirmary door. "So whatever happened to him is on you. He could have died. How in the hell do you think that would have made Sky feel?"

Because of course it was all about Sky, and not me. Oh no, I couldn't possibly get attached to this pair of ridiculous, pompous, overgrown children.

David seemed about to respond, but my glare silenced him. Sky slid between us.

"David's been through enough today," she said softly. "Let it go." She nudged me and I turned away, glad of an excuse not to look at David, leaving her free to talk to him. "You know you can stay here. Just pick a room. We'll be back tomorrow, and if you need anything Kelly will help you. She won't go home."

We were walking out the door when Winter strode in, a look of fury on her face.

"How did they get past the ward?" she snapped at David.

Sky sighed, grabbed Winter's hand, and drew her out of the room. I followed.

"No," Sky said to Winter. "You're not going to yell at him too. He realizes what he did was wrong. Please don't kick him while he's down."

"Trent is okay, right?" Winter whispered, her voice full of

worry. "When Kelly called me, she told me he was going to be okay."

"He should be okay. If you go in there, you can't yell at David. I'm sure he's feeling like crap. He doesn't need more from you two."

She looked at me with disapproval. I stood my ground. If David was going to survive in our world then he needed to toughen up, and he needed to learn to listen. Cushioning him now would be no help in the long run.

But I wasn't going to win that fight. Even Winter had given up on it, nodding sadly. She took a couple of deep breaths and closed her eyes, bringing her emotions back under control.

"Okay," she said. Her frown faded and she headed back to David.

"Come on," Sky said. "I'm exhausted, and we've done everything we can here. We should get home and rest."

CHAPTER 33

I sat on the sofa with my feet up, reading a draft of a legal textbook one of the legal partners was working on. Ever since our conversation, they had started seeking my input on a wider range of issues, from complex cases to side projects like this. It was as if, now that the tension between us had been addressed, they had decided to turn me into a guided weapon, offering insights and analysis wherever they were needed. I was enjoying it.

The morning was nearly over, and Sky had only just emerged from the bedroom. Tiring as the previous night's rescue mission had been, I was pretty sure that wasn't what had kept her there. She had been avoiding me, still angry that I refused to apologize to David, even though I had nothing to apologize for.

Of course, her anger at me didn't stop her from plowing through the heap of breakfast food I had laid out, now that she had emerged. There was rare steak to satisfy her vampiric side, eggs and milk for extra protein, and a side of red velvet muffins to soothe the savage Sky. But apparently nothing was going to win her over this morning, so I just got on with my work, flipping back and forth through the book, comparing sections and making notes in the margins.

Sky's phone buzzed.

"Hi, Jeremy," she said. "How are the patients?"

Even without using the speaker, my senses let me listen in on a phone call from across the room, and my ears pricked up at this one.

"Getting better," Jeremy said. "They're more resilient than they look. David can go home whenever he wants, though I think he's happier here for now, and I'm going to release Trent tomorrow."

"That's great. Let them know that Ethan can give them a lift whenever they want to head home."

That wasn't something I'd offered, but we could have that argument if and when they took Sky up on her offer. I carried on reading my book as Sky put the phone down.

She attacked the contents of her plate with renewed vigor, occasionally glancing up at me, then looking away any time she thought I had noticed. Loud sighs and the tapping of cutlery told me that this was a stalemate she wanted me to break, and I almost laughed out loud at the absurdity of someone giving me the silent treatment while simultaneously trying to demand that I talk. At last, she let out such a loud harrumph that I had to respond.

"Sweetheart," I said, putting on a sickly sweet smile, "if you're not going to speak to me, can you find a way of doing it a little quieter?"

I went over to the fridge, got out a carton of milk, and held it ready to refill Sky's glass.

"Do you like the almond milk?" I asked. I had heard a snippet of conversation on the radio saying that this stuff was good for expectant mothers. Not that I knew Sky was pregnant, but she was certainly eating more than usual, and there was that indefinable shift in her scent, something so subtle I doubted anyone but me would sense it.

"I'm not speaking to you," she announced.

"Yes, dear, and you are doing an exceptional job with it too."

She glared at me, lips pinched, her whole face folding in like a petulant child. I couldn't help laughing at it.

"I know that's your pissed-off face, and perhaps I should have told you this years ago, but your face is too round and your features too soft to pull off that look. It's not intimidating, and to give you an idea of how innocuous it is, Gavin refers to it as your 'angry doll face.'"

She growled, showing something more like real anger.

"That's more like it," I said brightly. "Now that's intimidating."

I feigned a dramatic quiver of fear, but she still didn't seem amused.

"How could you have spoken to him like that!" she snapped. "You scared him!"

"Good," I said, a flash of my own anger breaking through. "Maybe enough that they'll be more careful next time."

I started filling her glass with the almond milk.

"I want coffee instead."

"We've been drinking a lot of coffee lately. Let's try milk for a while."

Because expectant mothers were meant to avoid caffeine, and maybe, just maybe…

I poured myself a glass in solidarity.

"This silent treatment you're giving me; how long do you plan for it to last?"

Apparently the answer was a while longer yet, as she said nothing in response. I sighed and inched closer to her, pressed my forehead against hers and brushed aside wild strands of hair as I sought the connection that defined us. But when I went to kiss her, she moved away, and I had to make do with a peck on her forehead before backing off to a safe distance.

"What happens now, Sky?"

"You apologize."

"What exactly do I have to apologize for?"

"I don't know, maybe you can apologize for the new flavor of Lays. What do you think you should apologize for: yelling at him, threatening him? You scared him."

"Good. Then I may have saved their lives."

I made the answer cool and matter-of-fact, but it was driven by real worry. I didn't want our humans, the men who had taken so much care over our wedding, to get hurt, and if that meant delivering some harsh truths, so be it.

"You could have handled that differently," she said more softly.

"I'm not sure I could have. You can be upset with me if you want; I will accept that and deal with it. Sometimes you have to be cruel to be kind. I'm trying to keep them safe, instill in them the need for caution. If they die, they won't have to deal with your sorrow—I will."

Sky let out a long breath. She might not agree with my methods, but she knew just as well as I did what danger there was around vampires.

"I still think you should apologize."

There was a possibility that she was right. After this long with Sky, I had learned to admit that sometimes I could be wrong, and her perspective on the world could show me insights into things I might otherwise miss, especially where humans were concerned. But I had also learned that there were times when I had to stick to my guns.

"No," I said, pinching the bridge of my nose. Everything would have been so much easier if I could have said yes, but that would have been abandoning what I thought was right, and with it the best interests not just of myself but of David and Trent.

A new smell cut through the aromas of steak and cake, a

scent of rot and cologne. The all too familiar smell of one particular vampire approaching our home.

"Answer the door," I said. "I believe it's for you." I let out an exasperated breath. "They never came before."

She hurried across the room and answered the door, letting in a fresh waft of Demetrius's expensive cologne. I followed her warily, not wanting to leave her alone with him, even after everything that had happened.

He bowed to her, and she took a step back in confusion.

"Demetrius," she whispered.

Over her shoulder, I saw him blink, just once. Then he sniffed and handed her a black velvet envelope closed with a wax seal.

I froze. I had only seen envelopes like that twice before, and both times they had been heavy with significance. Was Demetrius really offering Sky the honor that I thought he was?

While she looked down to break the seal and draw out the paper within, Demetrius turned and strode silently away, his movements an absence in the world, almost a void created by his unnatural powers.

I walked up behind Sky and peered down at the single heavy sheet of bright-white paper, with Demetrius's full name written on it in an elegant, curling script. Written in blood.

I stared in disbelief. He really had done it. I must have made some sound, because Sky turned to look at me.

"What?" she asked.

I stared at the paper, and this time I heard my own small gasp of surprise. This was a thing between vampires, one of the most powerful bonds they could offer each other. Most would never use it in their whole life, especially not if they grew as powerful as Demetrius.

"I take it this is a big deal," Sky said, holding up the precious sheet.

"It's a promissory note," I said. "Equivalent to him saying he will protect your life with his blood and life."

"Okay, it's a nice gesture but—"

"No vampire has ever given one to anyone who wasn't another vampire. It's so untraditional—like if we made a witch the Alpha of our pack. That's how unlikely it is to happen."

I couldn't take my eyes off that single sheet of paper. I had been so sure that Sky was wrong to save Demetrius, but now that I saw the results, I had to think again. If the Master of the Northern Seethe was in debt to a member of our pack, if he felt a need to support and protect her, then the whole Seethe would go from being a threat we were constantly fighting off to a quiet, untroubling neighbor, possibly even to an ally in the end.

I would never use the word "Skyed" as an insult again.

Sky slid the sheet safely back inside the envelope and lined up the broken seal with all the care this moment deserved.

"Cool," she said.

"Cool?" I couldn't believe the flippancy with which she was treating this event. It gave her an unprecedented hold over the vampires of the Northern Seethe. It could transform the balance of power in our region, and for once I meant that in a good way. It made all of us safer than we had been in a long time.

"Yeah, cool. Now let's talk about this apology."

I stood in the middle of the living room, looking at the mess of random items scattered around the place. There were bottles of wine, all of them red, boxes of chocolates, elegant crystal glasses we could drink the wine from, and the latest iPad. On the coffee table lay a stack of first edition books, including Stoker's *Dracula* and Le Fanu's *Carmilla*. Littered around them were red ribbons and heaps of torn black tissue paper, from where some of the presents had arrived wrapped. When vampires came bearing gifts, they made sure that you would remember who gave them.

I could have lived with the clutter. Clutter was part of Sky's way of being, from the ice cream bowls piled up in the sink to the heap of half-read books and worn blankets she kept around her reading chair. The orderliness of my life had been overturned the minute she arrived, and that was a price I was willing to pay. But the lingering scent of vampires that clung around these presents, the aroma of grave dirt and cologne, that I really didn't want in my house.

The problem was, I had to accept it. This was tribute to Sky, a recognition of what she had done and how Demetrius had responded. Each of these gifts reinforced a pattern that would keep her safe and give the pack political leverage over the Seethe for years to come. That wasn't something I could even suggest she refuse.

It was the guinea pig that really made me wonder where the limits lay. Sable brought that one, turning up dressed in pink from head to toe, which at least made a change from the stream of black, red, and deep gray I'd been seeing. She handed the animal in its cage to Sky with a lost look on her face, then dropped a bag of feed on the doorstep and ambled away. Always a little detached from the world, Sable now looked completely broken, but that wouldn't stop her from doing her duty, as defined by Demetrius. She was paying tribute, a tiny, furry life for the woman who had saved her Master's life.

Sky set the cage down next to the first editions and we stared at it, while the guinea pig nibbled on a sunflower seed.

"This is weird," Sky said.

"Just the guinea pig is weird?" I asked, staring through the bars at the creature. Its eyes went wide as it sensed a predator, and it fled to the far corner of the cage, to bury itself in a pile of straw. "Not the slew of vampires coming to our house? Do you know how many vampires visited this home before you moved in?"

"Five," she said perkily. "No, six … two … seven. Final answer—three."

"None. Vampires never came to my home. You move in and it becomes vampire central."

"That would make a great bar name. Let's get a sign and charge a cover."

I growled. This was getting well past funny. Our home had been taken over by the vampires' grand acts of display.

A click of heels and a familiar scent announced another vampire approaching our door. Not just any vampire this time—Chris had come with whatever she considered to be suitable tribute.

"Another one," I said, then headed upstairs, seeking time alone in my study.

Through the floor, I heard a few words of murmured conversation, then the closing of the door and two sets of footsteps as Sky and Chris headed out into the woods behind the house. This visit wasn't just a present drop.

Through the study window, I watched them disappear between the trees. I still hadn't gotten used to what was going on there, this unlikely friendship between my mate and my ex, the Mistress of the Northern Seethe. Weres and vampires could sometimes manage to exist on speaking terms, when we weren't busy tearing each other apart, but an actual friendship, especially at such a high level? It was unheard of.

That was the magic of Sky. She fostered connections wherever she went, developing the most unlikely of bonds. It had caused trouble in the past, not least with Quell, but it was never badly intentioned, and in the end, it was a way of being that helped to bring peace. It wasn't a way that I could ever live, but I didn't need a mate who was just like me, I needed us to complement each other. Sky was becoming the glue that held together our supernatural community, through her instinctive concern for others. I loved her for that kind, compassionate nature, even if it meant that my house stank of vampires.

I still had no idea what we would do with a guinea pig though.

CHAPTER 34

I was willing to accept a house full of vampire gifts for Sky, but I still had limits, and of course she was finding ways to push them. In the few days since we rescued David and Trent, she had repeatedly pushed me to apologize to them for my attitude. Some of that had been direct requests, some of it attempts at subtlety, none of which felt even slightly subtle. I was increasingly frustrated at the whole topic, and at her unwillingness to accept that I wouldn't agree with her.

We had risked our own lives to save David and Trent after they ignored our advice and put themselves in danger. Without our intervention, Trent would have ended up dead, and probably David too. I wasn't going to apologize for pointing out their mistakes, or for being direct about it. If nobody ever set boundaries for them, then they were never going to learn, and they would continue to be a danger to themselves and anyone who cared about them, including Sky.

"Maybe you should call them to check on them," she suggested as we sat in the living room, a book open in her lap and a folder of case notes in mine. "While you have them on the phone, maybe you can apologize."

"I'm not going to check on them or apologize to David, because I think they're okay."

As if I didn't know it already, I could hear the proof coming from outside our house—the sound of David and Trent's car pulling up. I got up from my seat and opened the door, to reveal the two of them standing outside, a basket in their hands.

Sky frowned in confusion. I hadn't even left time for the troublesome two to knock.

"I heard their car," I explained.

David smiled and walked inside, bringing with him the aroma of baked goods. He handed Sky the small basket and a bakery box of cupcakes.

"Cupcake for my cupcake," he said, and kissed her on the cheek.

Trent followed his partner inside and I shut the door. The two of them had thoroughly recovered from their ordeal, and something else had them in the grip of excitement. They were practically buzzing with energy, their hearts racing and their grins twitching. While Sky attacked a cupcake like it had done her personal harm, I watched our visitors with suspicion. This wasn't just "invite to a party" or "we've got gossip to share" excitement, emotions I'd seen on both of them before when they visited Sky. They were up to something, and I couldn't escape the suspicion that I wouldn't like it.

Sky's heart raced. She had clearly realized that something was the matter too, and it was unsettling her, those wild emotions spilling out through the room. David and Trent were taking a long time to build up the courage to talk, and while they did that she stood tense, waiting for the worst, whatever that might mean for her. I walked over to stand beside her and took the hand that wasn't full of cupcake, offering what comfort I could.

"What brings you by?" Sky asked, her voice far calmer and steadier than her pulse.

David beamed at her. "We've decided we want to be wolves."

"*He* wants to be a wolf," Trent said with the self-importance of a child listing their favorite toys. "I want to be a jaguar. Maybe a bear, but before I decide, I have some questions."

"And I want to be a unicorn," Sky said sharply, drawing looks of confusion from the couple. Were they wondering if that was a real option?

At least now I knew what was going on, and it wasn't the stupidest thing I'd ever heard, given how these two were already tangled up in the pack. I stepped in front of them, forcing their attention onto me. Someone needed to treat this with the seriousness it deserved.

"We don't have a jaguar in our pack," I said. "There is one in the South, but if you are turned, it's better to be done by someone in this pack. I also strongly recommend both of you be changed to wolves. Either me, Sebastian, or Sky can do it." They needed to understand the seriousness of what they were asking, both in terms of the process and of the results. I only hoped that they were capable of being serious. "The first couple of days will be difficult for you. Similar to the way you felt when you took vampire blood. Also, you will have a bond with whoever changes you—it will be odd at first, but you will quickly adjust to it."

"No," Sky said softly.

We all looked at her, waiting to hear which part of this she didn't agree with, but apparently it wasn't that important, as she slipped back into silence.

I could see that there might be reasons not to make these two into wolves, though I doubted they would be reasons I found convincing. I could definitely think of reasons why I didn't want to turn them, not least because I didn't want to be responsible for the pack's two most irresponsible members. In different circumstances, I might even have objected to their request, but we had to live the lives we were given, and now those lives included David, Trent, and their unhealthy curiosity about the supernatural. This would save us some bother as well as making them safer.

"Were-animal life isn't like what you're used to," I continued. "You'll have obligations to the pack, a sort of part-time job on the side of what you normally do. We all contribute to keeping things running, and to keeping each other safe. Hierarchy is very important, so if you're going to join us, then you're going to need to learn how to—"

"No!" The word burst out of Sky in a howl of anguish that silenced me and made all three of us stare at her in shock. "Stop talking to them! Stop acting like this is going to happen! No! Just no!"

Her cheeks were red, her body trembling as her feelings ran out of control.

"Sky," I said softly, trying to soothe her, "it won't change things—"

"It changes everything. How can you agree to this? This will change them. They won't be human anymore. We can't take that away from them. Not in such a trite way. We're asking them to give up too much."

"You all didn't ask, we did," David said, looking as serious as I'd ever seen him. "It's what we want."

"You're making a mistake," Sky said. "A big one."

"I know you think we are entering this foolishly, but we aren't. It's been something we've been considering for a while. More so since we nearly died by that vampire attack. This is our life now, what we deal with. Isn't it better that we are prepared?"

"I won't do it! Or have anything to do with it." Sky turned

to me with an expression of unshakable determination. "You won't either. You will not do this."

"I'm sorry, Sky."

I was sorry she was upset, but not sorry enough to change my mind. It might be hard for Sky to lose this link to mundane life, but that didn't change David and Trent's decision or my view of what was best for the pack. What was best for these two as well, who had somehow slipped into the group that I got protective over, and so might as well be pack already. Everything would be easier if they joined us.

Sky flung away her half-eaten cupcake and ran from the room. The bathroom door slammed shut, but it couldn't block out the sound of her being sick.

"Oh no!" David stared after her. "Is she not well? Did we come at a bad time?" He stared at the box of cupcakes. "Did I give her food poisoning?"

My own suspicion seemed more likely than ever, but it wasn't something I was going to share with them. It wasn't even a thing that Sky and I had discussed yet.

"It's the stress," I said. "This business with Demetrius, vampires coming around at all hours with unexpected gifts…"

I struggled to think of what else I could say that would make sense.

"Oh, I know how that is," David said. "People mean well, but a gift can be so pressuring. My great aunt left us this painting in her will, and she loved that thing, but oh my god, it is just the ugliest."

"Such an abomination," Trent agreed. "But of course, we have to hang it up anytime family are coming around, just because it's Aunt Maude's painting." He glanced mischievously at David. "Honestly, if I'd known this was the price I would pay, I never would have settled down with you."

"And I never would have let myself live this long!"

"Listen," I said, cutting them off before they could get into their full flow. "It's good that you brought this to us, but I need to take care of Sky now. Leave it with me, and I'll talk to the pack about making you into weres."

"Will it be soon?" Trent asked. "Please say soon."

He pulled a pleading face, complete with doe eyes that almost put me off the idea.

"So we can look after ourselves," David added. "It's all perfectly practical."

I sighed. They might not be practical, but the point they were making was.

"Come to the pack's house tomorrow. We'll deal with it then."

"Yay!" They clapped their hands and made as if to hug me. I backed off hurriedly, almost knocking over the pile of first editions.

"Ooh, nice books!" Trent said. "Are you thinking of remodeling? Maybe going for a more old world theme? Because I have all sorts of suggestions for this place."

"You're not touching my house," I said, giving him a warning look.

"All right, no need to scowl! Come on, David, we should leave this brooding monster in peace. We have an important day to plan for."

The bathroom door creaked open, and footsteps padded softly from there to the main bedroom. I saw David and Trent out of the house, then went to find Sky.

She was sitting on the edge of the bed, her eyes bloodshot and puffy from crying.

"Feel better?" I asked softly as I stepped into the room.

"Are they still here?"

"No, they went home." I took a deep breath. She wasn't going to like what I had to say, but she needed to hear it. "But they will be at the pack's home tomorrow with Dr. Jeremy for the change."

I sat next to her, hoping that physical proximity might reduce the emotional distance between us.

"If a doctor needs to be present for something, it can't be safe," she said. "Do they know that?"

"They're healthy; there shouldn't be any problems."

I took her hand, but she pulled it away and crossed her arms over her chest.

"Tell them no. If you tell them you don't think it's a good idea, I know they will listen. They'll just think I'm overly cautious or sentimental."

"I'm not going to tell them that, because you are. There won't be any complications with their change. And they will be more equipped to protect themselves than they are now."

"Do they know they have to change during the full moon?"

"Yes."

"Vampires have killed were-animals before. Just changing them isn't going to make them immune to that."

"We'll make sure they can take care of themselves. Sky, no matter how they presented it, I don't think they came to this decision lightly. They've seen us change, they understand a lot of the pack's dynamics, and they aren't afraid. They aren't making this decision out of fear. Although I wouldn't care if they were, I know you would."

She kept shaking her head while I spoke, as if that movement could scatter the words and everything they represented. I sighed. There was going to be no persuading her on this, but it was a pack matter, and that changed the terrain.

"This is one of the times that will create difficulty between us. I'm not your husband or your mate when I make this decision. I'm the Beta of the pack, tasked with keeping friends of the pack safe. People who achieved that privilege because of you. It's going to happen, and I'd prefer you be on board for it and to do it."

She sat for a long miserable moment in silence, taking it

all in. Then she leapt to her feet and raced through to the bathroom, getting there just in time. I followed and stood by while she threw up what remained in her stomach. Then I offered a cool towel for her face, all I could do to help.

As I leaned against the sink, I wondered if I should suggest taking a pregnancy test. With the odd eating and now the vomiting, there were more and more signs pointing in that direction, and Sky seemed oblivious to them. But this didn't seem like the moment to mention it, when it might seem like I was distracting from an issue we disagreed on. I kept my mouth shut. A test could wait while we sorted this out.

"At least give them a week," she said. "Can you do that? They know it's going to happen. Before, it was just speculation. Let them live a week with the certainty."

I nodded. That delay wouldn't do any harm, and if it soothed her, then all the better, not just for us but for the emotional state of the pack.

"Sky, you know it's not going to change anything."

"I know, but at least it will give me time to come to terms with it."

Sebastian and I raced through the woods behind the pack retreat, the light of a half-moon illuminating our way. I was inches ahead of him as we rounded the last corner of our route and dashed for the building. But while I was a better runner over long distance, he was better in a sprint. With a sudden burst of energy, he accelerated, getting ahead of me just as we ran out of the trees, our traditional finish line.

He stopped in the open and turned to face me, teeth bared in a symbolic challenge. I bowed my head and lowered my tail, acknowledging the victor, before we both turned back to our human forms, laughing and grinning.

"I needed that," Sebastian said as he started getting dressed. "I feel like I've been cooped up inside all week, dealing with the latest inter-pack politics and advising Fallon on how best to run things out east."

"How's she doing?" I asked, buttoning my shirt.

Sebastian pulled a face. "Cole didn't do anything to prepare her for leadership, so now she's having to work it out from scratch. She'll get there, but it hasn't been easy."

I was very glad that Sebastian was our Alpha. He never made the job about him, but used his influence to make sure that things went smoothly for everyone. He was constantly challenging the ranking weres, creating opportunities for us to develop the skills we would need to run the place if anything happened to him, and watching out for other promising members of the pack who might one day be raised up. He understood that true leadership was never about one man.

"Sorry to drag you back into serious issues so late," I said, "but I've got one I want to talk about."

"David and Trent?" he asked, raising an eyebrow.

"David and Trent."

"Come on in, I think we'll need a drink for this one."

When we got to his office, he took a decanter from the shelves behind the desk and poured us each a glass of single malt Scotch whiskey.

"You know you're not the only one to talk to me about this?" he asked, sinking back in his seat.

"Sky?" I asked.

"Not yet, though I'm sure she'll be around to offer me her opinion with both barrels. But I've had two calls directly from David and Trent."

"Already? It's only been a day since they spoke with me."

"They're eager to get things moving, and a little disappointed that you delayed their change."

I sighed and sipped my whiskey, the mellow taste taking

an edge off the frustration I felt when dealing with this. It should have been over and done with already, but managing Sky made everything more complicated.

"You agree that they should join the pack, don't you?" I asked.

"Convince me."

"Basically, it comes down to the fact that we're better off with them on the inside than standing on our doorstep longing for something they can't have. Thanks to their connection with Sky, they've seen a lot of what goes on in the supernatural world, and almost been killed by it more than once. They're not going away, and if we don't invite them in, then they'll keep kicking up a fuss, and eventually they'll turn to someone else to make them more than human. Given their connection with Sky, and what they already know about us, that would make things complicated."

"That's all logical, as far as this goes. What do they bring to the pack?"

"Two well-paid professionals, so we know they can pull their weight, despite their ridiculous behavior. Trent's in PR, so that's a big plus. We could really do with someone to manage our public profile, both with the other supernatural creatures and in avoiding the wrong sort of attention from the press. David's event management skills don't fill a gap in the same way, but it's always useful to have project managers."

I stopped as I heard what I was saying, and took a big gulp of whiskey.

"Listen to us," I said, shaking my head. "We used to talk about how to fight back against the vampires or beat rogue weres into line. Now we sound like a damn HR department."

"A symptom of our success." Sebastian smiled. "The more secure we are, the more we're left to deal with bland details. I'm assuming these two won't add much in the way of magic or combat experience?"

I laughed out loud. "I think having them makes us worse in a fight. Just ask Winter, she's been trying to teach them."

"Well, we can't have everything."

I swirled the last of my drink around in the glass, caught by a thought that had almost slipped me by.

"Ultimately though, it's not about us," I said. "It's about doing the right thing for people whose lives we've touched, just like when we cleared out Dexter's test lab. David and Trent are too embedded in our lives to live safely without powers, and this is what they want. We have a duty of care."

Sebastian picked up the decanter and I held out my glass for a refill.

"Like you said, we sound like a damn HR department, but I can live with that if it means we're doing right." He raised his glass. "Here's to our latest additions."

"We should get an objective opinion about David and Trent," Sky said as we walked into the retreat the next day. "I'm thinking Sebastian."

"Of course," I said, keeping my real thoughts to myself. Unless Sky had some amazing new argument I hadn't heard, she wouldn't win Sebastian around, and I'd heard so many arguments from her that I was sure there couldn't be any left.

She glared at me as if I'd just disagreed with her on something important, not given her exactly what she asked for. I tried not to take it personally. Sky was clearly struggling with the situation, and with other things on top of that. She had been sick twice more since David and Trent's visit, and while she claimed it was triggered by stress, I was convinced that there was another cause behind it, one that was making the stress worse.

I was still excited at the prospect of becoming a father, but I was also feeling increasingly anxious. It was one thing to be responsible for a pack, with all the odd people and wild behavior that brought, but a child was a whole other matter. They would be completely dependent upon me, their personality shaped by everything I did and said around them. If I got that wrong, I could cause them problems for life. If my relationship with Sky had taught me anything, it was that I didn't always know how to handle people right. Did I really want to raise a kid to be as stubborn and detached from the world around them as I was? I'd only just started breaking those habits, and feeling better for it. Though the thought of having a child made me smile from the bottom of my heart, I didn't want to inflict my bad habits on someone else.

While Sky went to talk with Sebastian, I headed outside to the edge of the woods. I stood for a few minutes, enjoying the view and making sure that no one was around to listen, then pulled out my phone.

"Hello, Ethan," Joan said when she answered my call. "I wasn't expecting to hear from you. Can I help with something?"

It was a tribute to Joan's character that she dealt with me in such a calm and soothing tone. The last time I had called her out of the blue, it had been because Steven was in a world of trouble, but she didn't assume the worst now. She just took the call in her stride.

"I wanted to ask your advice about something," I said. "As a parent."

"As a parent?" Now Joan sounded surprised.

"You pretty much raised Steven, and you did it by yourself. He's turned into a great guy, so I figured you must have done things right."

"Thank you for that." Joan laughed. "I certainly tried, though as any parent will tell you, we all make mistakes."

There was an awkward silence as I tried to work out what to say next. I knew what I wanted to ask, but it was a difficult thing to express, especially when I didn't really know what was going on.

"It's okay, Ethan," Joan said softly. "Whatever's on your mind, you can talk to me."

I took a deep breath.

"Do you think I'd be a bad father?"

"What? No, of course not!"

"But I get angry and frustrated with people all the time. I shout and glare and force them to act like I want. That can't be good for a kid."

"Ethan, the person you are with your children isn't the person you are with the rest of the world. When the time comes, you'll see that. Being a parent brings out something you never knew you had inside."

"Then how can I know that I'll get it right?" The words caught in my throat, fears almost choking me.

"Because you're a good person, with good intentions. When you get firm with people, it's to set boundaries and keep others safe. Children need that, and you'll find a way to deliver it that works for them."

"So you don't think I'll fuck them up?" To my surprise, tears were welling in the corners of my eyes. I hadn't realized how badly this was worrying me until I started letting it out.

"You'll be a great father." Joan cleared her throat. "So, is this all hypothetical, or is there something you want to tell me?"

I shuffled from one foot to the other. This wasn't a conversation I should be having with anybody other than Sky yet, and I felt like I might already have given away too much.

"Hypothetical," I said. "For now. Don't tell anyone I asked about it."

"Of course not. But hypothetically speaking, congratu-lations."

I grinned. "Hypothetically speaking, thanks."

David and Trent stood in the middle of the infirmary, a space they must be growing all too familiar with by now. Last time they had been carried in pale and drained of blood, with Trent on the verge of death, but this time they walked in under their own steam, looking not just healthy but excited.

In the corner of the room, Jeremy stood with emergency supplies in hand, in case anything went wrong. It was seldom a problem, but there was no harm in being ready, especially after everything these two had been through. I didn't know how well they would initially deal with the transformation—the overload of enhanced senses could be a lot for some people to deal with, and they weren't exactly the most stable characters to begin with. But with me, Sebastian, and Jeremy there to talk them through it, as well as Sky bringing about the change, we were as well equipped as we could be.

Across the room, I could hear Sky's heartbeat racing. It was hardly surprising, given how anxious she had been about doing this to her friends. Suddenly, her breath quickened and she bent over, hyperventilating. I rushed to her side, her anxiety spreading to me as I worried about what was wrong. I cradled her face and looked at her with concern.

"Sky, are you okay?"

She opened her mouth as if about to speak, hesitated, and instead took a deep breath before nodding.

"Fine, just last-minute jitters." She turned to David and Trent. "Are you ready?"

In the time she had taken to bring her breath under control, the two of them had stripped down to their underwear. It would have been nice to see them showing concern for Sky, but I guessed that excitement at their impending change had kept them from even noticing what was going on.

"You can keep your clothes on until after the bite," she told them.

"I thought we'd be forced into a change," David said.

"Once the serum is in your system and works its way through it, then the change will be initiated. But you'll have time to undress. You should feel it once it starts."

They looked at each other and shrugged.

"We're half-dressed," David said. "Might as well get it over with."

They took off their briefs and stood naked, looking proudly around at anyone who would meet their eyes. Most of us were quite used to this sort of thing, but Sky still held onto mental habits from before she joined the pack, and she squirmed at the sight. I found it reassuring. In some ways, David and Trent were a poor fit with the other personalities in the pack. The old guard like myself, Winter, and Gavin tended toward a rough and stoic approach to life, full of combat training and time outdoors, in direct contrast with the way these two pampered themselves. While the Worgen represented another approach to living as weres, I didn't think that *Lord of the Rings* roleplay or *Halo* night were likely to be to the tastes of our new additions. But if they were comfortable getting naked, and so didn't make a fuss about our time together as animals, that would at least provide one way that they fit in.

Sky went into one of the recovery rooms and emerged a few minutes later in wolf form. She padded over to David and Trent, her claws on the tiled floor the only sound. Even Trent had fallen silent, the seriousness of the occasion finally hitting him.

For a long moment Sky stood facing them, her lips pressed together but her jaw hanging slack. I knew from my own experiences that she would be letting saliva pool in her mouth, ready to carry the werewolf serum into the bodies of the people she bit. It needed a good dose of the serum to ensure a transformation, to make someone into more than a human.

We had told David and Trent what was involved in the change, but nothing could really prepare them for this. David braced himself, then walked nervously over to Sky. He knelt in front of her and held out his arm. There was a moment's hesitation, then Sky bit down on the offered limb, and David yelled in pain.

Trent watched, eyes wide, and for a moment I wondered if he was changing his mind. That would make things very complicated, not least for their relationship. But he knelt down too and held out his arm, keeping his eyes fixed on Sky. He didn't even make a sound as her teeth sank through his flesh, but when she let go and he sank to the floor, the serum running through his body, reshaping it from within, he then let out a cry.

Sky rushed back into the recovery room and slammed the door shut behind her. Knowing Sky, this had to be hard for her to watch, seeing her friends in pain at her hands, even if it was for their own good. None of us would challenge her decision to get away from the sight.

"It'll be all right," Jeremy said, kneeling next to the trembling David. "This just might take a while."

David and Trent lay close together, writhing, twisting, and moaning as their bodies fought to achieve their first change. Bones crunched and muscles spasmed, and they gritted their teeth in pain. Trent's eyes went wide, while David shut his, curling in around himself and whimpering.

The first transformation was never a pretty process. A body that was only used to being human resisted what was happening to it, causing a battle between muscles, organs, and even individual cells. The serum didn't always spread evenly through the system at first, making the effect messy and disjointed. A bone might try to grow before the muscle around it was ready. Fur might sprout under skin that couldn't yet let it through.

David and Trent seemed to be having a particularly difficult time. They turned and twisted, groaned and moaned. After nearly an hour, Jeremy started gathering sedatives and pain killers, in case they needed help toward the end. Sebastian crouched between them, exerting his influence as Alpha to ease them through it, but this was still taking a long time. Not long enough for me to worry that the change might not take, but enough that this was one I would remember.

"I knew they were stubborn," Jeremy said, "but I didn't think that would go down to the cellular level."

I laughed, but it sounded hollow. For all the times that I had wished David and Trent out of my life, I had never wanted them to suffer, and that was what I was seeing. The upper halves of their bodies had taken on their wolf form, but the lower halves were still human, and nothing Sebastian did seemed enough to tip them over.

Sky emerged from the recovery room, human again and fully clothed. She knelt down facing Sebastian and laid a hand each on David and Trent, stroking their fur. They howled, a sound as trapped between human and beast as they were. I could feel Sky's distress in the air around us, could sense the two of them picking up on that emotion, amplifying it through the horror they were going through.

"Sky, step back," I said.

For once she didn't resist, but backed away, still staring. I wished there was some way to balance this out, to find a calm that could counter the chaos whirling out of Sky.

David and Trent kept writhing and howling, but without the intensity they had shown in contact with her. Inch by inch, their bodies altered, bones cracking and reforming, muscles twisting, fur emerging in patches, then more densely, covering their skin. It was at once both a difficult spectacle to watch and a life-affirming one. This was the creation of two new weres, the extension of our pack, a chance for two friends to join us in the only life I could ever want. Like so much about being a were-animal, it was the glorious and the monstrous rolled into one.

At last, two hours on from when Sky had bitten them, David achieved his full wolf form, and a few minutes later Trent joined him. They stood on all fours, briefly sniffed at each other, and almost seemed to giggle. Then they started bouncing about, howling and skittering across the floor, darting between me and Sky in mad circles.

"Trent and David, calm down," Sebastian snapped.

They tried but didn't seem able to control themselves. The closest they could manage was to back up next to Sky, rubbing their heads against her legs as they kept howling.

"What's wrong with them?" Sky asked over the din, her expression one of worry.

Sebastian and I exchanged a look, and I could see that this one would be mine to answer.

"It's you," I said softly. "They don't know how to discern your emotion. It's your unease. It's humming so much they can't relax. They're distressed because you are."

"I'm okay." Sky knelt and stroked the fur of the newly made wolves. "Shhh. I'm okay. You're okay. We're okay."

It clearly wasn't true. She sat down, looking exhausted, and David and Trent curled around her body, whining as they nuzzled at her. I had a good idea what was causing all of this, a topic tied in with Sky's untamed emotions. To tackle it, I needed to talk with her, and I couldn't do that with a pair of wolves butting in between us.

"David. Trent," I said slowly and firmly. "I need to talk to my wife."

They whimpered but wouldn't move.

"Now," I snapped.

They lowered their heads and backed hesitantly away, glancing at Sky for reassurance.

"I'm okay," she said, but still they moved slowly, resisting my command.

This was a matter of pack discipline and it needed to be nipped in the bud.

"Trent, David," I commanded with cold finality, channeling all my influence as Beta.

At last the message got through. Together, they slunk into a corner.

I went to crouch in front of Sky, closing the space between us, so that it seemed like there was just the two of us in the world.

Two, or three now?

"Tell me," I said softly. She looked at me blankly. "You didn't have a period last month."

"I did."

"No, you had one for one day. That's not normal for you. And you missed your period this month. You've been nauseous in the morning for the past six days and it only got worse with the situation with David and Trent. Sky?"

Sky looked as if she was about to burst into tears, but she forced the words out.

"I think I'm pregnant."

"You're afraid," I said, hearing the quiver in her voice. It had never occurred to me that she might react like this. Was she not ready yet?

"Not of having a child." Tears ran down her cheeks. I wiped them away.

"You don't have to worry, you are going to be a great mother." I meant those words with all my heart. No one in the word had more love, more kindness, more compassion, than my Sky.

She shook her head.

"I struggle daily to keep Maya in check. She forced me to place a curse on you." She looked at Sebastian and then back at me. "What will she do with a baby who isn't able to protect itself? We don't know the extent of her magic. Can she perform magic through our baby?"

She pressed her face into my hand, looking so lost and frightened that it broke my heart. Caught up in other concerns, I hadn't considered the spirit shades or what effect they might have on all of this. But I had mastered them and their creators before, and I would do it again for our child, no matter what it took.

"You need a spirit shade to survive," I said. "I have one. She will not hurt our baby."

"I'll talk to Ariel," Sebastian said. "The witches suppressed her magic before, they can do it again."

At last, Sky relaxed, leaning into me as she let the worst of her fears go. Just talking seemed to have lifted a weight off of her. I felt better too, now that this wasn't some secret but was a thing we shared.

I was going to be a father. I smiled at the thought. Another life, part me and part Sky, the fulfillment of what we were together. A family of my own. Even after days of wondering, it still hit me like the most amazing and wonderful surprise.

In their corner, Trent and David stopped whimpering. They curled up together, eyes fluttering, as they failed to fend off the sleep their bodies desperately needed.

"That's great preparation and an excellent idea," Jeremy said with a shrug and a nod toward an ultrasound machine. "Should we determine definitively whether or not she's pregnant?"

I pulled away from Sky, feeling embarrassed at how much we had made out of what was still just speculation.

"Yes, we should find that out as well," I said.

CHAPTER 35

"And where is your lovely wife?" Claudia asked as I took my seat. The fusion restaurant was bustling, but she had managed to book one of the better tables, discreetly tucked away at the back, with space for her, Josh, me, and, theoretically at least, Sky. But as a waiter approached with the wine list, there were only three of us.

"Yeah, bro," Josh said, grinning. "Where's the woman of the hour? We didn't invite you two out just for the company of the surly Beta."

"You didn't invite anyone," Claudia reminded him. "This is my treat, a family outing before Ethan's family expands. Babies and restaurants don't mix."

"I believe that's what family restaurants are for," I said, a small smile curling my lip.

"Please." Claudia shook her head. "Don't even joke about those ghastly places." She picked out a wine, then turned her attention back to me. "And you haven't answered my question."

"Sky says sorry for missing this, but she doesn't feel well." I remembered her curled up on the sofa, clutching a hot water bottle, a big slice of cake only half eaten beside her.

Something was seriously wrong when she couldn't face a meal made up of dessert, and it had taken some persuasion from her to get me out of the door. "She's been sick a lot the past few days, and everything tires her out."

"The poor dear. I hope that you're taking good care of her."

"When she'll let me, yeah."

The wine arrived and we turned our attention to the menus, taking the pressure off me for a few minutes. But once we finished ordering, I could see that I wasn't going to be let off easy, and I had to admit, given the topic of conversation, I didn't entirely mind.

"So how are you doing?" Josh asked. "Feeling psyched for parenthood?"

I grinned.

"Yeah, it's pretty awesome to think that I'm going to be a dad. I mean, it's not something I ever planned on, but then I never expected to get married and you were both there for that. Sky really has changed my life."

"Imagine it, a teeny tiny were-pup biting at our ankles." Josh grinned at Claudia. "It's almost worth putting up with all his nonsense for that."

"Don't be mean to your brother, Josh," Claudia chided, though she smiled gently at him. "He has quite enough to deal with already." She must have seen some of the worry I was trying to hide, because she looked at me with concern. "Is something the matter, Ethan?"

Where could I even start? There were worries about Sky's body, part were-animal and part vampire, and how well it might endure pregnancy. There was the issue of the spirit shades lurking in both of us and what claim they might try to stake on our child. There was the attitude of the rest of the supernatural world, many of whose denizens had taken a dislike to our mating in the first place. I had no idea how they would react when the prospect came along of a child combining our different powers, but there was no chance it would all be positive. This should have been one of the happiest times in my life, and instead it was turning into a period of fear and anxiety.

I tried to hide all of that from Sky. She had enough trouble controlling her emotions normally, and the pregnancy was making that worse. She needed support and stability, not for me to be brooding over worries we had no answer to. But here and now, surrounded by my family, I had the chance to let some of that out.

"There are a lot of people watching us," I said. "People who didn't want us together for this exact reason—because we might breed. By now, word is getting out, and they'll be making plans against us. How can I keep my child safe when their very existence stirs up hate? How can I keep Sky safe from that?"

Claudia reached across the table and took my hand, the silk of her glove smooth against my skin.

"Throughout history, there have always been people who hate others for who they are. It's not an easy thing to deal with, but you're not alone. You have friends who will stand by you no matter what."

"We'll be here," Josh said. "Me, Claudia, the whole damn pack. London too, and all our friends in the Creed."

"Not to mention Demetrius's extraordinary gesture toward Sky." Claudia squeezed my hand. "I'm not saying that this will be easy, my dear, but there are a lot of people standing ready for you."

I smiled. I was used to thinking of myself as someone who fought alone, or at best alongside the pack. But I had more friends than I had realized.

"Anybody tries to hurt my niece or nephew," Josh said, hands waving in the air, "I'm gonna curse them so bad they won't even remember what it felt like to live without pain."

It was good to hear, but didn't put all of my fears to rest. Nothing could, given how wide those fears went.

"What if those people are right?" I asked. "We're talking about a child whose lineage includes weres, dark elves, vampire blood, and the influence of two separate spirit shades. That's a lot of darkness and power. What if my kid turns out to be a terrible monster?"

"You and Sky love each other more than anyone I've ever known," Claudia said. "Nothing born from love like that could possibly be monstrous."

"And if Demetrius can learn to chill out, then anyone can grow up good," Josh said.

"Demetrius has chilled out?" I raised an eyebrow, not sure what he was getting that.

"Didn't you hear? Biting attacks are down across Chicago. The big D has been reining in his own kind. I don't know if it's Sky saving his life or Chris's influence, but things are changing there."

"So what, vampires won't prey on people anymore?" I had trouble believing that, after all these years of dealing with them.

"It's not that good, but it's certainly an improvement. Ariel's pleased about it."

I was pleased too. If the vampires became more peaceful, then life would be easier for all of us. I wasn't going to stop despising Demetrius, but it was good to see him heading in the right direction.

Our food arrived and I tucked into a rare steak. The taste of nearly raw meat helped to turn me away from the dark thoughts that had been dominating my mind.

"Sorry for bringing things down," I said. "Really, life's good. I mean, I'm married to Sky, I'm about to have a kid, and now I get to have dinner out with my family for the first time in who knows how long. How could it get any better than that?"

I smiled at them, and they smiled back, Josh with a lopsided grin, Claudia with softness and grace.

"I agree," she said. "What could be better than time with family, and knowing that the family will soon be growing to include one more tiny bundle of joy?" She looked at each of us in turn, then brushed away a tear. "I remember when you two were tiny, it seems so long ago now. I suppose it's too late to ask you not to grow up?"

"Maybe for me," I said. "Josh though…"

"Hey!" Josh put on a look of mock outrage. "I resent that remark. Or do I mean resemble? They're so close together…"

I raised my glass, and the others joined me.

"Here's to family," I said. "May we always have each other's backs, no matter what life throws our way."

"To family."

We sat around a table in the Creed's headquarters, a large room in the back of a new age shop. It had been redecorated since Ariel took over, but retained the esoteric tastes of its inhabitants, with murals of magical scenes and symbols as well as large pots of burning incense, their drifting smoke taking on the shapes of spells. At the back of the room were more practical resources: laptops, shelves heavy with books of ancient wisdom, racks filled with esoteric ingredients. But around the conference table, the decor had been designed to create an air of mystery.

There was little space for the mysterious at this meeting. Instead, it was tension that clung to us, as senior members of the pack and the Creed watched each other warily across the table. There was a formality to proceedings that hadn't been there before, a sense that living by the rules, both the unspoken conventions of a business meeting and the formal laws of Creed and pack, was the only thing holding us together, as the pressures of a mounting crisis threatened to tear us apart.

"How many months are you?" Ariel asked, looking coolly at Sky.

I wasn't comfortable discussing our situation with the witches, but I knew that it had to be done. That was part of why I had called the meeting, and why I had accepted their terms for it, including meeting on their home ground.

"About twelve weeks," Sky replied.

Ariel took a deep, ragged breath and closed her eyes. "Do you think it's a good idea for you and Ethan to have children?"

"Well, it's a little too late now, isn't it?" Sky snapped.

Nia leaned forward. "It's not too late for you to—"

"You don't want to finish that sentence," Sky growled with all the ferocity I was feeling inside. That sort of talk was a threat to our child, and there would be consequences for anyone who suggested it again. Ever since word got out about Sky's pregnancy, we had been treated to nervous glances and fearful whispers from within the supernatural community. While Josh, Claudia, and the pack rallied around us, others watched with suspicion, as if Sky was growing a superweapon, not an innocent infant. Even our supposed allies seemed to have changed their tune.

Nia straightened, as if she was distancing herself from a wild animal. Sky's anger was a tangible force in the room, a presence as thick and unmistakable as the smell of incense. Nia's hand shifted, ready to put up a defensive spell, but Ariel reached out to touch her and she sat back, her fingers slowly uncurling.

"With everything that is going on, it would have been a better idea to be more cautious," Ariel said. "You two are under a microscope; the world is watching, apprehensive and afraid." She turned her attention to Sebastian. "You are all being watched."

"That's not new information, Ariel," Sebastian said in a warm, relaxed tone. "What's really going on?"

Ariel looked down at a metal disk lying on the table. It was made of something like dark bronze, small enough to fit neatly in the palm of her hand, and it had a red mark in the center. When her gaze rose from the disk, it was to look at Josh, and I could smell her fear even through the incense.

This wasn't just about us.

"You got one too, didn't you?" Josh asked, pulling out a matching disk.

"We all did." Ariel nodded. "Every one of us in the Creed. It's the sign of betrayal of our kind. Denouncing us. Rayna said our alliance with you is sedition and paramount to betrayal, and we need to be held accountable. Now she has more followers, enough that she feels confident doing this. There's about to be a war, something I wanted to avoid. No one ever comes out a true victor in one. Too many casualties, and the winner is always left compromised."

Her distress was clear, but that wasn't what I cared about. I turned to look at Josh, bewildered and frustrated that this was the first I had heard about it.

"Why didn't you tell me about that?" I asked.

Josh shrugged. "It's nothing new. I've always been considered an enemy of some sort to Marcia's Creed witches. My loyalties have been divided since birth. I won't choose anyone over you. It's a nonissue. I'm your brother first, a witch second. If I'm their enemy, so what. They can bring whatever they have."

"We got you into this," Sebastian said, talking to all of the witches, though his eyes kept moving back to Ariel. "We will get you out."

"It's not that simple," Ariel said, smiling weakly. "We've lost witches who once supported us; they see Rayna as a stronger leader who will uphold our rules and their perceived 'purity' of magic. You two possessing magic is one of the 'impure' things they are concerned about. Those who were on the fence have now sided with her. She has the Aufero, and like Marcia, she's made no secret of her willingness to use it. I'm sure I will be on that list eventually and so will the rest of the Creed. So, even if we do decide to restrict the magic—she'll use it to hurt you. If she removes any of our magic, the mark won't work."

"Alliances work both ways, Ariel. We've had this discussion more than once, and you've even reminded me of my own advice. Don't be afraid to ask for help. The Aufero doesn't work on us. We can find a place for you until we fix it."

"We're running and hiding?" Nia looked appalled.

"You can devalue and reduce self-preservation to 'running and hiding' if you like. I see it as a strategic move to keep your powers until a threat is removed by people willing and capable of doing it."

For all the reassurance in Sebastian's words, the witches remained unmoved. Most sat wearing masks of indifference, while Nia's hostility was clear.

"Please give us a minute?" Ariel said, looking at us.

"Of course." Sebastian smiled and led us out of the room, into the shop that provided the Creed's cover. It was shut for the evening, no customers or staff around to watch what we did.

Sebastian closed the door behind us and we gathered around it. It was solidly made, a modern security door installed to replace one destroyed by Josh during his rampage against Marcia and her people, but while it might help keep out attackers, it wasn't thick enough to prevent were-animals from hearing what was going on inside.

I listened with growing annoyance as the debate between the Creed heated up, several of them accusing Ariel of letting her relationship with Sebastian get in the way of her decision-making. She tried to stay calm, but defensiveness crept into her voice. I wouldn't have been as steady in her position: her people were throwing away an offer of help for no good reason, and it had to be maddening to deal with.

"They are offering to help us," she said. "The Aufero can't be used against them. Why do you have a problem with it?"

"Because it's them we are handing our safety to," Nia said, incensed. "They are the very reason we are in this position. Distancing ourselves from them might be the best option."

"You don't see this as a power move on Rayna's part to claim the Creed for herself?"

"If it is, she has every right to want to see the Creed elevated to more than just the were-animals' lackey. And that's what we've been reduced to. They call, we come, and what have we gotten from this alliance? Our names tarnished, our fealty challenged, and our morals compromised, and believe me, I see it getting worse."

A long, tense silence was broken by the voice of another witch.

"I know you wanted to be different, to have a better relationship with them, but have we considered that after all we've seen, maybe there was a reason the others would distance themselves from them? Not just that Rayna considers them a blight on the otherworld? It's not as if she is truly an acolyte of Marcia's. She left them and chose to be alone, to separate herself from Marcia and the others. She's resurfaced for a reason."

"You two seem like you are ready to do that as well, maybe even join Rayna," Ariel said, her voice hard and sharp as a razor's edge.

"We are with you," Nia said. "When you decided to take over, I didn't follow blindly. When I said I was with you, I meant it. To the bitter end. But I don't want this to be our end. Not disgraced and stripped of our magic because we allied ourselves with them." Her voice softened. "When we decided to do this, you chose people who would challenge you, be the voice of dissent when necessary. You didn't want sycophants; you wanted challengers. You may not like what I'm saying, but I'm doing the very thing you said you needed. What's changed?"

"'I won't be one of the many who falls for his allure' was the first thing you said when you were warned about Sebastian," another witch said. "You assured us that you wouldn't, but you have. You're besotted and you don't see it, but we do."

Sebastian smiled, and I couldn't blame him. His charm had helped to forge this alliance, but it had done more than that for him personally.

"And don't forget the child," Nia said.

A sudden quiet fell, accompanied by the tingle of magic on my skin. An auditory cloaking spell to keep us out of the conversation. Someone had realized the limits of the door.

"Can you break it?" Sebastian asked.

Josh nodded. "But are you sure you want me to? It can't be done without them knowing. Will that help or hurt our case? If it were me, I'd consider it an insult to have it broken by someone I was supposed to trust."

Sebastian shook his head. I didn't know whether to feel relieved or annoyed. He had clearly done the right thing, but I couldn't escape the thought that people were discussing my child, my future, in my absence, and I wanted to know what they were saying, however terrible it was. I wanted to be ready for whatever came next.

We made conversation while we waited for the witches to finish, but it was hard to engage with anything else when so much was at stake. In their chamber, the Creed were deciding whether to sever ties with us. Just as relations were improving with the Seethe and things seemed to be going our way, our closest allies might be about to cut us loose, leaving us without support.

The shop door burst open. We turned to face it, tensed

and ready for action. For several seconds, nothing happened. Then the windows exploded, broken glass spraying across the room, shredding books on the mysteries of the universe and packets of magical herbs.

I watched the empty windows, their frames like open mouths with shards of glass for teeth. Was this an attack, or just an attempt to get the witches' attention, to sway the debate one way or the other?

A creature burst in, so big it could barely fit through the doorway. It was winged, with the face of an eagle and a horn emerging from its beak. Talons like knives gouged splintered lines in the floorboards.

The monster charged at Sebastian, who shifted as it came, shedding his clothes to embrace his wolf form. A clawed leg swung down at him, but he grabbed it between his jaws and slung the animal across the room, where it crashed into a display stand full of crystals.

Another travesty stomped in, this one a combination of rhino and Komodo dragon. I only knew of one place where creatures like this existed: Elysian. Someone elven was behind this attack.

Samuel appeared beside the creature, his narrow mouth fixed into a look of grim determination. A protective field glistened over him and the hide of the beast. For a guy who wanted to rid the world of magic, Samuel sure did like to use spells.

Josh, Sky, and I stood firm in front of the door, barring the way to the witches. Following Josh's lead, we flung magic at Samuel and the monster, trying to knock them out, but their protective field held. They stood in the doorway, leaning into the magic as if they were trying to walk through a strong wind, unable to advance but unwilling to give up.

With a swipe of his claws, Sebastian ripped the throat out of the mutated eagle, and it collapsed across the broken shelves. But two more were already flying in through the shattered windows, diving at him.

Realization spread across Sky's face.

"Josh, do you have this?" she said. "I need to try to get the Aufero. It's near. Rayna's near."

"Sky, don't you dare!" I yelled, using the commanding power of a pack leader. She paused, frozen for a moment by her own instincts. I didn't like to use my power on her like that, but I would do whatever it took to keep my wife and child out of danger.

Behind us, the door to the witches' lair flew open. London strode out, her bright hair flaring out behind her in waves of powerful magic. One of the eagle creatures leapt up and flapped its wings, buffeting her with a blast of wind, and she was knocked back for a moment, but stood her ground, eyes black as night and shining with anger.

The others emerged and spread out beside her, wreathed in wrath and magic. Ariel waved her hands and the rest followed suit. A wave of magic crashed across the room, knocking all of us to the ground, annihilating the protective field around Samuel, shattering the last shards of glass from the windows.

Even struck to the ground, Sebastian was still grappling with one of the eagle creatures, blood and feathers flying. Sky leapt around him and slammed into Samuel just as he was stumbling to his feet. The force of the collision knocked him to the ground, Sky landing on top of him.

I followed, teeth bared and fists raised, ready to deal with anything that threatened Sky. If our enemies thought that they could catch us at a vulnerable moment, they would see how wrong they were.

One of the winged monsters lunged at me. I dodged past its beak and slammed a fist into the side of its head, then grabbed a fistful of feathers and pulled. The creature squawked as the feathers tore free, and backed off, blood running into its eye, only to be caught by a blast of magic from Nia and Ariel.

Sky had her hands around Samuel's throat. Magic poured from her, as thick and powerful as her rage.

"You behave as if this is a fight you are ready to die for. Is it?" she whispered.

Samuel shook his head.

"You're going to leave and be done with this fight," Sky said. "You don't want to be on this side of the war you've chosen. This world you want without us in it isn't going to happen, Samuel."

I could sense the battle between the beast and the woman within her, the need to destroy him against the desire for mercy, the longing for a kinder world. And in the end, Sky would always be Sky.

"Samuel," she said. "This will be your last warning and the final time I ever grant you clemency."

Eyes wide with fear at the dark and powerful magic flowing over him, Samuel nodded. Sky released her hold and stood, letting him stumble away.

The creature he had arrived with remained. As Sky rushed out after the Aufero, the rhino-dragon swung its head at me. I grabbed the horn and planted my feet, pushing all my strength into holding it in place, into keeping it from hurting anyone else around me. The two of us strained and grunted, a wrestling match between man and beast, while I watched from the corner of my eye to see that Sky was safe.

Rayna stood in the street, the Aufero clutched in her hands. Sky stopped, facing her.

"This won't end well for the weres," Rayna said. "Do the spell. You have the power to end this. The Clostra was left for you."

Sky reached out for the Aufero with her magic, but a counter-blast from Rayna knocked her to the ground.

"I guess you've made your decision," Rayna said, and disappeared.

A wave of terror flashed over me. What if the baby had been hurt? The adrenaline spike gave me extra strength and I twisted at the rhino monster's head with all my might. It roared in pain, but could do nothing more, its body held in place by magic from the witches. I twisted again and, with a loud snap, its neck broke. The beast slumped to the floor.

Sky walked back into the ruins of the store. To my relief, she seemed to be fine. Whether through her magic or her natural toughness, she had gotten through the encounter unharmed.

The fight was over, the elven creatures dead, Samuel and Rayna gone. The shop was ruined, but that seemed like a minor issue next to everything else.

"Liam has chosen a side," Sebastian said.

"Are we sure he has, or is he just indifferent?" I asked. "I think Mason and Abigail are the ones to watch. She would have access to the dark forest."

Either way, we knew that there were elves acting against us now.

Sebastian sighed and turned toward the witches. They looked exhausted, leaning against each other for support as they let go of the powerful magic they had wielded.

"Are you willing to accept our help?" he asked.

Ariel, usually the first to speak for her people, stood mute, watching to see how they would respond. Their disputes weren't yet resolved, but perhaps this attack could swing the argument. After all, we had protected them, driven off a rogue witch and killed the monsters she brought with her. That had to be worth something.

"How the hell did we get here?" Nia whispered as she looked around at the destruction, weary and wounded. She looked us over, still unwilling to simply trust in our support, all too aware that it could bring trouble with it. Had they been attacked because they stood with us, or would they have been attacked anyway? Had this alliance protected them or put them in danger? She was weighing the balance, and it was more difficult than ever.

Sebastian let out a deep breath, pausing for a moment before he spoke.

"What you see as acquiescing and a sullied compromise of who you are as witches, isn't. Marcia's flaw was that she held to old ways, faulty ways that led to her destruction. Your strength is in the fact that you haven't. You won't be bullied into siding with someone who doesn't share your beliefs. That is a strength, not a flaw, and it will serve you well to remember that. We have resources that you don't. I have had years to build them."

He brought the full weight of his attention onto Nia. "You weren't wrong—this alliance has benefited us disproportionately, but if you never give us a chance to help in an area that we excel in, then it will remain that way, unequal. I question whether your biases and fixation on our past and our flaws have narrowed your vision. If that is the case, perhaps you're not really what Ariel or the Creed needs. If you care about the strength of the Creed, then you'd care about its survival."

Nia watched him with deep, pensive eyes, evaluating his words, his offer, and the man himself. If she was charmed, then it didn't show. At last, she raised her hand.

"I vote that we go with Sebastian," she said.

CHAPTER 36

With Nia's vote gone our way, the rest of the Creed fell into line behind Ariel. Within days, Sebastian had moved them out of the city and into a safe house, one so secret even I didn't know the details.

"They'll feel more secure that way," he explained. "If I can say that only one person knows where they are, it feels like a true secret."

I couldn't argue with his logic, though I wanted to. I was used to knowing all of the pack's arrangements. Knowing that we were sheltering a group of powerful witches but that I had no idea where, that was the sort of thing that could have been designed to stress me out.

In an ideal world, I would have taken it out on Rayna. I was convinced that she was hiding in Elysian, behind the protection of whichever elven leader had taken her side. But storming straight in to grab her would cause a huge dispute, at a time when we were just hanging onto Gideon's neutrality, trying to edge him toward passive support. I wanted to rip the Aufero out of her cold, dead hands, but I would have to bide my time.

Weeks passed, the whole supernatural world holding its

breath, waiting to see what came next in the witches' civil war. Meanwhile, Sky and I had concerns of our own, concerns which crystallized around a fifteen-week scan and checkup with Dr. Jeremy. As we drove home, Sky stared at her flat belly, one hand resting there as she battled her anxieties. Jeremy had assured us that the upcoming full moon change would be perfectly safe, that plenty of were-animals had gone through pregnancy without any danger. There was no reason, he said, to think that Sky should be any different.

Except that this was different. The strange magics surrounding the two of us meant that anything could happen, that the usual rules might go out the window at any moment. Precedent was fine for showing the likely outcome, but there were no certainties, especially when politics and the threat of violence continued to shift around us.

I took Sky's hand on the drive home, rubbing my thumb gently across her skin, seeking to reassure myself as much as her. But I couldn't find the words to tell her that everything would be all right, and my failure there made me feel even worse.

A tan Suburban was parked in the driveway of our house. I glanced at the time and realized that we were running late, but I doubted that Tracy would mind. I was paying her well to plan and execute the redecoration of our house, well enough to cover a little waiting.

I parked in the garage and led Sky out onto the driveway, our fingers intertwined. She still seemed tense. I hoped that this surprise would at least help a little.

Tracy was waiting by the front door, wearing a green dress, chunky jewelry, and two pairs of glasses, one on top of her head and the other hanging from her neck by a chain. She smiled brightly as we approached.

"Hi, you must be Ethan's wife." She shook both our hands, then turned her attention to Sky. "I'm sure we can have all the changes made in two months. Don't you worry about a thing."

One of Tracy's team got out of the car. He was wearing jeans, a button-down shirt, and a tool belt, and carried a notepad and measuring tape. I opened the door and led them inside.

"It still looks great," Tracy said, looking around the house. She had been involved the last time I decorated, and rightly took pride in her work. "You're sure you don't want to consider getting a new house?"

"No," Sky and I said in unison. I would have considered the option, but Sky was determined, and I was happy not to have that discussion again. Letting some things stay settled made it easier to deal with the other issues.

"Changes?" Sky asked, sounding strained as she turned to look at me.

"I'm getting an estimate on moving the bedrooms downstairs," I explained, "ours and another for the baby, and the offices upstairs so you won't have to go up and down the stairs while you're pregnant." Sky didn't say anything, so I continued. Hopefully the details would reassure her, knowing that I had everything in hand. "I also have a list of cribs—one for the baby's room and one for travel—strollers, and car seats. You should look over them so we can have a decision by next week. Tracy will sit down with us to go over some colors for the rooms."

"Ethan." The sharpness in Sky's voice brought me to a crashing halt, and I looked at her in concern. "I'm three months. We have time…"

"You're almost four. We don't have lots of time, it's better to be prepared than rush to do everything at the last minute."

She sighed. "I'm pregnant, I'm not going to be an invalid. I will be able to walk up stairs and I'm sure I can carry a baby that only weighs a few pounds. Stop Tracy—"

She stopped and stared at Tracy and the contractor, who

were wandering around the house, taking pictures, measuring distances, and making notes. Tracy gestured excitedly as they looked at the stairs, and I felt better knowing that these skilled professionals had it all in hand, but Sky looked deeply unconvinced.

"Okay, but we'll look at the list later?" I said, hoping she would deal with it better once she'd had time to adjust. "We need to get prepared."

I looked around the living room, considering how much had already changed. Sky's arrival with all her things had already disrupted the tranquility of what had once been just my home. Remodeling wouldn't just let us prepare for the baby, it would let us find a better balance between our two tastes, making this a properly shared home, not just my house messed up by her clutter. Of course, the anxiety I was feeling didn't just come from our living arrangements, or even from me. I was feeling Sky's emotions and struggling to keep them in check. Working on the house gave me a way to release them productively, and not to create a feedback loop of stress between us.

"Ethan," Sky said softly, taking my hand in hers and squeezing it. "Everything will be fine. We'll go through your list and pick out a stroller, crib, brand of diapers, baby mobile, diaper bag, or whatever else you have there. I'll sit down with Tracy to pick a color for the baby's room—spoiler alert, I want yellow."

"It's a good color," I said, pleased to see that this was working, that I'd found something I could do that suited Sky, perhaps even soothed her.

"See? We have it covered. Everything's going to be fine."

But the tension was still there in her voice, and how could it not be? There were so many uncertainties surrounding her, from the pregnancy to the politics of the pack to how David and Trent's first full moon as werewolves would go.

Everything was in flux, and some of it put the two of us and our baby in real danger.

I turned to face her and ran my fingers lightly over her shoulder, before resting them against her neck, feeling the racing of her pulse.

"You don't believe that," I whispered.

"No," she admitted. "Once I'm marked, I should be fine. It will be fine. The pregnancy will go on without any problems."

We had talked about marking her with the *interdico*, the spell to suppress her magic, as a way of limiting its impact on the pregnancy. While it was a good plan, it didn't seem to be reassuring her as much as she claimed.

"Your ordinary respiration rate is seventeen," I said with a frown. "It used to be fifteen, but since the pregnancy it's been consistently seventeen. When you weren't giving the full truth, it decreased to thirteen, now it's fifteen. Six times you've blinked; it's usually eight times. Your heart rate is a little higher since the pregnancy—it's sixty-nine, instead of sixty-four—it's now seventy-six and has been since you started claiming everything is going to be fine." I rested my forehead against hers, establishing a connection, trying to soothe her with my touch. "If you're concerned, don't pretend not to be, okay?"

Sky nodded, and for a moment I thought that it was settled. But then she started talking, and as she did, she picked up speed, the words tumbling over each other in an unstoppable rush. All the concerns we had talked about and the ones we hadn't: her worries about the pregnancy, about the magic, about the way people were treating us, about the politics that seemed to bear down on us just because we were having a child. All her fears and uncertainties burst out like a thundercloud releasing long-threatened rain.

"Finally, I'm afraid I'm going to start hating red velvet cake," she said. "I've read and heard the stories about women despising the foods they once loved. What if our baby hates red velvet cake!"

I'd made it through the rest in seriousness and sympathy, despite the rising speed and pitch of her voice, but that one made me laugh out loud.

"Making sure you can eat red velvet for the rest of the pregnancy is at the top of my list, and the whole keeping Maya in check, handling Rayna and the others thing will be a strong second."

"That sounds about right."

At last, her shoulders sagged and she seemed to relax. Smiling, I went to talk with Tracy, who was standing in the kitchen with the contractor, carefully not looking at us. She gave a surprised smile as I approached.

"What do you think?" I asked.

"It's a fantastic opportunity," she said. "The things we could do with this place! Where would you like to start?"

"Let's look at the offices."

We walked around the house, Tracy talking me through her initial ideas, checking that they fit with what I was after, while the contractor brought us down to earth with practicalities and costs. We kept clear of the main bedroom, where Sky had taken shelter, but by the end, I was confident that a good plan was in hand.

"I'll leave you to pull the details together," I said as I showed them out the door. "Send me costs and options to consider, and we'll go from there."

"Will do," Tracy said, beaming. "This is going to be so much fun! Your family will have the loveliest home."

I made my way quietly to the bedroom, where Sky was indulging in a feast only a pregnant woman could possibly consider.

"Frosting and pretzels, the meal of champions," I deadpanned.

"I've seen you eat a deer," she replied between bites.

"In wolf form." I smiled and sat down. Sky moved over to sit beside me.

"This has to stop," she said. "It's too soon. I should be getting cravings at five and six months. Not three. What am I going to be like at five months?"

"I've read the cravings start early, then they get better in the late second or third trimester."

I couldn't do anything to change how her body behaved, but I could at least do the research, and offer whatever other comfort was mine to provide. I pressed my lips to her forehead and lingered there, feeling the warmth of her skin.

"Better?" I asked.

Sky scowled and kept eating her frosting-coated pretzels. It was going to be a long five-and-a-half months.

CHAPTER 37

Time seemed to move differently with a baby on the way. The hundred different things I wanted to get done before the arrival crowded up against the jobs of a lawyer and Beta, yet somehow reality stretched around them and I found time for the things that mattered.

It helped that the conflict among the witches had gone quiet. With both sides hidden, there was little chance for fighting, and the rest of the supernatural world had been waiting to see how it would play out. Rayna had disappeared so far off the grid that the others were now considering coming out of hiding, to take the life of the Creed back to something like normal. That had left me with time to focus on the rest of my life.

For the most part, that meant getting the house ready for the baby. Tracy and her team did a fantastic job, and two months after they started work we were comfortably settled in the new setup. Furniture and equipment for the baby were coming in steadily, filling up our house with everything we might need as parents. With Sky falling asleep early and waking up late, I filled a lot of the time on my own with sorting out the deliveries and finding places for everything in our newly decorated and warmly welcoming house, a more colorful place now that Sky's input had shaped it.

"You're like a little boy with his toys," she said, coming into the baby's room with a bowl full of ice cream and a hand resting on her belly. At nearly five months pregnant, she couldn't fit into most of her regular clothes anymore, so loose and baggy were the order of the day, and this evening that meant Hello Kitty pajamas and a fluffy blue robe with matching slippers. "What are you playing with today?"

"Baby monitors," I said, holding up an instruction book. The monitors themselves were laid out on the floor in front of me, along with the batteries and a screwdriver. I wanted to make sure that I had everything, and that I was doing it right, before I started setting them up.

"Do we need so many?" Sky asked.

I nodded. "This way, we can have them set up in different rooms, to make it easier to listen in."

"We've become the surveillance state!" Sky put on a tone of mock horror. "They're not even born yet, and Big Brother is watching our baby."

"Very funny." I got up off the floor and went to kiss her. She tasted of ice cream and pickles. "Have you been dipping gherkins in the chocolate fudge ripple again?"

"I couldn't find a clean spoon, so how else was I going to eat it?"

I looked pointedly at the spoon in her bowl.

"I found this one afterward," she explained. "It had been hidden away."

"Hidden away in the cutlery drawer, by any chance?"

"Who would think to look there?"

The back door opening resounded through the house, followed by footsteps and excited laughter. David and Trent walked in, smelling of fur and sweat, their shirts still unbuttoned from a run in the woods.

"You could have knocked," I said sternly.

"You knew we were here," David said. "We just had to pop outside for a quick run."

"That was hours ago."

"Guess we got carried away."

There was something sweet about the way these two interacted after running around in wolf form, something that meant even I couldn't stay grumpy at them for long. Exploring their wolf bodies together had brought a new level of closeness between them, and their affection shone through in the smiles they offered each other, the way they held hands when they stood close.

"Ooh, is it craft time again?" Trent asked, looking at the boxes piled up around the room. "Can we help? I'm a wonder with a glitter pen."

I tried to imagine Trent assembling a cot. I could imagine him posing in a tool belt, but not making effective use of its contents.

"I've got this under control."

"Let them help," Sky said, then yawned. "I'm too tired, but you shouldn't be doing all this alone."

"I like working alone."

"Everybody needs a hand sometimes." She kissed me softly, then waved at David and Trent. "Goodnight, all."

Leaving her bowl half-finished on a chair in the corner of the room, she headed for bed.

"Did Sky just leave ice cream behind?" Trent whispered in exaggerated shock. "These must be the end times!"

"If you want to help, you could wash that up," I suggested. The two of them had been eating here often enough, maybe it was time they helped with the chores.

"I was thinking more like we could put together a playhouse, or make a tasteful arrangement out of stuffed toys?"

I looked at the selection of soft animals that had already accumulated on a shelf, months before the baby was due to arrive. None of them were what I would have called tasteful, or a realistic depiction of what those beasts were really like. I had met bears, they had far sharper claws and didn't smile half as much.

"You could help build a storage unit," I said, pointing to a cardboard box that was leaning against the wall, full of flat pack pieces. I wasn't going to let my child sit or sleep in anything built with these two's haphazard DIY skills, but building shelves seemed fairly safe; the worst that could happen was that one of those inanely grinning bears got their stuffing crushed.

"I don't know, that doesn't sound like a lot of fun."

I held up one of the baby monitors. "The fun comes later. Right now, I'm trying to make a safe, comfortable home."

"We should probably go," David said, casting a disinterested glance across the flat pack box. "Dinner won't eat itself."

"Never mind," I said, trying not to sound too openly relieved. "Maybe you can help another time."

The next morning, I sat in a chair in the corner of the baby's bedroom, drinking my first coffee of the day, surrounded by the baby monitors, a sound machine, and several pieces of furniture, the latter in the dark wood that was still a motif of the house, and that contrasted nicely with the room's soothing white and yellow.

Sky appeared in the doorway, wearing yoga pants and an oversized t-shirt. She stared at my coffee with the hunger of an addict missing her fix, before her gaze drifted across my naked chest.

There were signs of Sky's addictions there as well, in the form of bite marks. Her craving for more blood wasn't one I had expected, but it made sense. If she needed its vitality to sustain her normally, then she must need it even more with a second life growing inside her. It made me worry, just a little, about whether the baby might inherit her vampirism, but there was nothing I could do to change that, while there was something I could do to support Sky, and so I encouraged her more frequent feedings, even as their sapping effect slowed down the healing of the bite marks.

"Did Trent and David help?" she asked, looking at what I had gotten done the previous night.

I shook my head. "They went home before I started."

"Did they leave, or did you kick them out?"

I smiled and made a noncommittal sound. David and Trent were a lot more tolerable now that they were part of the pack, and so more vulnerable to my influence as Beta. "They wanted to leave."

"Sure." She rolled her eyes. "We knew they were going to be around once they were turned. You can't be irritated by that now."

"It has nothing to do with that and you know it. They're handling things exceptionally well."

I'd thought that, living with Sky, I would quickly get tired of David and Trent coming over all the time to see their friend, who they had formed an even closer bond with when she turned them into weres, but while they were frequent visitors, that was more for the chance to run free across my land than to lurk around the house gossiping. Turning had been really good for them, and their presence in the pack was helping to keep people's spirits up as the cloud of a potential witch war loomed over us.

"Well, I could have helped you put everything together," Sky said, looking over the furniture, apparently forgetting that she had ducked out of that opportunity the previous night. She leaned in and kissed me deeply, her tongue exploring my mouth.

"I'm going to miss those peculiar morning kisses when

you're able to have coffee." I grinned and uncrossed my legs so that she could sit on my lap.

"We should have put in a sofa instead," she said, leaning back against me.

"Hmmm, like I suggested. We can change it out, but I like this. It's cozy." I surveyed the rest of the room, full of toys and contraptions for the baby, all chosen by Sky. "You did a great job picking things out."

"Yeah, I'm amazing. I just pulled out the list you gave me with the pros and cons of each product, available colors, and reviews, and enlisted the eeny-meeny-miny-moe strategy."

"Yet it took you over a month to choose," I teased.

I pulled her closer, laying my hand on her stomach, holding her and the baby tight.

"I wonder why Rayna's silent," Sky said.

"Perhaps her recruiting efforts are diminishing. Now that she has the Aufero, people seem content." It was something I'd been considering too, a piece of the political puzzle that didn't quite fit, especially after the attack at the shop. "I'm not sure why people are so comfortable with that zealot having it and not us. And Liam adhering to his belief that her having it constitutes ownership is concerning. He believes it shouldn't have been in your possession in the first place. The righting of a wrong."

That was a point we hadn't argued back on, not because anyone in the pack agreed, but because it was a fight we weren't willing to pick yet. There was too much risk of seeing the elves rally behind Liam if we took him on, undoing all our work in winning Gideon around and dividing his faction from Abigail. Sebastian and I had come up with plans for storming Elysian to get at Rayna, if it ever became necessary, but we were still waiting while we tried to work out if the risk was worth the reward. As long as Rayna kept quiet, the answer was probably not.

"I hate this," Sky whispered, settling in closer to me.

I hated it too, and I wasn't even the one our enemies would attack if they wanted to kill our unborn child. But there was nothing to be said that we hadn't covered a hundred times before.

"Are you ready for today?" I asked, trying to distract her.

"We're still doing that?" She groaned.

"You said you would at least look. We are just looking and…"

I was keen to find Sky a better car, not just something safer but something with a little more style. Her reluctance to engage with this had almost reached the point of active resistance.

"The baby will probably be less than ten pounds and, even as a toddler, how much room will it need?" she asked. "My Honda is just fine. I don't need anything bigger."

"Must we debate this again? Winter."

It was a cheap argument, perhaps, but a good example. Winter had slammed her Navigator into a creature that attacked her, crippling the beast and saving her life. Sky's car was nowhere near up to that kind of encounter.

"We don't know that my Civic wouldn't have stopped it."

"Yes, we know." I had to keep myself from scoffing at the very suggestion. I'd looked up the crash reports and seen what happened when a Civic hit anything tougher than a twig. It wasn't pretty.

"I guess I need a larger back seat so our child can roam free?" she asked sarcastically. "Because if the baby's in a car seat, a lot of room isn't needed."

"We're only going to look. Besides, you need more room for the baby bag, travel bed, toys, and supplies."

"You know babies are small, right? Tiny? They don't need a lot of room. Even as toddlers they require very little space." But her tone was finally shifting from combative to accepting. "Fine. I added cars to the list and I want to look at those."

"I saw that you had. Of course we'll look at them."

And then we would move on to somewhere that sold better cars, because Sky's taste in these matters was atrocious. But if this was what it took to get her out and considering the options, then this was what I would do.

"I'd like to go to my choices first," Sky said. "If I find something there, then we don't need to go anywhere else. I love the Pilot—it's cute."

With an unexpected level of effort, she pulled herself into the front seat of my Range Rover, a new addition to my collection that I'd bought in preparation for the baby. It had more space than my usual cars, and would be tougher if anything went wrong.

I frowned at the wrongheadedness of Sky's tastes in transport.

"Just because it cost the equivalent of a house doesn't make it better," she said.

"It's not the cost, it's what I like, Sky."

"And since it's for me, we should get what I like. I like the Pilot."

I was fighting a losing battle and needed something to swing the argument around. Thinking on my feet, I jumped out of the driver's seat.

"You drive," I said. "If you like the way the Pilot drives over this, we get the Pilot."

I felt dirty just saying that, and not in a good way, but I had to give some ground in hopes that she would also stop digging her heels in. Then the car could speak for itself.

Sky took the wheel and we headed out onto the road.

"The woman pulls out of her driveway, protected only by the steel of the Range Rover," she said in the deep voice of an action movie trailer. "Hoping it will lead to her survival in the terror-torn streets of suburbia, aware that behind the brick walls and manicured landscapes lurk the infidels. They might look innocent, pushing their strollers, jogging through the trails of danger with lattes, but the woman knows the horrors. She's aware that little girls in brown-and-green garb are just beacons of mayhem and horror. The woman is protected from those cunning, cookie-toting monsters because she is in her big, powerful, four-wheel-drive vehicle. But she remains vigilant behind the wheel of her aptly horse-powered military grade transportation, ever aware of potential threats. Constantly on the lookout for those hooligans carrying their netted sticks, claiming they're for lacrosse though she knows they are weapons of pure evil and destruction. The woman remains steadfast. With her grand Range Rover, she knows she stands a chance of surviving the mean streets—of suburbia."

At last, there was a break in the speech.

"Are you finished?" I asked.

"Until I can think of something else clever to say."

"Clever? I think you're using that word wrong."

"It's still unnecessary," she said firmly, "and I still want to test-drive the other cars."

Suddenly, cold swept through the car. Frost crackled across the windows and we started sliding across a road where there had previously been no ice. I looked around in alarm as Sky pumped the brakes and gripped the steering wheel.

Then there was a thud that shook the Range Rover and jolted us sideways across the ice. A bipedal creature covered in shaggy brown hair had slammed into my side of the car. It climbed up over the roof and punched through the front window, and I raised my hands to shelter my face as we were showered with shards of broken glass. Then a clawed hand reached through the gap and snatched at Sky.

I hit that grasping hand as hard as I could in the confines of the car, then grabbed hold of it, holding it back from Sky.

She snatched a flashlight from the back seat and swung it at the monster's arm, battering away until the long claws broke. Its other clawed hand sliced at me, and blood flowed from my arm.

"Let him go," Sky said. "He's trying to escape."

I didn't dare. What if she was wrong and the creature forced its way into the car, to attack her and our unborn child?

"Release it," she said louder.

I released my grip but kept both hands ready to dive in again. Immediately, the beast fell back off the Range Rover and rolled to the ground. I had a better view of it now, a disturbing combination of a gorilla's body, an orangutan's long fur, and a sloth's curved claws, with shell-like armor over its hips and shoulders. A mutated combination of different creatures.

A monster from Elysian.

Clutching its injured arm, it started to run away. I leapt out of the car to pursue it, then turned back as I realized that Sky would want to follow me.

"Sky, no," I said. "Go to the house. No. Go to Josh."

She hesitated, looking from me to the beast.

"Please," I said, looking at her belly.

She looked at me across the melting ice of elven magic, and it seemed that the reality of the attack was sinking in.

"All right," she said and brushed away broken glass before she turned the keys in the ignition. "But you be careful."

I couldn't promise her that, not after what had just happened. I was too angry. Instead, I turned and ran.

I chased the beast across the countryside, my heart racing, blood pounding to the rhythm of my fury. Someone had tried to kill my wife and child. Someone was going to suffer.

We ran through a patch of woodland, then across an open field. The creature wasn't just running away, it was running toward someone, the owner of a sleek blue BMW sitting by the side of the road. I caught a glimpse of a uniform in the driver's seat, a uniform I recognized: the guards from Gideon's house. Then the engine started, the car turned, and I saw who sat in the passenger seat.

Abigail. That was who had created the ice and sent the monster against us.

Fuck the fragile peace. I was going to tear her apart.

The car roared away, the creature staggering after it, still clutching its injured arm. It stumbled and howled, a sad and broken sound, as its mistress abandoned it. I almost felt sorry for the beast.

Almost.

It kept running, loping through woods and across fields, heading for Elysian. I followed, slowly gaining ground. I could have caught up faster if I became a wolf, but I wanted the control my human body offered, wanted to feel its death at my hands.

I caught up with it at last and leapt, smashing into it from behind. We tumbled across the deserted road, knees and elbows scraping against the asphalt, rolling to a stop with me on top. Then I wrapped both my hands around the creature's head and twisted. There was a crunch as its neck gave way and it flopped down dead.

I rose, trembling, to my feet.

"You're nothing but a weapon," I said, staring down at the hairy corpse. "And now it's time to disarm Abigail."

I looked around. The route to Elysian was always a strange one, the distance a matter less of geography than of magic. I wasn't surprised to see that, pursuing a mutant born from that place, I had almost reached its edge. Ahead of me, a barrier of magic shone through the woods, the wall between the mortal world and the one where the elves bred their abominations.

A storm billowed around me, lightning flashing across the sky, rain lashing down. I strode through churning mud as water plastered my clothes to me. I didn't care about anything around me, only my goal.

As I approached the barrier, rain turned to snow, mud to ice. I wrenched my feet out of the morass, leaving my shoes behind. I barely felt the jagged cruelty of the frozen ground beneath my feet as I took the last few steps and pressed my hands against the barrier.

Power rose from the dark pit that my heart had become. The power of the dark elves. The power of the spirit shade. The power of an Alpha, filled with primal fury, channeling the other magics into a force that could sunder the heavens and break open the gates of Hell.

Hail pounded my skin, bruising me down one side, as I let the power flow out of me and into the barrier. It began to buckle beneath the pressure, spells unraveling, frayed ends of magic breaking free. The hail stopped and in its place I felt power growing on the other side of the barrier, as the elves there fought to keep it intact. The holes I had made closed up. Loose ends wrapped together. Broken spells were reworked from out of the air.

I howled in frustrated fury. I was full of power, but the elves had long years of practice, and this magic was theirs. I was so close to my quarry, and I was going to be defeated.

Then there was a flash, a bright doorway appeared, and Josh emerged next to me. He looked like I felt, his whole body quivering with tension, face grim and determined. He spat words of magic and scythed his hands through the air, bringing them down in a chopping motion. Magic flared from them and into the barrier, slicing it open. The severed edges of the barrier peeled back like flesh from a wound and we stepped through, into the twisted forest of Elysian.

Around us stood the same strange trees and unnatural flowers I had seen before, the same still pools standing between them. But instead of a place of uncanny beauty, it had become one of darkness, reflecting my own menace back at me. The plants dripped with venom and the edges of jagged leaves twitched in a bitter breeze.

A dozen elves stood facing us, their hands raised and magic flaring between their fingers. Beyond them, their mutated beasts were waiting, a vast herd of them, no two the same, every one made to kill.

"Those things are weapons," I said, pointing at the beasts. "And one was just turned against my mate and unborn child. Stand back and let me destroy them, or I will destroy you."

In response, the elves unleashed a flurry of magic. Wind howled, hail battered my body, and lightning crashed down around me and Josh, charring the grass at our feet.

"Your mistake," Josh snarled, sounding more like a were-animal than I had ever heard him.

He chanted and a barrier rose around us, blocking out the weather magic. Then the barrier rushed outward, a wave of magic that slammed into the elves, knocking every one of them from their feet. As they fell, the glowing remnants of that spell wrapped around them, binding them in place.

"Go," Josh said through gritted teeth, sweat beading on his face as he struggled to keep twelve magic users bound. "Finish this."

I turned into a wolf, clothes tearing and falling away as I leapt at the beasts. Then I was in among them, lashing out with teeth and claws, rending and shredding anything that stood in my way. A great fist slammed into my side, and I sank my teeth into it, ripping it open, spilling thick black blood. Tentacles wrapped around my waist and I sliced them with my claws, reducing them to a tangled, blood-soaked mess.

For a long while, my world was nothing but violence. I

twisted and turned, dodging attacks, striking back at anything within reach. With my nearest targets gone, I widened my circle, howling in fury, lunging at anything that moved. Something with a horn charged at me, but I leapt over its head and landed on its back, then snapped its spine between my teeth. A bird covered in eyes swept down and I swatted it out of the air, then shredded it in the dirt.

These weren't the enemy, just their weapons, tools of cruel and merciless lords. I didn't care. All I wanted was to destroy, and if I couldn't reach the hand that wielded it, then I would smash the weapon itself.

At last I stood, panting and aching, in a circle of broken bodies. There were still monsters in Elysian, and they still crowded around, watching me while staying out of reach. If I darted closer then they fell back, receding from my rage.

I was slicked with blood, only a little of it mine. I could taste the foulness of the place, and the gaps between my claws were clogged with fur and feathers.

It still wasn't enough.

Could anything ever be enough?

Perhaps.

With a low growl, I shifted, muscles twisting and fur retreating, until I stood on two legs, still blood-soaked, feathers falling from between my fingers. Josh's mouth hung open as he saw the look on my face.

"This isn't your fault," I said to the monsters, not knowing whether they understood. Not caring either. The words were for the captured elves, for any other witnesses who somehow saw what happened there. "But your time is over."

I took a deep breath. As I exhaled, my magic flowed out of me, down through my feet and into the ground. As I had done once before, I unleashed the power of death and destruction into the dirt of Elysian. This time there was no holding back. Every ounce of my power went into that magic. It flowed through the realm in an ever-widening circle, a pool of darkness that rippled out without end. As it touched the mutated creatures, they fell, bodies twisting and spasming before falling still. Some tried to flee, running away or taking to the air. But the magic was there too, stretching out through the treetops, bringing them tumbling down. Those that ran reached the barrier at the edge of their world, only for the darkness to suck away the last of their life.

At last, Elysian was still. Dead bodies lay sprawled across infertile ground. The only things moving were me and Josh.

He released the bonds on the elves, who stared around them, speechless, then looked at me in terror before running for their lives.

"We're done here," I said, looking in satisfaction at centuries of magical breeding programs brought to an abrupt end. But I didn't feel done. The need to fight was still inside me, even with no opponents left.

"No," Josh said. "One more thing."

He raised his hands. Magic flowed from them, bright and shining where mine had been dark and consuming. It formed a thousand glowing spikes that hit the barrier around Elysian, shattering it. The barrier fell away, shreds of spells dispersing on the wind, leaving the elves' private playground exposed.

As I pulled on my bloodstained pants, Josh nodded in satisfaction. Magic still sparked around his fingers, and his eyes had turned a cloudy gray.

"Now we're done."

CHAPTER 38

I paced back and forth in the front room of our home, drawing ragged breaths as I tried to bring my body and my powers back under control. Since unleashing my wrath in Elysian, I had felt my strength fading and returning over and over, like a tide rushing up and down a shoreline. I had poured so much of myself into that act of destruction, my body was struggling to manage what was left. Part of me wanted to fight on against someone, to use the fury I still felt at the attack on Sky. Another part of me felt exhausted, on the verge of collapse. As long as I kept moving, I hoped that I could at least hold that part back.

The attack on Sky was still at the forefront of my mind. The car skidding across the road. The wild beast smashing the windshield and reaching in for her. The fear and rage I had felt as I realized that someone was trying to kill my mate and our unborn child. If I got a hold of the people behind it, there was no limit to what I would do to them. Our enemies, those arrogant, pure-blood elves and their allies among the rogue witches, had gone too far. Nothing I did could be enough of a punishment.

Josh leaned against the wall, magic sparking around his

fingertips, his eyes still grayed over. He had been leaning there since we came back to the house, only fifteen minutes before. If I was struggling with the waxing and waning of my own power, I was truly worried about his. He had tapped into a deep reserve to break down the barrier at Elysian, the most incredible show of magic I had ever seen from him, but he seemed unable to let that magic go. It had some hold over him, and I didn't know what that might lead to.

The whole time, Sky had watched us nervously, waiting to see what came next. I didn't even have the words yet to tell her what we had done, never mind to contemplate what it might unleash.

The elves had deserved everything we had done to Elysian, but that didn't mean that there wouldn't be consequences.

There was a knock on the door. I stalked over and flung it open.

Sebastian walked in and closed the door behind him, then followed me into the front room. He stared at me, then at Josh. His brow furrowed, he frowned, then ran a hand over the lower half of his face, as if he was trying to force his expression under control, and with it his emotions.

"Do I want to ask?" he said.

"They attacked Sky." It was all the answer I would ever need to give. Sebastian looked over at Sky, her stomach bulging, and he understood, even if he didn't like what was happening.

"Liam has been calling me," he said. "I haven't spoken to him yet. What do I need to know?"

Three sharp knocks on the door cut off the conversation. Sebastian peered out the peephole, tensing as he did so.

"It's Chris."

"I called her," I said.

I wasn't entirely sure why I had taken that choice. I had known that someone needed to help Josh bring his power back under control, and perhaps London or Ariel might have been a natural choice, witches to help a witch master his magic. But this wasn't ordinary witch magic, and it didn't seem like ordinary solutions would do, even if I had known how to get a hold of the hidden witches.

Chris had been another logical option. She and Josh had bonded when he let her drink his blood for a while, at a time when she didn't have access to the Seethe and its garden. I knew from my experience with Sky that having your blood drunk could be a draining experience, so perhaps it could be used to tap off some of what was flowing through Josh. It might not have seemed like a good idea, bringing a vampire into our business, but if Sky trusted Chris, then perhaps I could put my trust in Sky's judgment.

Sebastian opened the door and Chris walked casually in. She looked sternly at me and Josh, her eyes as black as the deepest pits. With a scowl, she crooked her finger at Josh, gesturing him to come to her, but he stood unmoving, too lost to the world to even respond. Instead of waiting, she walked over to him, moving slowly as if to avoid causing alarm, trying not to trigger whatever power was swirling around behind those gray eyes.

"Josh," she said softly.

His eyes lifted, but nothing else moved. He seemed caught in a web of darkness, unable to drag himself from its threads.

Chris pressed her lips to his neck, then bit down hard. Josh grimaced, but he still didn't move, except for a shaking of his hands as the magic around them started to disperse.

It was a sight that had appalled me a year before: my brother being drained by a vampire. Now it was strangely fascinating, seeing a different version of something that played out regularly between me and Sky, watching for what was different and what was the same. There was none of the closeness that Sky and I shared, none of the intimacy that came with the act. This was purely a practical matter, a trade of blood for calm.

Josh drew a deep breath and held it, while Chris kept feeding on him, filling the room with the quiet, unsettling sound of her sucking at a vein. The cloudiness faded from Josh's eyes, leaving a vacant, hypnotized look, and a darkness that hadn't been there before Elysian. His hands moved as if of their own accord, heading for her waist, before he jerked them back. Startled by the movement, Chris pulled away, leaving small tears in his skin instead of the neat puncture marks I was used to.

Josh backed away from her. There was still that hint of darkness to his eyes, something that hadn't been there before. Whatever power he had tapped into, it had changed something in him. I hoped that, in coming to help me, he hadn't done himself some harm.

"Want me to close them?" Chris asked, pointing at the wounds.

He nodded and leaned over to give her access to his neck. She licked at it with comical exaggeration until the wounds closed up.

"Gross," Josh said with a frown.

Chris chuckled and stepped back from him.

"Thank you for coming," I said.

"I've been called upon by quite a few people in regards to you all." She came to stand in front of me, spearing me with a look of terrible intensity. I was no longer just dealing with my ex. I was being judged by the Mistress of the Northern Seethe. "What. The. Hell. Did. You. Do?"

"They tried to kill Sky." I said it with finality. It was the only reason I needed, the only one I would be giving anyone. I loved Sky, she was my mate, and I would protect her with my life. I expected the same of anyone who saw their mate hurt or threatened, doubly so when that mate was carrying their child. Anyone with the least understanding would anticipate my fury and know that an attack on her would bring terrible consequences. The elves had crossed a line, and they had earned everything that came back at them.

"You have every right to be pissed, but Elysian will never be the same. Their animals are all destroyed—"

"They shouldn't have been creating them in the first place," Sebastian said. "Us overlooking the creation of such dangerous animals was a courtesy. What was their purpose? Fun? Most of those creatures were too dangerous to exist. If anything, Ethan provided an overdue service."

Chris harrumphed.

"Let's see if you get some type of acknowledgment for your acts of altruism," she said, then turned to Josh. "And you, whatever magic you used to break their ward and prevent them from erecting it again needs to be reversed."

"I'm not reversing anything until they tell us how to find Abigail. She was there at the attack. It was her magic that initiated it. I want her stopped."

Chris sighed and started to pace the room, taking on the same posture I had a few minutes before.

"Ethan, I'm on your side," she said. "This coalition they've founded is unnerving. I've never been one to employ the preemptive approach. They are acting out of fear, and it's a great motivator and causes people to behave erratically. Rayna's smart and calculated and has enlisted some magical heavy hitters. Even witches that wouldn't fall in line with Marcia and left under her governing have allied with her. They probably would have eventually fallen in line with Ariel, but she's convinced them that the new Creed are ineffectual. You are what they fear, and you've confirmed the need for it to be a concern by displays of powerful magic."

My anger, which had lain just beneath the surface of the conversation, bubbled to the top. This attitude was ridiculous. Sky and I had only ever been a threat to the people who hurt or threatened us. Our baby wasn't even born yet, completely incapable of harming anyone. These people had stirred up fear over nothing, then used it as an excuse to intimidate, threaten, and attack us. If this was what they were like before our baby had even been born, how much worse would they get as the child grew up? I had to stop this now.

"They tried to kill me and Sky. What exactly should I have done? Let it go unchecked? I don't care about their fear—"

"You should care because it's not just them. If I wanted you dead, other than myself there are three people I would call. They've been hired. Ethan, this is only going to get worse. Do something about it." She turned to Sebastian. "You all need to try to handle this diplomatically, because all hell's about to break loose and the very lives you are trying to protect will be the casualties of it."

"I did nothing wrong," I said, clenching my jaw as I struggled not to shout at her, not to scream and rage at the world. "I fell in love and I'm having a baby. Why should that be something I need to handle diplomatically?"

"As of four hours ago, you hadn't done anything wrong and others were hesitant to feed into Rayna's and the others' paranoia. With you putting on a full display of what you and your brother are capable of, they are concerned about your offspring. It's a valid concern, especially if your child will be able to do more as a combination of you and Sky and be impossible to constrain. Have you considered that your child might be able to perform magic in animal form? Be immune to it even in human form? Immortality? How hard was it to kill the Faeries? These are the concerns people have. Will you stop at one, or can they expect an army of your children, who could be dangerous and nearly unstoppable?"

She paused long enough to move over to the side of the room, where she leaned against the wall, watching us all, evaluating our reactions.

"I'm team dud," she continued. "Because honestly, that

could be an option too: everyone on high alert for the unstoppable being of great magical aptitude, and you get an absolute dud. One that can't even shift. There have been cases where two shifters had a child that wasn't able to change, right?"

"That's only happened when one was a changed were-animal," Sky said. "It's never happened with two born weres."

"That one has a lot going on," she said, with a nod of her head toward Sky. "No telling what you have baking in that oven. It might just come out a pup, for all we know. Use that obscurity to your advantage."

She was right about this one: we had gotten too caught up in the situation to consider what other options it offered. Though half the supernatural world seemed convinced that our mixed magic would create an abomination, it was just as likely to produce a perfectly ordinary baby, a normal were, or even a human. Mixed powers could cancel each other out rather than combine. This was an unprecedented situation, and we shouldn't let others treat it as though the outcome was set in stone.

"Would you be able to set up a meeting?" Sky asked. "I'd like to talk to Rayna and Abigail."

"Rayna, possibly. After what your mate did to Elysian, I'm sure Abigail knows he wants to talk to her and she's not amenable to listening. But without Rayna, she won't have support. Rayna's not foolish enough not to recognize that Abigail has an ulterior motive. This isn't about the health and security of the others in this world but the preservation of her people, and her people only. She's vying for her brother's position, and now that the rules have changed about women holding the position, he will not seek reelection so that she can have it." Chris looked from me to Josh. "Some siblings will do anything for each other. I'll see what I can do."

"How will you be able to get to her?"

"Demetrius and I were invited to be part of the conventicle and we accepted."

I growled, deep and low, my voice joining with Sky's. All this time, Chris had been making out like she was helping us, when she was in bed with the enemy, plotting against our child.

"Oh, calm down, wolfie," she said with a roll of her eyes. "I've made my position known but I'd be remiss in not hearing their side, nor would it look good if I sided with you all without hearing it. They are aware I don't agree and that I don't plan to take action. Their goal was to convert me; they were unsuccessful. I told them if something was an imminent threat to the Seethe, we would handle it. Your unborn is not a threat."

She headed out the door, leaving us with that thought. It all came down to making it clear that our child wasn't a threat, that nobody needed to worry about what we were doing or what we represented. We were just a family, even if it was a family with some extraordinary powers, and we weren't going to hurt anyone. If we could convince them of that, perhaps people would leave us in peace.

CHAPTER 39

I rolled the Range Rover to a stop, and the cars of other pack members fanned out around me. I glanced at the satnav, and again at the message on my phone that had given me the location. Unlikely as it seemed, they all matched. We were in the right place.

I peered out at a large, rundown farmhouse built from gray stone. The land around it lay fallow, long grass and weeds filling the space between groves of dying trees. The smells of manure and farm animals told me that there was a working farm nearby, but this certainly wasn't it. Ravens spread their wings and watched us from bare branches, eyes gleaming with hunger.

"Why don't you wait in the car?" I said. "This doesn't look like a healthy place."

"Nothing about this situation is healthy, Ethan," Sky said, giving me a stern look. "That doesn't mean that you can talk me into sitting it out."

We'd had this conversation a dozen times already, but I was still willing to give it one more round, to try to persuade Sky that she could miss the negotiations with our enemies. She didn't need to be there, and putting her close to them, visibly pregnant, seemed like a way to remind them of every-thing they feared, as well as putting her in the firing line if things turned violent. But Sky wasn't going to be deterred, and in the end, I'd faced a choice between bringing her myself or knowing that she would follow anyway.

Still, one more try…

"It's different now that we've seen the place," I said. "There's something unnatural going on here, it can't be good for you or the baby."

"There's something unnatural about almost everything in our lives." Sky opened her door. "I can't avoid that forever."

"I'm not saying forever, just a few months."

"A few months that could decide our family's fate?"

"Stay." I didn't even mean to put my Beta authority into my voice, it just emerged that way.

Sky froze, then glared at me. "Did you just—"

"I didn't mean to. It was instinct. I don't want to see you in danger." I laid a hand on her belly. "Either of you."

"That's sweet." She took my hand off her belly, kissed it, then set it aside. "But we'll be well guarded. I hear that the Beta of the Midwest Pack will be there, and he's quite a bruiser."

Sebastian was already out of his car and peering up at the trees, like he was in a staring match with the ravens. Other weres spread out into the surrounding countryside, sniffing around for any signs of an ambush, while in the back seat of Sebastian's car, Quinn and Tabby sat with laptops, satellite phones, and gadgets I didn't recognize, scrutinizing the airwaves for evidence of surveillance or technological traps.

"What do you think?" I asked as I approached Sebastian.

"I think it's like something out of Poe," he replied. "Apparently Rayna has taken a turn for the gothic."

Another car pulled up and Ariel stepped out. She was less elegantly dressed than usual, in flats, fitted jeans, and a simple white shirt. Did this reflect the weariness that lay heavy across her face, or was she showing Rayna that she didn't consider her worth the effort? Gavin and Steven emerged to either side of her and took their animal forms as the three of them approached.

"This is where Rayna wanted to meet?" Ariel asked, looking in disdain at the dilapidated building.

Sebastian moved to stand beside her. "Yes, it's not what I expected."

"I'm not surprised," Ariel said after a moment's thought. "I'm more surprised that she agreed to the promise of no violence. Perhaps she's more prudent than she's demonstrated."

As we approached the building, rats scurried away, seeking shelter in the long grass. Other cars sat to one side of the building. We weren't the first to arrive.

The front door opened and Chris stood there, watching us impassively. She stepped aside to let us in, and took up position next to Demetrius at one side of the room, the two of them black-clad guardians, referees for what should be a peaceful contest. The interior of the house was barren, unfinished, nothing but drywall and bare boards. Whoever had once dreamed of living here, fate had gotten in their way before they even got started.

A thick magical barrier ran down the middle of the room. Behind it stood a dozen figures. Most were rogue witches, headed by Rayna, but Abigail and Mason were there too. Samuel wasn't. It seemed that he'd taken the last chance Sky had given him and prudently gotten out of the fight, or perhaps had simply realized that witches weren't really allies in his cause.

The air smelled so thickly of blood that it must be making Demetrius desperate with hunger, but this wasn't blood for the drinking. It had been used to build the barrier in the middle of the room, a blood ward, powerful in itself, even more so when it had been created by ten witches. However paranoid we were about our opponents' intentions, they were equally worried about us.

Rayna cleared her throat, then rolled her eyes as she saw the pack of weres streaming in through the door behind us.

"Always a display of power with you all," she said with disgust.

"Like your wall," I replied. Or like the group of witches she had brought along. It seemed that Rayna ran as good a line in hypocrisy as Marcia had done.

"It is for our protection. I know we agreed upon a truce but, knowing your history, I considered it prudent to protect ourselves for the moment when you all have exhausted your restraint—something you seem to do regularly." She turned her fiery look on Ariel, and a disapproving sneer fixed itself on her lips. "Ariel. I'm sure you know as much of my history as I know of yours. When I heard you and yours were going to make the long-needed power grab of the Creed, I was elated. Even considered returning to the witches, to be one with you all, with the confidence it would be led by one who believed in the purity of magic, the rules, and the importance of not abusing magic.

"Top of your class in magic school, gifted beyond what had been seen in years"—she looked at Josh, who had come in quietly behind us—"gifted for someone who would use their magic for more than being the pack's magic-wielding lackey. So much promise. How long did it take before you were allied with the pack and *allied* with Sebastian?"

Ariel flushed, just a little, but enough to show that the comment about Sebastian stung. Rayna smiled maliciously, seeing that her words had hit their target.

"Her personal life has nothing to do with her ability to lead," Sebastian said, his voice steady, but I could sense the anger underneath. He didn't like to see their relationship judged in this way, to hear it reduced to a political play.

"Of course you'd say that; it benefits your pack. Not only

do you have Josh but a group of powerful witches at your beck and call. And"—she waved at Sky's stomach—"whatever that will be."

"Do you really think she's going to weaponize their child?" Ariel's incredulity was clear. "I don't agree with a lot of things they do, and they don't have the same reverence and respect for magic as we do, but they aren't as careless or callous with it as you want people to believe. They make a mess, they clean it up."

"Not out of virtue or acceptance of responsibility," Rayna said angrily. "It's to save their asses. If we all came together to punish them for the carelessness and crimes, they wouldn't win."

"Who cares about the reason they do it, as long as it is handled? That's the difference between us. Why we have control of the Creed—"

"For now," Rayna said, glaring daggers at Ariel.

This was going nowhere, but it needed to happen. For months, these two had been caught up in a struggle for control of the Creed but had been unable to face each other. Some of their aggression and frustration would have to be spent if they were going to move on.

"I'll agree to be marked," Sky said, interrupting the back and forth. "That will restrict my magic. You win, I won't have access to magic. I will be as you wish, a wolf without magic."

As offers for our side to make went, it was pretty much perfect. Sky and I had discussed the possibility already, as a way of restraining Maya's influence as the baby's arrival drew near. If it also appeased Rayna, then we gained ground while conceding nothing we hadn't already planned. At the same time, it seemed like a huge gesture, especially to witches, who were reliant on their magical power.

"You know that's not all I want."

"That's why it's called a compromise. I'm not making a decision for my pack or any of the weres who enjoy what they are and are content to live in both worlds. You don't get to make the decision of whether or not they get to live that life. That's not how things work. Just like I wouldn't agree to Samuel's desire to wipe the world of magic."

There was a long silence. We did know what she wanted, and it was to take away what made us ourselves, to turn us into ordinary humans. Perhaps that would have been enough for those who had grown up that way, but to me it would have been like chopping off a limb, or like lobotomizing myself. A crucial part of who I was and what I could do would be gone. I wouldn't even be me anymore, in many ways that mattered.

And this was the thing on which Rayna was refusing to compromise, refusing to respond to Sky's offer.

"Do you really want this?" Sky asked, looking at Abigail.

"More than she does. I've watched you all for years, knowing the menace that followed in your wake. But the return of the Faeries was the last straw. You all need to be put down, like the animals you are."

I stayed silent, stayed back, letting Sky do the talking. She could at least exert some control over her anger, though it hung around her like a miasma, clouding the emotions of anybody nearby. If I tried to speak, I didn't think I would be able to say anything other than threats. Not to people who had tried to kill my unborn child.

So often in the past, I had been the one trying to make Sky see reason. Now, in spite of everything, she was the reasonable one.

She pressed her hand against the barrier, not interfering with it, just sensing it, testing it. I watched to see if it would give beneath her touch, and realized that was what I hoped for, a breakdown in negotiations and a swift, brutal resolution. With the smell of blood all around, how could I want anything else?

"Ethan and I will get the mark," Sky said, "our child will

wear an iridium brace once of age, and you will surrender the Aufero to someone who can't benefit from its use. Maybe the vampires. They can't use it."

"You speak on behalf of the witches now," Rayna said with amusement. "You do have your nose in everything, don't you?"

"I won't allow you to terrorize the Creed for no other reason than they've helped us when we needed them."

Rayna chuckled darkly. "You won't 'allow' it. How presumptuous of you."

"Yes, you heard me correctly. Nothing's wrong with your ears, it's your heart and values that have the dysfunction."

Sky pressed against the barrier again, and this time it gave way, stretching out around her hand like a rubber sheet. She pushed forward until she and Rayna were almost touching. While Rayna maintained her look of control, behind her, the witches' mouths fell open and they stared at Sky in horror.

"That's the offer," Sky said. "You are going to want to take it."

"And if I refuse?"

We were so close, but instead of accepting a solution, Rayna was determined to push, to provoke, to prove that she was right. My own stubborn aggression receded as I saw it reflected in her and realized how stupid it was. Compromise was the way out here. Both sides had to give.

But the other side weren't going to budge an inch. I could see it in their faces. Rayna's followers might not have the absolute certainty she did, but they would follow her, because she offered a world in which they felt stronger, more secure. It was the same with Abigail and Mason. The power and the prestige of the elves had been weakened. If they could bend Sky to their will now, then they could restore the feeling that they ruled the world. Without that, they had to accept that others were their equals, and that thought was too much for them.

The barrier rippled as Sky leaned into it, the strength of her emotions pressing against the magical world. The witches cringed as a power tied to their blood came under attack.

"Sky," I said softly. "Step back from the barrier."

She didn't move. Her eyes were closed as she fought to control her inner turmoil.

"Sky, please, there's still a chance to talk this through. Come back to me."

She opened her eyes, but if she had heard my words then there was no sign of it.

"Take the offer," she whispered.

"Begging is hardly going to change anything," Rayna said. "Constant compromise has led to where we are now with you. Marcia was power-hungry and at times tyrannical, but she understood and did what was necessary."

A burst of magic from Sky hit the barrier, and its impact struck Rayna. Shocked, she stepped back, clustering together with her witches and their elven allies.

"What she thought was needed was cruel and unnecessary," Sky growled. "Fine, offer rescinded. Know this: It is over. You come after me, Ethan, or anyone I care about, you make goddamn sure you say goodbye to everyone you care about, because you won't be seeing them again!"

Sky clawed at the barrier, and it flashed and trembled beneath her fingertips, but held. She slammed her fist against it.

I could see disaster coming, not just for these talks but for my family. If Sky over-strained herself, anything could happen to our child. If she gave in to the deep, dark magic within her, that could do as much harm. I grabbed her around the waste and pulled her, struggling, away from Rayna.

Chris stepped into the gap, looking sternly at the witches.

"You should reconsider; it's a good offer," she said in a professional tone. "Is the possibility of a magical abnormality worth a war that may come of this? You made an attempt on Sky and Ethan. What will be your punishment if their child is just a simple were-animal, undeserving of whatever you have in store?"

"How can you be so optimistic?" Rayna snorted. "Oh, because you all likely won't be affected. Pardon me for not taking your feedback into consideration. This was a courtesy in hopes I could get you to understand the importance of our stance. Obviously, your vampire conversion has changed you from the type of person I would want on my team."

"Then obviously, the rumors you heard were false. I never supported measures like this, nor will I ever. I didn't condone it when the witches did it, nor when the elves did it."

Chris glared at Abigail and Mason.

I was battling to keep my breaths steady, to calm myself and to soothe Sky, who I still held pressed against me. I had stood by and listened through everything Rayna had to say, containing my anger despite her attitude. I had let her talk about my child as if they were something toxic, and I had held back my anger. We had tried to negotiate in good faith, offering a compromise that restricted us just to settle her fears. We had done the best we could, while all Rayna offered was hateful rhetoric and an unwillingness to listen, to bend even a little toward a solution. Through an effort of will, I had stayed calm through it all, had even tried to soothe Sky. But what was the point in staying calm when we were here under false pretenses, the negotiations a complete sham? If the other side never intended to give any ground, then there was no point in talking.

"Let's break the field," I said and let go of Sky.

She pressed her hands against the magical barrier, and the

air thrummed with magic. I expected to see the barrier wobble and break, to see the blood magic dissolve or shatter into pieces. Instead, it was the people behind it who changed. The witches gasped and clutched at their throats, sweat breaking out across their faces, eyes reddening as blood vessels ruptured. Sky was reaching them through their blood magic, choking them, killing the people who had tried to kill her.

Good.

Abigail and Mason sank down next to the witches, looking at them in fear.

"Let the protective field drop," Abigail said.

For a long moment, Rayna didn't respond. She stared at Sky with bloodshot eyes and an expression of unadulterated hate, unable to see past that hatred long enough to save herself.

Electricity jolted from Abigail's fingers, shocking Rayna out of her obsession. She gave a wave of her hand, and the other witches followed the gesture. The barrier vanished. So did the witches and elves.

It was hardly the victory I had wanted. The problem wasn't resolved. There was no negotiated peace, and our opponents were still out there. At least we could hope that this might scare them out of attacking us.

Chris frowned as she surveyed the aftermath. "Did that go the way you wanted?"

"What were we supposed to do?" Sky snapped.

"I'm on your side on this," Chris said sharply. I reminded myself that she had arranged a peaceful negotiation, probably pulling in several favors to make it happen, and that, while the other side had been uncompromising, we were the ones who had broken the peace. She had a right to be angry.

"I'm sure that stunt didn't help to change her mind," Ariel said, rubbing her face. "We are returning home; when you are ready to have the *interdico* placed, just let me know."

She backed out of the door and Sebastian followed close behind. The rest of us hurried after them.

"What do you mean, you're going home?" he asked.

"I'm removing my witches from the pack's protection. The price is too high. We will protect ourselves."

Gavin was standing by the car Ariel had come in, ready to drive her back to the safe house. But when she approached, he looked at Sebastian, who shook his head.

"Drive me home," Ariel said.

"No," Gavin said, leaning unmoving against the car door

Ariel turned, her face red with fury, and strode up to Sebastian.

"You don't get to make decisions for us. Do you understand? I am declining your offer of assistance."

"Once again you are putting your pride before your safety. It's a foolish way to lead."

"We are not in the same situation. You've had years to establish yourself, to earn the respect that you enjoy and often exploit. I don't have that, and with Rayna commanding so much loyalty from others, I am now the cause of the very civil war I was trying to prevent."

"You let her get to you—"

"Damn right she got to me! Did you see the witches she has with her? Older, more experienced witches who had distanced themselves from Marcia and the former Creed's ways and aligned with her. I'm not enough—*we* aren't enough. They don't trust me."

She sagged, visibly battered by the weight of her responsibilities and the impossibility of her situation.

"We trust you to do the *interdico*," Sebastian said, "and we will need you all at full strength for the safety of Ethan and Sky's child. If Rayna gets to you all, she will take your magic. How is that better?"

"We'll protect ourselves." Ariel started for the car again.

"Sebastian, I'm going home. Don't instruct Gavin to do anything other than that."

Sebastian dashed after her, so swift and silent that she jumped in surprise when he appeared in front of her.

"What are your plans?" he asked, his voice mild, without a trace of the frustration he must feel at her disagreeing with him.

"That's between me and the other Creed."

She was quivering with anger, while Sebastian was calm and composed as he stepped closer.

"It's just us," he said quietly.

I pitied her. She had taken charge of the Creed with such confidence, but her position was crumbling. Taking our protection was the right thing to do, but it also made her look weak, and Rayna had skillfully used that to peel off some of her supporters. The longer she stayed in hiding, the worse that situation became.

She looked at me and Sky, and I could imagine the comparisons going on in her mind, considering how a romantic relationship with a powerful were-animal had reshaped Sky's life, for better and for worse, considering how it might affect her.

"Things between us have to be strictly professional," she said, pressing her lips together as she stared past Sebastian.

"How do you want to handle the arrangement with the witches?" he said, finally letting go of his attempt at control.

"We stay together—but not at one of your homes. At mine."

I tried to imagine all those witches crowded together in Ariel's apartment, and I hoped that it was more spacious than it had looked. At least the cat would get plenty of attention.

"Okay," Sebastian said.

Ariel exhaled, then some of her confidence seemed to return.

"I would like to ask the help of Gavin, Steven, and maybe

a few other were-animals to track the Aufero. Rayna's witches are more experienced but not stronger—I'd feel better with that threat out of the way."

Sebastian nodded his assent. "Will you be warding your home?"

"Of course."

"Can Josh do a second one?"

Ariel considered it for a moment, then nodded.

"It sounds like a solid plan," Sebastian said. "Gavin and Steven will be with you the entire time you look for it—their ability to track is better than yours."

"I agree."

There it was. Ariel got to protect her pride, and her public image, while still having the pack lurk around the whole time. At least one compromise had worked out today.

Sebastian touched her hand. She didn't move any closer to him, but she didn't pull her hand away either.

"Fine," she said at last, then headed for the car.

CHAPTER 40

*J*osh had made some alterations to the bar when he reopened. He claimed that they were about market awareness and recognizing how Chicago's night life had changed, but I suspected they had as much to do with him aging and mellowing along the way as they did with market considerations. Josh was starting to settle down. He and London were moving in together, and a steadier, more stable business aesthetic matched a steadier, more stable manager.

The end result was a calmer place than before, better lit but still relaxing. The dance floor was smaller, making space for more tables. Sugary drinks to keep late-night clubbers going had been replaced by artisan ales and a more extensive cocktail menu. It was a place for sophisticated, discerning drinkers, though of course there was still plenty of space for were-animals in need of a night off.

The new style suited Sebastian better, and for the first time that I could remember, he was making a regular habit of going out to the bar. I saw him as I walked in, relaxing at his regular table in the corner, sipping at a German lager. I got myself a glass of Scotch and went to join him.

"This makes a nice change from meeting in your office," I said as I sat down.

"It certainly does." Sebastian nodded. "And my days have been pretty busy recently."

"Dealing with the witches?"

"A little. More dealing with the tensions in the pack."

I frowned, annoyed at myself. I'd been so preoccupied with the coming baby, I'd almost stopped paying attention to the personal dynamics of our ever-growing pack. That left even more work on Sebastian's shoulders.

"What's the latest?" I asked.

"So many things." A small, rueful smile tweaked up the corner of his mouth. "Not enough space in the gym. Jealousies over who gets to train with Winter. Disputes over who's using the spare rooms in the retreat when. The Worgen have fallen out with each other over something called Eve Online, and I don't even know what that one is, but I know I'll care less and less the more they tell me."

"The Worgen are pretty special."

"They certainly are."

We both grinned and took a drink. I'd missed these moments, the two of us working together to organize the pack. It made me feel like I had purpose, like I belonged.

"Of course, there's more to it than that," Sebastian continued. "Steven's started to get itchy feet. He doesn't complain, and he hasn't argued with anyone, but the restlessness is there. I'm not sure he realizes himself that it's his deepest instincts, the desire for more status, to be running his own pack. Even Gavin could do with more authority than he has, and there's a line of younger weres behind them. We need to offer them more purpose."

"Will this hunt for the Aufero help?"

"It's a start, but not enough. And the minute it's finished, we're back where we started."

I rubbed my chin, considering the options.

"I'm happy to take some of that stuff back on," I said. "Perhaps I can get more of the pack involved in watching out for threats like the Faeries, and put Steven and Gavin in charge of groups for that. Or we could—"

"I've already got a solution," Sebastian said. "That's why I wanted to meet."

"What is it?"

He hesitated, then waved for more drinks. I waited, watching him, while the bartender came over. Something was up, and even Sebastian was reticent to share it with me. Did I need to be worried?

"We've been following the same strategy for the past decade," he said. "Constantly growing, absorbing smaller packs. It's been good for maintaining order."

"I still think it was our best option," I said, thinking back to my early days as Beta. "Compared to where we were before, the whole region is calmer. I know we had that trouble with Red Blood and Steven, but we hardly ever have to rush in to cover up for someone's sloppy behavior anymore."

"You're right, it's worked well. It's helped us bring peace and calm, and now other weres know to behave themselves. North America is a far more peaceful place to be a were than it was when I was young. But that strategy has also created this vast, unwieldy pack, and now that's the problem. It's something we need to change."

"How?" I asked warily. I didn't like the way this was going, abandoning an approach that had gone so well.

"I'm considering breaking up the Midwest Pack into smaller packs. As Elite, I'll still have some control over them, and can reabsorb them if they start getting sloppy, but it will make for less work in running the Midwest. It will also create a lot more positions for ranked weres, which means opportunities for those who need them."

"Now hardly seems the time. We're hunting for the Aufero, the witches' civil war is still ongoing…"

"I know. I'm not planning to do this straight away. It will take time to plan and organize. I expect the first breaks will come in a year or two, which means you also won't be worrying about Sky's pregnancy when we do it."

I hated to admit it, given how much fuss outsiders were making about the baby, but that was a factor for me. I didn't have the spare mental energy to deal with this right now. Hell, I wasn't even sure it was a good idea. I trusted Sebastian, and I knew that part of my resistance was just clinging to what I was familiar with, but still, there were risks in stepping into the unknown.

"I guess it might work," I conceded. "Though it's the end of an era."

"It certainly is. I'm going to miss having the ranking group I've worked with for so long."

At that, I stiffened. I was one of Sebastian's ranking weres. This was very much about me.

"What do you mean?" I asked quietly, afraid of what I might hear.

"That some of you will move on," Sebastian said. "Not Winter, she tried being a Beta and it wasn't for her. But Steven is too capable to stay stuck as a fifth, he'll make a good Alpha for one of the smaller groups. I expect Gavin will become a Beta somewhere: he doesn't have an Alpha's leadership skills, but he's got great strength for a second in command."

"And me," I said, keeping my voice flat. "Do you expect me to leave?"

I dreaded his answer. We both knew that, if not for him, I would already be an Alpha somewhere. I had briefly taken control of the East Coast Pack, and could have dominated almost any of the other packs in North America. If we were scattering to the winds, I was the most natural choice to give a new pack to.

But I didn't want to go. The Northwest Pack was my home. It was where I had friends. It was where my heart lived. My early life had been thrown into turmoil by a curse and family loss. This was the place that gave me stability.

"If you want to move on, then I think you should," Sebastian said, looking into his drink rather than meeting my eyes.

"If you think I should, then..." The thought made me miserable, but I trusted Sebastian's judgment. If he wanted me to move on, then surely I should accept that. And it was his pack to make these decisions about.

We sat in silence, staring at our drinks. That was it. This time I really would become an Alpha. I would leave the Midwest behind, settle somewhere new, with whichever weres wanted to leave. A new house, a new retreat, a new job to go with them. Not only would the pack scatter, but I would leave behind almost everything that I had now.

"Well then," Sebastian said. He let out a deep breath. "We'll factor that into the planning. Give you a big breakaway group, some good people and territory. We'll—"

"Dammit," I snapped. "Can't I stay? We work well together. I don't want to—"

"Of course you can stay!" Sebastian stared at me. "I said if you want to."

"I thought you meant that—"

"I was trying to show that—"

For a tangled moment we were talking over each other. Then we stopped and both laughed in relief.

"Ethan, you will always have a place in my pack," Sebastian said. "And if you ever want to leave, then I will support that too. I can't think of anyone better to work with, I just don't want to hold you back."

"You're not," I said. I was so relieved I almost laughed out loud. I would get to stay. I could raise my child around the pack house, have them learn from Sebastian's example, take them to all the places that mattered to me. I could still see Josh and Claudia whenever I wanted, while Sky and I would be close to all those friends that remained, and see any that visited, as I was sure most of them would, for a break from their new packs. I could hang onto the life I had built. "I have everything I want."

"Well then." Sebastian raised his glass with a smile. "Here's to the end of an era, and to the beginning of a new one."

Sky was in the front room when I got home, dressed in yoga pants and a loose t-shirt, one of her scruffy blankets spread across her lap. In a bowl next to her, jelly bears and mini pretzels were mixed together, and her Kindle was resting on her bump. She flung the e-reader aside when I came through the door and tried to leap to her feet, only to be stopped by a mixture of blanket and bump.

"You're not going to believe what happened today!" she exclaimed, wide-eyed with excitement as she looked at me.

"You found a disgusting new pregnancy craving," I said, looking at the bowl of salted snacks and candies.

"No! Well, yes, but that's not what I mean."

"You beat Tabby at that weird card game she's obsessed with."

"Of course not." Sky rolled her eyes. "And tomorrow, can I please have some guards who aren't Worgen? I've had a whole day of cartoons and sci-fi shows, I want to watch trashy reality TV."

"When people are here to guard you, you don't have to let them choose the entertainment."

"I know, but I feel rude making it about my choices when

they're here to keep me and the bump safe, and some people…"

"Tabby doesn't recognize when you're not having fun."

"Exactly!"

"Well, tomorrow it's David and Trent all day, so you should be fine." Whether I could stay sane when I got home to them was another matter.

"Yes, you are the best Beta in the world." She flung her arms wide, and I leaned over to receive a grateful hug. "But you still haven't guessed my thing yet."

"Can I possibly guess?"

She popped a handful of pretzels and gummy bears into her mouth, then chewed thoughtfully. "Probably not."

"One last go then. You were elected president, and you're leaving me to go live in the White House."

"No, though if the beds there are any comfier than ours, I'd consider it." She sighed. "I am so tired of not sleeping through the night."

"Sorry, I bought the best mattress money could buy, after you said you were struggling."

Sky sighed again and pulled a sad face. It didn't last long, as she stuck a gummy bear through the hole in a pretzel and then bit through them both.

"Ah well, someone else will have to run the country."

"So what is your news?"

"Abigail and Mason interrupted my lunch with Claudia. They—"

"Did they hurt you?" I bolted to my feet, adrenaline coursing through my veins, ready to leap into action. Our enemies had been given more than enough warnings about what would happen if they touched my mate, now they were going to face the consequences. "Do you know where they went? I'm going to finish this now, once and for all, I swear."

I was seething with fury, ready to take on the world for the sake of my family. To my shock, Sky burst out laughing.

"It's fine," she said. "They didn't hurt me. They couldn't." She patted the seat next to her on the sofa. "Please, sit down, let me finish the story."

I set the bowl of snacks aside and sat down next to her, feeling bewildered. How could a visit from those two be anything but bad news, especially an unannounced visit to where Sky was relaxing with my godmother, a clear signal that they could get to my family?

"Like I was saying, I was having lunch with Claudia when Abigail and Mason burst in. They've had powerful magic laid on them, and it's on Rayna and Liam too. It stops any of them from using magic. They've been neutered."

"What?" I stared at her, incredulous, not knowing what to say. After a minute, a huge grin spread up my face. Our worst enemies had been stripped of their power. They were every bit as vulnerable as they had wanted to make us, just as robbed of their supernatural essence.

"Claudia said that magic like this could only be cast by three sisters called the Roho. Their magic is so old and powerful, it gets around all the wards the witches and the elves can set up. But the Roho will only cast it for people who prove themselves by passing their trials. Abigail and Mason and the rest can't just have it removed. They would have to face that challenge, and if they failed, which they probably would without their magic, then the result is death. Claudia told them how to go about it, but..."

"But even if they succeed, they'll know that this could happen again, and that it only happened to the people who threatened you."

"Exactly!"

Could this really be it, the end to all our struggles? With our enemies powerless, we were safe, for a while at least. I could relax and enjoy the prospect of becoming a father.

Except that it all seemed too easy. How the hell had this happened? I hadn't even heard of these Roho, never mind faced their trials, and no one in the pack had gone missing recently to arrange it. I could see Winter taking on ancient powers for a chance to protect us, but she had been busy around the retreat for weeks. She was even talking about giving up her job and becoming a freelance fitness trainer, so that she could fit her pack work in better.

So who had saved us? Sky could clearly see the question in my eyes.

"Chris and Demetrius," she said. I must have looked as dumbstruck as I felt, because she laughed. "They won't admit it, but they were the ones who went out to Africa, who faced the Roho's challenge, who got the curse laid on Abigail, Mason, Liam, and Rayna. They risked their lives to keep us safe."

I could hardly believe it. Demetrius, the pack's greatest enemy, had risked his life for us. That didn't make sense.

Except that Demetrius owed Sky a life debt, and Chris had been so grateful at having his life saved. What I had once thought the stupidest thing Sky ever did, bringing Demetrius back from the brink of death, had ended up being the smartest thing she ever did. Her friend the vampire Mistress, and her friend's partner the vampire Master, had faced a life-or-death trial for her.

I would never doubt the value of her compassion again.

"You made that happen," I said, my voice full of awe. "You saved Demetrius for Chris. Your kindness made sure that there was someone in the world to protect us and our child."

Overwhelmed by wonder at everything she represented, I leaned in to kiss her.

"You Skyed it up, and that ended up saving the day. You're amazing."

She smiled, then frowned. "If I'm so amazing, maybe you could stop using my name like that? It's kind of rude."

"Okay, I promise." I looked in disgust at the bowl of pretzels and bears. "Why don't I cook us some dinner? Steak maybe?"

"Sounds good," Sky said with a smile. "Extra rare, in honor of our friends."

I shook my head as I walked into the kitchen. I was friends with a vampire. How had that ever happened?

From the front room, I could hear the answer shaking a bowl full of pretzels.

It was all down to Sky.

CHAPTER 42

Constantly looking out for trouble was a hard habit to break. I had gotten used to watching for suspicious strangers at my office, people following me in the street, any sign of elves or unknown witches within reach of our house. A steady, low level paranoia was useful when you were being spied on, when there was a constant risk that the enemy might make a move against you. When that ended, it was a waste of energy, but that didn't make it easy to let go.

I started to feel safe when Stacy told me that the attempts to spy on me at work had stopped. There were no more strangers tailing her or trying to sneak into the office, no more crude hacking or malware attacks specifically targeting my account. The alarm wards Josh had discretely installed on my desk and filing cabinet didn't go off. As the reality of it sank in, I became more focused in work and more relaxed at home. I watched Sky with admiration, knowing that she had made this happen. But still, it didn't seem entirely real. After all, Rayna was out there somewhere. What if she was still plotting her revenge?

I didn't recognize the footsteps approaching up the driveway, uneven and uncertain, or the scent of the person, masked as it was by blood and sulfur. The strange arrival triggered warning bells in my brain, and I rushed out of my office and down the stairs, too late to stop Sky from being the one who answered the door.

She froze when she saw who was on the other side, and I tensed behind her at the sight of Rayna. I prepared to fend off an attack.

I didn't need to worry. This was an empty shell of the witch we had met before, her skin ghostly pale, hair wild, bags under her eyes. The magical energy that surrounded most witches was gone, making her whole essence seem muted. Her hands, covered in a chaotic jumble of magical symbols and scars from drawing blood, reached out toward Sky, offering up the Aufero.

This was the woman who had plotted to kill Sky, who had wanted to wipe our unborn baby from the world. I could have torn her throat out and never felt the faintest twinge of pity. Seeing her so lost and broken, I felt no empathy, but I was able to hold back my aggression. What was the point in killing someone so pathetic? I would be putting her out of her well-earned misery.

The Aufero pulsed with bright light, running through orange, maroon, silver, and blue, responding to the power of Sky's presence. Sky hesitated, staring at it.

"You should have it," Rayna said, trying to muster the dignity with which she used to hold herself. "I want Ariel and hers to know there isn't a threat of me taking their magic."

As if that was even a possibility, when her own power had been stripped away.

"Thank you." Sky took the Aufero but held it away from her. The baby was subject to enough strange powers without bringing the Aufero close.

Rayna looked carefully at both of us, still calculating, still trying to assess her situation, still desperate for a way to cling to what she had been.

"When will my magic be returned to me?"

"I don't know if it will," Sky said. "I had nothing to do with it, and I'm not sure how to have it returned."

Rayna narrowed her eyes as she looked at Sky's face, then down at her bulging stomach.

"Your baby is safe, I've given you the Aufero, and I've made it known that you are not to be touched—I think I've more than earned it back."

As if she had chosen for those things to happen. Our baby was safe despite her. She was giving us the Aufero out of desperation, and because it was now useless to her. Even if it had been within our power to return her magic, I wouldn't have done so. She deserved to stay like this.

"We aren't able to return your magic, and I think it's a good thing," I said. "Your change of heart is a result of your change in circumstances. Is there anything else you want?"

She pressed her lips together, holding back her first response, burying the anger that flashed in her eyes. But in the end, she couldn't help herself.

"Just because I don't have access to magic, doesn't mean I can't be a thorn in your side. In the pack's side."

"You're right," Sky said. "But you are a cautionary tale for those who might try to follow in your footsteps. It's quite a deterrent to getting the backing you need. Abigail, Mason, and you are what happens when you screw with us. Leave us alone and we'll leave you alone. You came for us; it wasn't the other way around. Contrary to how you depict us and our history, we've done more good than bad. Goodbye, Rayna."

Sky closed the door in Rayna's face, then turned to me. I wrapped her in my arms and held her close as we sought the steadying calm of each other's heartbeats.

None of our enemies could hurt us anymore. Our baby was safe. Now all we had to do was survive the pregnancy.

"Come on," I said, taking Sky's hand and leading her into

the kitchen. "There must be some weird food combination you've been craving. Now's the time to give in and enjoy it."

She set the Aufero down, its light shining across the counter, and smiled.

"I haven't tried steak with chocolate spread yet."

$\mathcal{I}$ didn't know what a delivery room normally looked like, but I was sure it wasn't this, with nearly a dozen witches spread around the infirmary and Winter lurking in the doorway, like she was a bodyguard ready to protect the mother from the arrival of her own baby. While Sky cried out at the pain of her contractions, and Jeremy inspected her to decide whether she needed a C-section, magic swirled through the air: the magic of Maya, struggling for dominance over Sky; Sky's magic, as she tried to hold Maya in check, to keep her from occupying the baby; the magic of the witches, pouring all their power into reinforcing an *interdico* mark that had already been wiped away by Maya three times that week.

Almost everything that mattered in my life was at stake. There were the dangers of a difficult birth, which had Jeremy's and Kelly's faces crumpled into frowns, though they tried to hide their concerns from Sky. More than that, there was the possibility that Maya might transfer from Sky to the baby as they were born. Without the spirit shade inside her, Sky would die, and I dreaded to think what effect it would have on our child. Amid the blood and pain of birth, the spirit shade was trying to enter a new body, one it could control. If it succeeded, I would lose my family, and my heart broke just thinking about it.

The whole thing was made a hundred times worse by the fact that there was nothing I could do to change events. I had no power over this situation. All I could do was stand by Sky, grip her hand, and offer her all the comfort I could provide.

"Why are we here?" Nia asked. "The *interdico* didn't work and apparently she's no longer immune to iridium, so what are we expected to do?"

"Just in case, but it will be fine," I said, hiding my anger at her and my fears for Sky behind a mask of confidence. If this was all that I could offer, then it was what I would give: confidence, strength, hope for Sky to hold onto.

In the quiet between contractions, a look of fear crossed Sky's face.

"Everyone's coming out of this," I said, leaning in close to talk quietly to her. "I promise."

Sky closed her eyes, fighting back tears. I felt as though my chest was being crushed in the fist of a dark and powerful spirit, as if the spirit shades were tearing at me, shredding away my happiness, leaving me with just the fear of loneliness and misery, of a life without Sky. A life I couldn't stand, now that I knew what it was to be with her.

Across the room, Josh waved his hands through the air, struggling to maintain the *interdico*, to keep some limit on Maya's power. His face showed the worries I was hiding. It made me feel sane.

"Ethan," Ariel said softly. "Do you have a worst-case scenario? Even with a C-section, Maya is still active. If at any time she can get the baby to accept her, she can be hosted. If Sky is de—"

"We know that," I snapped. I wouldn't let her finish the word. Sky didn't need to hear it. I didn't need to hear it. I was all for brutal honesty in most things, but not today.

By now, the epidural should have kicked in. Jeremy had explained that he couldn't give Sky a full anesthetic, but now that he had decided that a C-section was needed, she had to have something for the pain. With the baby struggling to emerge, the time for other options had run out.

He picked up his scalpel.

"I'm going to cut you," he said, using his most soothing doctor voice. "You might feel it a little—but you've had worse, haven't you? You are going to do just fine."

Sky nodded and gripped my hand so hard it was going to leave bruises. We looked into each other's eyes, and I found love there, the love that had made me a better man, that had let me make peace with so many people in my life. And then I realized that I might lose that love, and I felt a greater fear than I had ever known before. I had someone worth committing my life to, and that meant that I had something to lose.

"Ready?" Jeremy asked.

We both nodded. Kelly moved a portable curtain across Sky, blocking the view as Jeremy made his incision. Josh's invocation flowed softly across the room, and I realized that there was something I could do, a way of making use of my magic. I joined in that chant, offering Sky peace and protection, holding the powers in place around her. I wasn't a witch, my words wouldn't do as much as theirs, but it was something, and it gave me hope.

The power in the room shifted as we pressed at Maya with our power, and Sky joined in, exerting all her will even as her body was sliced open. I could feel Maya trying to take control, to seize her moment. But we had hold of her, pushing her down, squeezing her into a corner of Sky where she would still sustain her but couldn't ride through her body as she had done before. Maya writhed and twisted, trying to break free of the spell, to reach the baby as Jeremy reached inside to lift it out. We chanted louder, stronger, as Maya clawed at Sky's soul, clinging on for all she was worth. Sky howled in pain, then sank back onto the bed.

A baby's cry broke through the stillness that followed, and that sound made me look around in wonder.

"It's a girl," Jeremy said, holding her out for us to see.

The baby was slicked with blood and fluids, her mouth open wide in a scream, her tiny eyes screwed shut and fists bunched up. Somehow, she was the most perfect thing in the world.

"Isn't she amazing?" I whispered.

But when I looked down at Sky, she was unconscious.

CHAPTER 44

"Why isn't she moving?" I asked, looking at Sky.

My heart was thundering. With one hand, I held Sky's hand, which had gone limp and pale. The other was a fist clenched at my side, fingers digging into my palm, the pain barely cutting through the stunned bewilderment I felt. I couldn't look away from her, not even for a moment. She had been lying unconscious for ten minutes, and the whole time I had been fixed in place.

I was aware of movement elsewhere in the room: of Kelly cleaning up my crying daughter; of the witches still weaving some sort of spell; of Jeremy sewing up Sky's incision, a worried look on his face. But none of it sank in. My whole mind was filled with grief and horror, with facing the unbearable reality of losing the love of my life. Nothing else could get through. That one thought was too huge for all the rest.

She wasn't dead.

She couldn't be dead.

"Winter, step back," Jeremy snapped, as Winter walked into the room, staring around, looking as lost as I felt.

"Why isn't she moving?" I asked, my voice quivering with fear. "Why isn't she moving?"

I looked up and saw Josh. Desperate for an answer, I fixed my gaze on him. He had led the magic. He must know.

"Give her a minute," Josh said.

"It's been minutes," I snapped, glancing at the clock. "Nine to be exact."

Panic was taking hold. I had to do something. I couldn't do anything. What the hell was I meant to do?

Why wasn't she moving?

A machine started beeping, a frantic cry of alarm.

"Ethan, move." Jeremy shoved me aside and reached for Sky's pulse.

"It had to have worked," Winter said, her voice gravelly and cold, "because if not, she wouldn't be breathing at all, right?"

I stumbled back, still clinging to her hand, broken and bewildered. All my strength had fled me. All my focus. They had been turned to supporting Sky, and now she was... She was...

Someone was sobbing. Not me, though I wanted to. My chest heaved, but nothing came. The wound was too deep, the pain too deeply hooked inside me to be released.

My daughter whimpered.

My daughter.

I had to pull myself together for her. I had to.

But Sky...

"Josh," I whispered. "What do we do now?"

He shook his head, every inch of him trembling, hands clawing at his hair as if he was trying to pull fresh magic out of his head, to fight off tragedy with any last scrap of power he had left.

"It should have worked," he said.

Magic had failed us. Medicine had failed us. In spite of everything we had done, everything we had mustered to keep Sky alive, she was fading. Her breathing was rapid, erratic, out of time with her heartbeat and the beeping of the machines. Her lips were starting to lose color. Nothing Jeremy did seemed to make her better, only to slow the rate at which she was slipping away.

After all we had been through, all the threats we had faced together, all the struggles to save each other's lives, I was losing her. It wasn't fair. It wasn't right. The crushing weight of it pressed down on me until I could hardly stand.

The sobbing grew louder as Kelly turned toward us.

"Stop with the damn crying or leave!" Winter snapped.

Kelly stared at Winter, then past her to where Gavin stood, his teeth bared, his hands curling into fists.

"She's upset, Gavin," Kelly said softly, fighting back another sob, and he retreated as surely as if Sebastian had ordered it.

Kelly turned away again, making soothing noises to the baby, giving comfort to my daughter. I wanted to reach out and take that tiny bundle, to wrap her in my arms and hold her close, safe from all the world. Except that the world wasn't a safe place, not if I couldn't protect her mother.

I had to pull myself together, for my daughter's sake.

"Josh," I said, finding the firmness of command with which I normally handled pack business. It became like armor, a hard shell around the vulnerable places where loss lay.

My brother's eyes were closed, his expression lost in thought. I watched him and clung to hope. Josh had dedicated his life to magic. He had shattered Marcia's hold on the Creed, had unleashed unprecedented power in tearing down the walls of Elysian. If his magic could do that, surely it could help with this.

His eyes opened slowly. "We'll do a spell reversal. That's the only thing that can work."

Not the only thing. One other possibility remained: *rever*

tempore, the magic to turn back time. But its consequences were too grave, the results too terrible. Neither of us could consider inflicting that on anyone, no matter what was at stake.

"It's like her body is rejecting the shade," Jeremy said, looking up from Sky.

"It is." A flicker of excitement lit up Josh's eye. "Logan. When she shifted the shade from her to him, it changed dynamics."

He paced back and forth, not looking at me, lost in his own thoughts. He was trying to work through a magical problem, to see the way that the pieces could be stitched together. It was the sort of challenge he and Sky had often faced together, poring over books in the pack library, each inspiring the other as they sought a solution. But she couldn't help him now, with her hand lying limp in mine.

I fought back the urge to howl in anguish, and instead kept my attention on Josh, watching, waiting, hoping.

He stopped still in the center of the room.

"We can't do the same spell because, unconscious, she's not able to accept the shade. So we'll have to do a spell reversal."

Ariel approached him cautiously, speaking in a quiet voice. "I want Sky to live, but—"

"Not the *rever tempore*," Josh said. "When we did the first spell, we technically had three witches, me, you, and Sky. Dormant dark elf magic and witch from you, and Faerie from you and Sky. That's a hell of a lot of magic. To do a reversal, the magic used has to be equal or greater than what was used to perform the spell. We have enough witches to help, but we're missing Faerie magic."

"What about Claudia?" I asked. She wasn't strictly speaking a Faerie, but her magic was part Faerie and part vampire, and I was willing to grasp at any possibility.

"She can help." Josh pulled a face. "I'm concerned that Claudia's vampirism will interfere with the magic."

"Sky is part vampire, so it's a better match, right?" Winter asked.

"Maybe." Josh scratched his chin. "That would be easier than trying to learn to mimic magic the way Sky does." He looked at Sky uncertainly. "I'll call her."

I tried to push his doubts aside as he walked out, phone in hand. I needed this to work.

In Kelly's arms, my daughter gurgled happily.

Crinkles formed around Claudia's eyes and mouth as she looked at me across the infirmary. Her tone was hesitant, not the firmly controlled presence I was used to. Was she afraid of how I might react?

"Ethan, you know I don't perform magic," she said.

"I know." I knew it for the half-truth that it was. Claudia avoided magic as much as she could, fearful of what might happen if it went wrong. But the power was still there, and she knew how to use it. I turned my gaze to Sky. "I think she's going to die if you don't."

"She might die if I do," Claudia whispered sadly.

I trembled at those words. Sky's death was all I had been able to think about while we waited for Claudia to arrive. If she couldn't help, then we were out of options. Senna, Sky's cousin, was a Faerie, but she lived too far away for us to reach her now, with Sky's life force growing weaker by the minute. It was either this or… No, I wouldn't consider it. This was the answer.

"Claudia, please try," I said. "For me."

I couldn't hold the tears back any longer. They ran down my cheeks, grief made manifest, an uncontainable symptom of my loss. Claudia slipped the gloves from her hands and gently reached up to brush the tears from my cheeks. We looked into each other's eyes, and for a moment it was like having my mother with me again, that gentle, reassuring presence that would make everything well.

I was painfully aware of the others around us—Winter, Sebastian, Jeremy, Kelly, the assembled witches, all seeing me in my moment of weakness. I didn't care. These tears were for Sky, and I wasn't going to hide my feelings for her from the world.

"Show me the spell," Claudia said.

Josh handed her a sheet of paper, hastily scribbled with Latin and strange symbols.

"My Latin." She flushed in embarrassment. "It's not as good as it used to be."

"Do you want me to—"

"No, no, no." She brushed Josh away and took a seat in the corner of the room. "I just need a few minutes to see how the spell works."

Time ticked by while she read and reread the spell, her lips and fingers twitching as she felt her way through it. I glanced nervously from her to Sky to the clock. Time was slipping away, Sky's pulse growing weaker. If we were going to do this, then we had to do it properly, but we could only wait for so long.

My heart strained as I struggled to contain myself, to patiently wait while my mate's life drifted away.

After nearly twenty minutes, Claudia finally looked up.

"I'm ready," she said.

"You can do this," Josh said, and some of his confidence rubbed off onto her. She stood taller, her back straighter, hands raised and ready to begin.

I could still smell her fear, still feel her tension nearly as intense as mine.

She began the incantation, the words almost musical as they filled the infirmary, her voice backed by those of Josh and his fellow witches. Magic swirled around her in currents so powerful I could almost see them. It settled over Sky, strands of dark and light, death and life, Faerie and witch magic.

As the magic took hold, Sky's breathing became sparser. The machine beside her started up its shrill, alarming beep as her vital sounds dropped.

Terror gripped me again. The spell was failing. All the power in the world would be undone by the willfulness of Maya, the spirit shade unwilling to be bound by mortals. That power was slipping away, stealing Sky's life with it.

"Claudia," Sebastian said, his voice low and soothing. I couldn't look away from Sky, not if this might be her final moment, but whatever passed between the two of them, it made a difference. The magic shifted, darker strands pulling back, death giving way to life. Claudia was battling her own instincts, narrowing the focus to a single part of herself, to give Sky a chance.

The beeping stopped. Sky's body sagged, and I stiffened, fearing the worst.

Then she groaned, and it was the most amazing thing I had ever heard, better even than our daughter's first exclamation at entering the world. That sound was the sign that Sky lived.

She opened her eyes and smiled at me. I almost collapsed as the tension left my body. I had been so afraid that I was going to lose her, but in the end, my family had come together to save her life.

She sat up, wincing as she did it.

"Remember, you've just had surgery," Jeremy said, his tone gentler than with most patients.

Surgery and a lifesaving dose of unprecedented magic, but that explanation could wait for later.

"Where's our baby?" she asked.

I pushed back her sweat-dampened hair, staring at her in

wonder and in fear. It seemed too much to believe that this had really worked, that she could be safe after coming so close to death. Tears welled again in the corners of my eyes.

"Ethan," she whispered, looking up at me. "I'm okay, Ethan. I promise."

I closed my eyes as I fought to bring my emotions under control. She reached up a hand and pressed it to my cheek, and I looked down at her again, smiling.

"I'm okay," she whispered over and over.

"I know."

I squeezed her hand, and she squeezed back. Somehow, that touch made it real enough for me to believe.

"Here she is," Kelly said, handing Sky our baby.

That small, red face was still scrunched up in distress, and she was wailing for all the world to hear.

"Hello, Sage," Sky said, and at last the crying stopped.

Sage looked up at us, and the whole world faded away. There was only my mate and my daughter, the two most precious women in my life.

In a life of pain and struggle, I had found a place of love.

CHAPTER 45

Sage lay curled up in my arms, making soft cooing noises as she slept. I could feel the warmth of her body through my shirt, hear her tiny heart beating, a fragile and beautiful sound. That sense of her next to me, the smell of her, the touch of her, the sound of her, it brought me a peace I had never known before. I could have sat there on the sofa in her room all night, just looking at her.

"It's her first night in her room," I whispered. "I don't think she likes it."

For the two months since we brought her home, she had been sleeping in our room, her cot set up next to our bed. It wasn't what we had originally planned, but being separated from her in the night had proven too much for me. I had been restless, jerking upright at the slightest sound from her, leaping out of bed at anything that could have been a cry of distress. It had taken some serious persuading from Sky to get me to accept that Sage needed to get used to her own room, to learn to sleep without us being there every time that she woke up. It wasn't what I wanted, and I expected we'd have a few nights yet before I could sleep properly in a

525

separate room, but it was for the best. I just had to convince myself of that.

I was never going to be the most relaxed parent, and we both knew it. When Sage became a teenager, I was going to become the sort of embarrassing dad who always wanted to know where she was going. I had seen how dangerous the world could be, and I was determined to keep my daughter safe. But at last, after many weeks together, I was ready to give her a little space of her own, as long as she kept giving me these moments of tranquility, her tiny hand wrapped around my finger, knowing just by looking at her that my world was complete.

I dragged my gaze away from Sage to look at Sky, who sat curled up beside me, smiling at the pair of us. I smiled back. If I had known that this was what happiness felt like, I would have sought it out years before.

I kissed Sage gently on the forehead.

"Thank you," I whispered, meaning the words for Sky.

There were so many reasons to be grateful to her. For putting up with me for so long. For carrying Sage around inside her and then giving birth, despite all the pain and danger that brought. For dealing with the situation with the vampires the way she did, and so creating a world in which Sage was safe. If we had been governed by my instincts, then Rayna and Abigail would still be out there plotting against us, gathering powerful magic to destroy Sage. Instead they were neutered, their power sucked away, their positions of leadership lost as they were shown to lack the strength their people relied on. Sky had "Skyed" the situation, and it turned out that was the best possible thing.

Sage's eyes opened and she looked at her mother. She let out a soft sigh of appreciation, then went back to sleep.

"She looks like you," I said, considering that round face and the large doe eyes, closed now until she got hungry again.

Sky sighed and laid a head on my shoulder.

"Are you sure you're okay with Chris seeing Sage?" she asked.

"I will have to be." I tried, and failed, not to show my tension. "You know your friendship with her is wrong on so many levels."

Sage shifted and made a small sound of agreement. She might not understand our conversations, but she was on the right side this time.

"The levels of wrongness and weirdness are insurmountable, but..." But without her we might all be dead, Sage included. "She keeps calling Sage 'the offspring.' 'How's the offspring?' 'Is the offspring a little Bambi?' Maybe if she sees her, she'll refer to her as Sage. It's so weird."

"I'm not going to be friends with Demetrius," I said, imagining with horror the possibility of double dates or dinner parties with the leaders of the Seethe.

"I don't expect you to. He didn't stop being an ass. In fact, it's a badge that he wears with steadfast honor. He's appreciative of me saving his life, despite him being one."

That was part of the miracle of Sky, not just fending off the rogue witches and elves, but taming the vampires. No one else in the history of the pack had achieved a coup like that.

"Chris and I aren't friends," she added.

Sure, of course not. They just met up for drinks and chatted about what went on in their lives. Not friends at all.

Sky fell silent. She had a lot on her mind, and I wasn't going to add to that weight by challenging her view of the world. I slid my finger out of Sage's hand, moving slowly so as not to alarm her, and rested my hand on Sky's leg. I stroked her with my thumb, trying to soothe her anxieties.

"There's still time with Steven," I said. "Even if he is Alpha of his own pack, you won't lose touch with him."

"No, I won't. I'll make sure of that. I want whatever makes him happy."

She almost sounded like she meant it, which was an improvement on the last time we had talked. Slowly but surely, she was adjusting to the new reality of pack politics.

"He's a future Alpha. You knew that, Sky."

"It's just the changes. They're still hard."

I kissed Sage on her chubby cheeks, then kissed Sky on her temple.

"I like the changes," I said. The world hadn't worked out how I expected, but I was learning to accept that as good. Not everything had to be under control.

CHAPTER 46

"Look who's up." I emerged into the front room with Sage in my arms. At two years old, she was big enough to start feeling like a weight in my arms, and opinionated enough not to settle back down once she had decided that nap time was over. Though she was still clinging to me sleepily, fingers curled into my shirt and head pressed against my shoulder, it was most definitely not nap time anymore. Sage wasn't a girl to let the world pass her by when she could be enjoying it. She had well and truly earned the title lovingly bestowed on her by Winter: "Mini T," short for "Mini Tornado."

"Hey, sweetheart." Sky pushed back our daughter's unruly curls, which had escaped her ponytail holder. Sage jerked her head away, wary of another attempt at braiding, and gave her mother a suspicious glare from steely gray eyes. "Do you want a snack?"

Now somebody was talking Sage's language. She climbed down from my arms, took Sky's hand, and tottered toward the kitchen. A few feet from there, she started bouncing excitedly up and down, while opening and closing her hands. It was what we called her "give me" gesture, the surest sign that something exciting was coming her way, or at least that she had spotted something she wanted. I assumed that was about the snacks, one of her favorite things in the world. But then there was a knock on the door, and I realized that another of her favorites had arrived.

Tiny legs working double time, a big grin plastered across her face, Sage hurried after Sky to the door. When it opened, she let out a piercing squeal, then flung her arms up and hurried forward again.

"Uncle Dosh!"

"Hi, Sage!" He swept her up in his arms and kissed her on the cheek.

Sky and I exchanged a look. For the past year, Sage had always seemed to know when Josh was approaching. Maybe she smelled him or heard him. Maybe something else was going on. However she did it, it was looking increasingly likely that she was more than just an ordinary human girl.

Josh sat cross-legged on the carpet next to Sage while she ate her snack and told him, in halting phrases of only a few words each, about the games she had been playing and the things she had seen. He treated it all with the seriousness a toddler appreciates from a grownup, a sign that he cared about her thoughts.

"Did you get it?" I asked.

Josh pulled a black leather jewelry box out of his pocket and tossed it to me. I recognized the quality of the stitching —someone else had been taking Claudia's advice. I snapped the case open, revealing a white gold ring fitted with a simple, pear-shaped stone. It would fit London perfectly, leaving her feeling like it had been made for her. That was the magic of Etsuko's jewelry.

"Nice," I said. "Claudia has the best taste."

"How do you know she picked it out?" Josh asked, as if it had ever been in doubt.

"When do you plan to give it to her?"

He shrugged. "We're going out tonight. I guess I'll give it to her then."

"What's wrong with you two?" Sky looked appalled. "Were you in fact raised by natural wolves? You don't just 'give it to her then.' You make it special. And it doesn't have to be anything big. You've been with London for close to three years. You don't just toss her a ring and say, 'You wanna?'"

"I wasn't going to say, 'You wanna?'" Josh said, a mischievous glint in his eyes. "I'd ask if she wanted to do this."

"Because that's infinitely better."

Josh leaned toward Sage. "Is Mommy always this demanding?"

"I'm not being demanding—I'm helping you not to repeat your brother's first proposal." Sky shot me a playful glare. "Just do something nice, okay?"

Josh nodded. I was confident he had a plan in place already. He might enjoy winding Sky up like this, but he had always been more of a romantic than me, and certainly more flamboyant in his gestures. Whatever London was presented with, it would be more memorable than just a ring in a box. In short, it would be better than I had managed on my first attempt.

Her snacks finished, Sage got up and did the little dance that told us she was ready for some time playing with Josh. She grabbed her favorite bear, the purple one Kelly had given her that played music and told stories, hugged it to her chest, and then reached for Josh's hand.

Before they could leave the room, Sky stopped them and started patting Josh down, like a police officer frisking a suspect for drugs.

"I'm flattered," Josh said, "but your husband's right there and I really love London...so, I'm going to pass."

"You know what I'm looking for," Sky said sternly. "The

last time you were here, Sage smelled like Twizzlers. No candy."

I restrained myself from commenting on the irony of Sky's anti-junk food stance. It was good for Sage to grow up thinking of healthy food as normal; she could learn about her mom's cake addiction later.

"She took it from me," Josh grinned. "I had no recourse. Mini T is assertive. She's like a mob boss. She asks and you have to give it to her. No questions asked."

"Nope. I haven't sanctioned that name. It's Sage. Not Mini Tornado. You and Winter are going to give her a complex."

Sky huffed and puffed, but seemed satisfied with her search, and let them past the border post.

"Okay," Josh said, "come on, Sage, let's go to your room and play." He lowered his voice. "It seems like Ethan's the nice one now."

"I heard that," Sky snapped.

Josh laughed. "You were supposed to."

Once they were out of sight, Sky and I finished clearing away the debris that Sage always seemed to litter the living room with, a scattering of toys, cushions, and the occasional discarded snack, usually half-chewed so that it really stuck to the carpet.

Sage was growing up to be just as willful as her mother, and dragging the pack into line with her desires in the same way. Winter would curl up to have a nap with her on demand, as if that was just something adults did. David and Trent let her run riot, to the point where they didn't get to babysit anymore. Kelly and Jeremy let her raid their cupboards for bandages to treat her stuffed animals. Even Sebastian was unable to resist when she put a crayon in his hand and demanded that he draw her a kitty.

But their interest in her wasn't just friendly. Until she too became pregnant, Kelly had been a constant visitor to our house, in a way she never was before. She cooed over Sage and played with her as long as the little girl wanted, but all the time she was watching, evaluating, observing her growth and behavior. The whole supernatural world was watching our pack, and the whole pack was watching Sage, to see what she turned into. As far as I was concerned, all that mattered was that she had turned into a healthy, adorable little girl, but it wasn't my opinion that had almost triggered a war.

"Ethan, Sky," Josh called from upstairs, his voice strained. "I need you both to come up here. I need to show you something."

We rushed upstairs and into the nursery, trying not to panic at the tone in Josh's words.

A small ball of gray fur lay in the middle of the floor, a purple bear under her head. A wolf cub.

I relaxed. This I was ready for.

"She changed earlier than expected," I said. I'd expected it to hit her earlier than me or Sky, on account of both parents being wolves. That tended to bring out the were-animal side sooner.

"Yeah, but *that's* not the headline of this event."

Josh knelt down beside Sage, pried the bear out of her paws, and came to stand beside us.

Sage's head popped up, revealing a flattened little snout and sleepy eyes. She whimpered and waved one of her paws. The bear was dragged from Josh's hands and floated through the air, across the nursery, before landing in front of Sage. She narrowed her eyes at Josh, settled back down, her head on the bear, and drifted off to sleep.

"Hmm," Sky said.

"Yeah, hmmm," Josh replied, sounding serious.

"A were-animal who can perform magic in wolf form," I said, stunned.

This wasn't an option we had predicted, and there was no way of foreseeing all the possible implications. Could it mean that she was immune to magic in human form? That would fit with the fears so many others had about us, creating a were-animal who was immune to their powers, a threat they couldn't take down. An outcome like this could cause real trouble once it became public.

At least we had made some preparations for the unexpected. I walked to Sage's dresser, opened a drawer, and drew out an iridium link bracelet. We hadn't thought that we would need it yet, so it was far too big.

"I think we are going to need a couple links removed," I said.

"And a meeting with Sebastian too."

We all looked at one another, and the thought remained unspoken. Sebastian was the only person we would tell. No one else needed to know that Sage was anything other than an ordinary werewolf cub. She would get a childhood without others' fears and obsessions bearing down on her, without being treated as a threat. We, her pack, would protect her.

I looked at the sleeping pup and smiled proudly, considering how amazing she had turned out to be. One more woman who had changed my life.

<<<<>>>>